The Hemsworth Effect

The Hemsworth Effect

JAMES WEIR

SIMON &
SCHUSTER

London · New York · Sydney · Toronto · New Delhi

THE HEMSWORTH EFFECT
First published in Australia in 2022 by
Simon & Schuster (Australia) Pty Limited
Suite 19A, Level 1, Building C, 450 Miller Street,
Cammeray, NSW 2062

10 9 8 7 6 5 4 3 2 1

Sydney New York London Toronto New Delhi
Visit our website at www.simonandschuster.com.au

A catalogue record for this
book is available from the
National Library of Australia

NATIONAL
LIBRARY
OF AUSTRALIA

ISBN: 9781761104084

Cover design: Alissa Dinallo
Cover illustration: Diego Catto/Shutterstock
Typeset by Midland Typesetters, Australia
Printed and bound in Australia by Griffin Press

MIX
Paper from
responsible sources
FSC
www.fsc.org   FSC® C009448

The paper this book is printed on is certified against the
Forest Stewardship Council® Standards. Griffin Press holds
FSC® chain of custody certification SGS-COC-005088. FSC
promotes environmentally responsible, socially beneficial
and economically viable management of the world's forests

To my little friends . . .

Sascha
Eva
Harry
Georgie

ONE

Nothing attracts rich white people like the *Big Little Lies* theme song. The long instrumental intro started playing over the speakers in the cramped bookstore and Aimee Maguire made a mental note to remove it from the playlist. This mental note was made every day. She didn't know it was the *Big Little Lies* theme song when she first heard it – it had been automatically added into the Spotify mix one of her store casuals had set up to stream over the speakers. But she was quickly informed. Every time it played, the notes drifted out past the racks and stacks of books and the novelty toys into the street and, by the time the moody chorus hit, a steady line of wealthy city folks had stumbled inside, like zombies but with all-linen outfits and blow waves. On cue, one strolled in. She was accessorised with the summer's oddest new trend, a $4,650 limited edition Louis Vuitton tote with the town's name emblazoned across it: Byron Bay.

Aimee sighed. 'They all end up going back to wherever it is they came from.' She swiftly picked up a cardboard box of stock off the floor, placed it on the antique pine shop counter and used a Stanley knife to slice open the top. Her arms flexed and showed off the natural tone that came with having spent a lifetime swimming in the ocean. She flicked her warm brown shoulder-length hair out of her face and looked up to see the journalist opposite her scrawling the sentence down on his notepad. Ever since *Vanity Fair* profiled the town in a glitzy feature about its Hemsworthification, the streets had been crawling with media outlets trying to capitalise on the world's new obsession.

They all end up going back to wherever it is they came from.

This sentence tumbled out of Aimee's mouth with the same rhythm and ease of an ancient mantra chanted by monks during meditation at dawn. It almost *had* become a mantra for Aimee. She'd found herself repeating it in her head every time she walked down the main street. Sometimes even muttering it, a little too loudly, when she saw obnoxious teenage weekenders littering. Or influencers blocking footpaths while taking photos. Or wealthy out-of-towners jamming up intersections with their bumper-to-bumper Range Rovers and Bentleys and Teslas. It was a reassuring reminder that, by the end of the summer holidays, most of the intruders would be gone. *They all end up going back to wherever it is they came from.* Just beneath the jaded weariness, there was almost a sense of acceptance and surrender. Aimee had thought about screen-printing it on a T-shirt – a more cynical version of those annoying slogan tank tops from Lorna Jane.

They all end up going back to wherever it is they came from.

The phrase had also become Aimee's go-to quote for the many journalists who'd started skulking into her store. They loved that quote. The reporter standing opposite her – in his linen shirt with the rolled-up sleeves, the typical uniform visitors seemingly thought was a requirement in the town – pushed his dictaphone across the shop counter and probed for more soundbites about the gentrification of paradise from a cranky local. *Oh god*, she thought. At thirty-six, when had she become a cranky local? It could probably be traced back to the day the town introduced paid parking meters. Cranky locals hated parking meters. Really, they just hated anything that stopped them from living their lives the way they'd always done. Cranky locals liked their routines. Cranky locals didn't like change. Cranky locals got very worked up when other people who were not true locals told them what to do. But wasn't that everyone?

She took a sip of her takeaway coffee and the journalist locked his eyes on the cardboard cup. She knew what was coming. In five, four, three, two . . .

'No KeepCup?' he asked.

Aimee kept sipping while shaking her head. She had tried KeepCups in the past and she knew she should use them but, every time she did, she'd take the cup home and it'd sit on the sink, unwashed for days. And the longer she left it, the more scared she became about popping off the rubber lid and seeing what organisms had started to grow inside. Eventually, she'd just throw it out and buy a new one. And then it happened again. After careful consideration, she'd decided her twice-daily single-use takeaway card-board coffee cups were much better for the environment.

'Oat milk? Hemp milk? Macadamia?' He was desperately trying to pin Aimee to at least one Byron stereotype that readers could gleefully ridicule.

'Regular.' Aimee drained the final drops of coffee into her mouth and tossed the cup into the recycling bin behind the counter. 'I should be run out of town any day now.'

She'd lost count of how many journalists had come into her store over the summer – all covering the skyrocketing property prices and the celebrities and rich city people buying up the town. Every time, Aimee told herself: Don't be the cranky local. The journalist opposite her probed further about out-of-towners trying to recreate the paradise they'd seen on Instagram. Aimee smiled.

'If they're not the soul that's meant to be here, they get spat out.' She winced slightly at the blunt statement and picked up one of the rubber fidgets she'd just unpacked. It fulfilled its purpose.

'I just wanna live my life in the town I love,' she said, pushing and popping the round buttons on the pineapple-shaped toy. 'Take a dip in the ocean I've swum in since I was three. I just wanna be happy.'

'What do you mean "spat out"?'

A seductive growl purred through the shop doorway and the glass in the display windows rattled as a sports car pulled up in the loading zone at the front of the store. That happened at least twice an hour all through summer. Aimee looked up at the clock above the entrance: Ten to three. She huffed before-realising she probably looked cranky, so she tried harder to seem breezy but then she just felt stupid. 'The town has a way of telling you it's time to go.'

A middle-aged man talking loudly on his phone burst into the store and the timber floorboards creaked under the weight. His whole presence seemed at odds with the childlike fantasy land he'd intruded on. He didn't belong. It was as if a grizzly bear had squeezed inside a cubby house.

'I've always liked the old F355 Ferraris,' he said, as if to impress the nearby plush toys with his yen for the collectable mid-nineties Italian sports cars that fetched upwards of $300,000.

Aimee called out from the counter, 'You can't park there.'

The man pushed through the mounds of costumes hanging from the ceiling and leant against a giant five-level doll house filled with hand-crafted miniature furniture that was nicer than the decor found in the real-life homes of most adults.

'I have a stock delivery coming and the truck needs that space.'

'Kids? Husband?' The journalist carried on with his questions.

Aimee stared at the oafish Ferrari guy, trying to get his attention, and mindlessly answered, 'No. Well, no kids. I'm engaged.' She shook her head and fidgeted with the fidget before placing it down on the counter. 'Actually, can you not include that?' She walked away from the counter and started following the Ferrari guy, who was meandering around the store, pulling out random books from the shelves and barely glancing at the covers before shoving them back in the wrong spaces.

'What do you think of the Hemsworths?' the reporter asked, glancing over the top of his retro-looking horn-rimmed glasses, which added an unnecessary touch of gravitas to the topic at hand.

'I love their music,' Aimee called back.

Confused silence.

'I'm joking.'

Aimee dodged around the Ferrari guy and stood in front of him. 'Hi, you need to move your car, like, now.'

The Ferrari guy stopped mid-sentence, glanced at Aimee, and then turned around to continue the phone call.

'I saw you pull up. Now please move it.'

He ignored her again. She tucked the front of her white tee into her faded blue skinny jeans and considered just walking away. Instead, she reached up and snatched his phone.

He scoffed and grabbed it right back. 'Fuck off, you fuckin' hippie.'

Aimee's brow shot up and her jaw dropped. *Fuckin' hippie?* Cranky local, she may be. But a fuckin' hippie she was not.

She looked at the pyramid stack of acid green plastic tubs with hot pink lids in the front display window of the store. Walking over to the merchandise, she stared the Ferrari guy dead in the eye and plucked a container off the very top of the pile before heading straight out the entrance. The journalist scampered behind her.

By the time the Ferrari guy followed them outside, green slime was splattered on the hood of the coupe. Against the light grey paint, the neon sludge looked radioactive. Aimee stood in front of the car – the empty container in one hand and the lid in the other. A small laugh bubbled up out of her chest.

'Whoever drives that car's gonna be pissed,' the Ferrari guy laughed from the doorway. He looked down the footpath.

The keyless entry on the car bleeped and all the lights blinked twice. Aimee stopped admiring the glowing mucus that continued to crawl out to the edges of the bonnet and looked up at the woman who was now standing on the driver's side.

'Is this your Ferrari?' Aimee asked. Her eyes widened and her stomach started to ooze like the slime.

'It's a Porsche, but yes.' The woman laughed as she replied, as if mistaking a $240,000 sports car for a $300,000 sports car was something to be embarrassed about.

Aimee stepped back. 'I accidentally slimed your car.'

The woman walked around and took a perfunctory glance. She waved a hand in the air. 'I don't care, it's just a rental.'

'I'm Aimee, I can give you money for a carwash—'

'Oh! Aimee!' the woman interrupted. 'Bookstore Aimee! Oh, good. I'm here to see you!' She switched her tan leather handbag to the opposite arm, straightened her Chanel sunglasses and laughed as if she'd just unexpectedly run into her best friend from primary school. 'Yeah, so Lang – he's been your store's landlord . . . forever? Well, he died. Yeah, so, I'm selling off all his properties. You're gonna have to move out.'

'Wait. What?' Aimee shook her head like a cartoon character who'd just been hit on the head with a comically-large wooden mallet. 'You're a real estate agent?'

'God no. I'm a lawyer,' she scoffed. '*And* I'm Lang's daughter. Or *was*. Anyway, I came down from the Gold Coast for the morning to deal with things. I'm selling everything off because he's—'

'Dead,' Aimee finished the sentence with a nod. 'I . . .' She looked across the road at the surf store for a moment before returning her focus to the splat of green slime that had started to fry like an egg on the car hood in the sun. Gooey and bubbling in the middle. Crispy around the thinning edges. At one point, it may have even sizzled.

The woman was still smiling but her frivolous demeanour developed a tinge of awkwardness as Aimee remained silent. Reports of rocketing property prices had clearly soothed whatever grief she'd been feeling since her father's death. She pulled a property flyer out of her handbag and held it out. When Aimee didn't reach for it, she stepped forward and tucked it into the waistband of Aimee's jeans. 'Just . . . in case you want to know more.' She waved a limp hand in the air as she turned and walked back to the driver's side. A few seconds later, she ducked her head up over the open door. 'Great song!' The end of the *Big Little Lies* theme drifted out into the street.

Aimee looked up into the sun and closed her eyes as the engine of the Porsche thundered. The summer heat seeped into her cheeks.

The journalist was basically frothing at the mouth. He looked up at the shop awning and wrote down the name of the store: The Dream Explosion. 'How would you like to be referred to in the article?'

Aimee lowered her head and opened her eyes just enough to keep the sun blocked out. 'Aimee Maguire. Cranky local.'

TWO

The outside of Aimee's apartment would've still been beautiful if one of those discount super-pharmacies hadn't moved in below and painted the entire building clashy primary colours. She'd been living above the old pub since before it stopped being a pub. In the middle of town and on a sprawling corner, she'd wanted to live there since she was little. Now, she did. The murmurs and cheers of revellers packed inside until the early hours no longer drifted up through the floorboards, lulling her to sleep. And the glossy old bottle-green tiled walls that cladded the exterior had been covered up in red and yellow signs advertising cut-price incontinence pads and anti-fungal ointments and prescription deodorant. But upstairs, it had remained the same.

Aimee had shut The Dream Explosion early and ducked home to grab her swimmers so she could go dunk her body in the ocean. It's what she did whenever something bad happened in her life. Lately, there'd been a lot of swims. Far out in the ocean, if she plunged under the water, sunk down to the sandy floor and held her breath, her problems wouldn't find her.

She opened the dark stained front door and exhaled. The afternoon light streamed through all the window-lined walls of the open-plan apartment that was piled high with a weird mix of chic antiques and bizarre finds. Her apartment was so cool it put nineties sitcom apartments to shame. A collection of art deco mirrors hung above an old workshop bench. A faded metal Coca-Cola sign stretched across an entire wall. On another was a neon light from a strip club: LIVE NUDE GIRLS. The pink cursive writing glowed. Aimee walked past a row of six red leather upholstered seats salvaged from an old theatre, and threw her satchel on one of the chairs. Her scuffed-up cream Converse sneakers squeaked on the hardwood floors as she walked through the living room, past the old dining table and into the bathroom to get her swimsuit. A few seconds later, she emerged empty handed. She walked to her bedroom, rummaged around, and then walked out – heading to the other end of the apartment to Charlie's bedroom, where she upheld her end of the gay-guy-straight-girl housemate deal: Look, don't touch – and for the love of god, don't go digging through any drawers. From there, she whirled out and over to the spare bedroom before finding herself back in the kitchen where she picked up the receiver of the powder green rotary dial telephone on the benchtop. She knew the number off by heart.

'Hey, is Rob there?'

As Aimee waited, she reached up into one of the cabinets for a glass and, when she went to place it down on the counter, she almost knocked something over. She glanced down. A KeepCup. She furrowed her brow, leant over and rested her chin on the beat-up stainless steel counter to inspect the matte black BPA-free mug. Her face was close enough that she could feel warmth coming off it.

'Have you been to my house today?' she said into the receiver, her tone matching the confused look on her face. 'I can't find my swimsuit. The navy one I always wear. I wore it this morning, came home and hung it on the shower rod like every other morning. Now . . . it's gone.'

'Do you think it finally just disintegrated away?' Rob teased.

The years-old swimsuit had become a punchline for Rob and Charlie. Tattered and worn-out, Aimee refused to toss it. She'd tried buying new bikinis, but whenever she'd wear them in public, she always ended up self-consciously tugging at the straps. Her old one was just right. A little threadbare. But just right.

'Maybe a breeze came in through the window and blew the final threads of it away, like pollen.' Rob continued to amuse herself.

Aimee craned her head into her shoulder to hold the phone in place and used her free hands to fill up a glass of water at the sink. 'Charlie never moves it.' She chose to ignore Rob's jokes. 'And he left before me today.' She picked up the phone base with her right hand and walked over to the dining table, using her left hand to pour the water into a tall glass vase with a giant cherry blossom branch in it. 'Then I found . . .' she walked back to the kitchen bench and crouched down to stare at the foreign object that had invaded her home, 'a *KeepCup*. You know the deal with KeepCups in this household. And it's . . . still warm.'

'What'd the FBI say?' Rob gasped.

Aimee grabbed the phone base again, walked across to the living room, moved one of Charlie's acoustic guitars off the long peacock blue velvet couch and flopped into it. She pivoted her body until she was upside down – feet dangling over the back of the sofa, the top of her head resting on the floor.

'Maybe everyone in town finally got fed up with your refusal to stop using single-use coffee cups and this is all part of a menacing campaign to scare you into using environmentally friendly drinkware,' Rob chattered away before changing topics entirely. 'Ooh! I almost forgot: Music Club tonight!'

Aimee let her body collapse off the couch and onto the vintage Persian rug. 'I just want to go for a swim,' she blurted with the jittery impatience of a recovering smoker who couldn't quite find where they'd hidden their 'in case of emergency' pack.

On the other end of the phone line, Rob's voice snapped to attention. 'Oh god. I should've known – the obsession over a misplaced swim- suit and desperately needing to swim. What's happened? Do I need to come over?'

'Nothing, nothing.' Aimee batted away the quick-fire probing about what big bad thing had happened. 'No, don't come over, I'm fine. I'll tell you tonight.'

After hanging up, she ran her index finger back and forth over the intricately patterned teal and burnt orange wool carpet before getting to her feet and wandering back to the kitchen. There was only one thing that could replace an afternoon swim. She popped the lid off a bottle of tequila and poured it into a heavy crystal glass.

The afternoon light had already started to lose its spark. She picked up a framed photo off the nearby windowsill and took a sip while studying it. Even with the muted sepia tone, her store building still looked the same as it did back then. The only thing that had changed was the hand-painted sign above the corrugated iron awning: MAGUIRE ANTIQUES. She placed the photo back down on the windowsill and picked up the frame next to it. A photo of the same store, but a different era and a new awning. THE DREAM EXPLOSION. Two kids standing in front. One of them was a much younger Aimee – eighteen or so – with her then-boyfriend Tim. Aimee was dressed in low-cut jeans and Etnies while Tim sported a trucker hat and an SMP belt – a sartorial time-stamp of the early 2000s. He'd swooped her up in his arms for the photo, as if they'd just been married.

Aimee sipped from her glass and realised the photo was one of the last remaining signs that Tim had lived inside the apartment she was standing in. Well, he still *did* live there. Technically. Just not at that moment. He'd left one or two pairs of boardies in their bedroom's cedar chest of drawers. And the surfboard in the hallway – one of many he had, but the one he used the least. The rest had been moved out for the summer, but you couldn't tell. The apartment had always been Aimee's domain. Tim's décor offerings came in the form of soggy wetsuits, surfboards and grains of sand in the sheets.

She moved to the fridge to get some ice and opened the door before quickly shutting it again. She stood back and stared. A rectangular card with cursive font on it had been stuck to the stainless-steel door with a magnet. It looked like the fortune cards one of the roadside clairvoyants in town handed out to clients after doing their palm readings. She leant in and read it.

If you want to win your life you have to go wild and jump into the fire.

THREE

A slinky, distorted guitar riff buzzed through the bar and the *tish tish tish* of the hi-hat shimmered. Then the rest of the drums cascaded down and the too-cool bass line decided to shuffle in. Charlie purred the opening lyrics to Olivia Newton-John's 'Totally Hot' into the microphone, abandoning his sulky pout for just a split second to flash a smirk.

No one knew exactly where Charlie came from, but it seemed that everyone was glad he existed. Anyone watching in the bar when he was playing would quickly become jealous of his black electric guitar. The way he'd grind his narrow hips up against it and how his tanned biceps flexed when he moved his fingertips up the frets on the neck was truly something to behold, if you asked Aimee. Charlie's band, The Girly Boys, did surf rock covers of songs by female artists. Their version of Kim Carnes' 'Bette Davis Eyes' was used on the soundtrack to a *Grey's Anatomy* episode. In the three years that Charlie had been living with Aimee, she'd never once seen him go to the gym. He stayed fit through sex and surf. She would've hated him if it weren't for the fact he was as beautiful as the breakfast quesadillas he made her every morning.

A pouchy middle-aged guy who smelt of essential oils came over to Aimee's table in the back corner of the pub. 'Can I get you a drink?'

The pickup line was as dated as the tweed vest he was wearing. Music Club drew an interesting crowd. It happened once a week at The Palace Hotel – a grand old three-level pub with wraparound iron lacework verandahs. Local bands would jam. And the local Looney Tunes would slam whatever was on tap.

'Someone's already getting me a drink,' Aimee yelled over the music.

'Can I get a name?' he smiled.

'Rob,' Aimee nodded.

'I meant yours.'

'Aimee.'

'Is Rob your boyfriend, Aimee?'

'Rob's my barber.'

The cold metal edge of a knife jabbed into the side of the man's neck and his body seized up.

'You want a cut-throat shave?' a throaty voice whispered.

The guy froze with wide eyes.

Then the menacing voice broke into a laugh. 'Relax, it's a butter knife from the bistro.' Rob wrapped her arm around his neck.

'This is Rob. She has a hair salon in town called Barber Rob's.' Aimee closed her eyes and laughed. This routine had become unintentionally rehearsed over the years. Barber Rob was tall, thin and had a short blonde shag haircut like Meg Ryan in the nineties. She was the coolest person in Byron Bay.

The guy straightened his vest. 'You know, that's really not in the spirit of Music Club.' He pursed his lips and walked off.

Charlie's band had finished their set and the microphone screeched over the speakers, which meant it was time for Bada Bing. Bada Bing had lived on the streets of Byron since Aimee could remember. He was the town mascot – a grizzled, opinionated mascot – and his submissions to the Letters To The Editor page of *The Byron Times* were famous. In a way, he was the original Byron celebrity. People had tried helping him over the years but he'd never accepted because, as he explained, he didn't want to give up the luxury of being able to complain. To fund his low-key lifestyle, he'd carved out a very specific niche: Emceeing Music Club and presenting a Guess Who, Don't Sue segment between sets.

The game was simple: Bada Bing would present clues to gossipy tidbits and then the audience would yell out their guesses for who the blind items were about. His nomadic lifestyle meant that he saw and heard everything and, ever since the glitz-factor of the town had cranked up a notch, the things he saw and heard were juicy. The only rule of Guess Who, Don't Sue? If anyone who was named during the guessing happened to be in the crowd and started denying the allegations, they got booed. The town really had gone tabloid.

Bada Bing had kicked off. 'Guess Who, Don't Sue: Which Hollywood star got attacked by a flock of ibises while picking through a pile of discarded furniture on council kerbside collection day?'

Rob's voice rasped over everyone. 'Shelley Craft!'

'She's not a Hollywood star,' Aimee said.

'Well she should be. She's a ray of sunshine.'

Out of all the notable personalities who lived in Byron, Rob had a particular fondness for the *Block* presenter, who'd become somewhat of a local property mogul after flipping a few houses in the area. Judging by the face Shelley made whenever Rob saw her in town and yelled, 'Oi, Crafty!', the affection was not mutual.

———

Charlie bounded over to the table and wrapped Aimee in his arms. 'How's my little slime monster?'

'I didn't tell him.' Rob put her hands in the air.

'I saw the video,' Charlie laughed.

Rob held up her phone. 'There's a video? Send it now!'

Aimee closed her eyes and placed her head down on the round bar table – grimacing as her cheek touched the puddle of condensation that had pooled around the drinks.

Rob pulled Aimee's hair out of the puddle. 'What can I do? Should I finally get back on stage and scream-sing "Thunderstruck"?'

Charlie drum-rolled on the table with his hands and Aimee sat up.

'I mean, *yes*, you absolutely *should* do that again,' Aimee said. 'Just not tonight. The crowd still seems . . . *sensitive*.'

Ever since Ben Harper showed up one time and tested out new material while he was in town for Bluesfest, Music Club had started to turn into hipster territory with lots of baby-voiced twenty-somethings ruining classic songs. Tensions flared about a year ago when Rob got drunk and decided to annoy them by crashing the stage and performing the AC/DC anthem, acapella. It had become somewhat of a ritual.

Aimee shook her head in frustration. 'Let's just talk about anything other than *sliming videos*.'

'Ooh, let's talk about dicks!' Charlie flipped his phone around. The image of a naked man's bottom half was on the screen.

Aimee shrieked.

Rob grabbed the phone excitedly. 'It's huge!'

Charlie laughed. 'It's the big dick from that Netflix show – *Oceans of Angels*.'

'I *thought* I recognised it.' Rob studied the photo intensely as she used her thumb and forefinger to zoom in. 'Aimee, don't you recognise it?' She held up the screen.

Aimee raised her eyebrows and sighed defiantly. 'No.'

Charlie shot up straight. He didn't get shocked by much. But this was a topic he was passionate about. 'How do you not recognise it? It's *everywhere*!'

'*Everywhere*? Where's *everywhere*?' Aimee laughed.

'The internet, nan,' Rob teased.

'I don't even know what *Angels and Oceans* is.'

'*Oceans of Angels*,' Rob corrected. 'The first season just dropped and it's so bad but that's why it's so good. It's about a group of wannabe actors trying to make it in nineties Hollywood. The cast is a bunch of nobodies and the acting is *terrible*.'

'But the actors are also *hot*,' Charlie chimed in. 'And they get naked and have sex.'

Aimee reluctantly posed a question. 'And why is this *particular* penis getting talked about?'

'Because it's *big*. Jeez, Aimee, pay attention.' Charlie slapped the table.

'There are entire think pieces being written about it online,' Rob shared, as if she were talking about an investigative report she'd just read in the *New York Times*.

Aimee furrowed her brow. 'Think pieces about a dick?'

'Not just *a* dick, Aimee,' Charlie said. 'A *massive* dick.'

'It's the pénis de résistance of the entire show,' Rob chirped.

Charlie nodded. 'And it's not just *Oceans of Angels*. Every TV series these days is showing full-frontal penis. We're in a wiener renaissance.'

'Debate is raging about whether it's real or a prosthetic.' Rob pointed to the picture on Charlie's phone. 'And you wanna know the best part?'

'The big dick is getting its own spin-off series?' Aimee deadpanned.

'The show's second season is being filmed on the Gold Coast right now,' Rob informed her. 'Finally! Government incentives and tax breaks are being used for good.' *Gasp!* 'Maybe we could track down the big dick.'

Rob and Charlie snapped their heads up to glare at each other. 'Dibs!' they yelled in unison.

Aimee took a big sip of her tequila. 'Well, thank you for getting me up to speed with *Angels and Oceans* – I'll definitely be avoiding it.'

'Aimee, there's a whole world of TV out there at your fingertips and you reject it all in favour of watching YouTube videos about chiropractors cracking people's backs.' Rob waved a hand in the air.

'Hey, I stream TV shows as well,' Aimee informed her friends.

'Oh, sor-ry, Stream Queen,' Rob laughed.

'What TV shows are you streaming, Stream Queen?' Charlie piled on.

Aimee fought a smile as she ventured an answer she knew her friends would mock. In this trio, they all knew their roles perfectly and leant into them hard. 'A lot of the old episodes of *Just Shoot Me* are on YouTube now.'

'Aimee!' Rob covered her face in pain.

Aimee laughed. 'Same with *Becker*.'

Charlie was mid-sip and covered his mouth as tequila dribbled out. 'Oh my god, it's all making sense. I've lived with you for years and I'm only just realising this now: You're female Becker!'

'You are!' Rob yelled. 'Always so cranky and ready to embark on long rants about minor inconveniences at a moment's notice.'

Aimee closed her eyes and laughed as Rob leant over and playfully poked her. 'You're Becker, you're Becker! That's what we're calling you now.'

'You know, on second thought,' Aimee swatted her away, 'I think I'd rather talk about the sliming video.'

'Actually . . .' Rob reached into her pocket and cleared her throat. 'I know you said you wanted to avoid talking about your . . . *other* . . . news, but I'm breaking the embargo.' She unfolded the property flyer the rich Porsche landlady had tucked into Aimee's jeans.

Aimee snatched it. 'Are these being handed out?'

'No, I stole it from your handbag earlier. Serious chat: What are you gonna do?'

Aimee used her finger to jab the flyer into the puddle on the table. 'Not much I can do. It's being sold with approval for retail and a thousand levels of boutique apartments. And a goddamn . . . *juicery*.' She whacked the table with both hands and the playfulness that had bubbled just seconds earlier was gone. 'I've been there eighteen years. My parents had the store before that. Same landlord the whole time. Barely raised the rent, ever.'

Charlie dropped his jaw. 'What if I sell the taco truck?'

Aimee affectionately grabbed a chunk of his scruffy, curly-ish brown hair and suddenly remembered the missing swimsuit. 'Hey, did one of your Grindr hookups stay over last night? My swimsuit's missing.'

Charlie laughed. 'Why would they want your swimmers? And are you sure it didn't just disintegrate?'

Aimee ignored the running gag. 'And there was . . . a *KeepCup*.'

Charlie arched an eyebrow and smirked. 'Did you wash it or throw it out?'

Rob persisted with her theory. 'I still think it's the town trying to scare you into going green. A KeepCup on the kitchen bench is their version of a horse head in the bed.'

Aimee looked back down at the flyer. 'Once this sells, the rent will be . . .' she exhaled as she tried to estimate a price before giving up, 'I dunno. More than I can afford. And the other shops in town are now all the same.'

'You could move your store into my salon?' Rob offered. 'We could be like a cool barber-bookshop hybrid.' She jutted her shoulders back and forth. 'Like those cafes in clothing stores or—'

'Like Tim and his rooftop bar?' Aimee finished her friend's sentence.

Rob stopped shoulder dancing and scrunched up her nose. 'I'm not helping, am I?'

'Just don't tell anyone about it. I don't feel like being interrogated by everyone in town before I've figured out what I'm doing.'

The microphone screeched again. 'Guess Who, Don't Sue: Aimee's being evicted from her store and she's probably poor now.'

Aimee jumped off her bar stool and walked closer to the stage with a screwed-up face. 'It's not a Guess Who, Don't Sue if you just blatantly name the person outright,' she argued.

'Boo!' The crowd went nuts.

'Yeah, boo!' Rob joined in. 'Sorry,' she mouthed when Aimee shot her a look.

'My store's not *closing down*. It's just—'

'Whatever,' Bada Bing cut her off. 'And guys, out of respect for Aimee, can everyone stop texting around that video of her sliming the car?'

'Thank you,' Aimee said.

Bada Bing continued. 'For everyone's convenience, I've posted it to the town Facebook page. Remember to like and share.'

Aimee looked like she'd just been punched in the face.

'Ooh, found it!' Rob waved her phone in the air. 'At least you look hot in it,' she teased.

Aimee walked back to the table and grabbed for the phone but Rob pulled back. 'Wait up, wait up. Lemme see something again.' Rob dragged her finger along the screen, scrolling the footage back and hitting play. Then she paused. 'What did Tim say?' She held up the phone. Aimee squinted at the screen. There was Tim in the background: standing on the roof of his surf store across the road from The Dream Explosion, looking down as Aimee slimed the Porsche.

Aimee pursed her lips and looked at the floor. 'I didn't know he saw.'

Silence.

'We need more tequila.' Rob slapped the table and headed for the bar.

Aimee called out after her. 'Just one! I have a bank meeting in the morning!'

Charlie rubbed his head on Aimee's shoulder. 'I know your Tim time-out includes not even talking about him. But you can break that at any time with us.'

Aimee looked down at the wet real estate flyer that was now disintegrating into pulp and dug the nail of her right middle finger into the pad of her thumb.

The microphone screeched. A faint whisper began to build over the speakers. It was unmistakable: Rob humming the opening *ahhh-ahhhs* of 'Thunderstruck'.

'C'mon.' Aimee stood up. 'We gotta get down the front before she stage dives again.'

FOUR

Aimee winced under the glare of the bright fluorescent office lights and wondered why all banks had started making their offices look like Ikea showrooms. A little boy started playing with one of those pens attached to a chain on the nearby teller desk – whipping the metal rope against the laminated counter. She flinched at the clicks and clacks.

'Sick?' asked the woman tapping away on the computer behind the desk.

It took a second for Aimee to realise the question was aimed at her. 'Hmm?'

'Feeling sick? Your sunglasses and cap . . .' The woman waved a hand around her face with a laugh. She'd been talking to Aimee with a sense of peppy familiarity from the very second Aimee loomed into the office like a hungover black cloud.

Not even Aimee's short responses were enough to snuff out the chatty small talk. The Bomb had not worked. Two Panadol Rapid plus two Nurofen with a Gatorade chaser – a cocktail remedy Aimee and Rob had concocted one blurry morning after a night of drinking at Music Club – had been a sure-fire remedy until today. The Bomb usually wiped out any ache and regret that thrived the morning after. But The Bomb had failed to detonate and now sitting in a fake Eames chair, Aimee was a swirl of ache and regret. Regrets about drinking so much tequila. Regrets about booking an 8am bank consultation the morning after drinking so much tequila. This wasn't a regular hangover. It was a hangover involving administration forms. No one should endure such suffering.

Aimee's phone buzzed. A text from Rob: *I feel surprisingly not hungover!*

Aimee thumbed at her screen, typing out a reply. 'Me too!' she lied. She adjusted the baseball cap and tugged the brim down low over her face. She'd usually be wearing her sister's old beat-up leather Akubra – the one with the braided leather band and the red feather on the side – but when she went to grab it off the hook near the door that morning, it was gone. Missing, like her navy swimmers. *Did I drunkenly move it when I got home last night?* she wondered, haphazardly trying to come up with innocent reasons that wouldn't add to her stress. *Did I wear it to the pub? Maybe I left it there . . .*

She picked another plastic-wrapped Mentos out of the bowl on the desk, held it to her lips and pressed on one end of the wrapper until the other side burst open and the lolly shot into her mouth. Orange flavoured. Citrus helped ease nausea, right? She crunched it between her back teeth.

The woman continued tapping away on the computer keyboard while making mindless small talk. 'Can you believe it's been almost twenty years since Byron Bay High?' She smiled as she stared at the computer screen.

Aimee took a moment. Had they gone to school together? She squinted behind the tinted lenses of her sunnies and tried to recall the woman's face. She looked and dressed like she was about ten years older than Aimee. The weird satin bank teller neckerchief she was wearing didn't help. Aimee searched for a sign. Her eyes flicked down to a glittery yellow smiley-face sticker stuck to the woman's name badge. Nichelle. Aimee still had no idea. She decided to venture a vague response. 'The glory days.' She nodded.

Nichelle laughed. 'Yeah. I always thought you'd be one of the ones who got outta here as soon as you could. You always seemed like you . . . I don't know . . . had big things planned.'

Aimee shuffled in her seat and hoped her lack of response would end the conversation. Inside, though, her mind hooked into Nichelle's statement and paused. She had no recollection of ever having big things planned. One day she was in high school. The next, she was turning her dead parents' antiques shop into a bookstore. What had she imagined her life would look like? She could only think of two words: *Not this*.

Nichelle swivelled the computer screen around to show an online form and data. 'OK, so, from the store, you make enough to pay your salary and your part-timer. Any other assets?' She started to answer her own question, filling in the form before Aimee could reply. 'About $10,000 in savings. No stocks or investments. No property.'

Aimee looked around to make sure no one else was in the office, over-hearing the detailed list of her failings. 'My car?' Her voice went up at the end.

Nichelle winced. She shrugged her shoulders up around her head and whispered apologetically: 'That's not an asset, sorry.'

'Don't be sorry. You're right . . . It's really not an asset. Right now, it's broken down and at Moe's Garage.'

'Any other income streams?'

'Um. I . . . run a rollerball game in the carpark out the back of the bookstore. Once a week.' She cringed at herself. 'It's like basketball but on rollerblades.'

Nichelle laughed. 'Yeah, our kid used to play with you guys. Loved it.'

Aimee still had no idea who Nichelle was and had no memory of her kid. She kept the conversation moving. 'I've also got a garage full of antiques. From my parents' old store. They're worth . . . something.'

'I'm sorry, Aimee.' Nichelle took her hands off the keyboard and looked down. 'Just . . . what happened with your family and now the store and Tim—'

The mention of Tim's name snapped Aimee to attention. She shot up in her seat and took off her sunglasses.

Nichelle's eyes widened. 'Not that I know any details.' She began to babble. 'I just . . .'

Aimee closed her eyes and changed the topic. 'So, the loan . . .'

Nichelle sighed. 'You know, it seems like it's every day that shop owners – locals – are coming in. Same problem as you. Buildings are being sold off, rents are going up. Property prices jumped almost fifty per cent this year. Gleeson's Market – shutting down. Landlord sold the building last week. I think a . . . ah, what's it called . . . a . . . *stretch studio* is moving in.' She laughed. 'I don't know why you need to pay someone to stretch your body for you but, hey – the town's changing.'

'So what can I do?'

'Other clients I've been talking to are moving further out. The prices in Ballina are getting just as bad. Some are having luck in Grafton. Casino. An hour or so away, but at least you'd still be near Byron.'

'Would you move to Casino?'

'We own our house. Here in town. Bought about sixteen years ago. Way before it boomed.' She raised her eyebrows and shrugged. 'Tempting to sell now.'

Aimee nodded. 'Smart.'

The kid had ditched the pen and moved onto playing with the automatic sliding door that was right behind Aimee. It whizzed open. Hot air and noise from the banked-up traffic burst in. The door whizzed shut. Silence. Then it whizzed open again. Heat and honking. Whiz. Silence.

Aimee looked down at her scuffed Converses and tapped the rubber edges of the soles together. 'So . . . how possible is it to get a loan?' *Whiz. Heat. Honk.* 'Oh my god,' Aimee whispered, 'whose fucking kid is that?'

'Mine,' Nichelle said.

'Oh. Right. Of course.' Aimee turned over her shoulder to glance at the kid and forced a smile. 'I remember him.' She had never seen him in her life. 'You should bring him to rollerball tonight.'

'It's not *him*. It's *they*.'
Whiz. Heat. Honk.
'So . . . the loan?'
Whiz. Silence.

FIVE

The Dream Explosion was empty and Aimee was scrolling through online property listings. She searched 'Byron Bay' for what was probably the nineteenth time since she left the bank but no results showed up in her price range. Ballina was the same. She typed 'Casino' into the search bar, hit ENTER on the keyboard and made a face like she'd just stepped in something gross on the footpath. The results made her shut down the browser tab entirely.

She stood up from behind the counter, walked to the front of the store and leant in the doorway, looking out across the street at Tim's. BYRON BOARDS. The store name was painted in faded navy font on the awning. He'd started the shop long before it became cool for beer breweries and liquid body wash businesses and fake tan companies to incorporate the town's name into their product branding. The old two-level store had scaffolding around it. Tim had approached his landlord last summer about adding a rooftop bar and it irritated Aimee more than it should. He made surfboards and sold wetsuits – why add a rooftop bar? The annoyance turned to anger and it was mixing with the hangover and the two takeaway flat whites she'd just inhaled. She walked back to her MacBook and opened Google. There was something else on her mind. A growing paranoia about how her hat and swimmers went missing. And where the hell that damn KeepCup came from. It was still sitting smugly on the bench when she woke up that morning. *Tap, tap, tap.* 'Byron Bay house break-ins'. Search. No recent news articles had been published. She googled the details of the local police station to check its opening hours – it was Byron, you could never be sure – then grabbed her keys from behind the counter and walked out of the store, locking the thick, glossy red door. As she adjusted the cross-shoulder strap of her leather satchel and turned around to walk off, she looked over at the surf store again. Tim was on the roof. Change of plans.

———

The spiral metal staircase at the back of Tim's shop wound up to the rooftop and Aimee had to duck under a metal beam when she reached the landing.

'Not quite ready for happy hour yet.' Tim threw a load of construction crap onto a pile of more construction crap.

'Well, at least you still have a store.'

'Yeah, I heard. One more building getting sold. It sucks.'

'Heard? You *saw* it happen.' Aimee winced at the sharp delivery.

'If you wanna get into specifics, I actually *read* it. In today's newspaper. What I *did* see was you sliming a car.'

Aimee held her arms out and furrowed her brow. 'And you didn't feel the need to come outside and see if things were OK?'

His lack of frustration wound her up. 'We're *engaged.*' She hated that word but it was true.

He walked over and grabbed her hands. 'Hey. The store's getting sold, but the business isn't. It's not as bad as you think.'

'I think it still requires a call.'

'We both agreed to this time-out.' He tried to sound like the reasonable one.

The truth was, *he* proposed the time-out. And she'd only agreed to it because her hands were tied. When the guy you've been dating since you were seventeen tells you he wants to take a break from your relationship for a few months, your only option is to agree. Because if you don't? The *break* becomes a *breakup*.

'And we talked about the challenges: no contact over summer,' Tim continued. 'It's hard enough with our shops being across the street from each other. Yes, some things are gonna come up. But if we wanna do it right, we can't just give in and run to each other every time something happens. Especially if we're . . .' he let out a weird laugh and looked away.

'What? C'mon. *Especially if we're* . . .' Aimee forced him into saying the actual words.

'Hooking up with other people.' He said it in such a matter-of-fact way. 'If we're doing that and we're also in contact all the time, it's . . . confusing.'

Aimee had no response. Sure, part of the deal was no contact. No daily check-ins about mundane things. But that rule applied to boring everyday problems like getting a flat tyre or doing a late-night dash to the supermarket only to find they'd run out of double coated Tim Tams. (In Aimee's world, the latter was a regular topic of conversation. Who the hell bought *regular* Tim Tams instead of the double coated ones? Probably the same morons who bought regular Panadol instead of Panadol Rapid. Why would you not choose to get rid of your headache faster?) Her livelihood being completely destroyed was a little different to double coated Tim Tams being temporarily out-of-stock.

Tim broke the silence. 'Also. Moe called. He said he needs to speak to you about the car repairs.'

Aimee sighed. 'Losing my building isn't just an everyday inconvenience.'

'It's really not that big of a deal. You'll find another store. It's fine.'

'Um, are you gonna move to *Casino* with me?' Aimee backed off for a moment and paused. Tim's way of arguing always annoyed her. He'd stay calm and dismiss whatever the problem was with a shrug, like it was no big deal. Of course, by contrast, Aimee would look petty and irrational.

She was the first person to admit that, generally, she exhibited both of those qualities – but wasn't that why people got into relationships? So they'd have a dedicated person to rant all their petty and irrational grievances to? Still, this wasn't just one of her petty and irrational rants. Her entire life was now up in the air. This was worthy of breaking the time-out rules. Aimee had been seeing articles popping up relentlessly on trendy women's websites about gaslighting. Was Tim gaslighting her right now? She still didn't entirely understand what it was. Whenever she read those first-person articles about it – written by people detailing their crappy relationships – she'd always find herself closing the browser tab with a sigh while thinking, *You* both *sound like assholes.*

Aimee decided to change the topic.

'Also, how does some lady called *Narissa* know about our time-out?' She scrunched her face up in irritation.

Tim turned to her and squinted. '. . . Narissa?'

'Yes. Narissa.'

'Who's . . . *Narissa?*'

'The bank lady,' Aimee spelled out, losing her patience.

'*Nichelle?*'

'Huh?'

'*Nichelle.* We went to school with her.'

'Then why don't I remember her? And how could I *not* remember someone called . . .' Aimee paused and tried to remember Narissa's real name.

Tim widened his eyes and filled in the blank. '*Nichelle.*'

'How does she know about our . . . relationship stuff?'

'I dunno. My mum sees her mum around. She probably mentioned it.'

Ah, Aimee thought. *Tim's mum. Of course.* The mere mention triggered her temper again.

'That's not just something you casually mention in conversation . . . like, *Yeah we're going to Daydream Island for the weekend – we scored some cheap fares in the Friday Frenzy.*'

'What's the Friday Frenzy?' He picked up a long yellow spirit level and waved it through a cloud of dust that billowed in the sunlight.

They stood in silence and Tim turned around to look out over the street. It was the most they'd spoken and the closest they'd physically been since November, when Tim had pulled the rug out from under Aimee. They were just over a month into the time-out.

From behind, Tim's body still looked like it did when they first started dating in high school. His faded blue Quiksilver tee stretched across his broad back and shoulders and skimmed down his trim torso to his narrow hips. His muscular, lanky limbs always seemed to glow more golden with each day of summer. Still, not everything was exactly the same. There were the kinds of changes that naturally occur over twenty or so years. The sun beating down on the rooftop highlighted the silver strands that had, at some point, started flecking his shaggy brownish hair. On the sides, the colour had become more ashy. Aimee wondered when that had happened and if she was a bad person for not noticing until now. It was in those quiet moments when Tim wasn't looking that Aimee would stare at him and scour her soul, trying to find the feeling that used to flood her body at the simple sight of him. Like, when her biology class would drag on after the school bell and she'd look out the window and see him – in his untucked uniform – waiting for her with a cardboard carton of Oak chocolate milk. It had been forever since that feeling had been around. It was like a super complicated home Wi-Fi password, written down on a scrap of paper that you couldn't find when you really needed it. Aimee had it once. It was definitely there. She remembers. It should still be around. Somewhere.

Tim turned back around, looked at Aimee and opened his mouth – then shifted his focus to something over her shoulder.

'Hey!' a voice perked up from behind Aimee. The girl it belonged to walked into sight and over to Tim. Twenties. Cut-off denim short-shorts that frayed around the leg. Tanned. Hot. One of those fake vintage band tees. She was holding two coffees – both in KeepCups. She handed one over, stood close to Tim and put her free hand in the back pocket of his dusty black boardshorts. He pulled away. He didn't have to – summer time-out: no contact, no rules. But Aimee was glad he did.

'Make sure you wash them straight away,' Aimee said out of nowhere. 'The KeepCups. If you don't and you leave them for a week, the cup just clouds up with mould. They don't tell you that when you buy them. It should really be on the label.'

The hot girl scrunched up her face. 'Ew.'

———

'Oh, fuck the Hot Ew Girl!' Rob's voice shrieked through Aimee's iPhone. 'Did she at least have split ends and patchy fake tan around the knees?'

'The whole . . . *putting her hand in his back pocket* thing . . .' Aimee marched down Jonson Street towards Moe's Garage and the police station, getting progressively crankier with each step. 'Just . . . the gall of Gen Z . . . Wait, what's the age range of Gen Z again?'

'Can I say something you're not gonna like?' Rob strained her voice. 'Remember, this is what you agreed to. I know it sucks and I hate the Hot Ew Girl even more than you do, but I just need to remind you of that. OK, now let's go back to hating the Hot Ew Girl.'

'Oh my god. You like the Hot Ew Girl better than me.' Aimee covered her face and laughed. 'It just—'

'Sucks,' Rob jumped in. 'It really sucks.' The bell from Rob's shop counter pinged in the background. 'Ughhh. Sorry, client—'

'No, you go,' Aimee cut her off.

'But call me if you need to and I'll see you later this arv. Also, I still can't believe how *not* hungover I am today!'

'Ohhh, me too, I feel amazing.' Aimee hammed it up and tried not to hurl into a street busker's guitar case.

They all end up going back to wherever it is they came from.

Maybe, in a few weeks, the Hot Ew Girl would crawl back to whatever metropolitan City Beach store she crawled out of. Was City Beach still even a thing? She'd always see the store's logo on giant banners for events it sponsored each year during Schoolies. Aimee cringed at herself for sounding ancient. A queue snaked out of a fancy new sushi train restaurant and, after a few metres of polite orderliness, the line turned into a feral crowd that blocked the entire path. Foot traffic came to a standstill. Aimee dodged through.

They all end up going back to wherever it is they came from.

A mum in a billowy Camilla kaftan scrolled through her phone as she mindlessly dragged along three little boys who were all dressed in matching white-and-blue outfits and wearing identical shark tooth necklaces.

'Yeah, we're Airbnbing next to Chris Hemsworth's house. CHRIS HEMSWORTH'S HOUSE,' a guy wearing cuffed cream chinos said into his phone, just loud enough to score glances from intrigued pedestrians.

You couldn't escape the guy. Chris Hemsworth. Even when he wasn't in town. Aimee had heard someone in the coffee shop that morning say they saw online that Chris and the family had left for the summer to escape the crowds. Went to Lord Howe Island or somewhere else remote. *Just great*, she'd thought. *Too bustling for you, Christopher? Gee, that sucks. Wouldn't know what that's like.* She'd read one time that Lord Howe Island had a strict limit on how many visitors it could take at any one time. Four hundred or something. Now that the island paradise was getting Hemsworthified, maybe it would become the new hotspot. Aimee had vengefully thought of ways to drum up attention and get the word out. Maybe launch a guerilla marketing campaign online, touting The Top 400 Club. People loved clubs they couldn't get into. Especially ones with celebrities. Everyone would clamour to score a spot in The Top 400 Club and the island would book up years in advance. *Take that, Lord Howe Island! Enjoy the touristy buzz, Chris!*

Aimee marched ahead and, in the distance, saw a troupe of half a dozen fitfluencers. Oh no. Not today, fitfluencers. Not today.

They all end up going back to wherever it is they came from.

Inside her body, she felt a warm ooze, like the acid green slime puddle melting away on the hot steel hood of the Porsche yesterday. In her mind, she watched a big sticky bubble inflate and then burst. *They all end up going back to wherever it is they came from.* She exhaled. The mantra had soothed her into a trance. The anger that came to a boil after leaving Tim's had calmed to a simmer and then . . . it was still. This is what those know-it-all voices on all the wellness podcasts meant when they talked about acknowledging distractions and letting them go. *Oh my god*, Aimee thought: *I'm finally meditating.*

The fitfluencers were getting closer. Aimee could see their weird high-waisted lycra leggings – the kind she could never figure out how to wear without feeling like an idiot.

A few of them were holding their phones up to film each other. Shrieks and laughs echoed as one girl danced into the impromptu photoshoot – spilling out of her navy blue swimmers and tossing off her beat-up Akubra that had a braided leather band and red feather on the side.

They all end up—

Wait. 'Freya?' Aimee jolted to a halt in the middle of the footpath.

'Move!' The guy bragging on the phone about being Chris Hemsworth's neighbour shoved past. 'Fuckin' tourists.'

SIX

Petrol fumes wafted into the old red Holden Monaro and the high-pitched squeals from an electric drill echoed off the corrugated walls of the garage, making Aimee and Freya wince.

'Admit it: This is still better than #VanLife.' Aimee clutched the steering wheel and yelled across to Freya, who was sitting in the passenger seat of the broken-down car in the middle of the mechanic's shed. They each had their doors wide open and the backs of their sweaty thighs stuck to the black vinyl upholstery. 'How have you been living in a van and not telling me?'

'This car is a time capsule.' Freya laughed and plucked a cassette tape off the floor – holding it up like a dead rat. You could only just see the artwork through the scratched plastic box: Def Leppard.

The drilling stopped as Aimee snatched it and also laughed. 'This was in the glove box when your mum bought the Monaro when she was . . . like . . . *eighteen*. We used to drive around, blasting it as a joke.' She closed her eyes and clutched it to her chest before opening one eye and mumbling, 'Then we kinda began to secretly like it.' She smiled at the memory. '*Hysteria* was our favourite.' Aimee placed her right hand on the steering wheel and made a power-fist with the other as she mock-belted the lyrics of the eighties glam-rock hit. 'Hys-ter-i-a, when you're *near-ear!*'

'Gross, stop it.' Freya shoved a palm in her aunt's face.

Aimee turned the key in the ignition to switch on the stereo. The cassette was already in the tape deck and started playing automatically. She pushed one of the chunky black buttons on the stereo to fast-forward. 'This thing only had a tape deck, so we started going to garage sales and buying all these old cassettes and cassingles.'

'Aimee, you're thirty-six. You're too young to be saying words like "cassingle" . . . but, cassettes *are* becoming cool again. They're the new vinyl.'

'Well, that makes me feel decrepit.' Aimee hit play on the tape. 'Is your dad cool with you being here?'

Freya opened the glove box, ignoring her. 'What other relics are in here?'

Aimee reached across to slam shut the compartment just as Freya pulled out one of those tattered neon green paper wristbands you get at concerts and clubs and festivals. 'Please tell me he knows you're here and that I don't have to call him to say you've driven from Sydney and are sleeping in a van in the carpark above Main Beach?'

'You don't sleep in the van in the *carpark* – you get fined for that. At night, you drive around the suburban streets until you find an OK-looking spot . . . and you sleep in the van *there* before driving back to the beach in the morning.'

'Well, that sounds safe,' Aimee deadpanned.

'Sorry I didn't call.' Freya fake-pouted before reaching over to ruffle Aimee's hair like a dog. 'I just wanted to surprise my favourite aunt.'

'You didn't *surprise* me.' Aimee swatted her away while hamming up the paranoia of a potential break-in. 'You *terrified* me. When I couldn't find the hat this morning, I started to get paranoid and thought someone had broken in. I was on my way to the police station when I ran into you . . . you little . . . *thief.*' She rolled her eyes with a laugh and leant forward to fix her hair in the rearview mirror. Her flyaways appeared wilder with the orange sun streaming in through the dirty back window and she tried to tame them before giving up and reaching over to steal the Akubra off Freya's head. 'Also – *how* did you get in my house?' She plonked the hat on.

'I still had the key you gave me from last time I was here.' Freya held the neon green wristband up to her face and inspected the faded, inky text that was stamped on it. 'Jet?' she read before looking up in disgust. '*Now* I'm judging you.' She snatched the hat back off Aimee's head and flipped it onto hers.

Aimee closed her eyes and placed a palm on her chest to defend herself. 'Jet were *very* cool at the time. It was just before they got famous. And I still remember that gig. Me and Fleur. Thursday night at the Palace Hotel.'

'Jet and Def Leppard. Wow. The Maguire sisters were *cool*,' Freya mocked.

At the time, Aimee really did think they were cool. Fleur was three years older and the kind of Byron girl who everyone was now trying to be. She was the original Byron babe and had the looks of a chick who you might've seen in a nineties magazine ad for Pepsi. Sun-kissed and carefree with permanent beachy hair – the kind that people now screenshotted on their phones and showed to their hairdressers, issuing one instruction: 'Give me this'. Fleur was effortless. Indisputably delightful. Like the white frothy foam that covers the ocean after a mile-long wave rolls into shore at dusk – and everyone from babies to old people stop to stare at the natural beauty as it fizzes in the orange haze and invites them to be just as playful. She had a lightness and ease that Aimee didn't. It was a quality you had to be born with. The joy gene. Freya had it, a little.

The shabby green wristband was still intact – both ends stuck together to form a cuff. Freya squeezed her hand through and slid it to her wrist. She looked at it closely again. 'September 2002?' She held it in front of Aimee's face.

Aimee glanced. 'Huh. I guess so.' She knew it was from 2002. That's why she'd kept it. She also knew what Freya was about to say.

'That would've been just a few months before . . .' She didn't need to finish the sentence.

Aimee looked at Freya – sitting in her mum's old car, wearing her mum's old hat, with her perfect tanned skin and long brown hair streaked with natural golden highlights. She looked exactly like Fleur.

'Mum was twenty-one,' Freya said. To stop the mood from drooping, she twisted the dial on the tape deck and cranked the volume.

Twenty-one. It was a number Aimee thought about a lot. Time stood still for a moment whenever she saw the digits on price tags or number plates or letterboxes. One time, at the deli, she yanked a paper ticket out of the take-a-number dispenser and 21 appeared in big red inky print. That ticket had been tucked into her wallet ever since. Twenty-one was the age Fleur had turned on the birthday she celebrated at the Jet gig. Twenty-one was also the age Fleur was when she gave birth to Freya, just a few months later. She was still only twenty-one when the accident happened.

Aimee nudged the volume dial down a little. 'And *you're* twenty-one in . . .' she scrunched her face while counting the days in her head, 'seventeen . . . eighteen days? Christmas baby!' She reached over and poked Freya in the side of the stomach repeatedly. 'Is that why you're really here? You want me to throw your twenty-first birthday party?'

'Stop it.' Freya wiggled away. 'And it's two days *after* Christmas.'

Aimee started doing the Marcia Brady thumb dance and flipping her hair from shoulder to shoulder. 'You wanna spend your twenty-first birthday with your cool, glamorous aunt who lives in Byron Bay with the Hemsworths.'

'Go back to singing Def Leppard.' Freya turned up the volume on the stereo.

'Oh, well – seeing as you requested it – I will *definitely* be singing Def Leppard at your twenty-first. And Jet. Now, tell me, do you prefer the song "Roll Over DJ"? Or "Cold Hard Bitch"?'

'Go away, strange lady.'

'Ooh! We can duet!'

A thick, hairy knuckle tapped on the rear side window and an older man wearing oil-stained blue overalls appeared. He leant down into Freya's opened window. 'You're not Aimee.'

Aimee leant across Freya to glimpse his old, weathered face. 'That's Freya, Moe. My niece.'

'Oh.' He assessed Freya and nodded. 'You look like Fleur.'

'Tim got your call. Can we get this baby movin' again?' Aimee slapped the black plastic dash.

'Does this mean you're approving all the work that needs to be done?' he shot back.

'Can you just . . . do the important things? Like, only the stuff that *absolutely* needs to be done?'

Moe howled. 'Oh! Only the things that *absolutely need to be done*. Aimee, this piece of shit isn't roadworthy.'

'Noooo.' Aimee's voice went high-pitched as she dismissed his comments with a wave of her hand. 'It's just a crunchy sound from the engine. That's all it is.'

Moe raised his brow. 'The motor needs to be completely rebuilt, the strut towers have rotted out and weakened the front suspension, the entire brake system is shot, the wiring's burnt out *and* there's rust all through the floor pans.'

Aimee cracked a smile. 'Oh, you've been rehearsing that.'

Freya reached into her bag and pulled out a wad of hundred-dollar notes held together by a rubber band. 'Here.' She held it up to Moe. 'Just get started on the important stuff.'

'Hey!' Aimee reached over to grab the cash but Freya turned away and stuffed it into the kangaroo pouch pocket on Moe's overalls.

Freya grabbed her bag and jumped out of the car as Moe walked off to the other side of the garage to deposit the money in the office register. 'Sooo . . . after I surprised you . . . my plan was to ask if I could stay with you . . . till the end of January.' She slammed shut the door and dropped down to look through the open window. 'Consider it my rent for the summer?'

Aimee didn't know how to respond. 'Only if you sing backup next time Rob performs "Thunderstruck" at Music Club.'

The thin rubber soles of Freya's Vans were already slapping the oil-stained concrete as she ran out of the garage. 'I can't hear you, strange lady!'

Aimee looked in the rearview and watched her niece disappear into the endless afternoon. Seconds later, the sunlight blacked out as a group of people entered the shed.

'I told you, get those cameras outta here.' Moe waved an arm at the group.

Aimee squinted in the mirror. The glare behind the group rendered them shadowy, featureless stencilled-out figures. Then a tow truck pulled into the driveway and cut out the blinding orange blaze. Aimee's eyes adjusted and she could notice some details. A camera crew – all dressed in black – and some woman with a handbag hooked on her wrist, dangling, the way celebrities would carry their handbags while walking down the street in paparazzi shots. The lady walked down the driver's side of the Monaro and leant down to find Aimee.

'I'm here to pick up the G-Wagon.' She tilted her head to the side and smiled.

Aimee's eyes flicked from side-to-side as she waited for the rich lady to realise her mistake. The rich lady did not. 'I don't . . . *work* here.' Aimee furrowed her brow and looked around the shed.

'Oh.' The woman stood upright. 'I just . . . saw the junkyard car and the oil stains on your shirt and . . . *assumed*.'

'It's not *oil*, it's *food*,' Aimee said.

The woman let out an awkward laugh. 'So . . . is it ready?'

Moe grumbled as he walked out of the office. 'Your G-Wagon's not ready. I'll call you when it is.'

Then the fancy lady and the camera crew were gone. Moe put his right hand on the roof of the Monaro and leant back down through the open passenger window to look across at Aimee. 'Another fuckin' movie shoot. Or . . . TV shoot. Whatever.'

'The Julia Roberts one? Or the . . . the one with the . . . um . . . guy from the robot . . . superhero movie?'

'The reality show. The *Byron Brats*. Or . . . *Brats in Byron*?' Moe gave up trying to remember the title. 'The one that was on the Facebook group.'

'I've been avoiding the Facebook group.' Aimee shrugged.

'Oh. Yeah. The sliming video.' Moe nodded. 'Well, there's a reality show here now. Girls in G-strings, boys on steroids . . . they all sleep with each other and get drunk . . . it's a shit-fight. Disgusting. My grandkids were telling me about it. All the local business owners are refusing to grant the filming permissions on their properties.' He raised his hairy-knuckled index finger and pointed. 'If we don't grant permission, they've got nowhere to film.'

The Def Leppard song started to fade over the car's rattly speakers.

'Hey, Moe?'

'Yeah?'

'Can you never say the word "G-string" ever again?'

SEVEN

Aimee turned up the volume on the portable speaker and plonked it down on the concrete in the carpark behind The Dream Explosion. 'Cold Hard Bitch' blared.

A little boy wearing a too-big Mambo T-shirt put his hands on his hips. 'My mum says the music you play in this class is inappropriate.'

Rob began skating backwards around the group of about a dozen pre-teen kids, giving them the lowdown. 'Rollerball is simple! It's a mix of basketball and handball on skates . . . Kind of.' After several years of holding rollerball matches, Aimee and Rob still hadn't quite nailed down the details of the game they'd invented. All they knew when they first organised it was they wanted it to involve rollerblades. While the rules were murky, the group was basically split in two and each team had a goal on opposite ends of the court that they had to get the ball into without being intercepted. Sometimes there were two balls. No one ever really knew where the second ball came from. 'We play mean. We play rough. If you wanna be coddled, go back to your teachers at Byron Bay Community School. You're on Little Rippers territory now.' The kid who'd complained about the music ran back to his mum's Subaru Forester. Rob looked over at Aimee and held out her hands with a shrug. 'I'm disappointed. We usually get at least three runners after that speech.'

Charlie took over and supervised the group putting on their skates. Rob rolled over to Aimee and they sat on a stack of old timber shipping pallets. The sky radiated purple and orange and a flock of birds flew in a V-shape over the droopy black powerlines. The smell from the newly-opened Guzman y Gomez – the one that locals tried protesting (and the one that Aimee and Rob were first in line to when it opened) – wafted over from down the street. 'Here.' Rob handed Aimee a Gatorade bottle.

Aimee took a sip and almost choked. 'Tequila?'

'You need it.' Rob glugged down a mouthful from her own bottle. 'Nichelle told me your bad news.'

Aimee scrunched her face. 'How the hell do *you* know Nichelle?'

'She comes into the salon. Great gal. She bought before the boom.'

Rob and Aimee were wearing matching cut-off Levis and had silver whistles dangling from their necks. Aimee's Shania Twain tour merch tee was tucked into the front of her shorts. Rob was wearing a green Jim's Mowing T-shirt that she'd cut the sleeves off. The whistles had become redundant over the years at Little Rippers because the pair just blew them at random points in the game. They'd quickly lost all meaning, like the game itself.

'What'd Freya's dad say when you called him?' Rob unclipped the helmet strap from under her chin.

'He knew. He thought she'd called me before she left Sydney. And it's totally fine . . . I'm just . . .' She adjusted the Velcro on her hot pink elbow pads. 'She's turning twenty-one a few days after Christmas and that was the same age—'

'Fleur.' Rob nodded.

'Exactly. And on top of that, in a few weeks it'll be the twenty-first anniversary of Fleur . . .' She waved away the rest of the sentence with a hand. 'She's just graduated uni. She hasn't got a job. And this extra emotional . . . *thing* . . . she'll be dealing with. I'm just . . . aware that maybe she's feeling . . .' Aimee gave up on trying to articulate it. 'I dunno. She didn't say any of that. I'm just . . . conscious of it.'

The kids started tearing around the parking lot in a circle to warm up and Charlie laughed as he led the swarm. Something caught Aimee's attention. She nudged Rob with her shoulder and nodded over to the driveway of the carpark. 'Hot Ew Girl.'

The blonde chick with the fake vintage band tee from Tim's rooftop was slowly rolling by the parking lot on a powder blue retro-ish bike. The streetlights had just flickered on. They lit her up before she cruised out of sight.

'Whoa, spooky.' Rob stared. 'Iron Maiden.' She'd noticed the shirt.

'She probably can't even name one of their songs,' Aimee said.

Rob whacked her helmet back on, grabbed the Gatorade bottles, shot to her feet and started skating backwards while grinning at Aimee.

'What are you up to, Roberta?' Aimee laughed.

Rob shrugged. 'Let's go ask what her favourite Iron Maiden song is.'

'No,' Aimee instructed, serious, like an owner would to their dog when they saw it gearing up to jump on the bed.

Rob cackled and started skating in a zig-zag, slowly heading towards the driveway, tempting Aimee to stop her.

'Hey!' Aimee hopped off the crate and skated after her.

The dog jumped onto the bed. 'Guys, Charlie's in charge!' Rob declared to the kids. 'Don't make him cry again.' She whizzed out of the carpark and jumped off the gutter onto the black bitumen of the quiet side street. By the time Aimee caught up, Hot Ew Girl was gone.

'Quick!' Rob tossed Aimee her Gatorade bottle and kept going, determined to find the alleged Iron Maiden fan.

'You are not doing this – I'm turning around,' Aimee whisper-yelled. It was a false threat.

They rounded the corner and skated down Jonson Street. The main drag was buzzing with people heading out for the night and others heading home from the beach. The pair dodged through tourists eating YoFlo and weaved between the banked-up luxury vehicles that were heading towards Main

Beach. As they rolled past the Beach Hotel and into the carpark above the water, a crowd came into view on the grass under the pine trees. About a hundred people. Lots of them holding big cardboard signs with slogans scrawled on them in black pen.

BIN THE BRATS

BRATS ARE TRASH

BAN INSTA BABES IN BYRON BAY

Some of the signs were less creative.

#FUCKOFF

'Aimee!' yelled Xanthe, a fellow business owner in town who had a store that only sold things made out of burlap. She was standing at the front of the crowd on a bunch of milk crates that were pushed together to make a platform. The group parted. Aimee clomped her rollerblades across the grass. When she got to the front, she saw TV news cameras filming everywhere. Xanthe lifted a megaphone to her mouth and addressed the camera directly. 'Aimee has been living here since she was born. If anyone understands the destruction a TV show like this will do to our town, it's her.'

Aimee moved closer. 'What is this about?' she whispered.

Xanthe bent down. 'The *Brats of Byron Bay* reality show that's filming here. We're protesting. If local business owners don't grant filming permission, they can't—'

'Yeah, I know, then they can't . . .' She closed her eyes and didn't finish the sentence. '. . . Moe told me.'

'Come on.' Xanthe held her hands out to pull Aimee up. 'Say something. It means more coming from you.'

Rob had clomped to the front of the crowd – just as Aimee hoisted her rollerblades up onto the makeshift platform – and pulled her phone out to film, clearly loving every second of what was unfolding.

A reporter fired a question. 'What do you think of a sexed-up reality show filming in your town?'

Aimee held out her arms and fluttered her eyelids, trying to find the energy to engage in the absurdity. 'I think . . . it's . . . ridiculous?' She shrugged. 'The last thing we need is reality TV trashbaggery – what's it called? *Twats of Byron Bay?*'

The crowd whooped and Xanthe handed Aimee the megaphone. The news camera people pepped up and manoeuvered into better positions. Aimee filled the space with more talk.

'. . . They're running around in those . . . weird G-string bikinis with all the thin straps. Are those bikinis only single-use? They look like they'd tangle up in a knot like a pair of headphones when you pull them out of your bag.'

Applause. Cheers. Aimee had warmed up. Her shoulders loosened and she gripped the megaphone comfortably.

'I swear to god – it's The Hemsworth Effect. *That's* what's ruining Byron Bay. Now no one who grew up here can even afford to live in the town anymore. Do *you* wanna move to Casino? That's where we're gonna end up. We may as well just move there now and start the revolution. And did you see Hemsworth's crapped off for the summer? Went to Lord Howe Island and left us to deal with the mess. King of The Top 400 Club.'

'Yeah, right on!' Rob started blowing the silver whistle that was strung around her neck. It egged on the already-rowdy group.

'You know, first came the Hemsworths, then the limousines. The night I saw a limo pull up out the front of Orgasmic Falafel in Bay Lane is the night I knew this town was gone.'

The crowd went nuts.

'Who the hell rides in a *limousine* to get *falafel*? I mean, *really*.'

'What about Freya?' a voice yelled. It was familiar. The crowd parted to show Bada Bing. 'Your niece. Freya. She's one of the Brats.'

Aimee stared blanky ahead and the world around her started to spin. Suddenly, the crowd of protesters and the news cameras seemed to multiply until the glare of the setting sun turned her vision to white. She felt one of her rollerblades slip involuntarily and shoot forward. Then the milk crate busted out from underneath her and she collapsed to the ground.

The crowd gasped at the spectacle and the news cameras pushed closer.

'Guess Who, Don't Sue,' Bada Bing said with a wry smile.

EIGHT

Aimee took a sip of her champagne just as the frost from the packet of frozen Potato Gems she'd placed on her bandaged knee began to drip onto the velvet couch. Onions spattered from the kitchen, where Charlie was being attentive and cooking up a Mexican dinner to distract Aimee from her public face-plant. Rob was scrolling through Stevie Nicks songs on her iPhone and playing them loudly over the wireless sound system.

'Is this the seven dollar Aldi champagne or the twenty-one dollar Aldi champagne?' Rob smacked her tongue on the roof of her mouth while holding her glass up in her left hand. The opening guitar riff to 'Edge of Seventeen' chugged in the background. 'Because the seven dollar Aldi champagne actually tastes better than the twenty-one dollar Aldi champagne. A lot of people don't know that.'

Aimee nodded. 'It's the seven dollar Aldi champagne.'

The music jumped and skipped and blipped as Rob switched and scrolled between songs. 'OK, how about we perform "Little Lies"?' She scrolled through the song until it started playing the chorus.

Aimee shook her head. 'That's a Christine McVie song. I thought you wanted Stevie?'

Rob held up an A4 music festival flyer. HOT CANYON NIGHTS was printed in big swoopy seventies-style font at the top and below was the artist line-up – rows and rows of band names that shrank in size the lower down the page they were. The Girly Boys were somewhere near the bottom. A big illustration was splashed across it in pinks and oranges and blues, loosely resembling Byron. *Loosely.* The lighthouse was the only vaguely recognisable thing. And there weren't really any canyons in the area. Every electrical pole in town was plastered with the poster, advertising one of the biggest music events of the summer. It always fell on the third Saturday of January – just before holidaymakers started packing up and returning to their normal lives. The first time Charlie's band played it, Rob and Aimee crashed the stage after too much tequila and performed an impromptu cover of Concrete Blonde's 'Joey'. Their special guest appearance had become an annual tradition and Rob spent far too much time throughout the year selecting the song they'd sing. 'We need to stand out. Stevie Nicks is hot again ever since that viral video of Cowabunga Cat. I mean, obviously she's never *not* been hot. But Cowabunga Cat got her to number one on the charts again.'

Aimee sighed. 'I have no idea what that is.'

Rob closed her eyes. 'Are you seriously telling me you haven't seen the video of that Sphynx cat riding a surfboard while Fleetwood Mac's "Dreams" plays?'

'Jeez Aimee, read the news,' Charlie teased.

'Anyway, the video sent the song back to number one so I really feel like we should do a Stevie song, but not an obvious one. Other people will probably have the same idea and do covers of "Dreams". Which is annoying. I mean, it's almost as if Gen Z doesn't realise *our* generation already stole Stevie and reclaimed her as our own. That's why "Little Lies" is a genius choice.' She jumped to her feet and started doing on-the-spot twirls while playing air tambourine. 'A lot of people think "Little Lies" is a Christine McVie song just because she wrote it and sings lead – but Stevie steals her thunder with that one-line monotone harmony in the chorus.'

Her voice went all nasally as she impersonated Stevie. She twirled over to the kitchen to dance with Charlie. He played air guitar on a fry pan.

'No Christine songs.' Aimee tore open a corner of the Potato Gems bag and picked one out to see if it tasted OK raw.

Rob skipped back to the living room, flopped on the floor, and then popped her head up in Aimee's lap. 'Is this because, deep down, you know that you're the Christine and I'm the Stevie?'

Aimee almost choked on her uncooked Potato Gem. She picked more of the carby balls out of the packet and started throwing them at Rob, who crawled away and cowered behind an old tan leather club chair.

'You're the Christine!' Aimee yelled as the Potato Gems shattered everywhere.

Rob poked her head out. 'You're the Christine! Always living in my shadow!'

Charlie stepped in. 'Guys. It's my band. I'm letting you guest star on one song. And, because of that . . . *I* get to be Stevie.'

'He's the Christine!' Rob tackled him onto the couch.

Freya opened the front door to the apartment and Aimee popped her head up to look over the back of the sofa.

'Um, hey TV star,' Aimee said.

'Hey Byron Karen. Aren't you the lady from the memes?'

As Aimee tried to comprehend what the hell any of that even meant, Rob had already started tapping away on her iPhone.

'Oh. My. GOD.' Rob held up her phone to show the Twitter trending chart. 'Byron Karen' was number one. Rob scrolled through the tweets and news links. She paused Stevie and pressed play on a video news report.

Reporter voiceover: Once known for peace and love, Byron Bay is now in the grips of a battle – with furious locals taking to the streets to protest the rise of celebrities and influencers. Tension erupted today at a rally opposing a controversial new reality show set to film in the sleepy paradise.

The video clip cut to Aimee holding the megaphone at the protest – and the footage had been clipped up to showcase her best bits.

The last thing we need is reality TV trashbaggery. *Twats of Byron Bay. I swear to God – it's The Hemsworth Effect.* That's *what's ruining Byron Bay. First came the Hemsworths, then the limousines. The night I saw a limo pull up out the front of Orgasmic Falafel in Bay Lane is the night I knew this town was gone. Who the hell rides in a* limousine *to get* falafel? *I mean,* really.

Aimee knew what was coming next. She watched through barely-opened eyes. In five, four, three, two . . .

The footage cut to a wide-shot of her stacking it off the milk crates. Ooft.

Reporter voiceover: It seems the mecca of mindfulness and meditation hasn't rubbed off on everyone – particularly the cranky local the internet has now dubbed *Byron Karen*.

Aimee flopped back on the couch, picked up the bag of Potato Gems and plonked it down on her face. 'You know, I really thought having my loan application rejected by Narissa would be the worst thing to happen to me today.'

Rob put her chin on Aimee's knee. 'Really? Cause . . . I thought it'd be seeing your fiancé with a hot twenty-year-old who called you ew.'

Even with her face covered by a bag of freezer food, it was clear what look Aimee was shooting at Rob.

'Sorry,' Rob whispered. 'Also, it's *Nichelle*.'

'Wait.' Aimee sat up. She turned to Freya, pointed an arm and clicked her fingers. 'Reality show. Starring you. Explain.'

Freya walked to the fridge. 'I'm sure I mentioned it at the mechanic today . . .' She poured a glass of the Aldi champagne.

Aimee spun around on the couch to give her a raised eyebrow.

'Maybe you just didn't hear me say it. Def Leppard was playing very loud.' The champagne started frothing over the glass and Freya licked it up.

'Don't blame this on Def Leppard.'

Freya dipped her finger into the pan for a taste of the simmering red sauce and Charlie playfully swatted her away. She walked over to the couch and flopped on the floor with Rob.

'OK, so. I was at the beach a few days ago and a producer from the show came up and started chatting and talking about *The Brats of Byron Bay*. They're filming over the summer . . . It's about this family who've moved here from Sydney . . . and some of the daughter's friends . . .' she trailed off. 'I don't really know. But they asked if I'd be keen to be on it and I said yes. It's fun. And they pay me, even on the days I don't need to film anything.' She picked up one of the rogue Potato Gems off the floor and pressed it between her fingers. 'And . . .' She paused and smirked.

Rob pepped up. 'They're looking to cast a hip, fun local hairdresser – who looks much younger than she is – to also be one of the rich daughter's friends?'

'Close . . .' Freya nodded facetiously. 'I was filming with them this arvo. And then everyone started seeing the Byron Karen memes on Instagram. And Heath, one of the executive producers, was talking about how he'd kill to cast you on the show . . .'

There was no way to even describe the disgusted sound that came out of Aimee's mouth. But everyone knew what it translated to: No.

It didn't deter Freya from pressing on with her pitch. 'And . . . I *may* have said that I'm a close, personal relation of Byron Karen . . .'

'Absolutely not.'

'And I also may have told him that it would take *a lot* to get you to agree . . . And he said he'd pay *big* to have Byron Karen on *The Brats of Byron Bay*.'

Freya jumped onto the couch and sat on Aimee's legs. 'Come on . . . I thought you were my cool, glamorous aunt who lives in Byron Bay.' She started doing the Marcia Brady thumb dance.

'How dare you use the Marcia Brady thumb dance for evil.'

Rob crawled up onto the couch with them. 'If Aimee says no, can I be Byron Karen?' She pushed her shaggy hair out of her face. 'And I wanna have a catchphrase. All the best reality show contestants have a catchphrase. I'm thinking something like: I'll have *that*, with cheese.'

Aimee pointed. 'Yes. Get Rob to do it. I'm sure Australia would love to follow her life – it's just too bad the TV cameras didn't catch her making out with that dorky dad at Music Club last night.'

Rob gagged. 'Ugh, the weird dad in the beige polo shirt. That was a lapse in judgement. We'll never speak of it again.'

'Nope. Charlie filmed you guys making out and that video clip needs to be messaged to me ASAP, please,' she called over her shoulder to Charlie.

Freya nudged Aimee. 'You've got a big problem. This is an easy solution.'

Rob agreed. 'Right now I'm reading Matthew McConaughey's memoir, *Greenlights*, and it's all about following the green lights when they present themselves. Admit it, Aimee: Byron Karen is your green light.'

'Are you really quoting Matthew McConaughey?'

'It was hard to do with a straight face.'

Aimee sighed. 'My livelihood may be—'

'Crumbling?' Rob interjected.

'My livelihood has . . . a *question mark* over it. But, before succumbing to a reality show that's ruining my town, I'm prepared to make money *another* way.'

Rob scrunched her face. 'So you're gonna start an OnlyFans?'

Aimee ignored her. 'I'm selling Mum and Dad's antiques.' The others moaned in protest but she raised her hands. 'They've been sitting in Tim's mum's garage since I was . . . what, eighteen?'

'Firstly, that's not gonna get you the amount of cash you need,' Rob said. 'More importantly: I think you'll regret it.'

Aimee talked over her. 'It's already decided. I've booked a stall at the markets.'

'What if *Charlie* starts an OnlyFans?' Rob proposed.

Charlie turned around from the stove and tossed a tea towel over his shoulder while strutting over. 'I'd totally do an OnlyFans.' He flopped down on the floor.

Aimee stifled a smile. 'I've *heard* the noises that come from your bedroom and I have no doubt many people would subscribe to your OnlyFans.'

Rob went back to the Stevie tunes. 'Dreams' started playing over the speaker. 'Hey Aimee?' Her voice cracked as the intro floated through the living room. She looked up at her best friend and drew circles with her forefinger on the couch fabric. 'I've got a serious question.'

Aimee's eyes softened. 'Yeah?'

'Hypothetical situation: You're held at gunpoint and told you have to live the rest of your life as someone else. Who do you choose: Christine McVie or Byron Karen?'

NINE

Opening the roller door disrupted the dust that had settled on all the worn timber surfaces of the antiques that filled the garage. The particles clouded the air, floating out around Aimee in the Saturday morning light. She stood in the driveway, staring at all the furniture stacked up on top of each other. There were old pine chests of drawers squeezed underneath farmhouse tables. A long cane daybed. Two or three marble-topped washstands. Mismatched chairs. Curios. Lots of those bluey-greeny glass fishing floats wrapped in old rope nets – the ones that had become very trendy in recent years and added to home interiors in order to give a beachy feel, no matter how far away from the beach the house actually was. Several church pews were lined up next to each other. Aimee had one of the benches in her apartment but couldn't fit the rest.

Tim reversed his old grey Toyota HiLux into the driveway behind her with ease – not even needing to glance around to make sure he didn't swipe the brick mailbox or the fence on either side of the tight space. It was the house he grew up in. Aimee remembered the times Tim would sneak her over after school, when his mum would still be at work at her wellness clinic in Bangalow. The low-set seventies-style brick house hadn't changed.

The roller door was still an unfortunate shade of brown. Everything about the house was an unfortunate shade of brown. It had started to look out of place in the cul-de-sac. Neighbouring houses had been getting sold in the property boom. Even ones that weren't actually for sale. Out-of-towners had just started going around the city and making offers on random homes. There was a rumour in Tim's street that the owners of the ugliest house on the strip got a call one day from some people in Sydney who offered a million dollars over the phone, just like that. Hadn't even seen the house. They'd accepted. Like most other recent sales in the area, the property was transformed to look like a weird spaceship house – all steel and glass and concrete.

Tim switched off the engine and jumped out. The silence was spiked by the tiny ticks and clicks coming from under the hood as the motor cooled down.

'Thanks . . . again. I know it's last minute. And I'm . . . *breaking the rule.*'

Tim walked around the back tray of the ute and unhooked the loop tabs of the canvas canopy. 'No worries. Mum's excited to have her garage back.' He let out a forced laugh.

'I have no doubt. Rozzie's found a way to bring it up every time she's seen me for the past twenty years.'

'I just need it back by this arvo,' Tim said of the ute. 'Round three.' He bundled up the canopy. 'Hey . . . I didn't mean for that to happen the other day. On the roof – at the shop. With . . . the chick.' He closed his eyes and shrugged.

'That's OK. It's . . . all . . . *within the rules.*'

Tim walked over, grabbed her hands and squeezed his fingers between hers. He looked into her eyes. Aimee stared back. She examined the lines that had started to form on his face from a lifetime of straddling a surfboard underneath the sun. She hadn't really noticed them before. His steely eyes were still identical to the ones she'd stared into when they were in high school and laying in the tray of the HiLux after wagging the last class of the day. She searched inside herself for *that feeling* again. The one she hadn't felt in years. She'd become obsessed with it – especially since the time-out started and she was suddenly forced to think about the pros and cons of her relationship, like it was one of those annual corporate evaluations employees had to submit about their workplace. It had to be there. That giddy feeling – almost like the one she'd get on a quiet weekday afternoon when she'd be walking home from the beach and the scent of jasmine would drift through the air for the first time of the season. Unexpected. She couldn't remember the last time she felt excited to see Tim. Most of the time, she just felt guilty. Guilty that she didn't feel the thing she was supposed to feel about her fiancé. Then she'd feel sad and terrible and try to overcorrect her lack of feelings by doing overly nice and thoughtful things for him. Somewhere along the way, she'd tricked herself into thinking that guilty feeling was actually love. A love that was maintained by tolerantly overlooking problems.

Aimee and Tim never really fought with each other. They got frustrated and exasperated – but that never led to one of those big gross fights where past resentments are dredged up and used as ammunition. The kind of fight that gets so petty, sobs turn to laughter as both people realise how ridiculous they're being. The closest they'd ever come – in recent years, at least – was that fight on the roof of Tim's shop, just days earlier. Sometimes she wished they would have those big gross fights. There were lots of things they could fight about but it was almost like they'd reached a point where neither of them could be bothered. At least a fight would show they cared.

Not even the suggestion of the summer time-out had led to an argument. Tim had adopted an annoyingly pragmatic attitude over the previous year or so – educating himself on start-up business culture and pop psychology with trendy books and cool podcasts – and proposed the time-out as a practical step for them to take before getting married. Well, it wasn't entirely his idea. It actually came by way of his mother – and *that* was something Aimee would've loved to fight about. He was staying at his mum's for the summer and Aimee hated how much Rozzie would've been relishing it. She also hated the idea of Tim telling his mum about their problems. When it came to marriage, Aimee wasn't even sure she wanted it. Tim, on the other hand, had become obsessed with the idea of marriage and kids, and the more he pushed, the more Aimee pulled back. Why couldn't everything just stay the same?

The time-out was a source of both relief and distress. Tim had pushed for marriage for so long and now it was like he was yanking it off the table. Aimee still wanted to be with him. At least she thought she did. But there was one question that kept creeping into her mind. Sometimes she fantasised about having one of those big gross fights with Tim, just so she could blurt it out: Do you even *like* me anymore?

The engine of a lawn mower ripped through the suburban Saturday morning silence and interrupted Aimee's thoughts. Tim's next-door neighbour rolled it out into the front yard and waved. Tim nodded back. When he turned to face Aimee again, he squinted and pursed his lips in a peculiar smirk while examining her.

Aimee was waiting for it. Tim hadn't brought up the Byron Karen thing all morning. She knew it'd get mentioned eventually.

'What's with your hair?'

Aimee jolted at the comment. 'I . . . ran out of product. I had to use a little bit of body moisturiser instead. I googled it. It's normal.'

Tim let go of Aimee's hands and walked over to the garage, glancing over his shoulder with that smirk. 'Is it?' He raised an eyebrow before turning his attention to one of the dusty relics in the garage: an old clown head – the kind from one of those carnival games where you put plastic ping pong balls into its mouth to win a prize. 'You really reckon someone's gonna buy this?'

Aimee sighed and fought a smile. 'Don't do that. Don't mock the antiques.' She walked over. 'I remember when Mum and Dad bought this and put it in the store. It just sat there in the same place forever. Me and Fleur used to think it was so creepy . . . Now I kinda hate myself for not putting it in our apartment.' She ran her fingertip around the chipped red lips on the clown's open mouth.

'You can still put it in the apartment . . . Just not in the *bedroom*,' he said. 'Maybe keep it in a cupboard. With a lock.'

'Nope.' She tapped the clown's head. 'Everything must go.'

Tim began separating some of the church pews and dragging them out. 'Rob helping you get these off the ute at the market?'

Aimee stopped, put her hands in the pockets of her old jeans and made a face. 'Huh.' She hadn't thought that far.

Tim slumped and hammed up a groan as he walked inside. 'I'll put thongs on.'

————

The Saturday markets on the grass above Main Beach had become overrun with buskers from big cities hoping to get discovered. Aimee blamed Tones & I. The scent of burning incense floated through the air mixed with the smell of freshly ground coffee and matcha waffles being cooked at a nearby cart.

Aimee stood in the back of the HiLux, lifted up one end of a turned-leg table and helped Tim shuffle it out. She looked around at the stalls and the business names painted on calico banners. 'Why do all businesses these days have to be branded as a "collective" and a "tribe" and a "co-op"?' She zoned in on one particular business name and read it aloud. 'The Mermaid Collective. What does that even *mean*?'

Tim shuffled backwards with the table. 'Why does it irritate you so much?'

Aimee squinted and shook her head. 'It's just *annoying*.'

'You just sound negative.'

She flinched, as if she'd just been flicked in the face with a rubber band. 'You used to like my negativity,' she said. 'Negativity is my best quality. Negativity is what fuels me. It's why I get up in the morning.'

He made a face.

'What?' Aimee let out a laugh. 'You know I'm just joking.'

They dropped the table down on the dewy grass next to the rest of the stuff they'd unpacked.

'Flatty?' Tim looked over at the coffee van.

'Double shot.'

Aimee started writing prices on little labels and sticking them to each piece of furniture. Then she heard a low, smooth voice from behind her.

'Tim told me I was getting my garage back.'

Aimee closed her eyes and exhaled. 'Rozzie.' She turned around and clicked the lid back on the black Sharpie.

Rozzie wore floaty outfits that swathed her body in fabric, and accessorised with crafty timber jewellery and multiple scarves. When she spoke, she insisted on emphasising random words. It was a unique skill. She could read a Woolworths receipt and make it sound so passive aggressive that you'd probably feel personally criticised and cry.

'I won't know what to do with myself now that I've got so much . . . *space!*' she said.

'You've been very kind to let me keep it all in your garage,' Aimee said. It took all her strength not to throw one of the glass fishing floats at her. She changed the subject. 'Just looking around the markets?'

'I've got a stall here for the summer. Holiday crowds – they wouldn't know about the clinic, so we thought we'd *bring* it to them.' She threw her hands in the air with a flourish.

Aimee wondered why the hell Tim hadn't warned her that Rozzie would be there. She looked around and clocked the sign on Rozzie's stall across the way. *One Life: Naturopathy and counselling.* The logo was a green sapling, which was ironic because Rozzie had a tendency to suck the life out of everything until it was a husk.

'How's the time-out going?' Rozzie's tone had the same carefree breeziness you might apply to a question like, *How's the new online meal prep service you've subscribed to?* She continued. 'I see the "no contact" part of the agreement isn't going well.'

Aimee forced a smile and went back to writing prices on the tiny stickers.

Rozzie barrelled on. 'Well, the break will be good for you both. I'm glad you took up my suggestion.'

Aimee hated that Rozzie thought she'd won some kind of competition. She looked smug – like she was waiting for applause or recognition that, after years of trying, she'd finally gotten her son away from the girl who'd been dragging him down since high school. Even if the time-out was just temporary.

A guy with a handlebar moustache piped up from behind the carnival clown head. 'I'll give you fifty.'

Aimee glanced over. 'The price on the sticker is final.'

Rozzie widened her eyes and pursed her lips as if Aimee was a toddler who'd just said a rude word. 'I just . . . *wish* you'd both come see me for a session.' Aimee opened her mouth to interject but Rozzie upped her volume and raced to finish her rant. 'I know you think it's *weird* to get couple's counselling when the therapist is the mother of one of the spouses. But it's actually beneficial. I know your *history*, Aimee. I know your history *together* and *separately*.' She closed her eyes and rubbed her brow, almost as if she was pretending like she didn't quite know what she was about to say even though it was always very obvious her criticisms had been premeditated and rehearsed. 'I believe you have a lot of past trauma that you haven't dealt with and it's affecting you, which affects . . . *Tim*.' She raised her palms and shrugged. She did this whenever she felt like she'd just dealt an earth-shattering truth.

'Sixty dollars.' The guy was still haggling.

'You should just give that *clown head* away. It's been haunting my house for almost *two decades*.' Rozzie chortled.

Aimee nodded across the alley and tapped the pen on the table. 'You've got people waiting at your stall.'

'Sixty-five.' The guy upped his bid.

Rozzie sighed. 'Let it go, Aimee. The clown head . . . *other* things.' She looked over at the coffee van, then flicked her gaze back to Aimee. 'Just let it go.'

'Seventy!'

'It's not for sale.' Aimee looked around at the people browsing the furniture. 'None of it's for sale. Sorry guys. Mistake. I'm not letting go of any of it.'

Rozzie opened her mouth to sigh another grievance, but Aimee cut her off in a low, direct tone. 'You're being very inappropriate.'

Rozzie snapped her mouth shut for dramatic effect and let out a half-laugh. She spun on her heels and walked across the grass towards her stall. 'You've gotta let go at some point, Aimee.'

TEN

Aimee sat on the timber steps at Wategos Beach, watching the TV crew film Freya and the random girls, who were wearing weird bikinis that looked like tangled headphones. It was the usual Saturday afternoon Wategos crowd. Cool out-of-towners and trendy families and hot twenty-somethings spilling between the beach and Raes – the ultra-cool boutique hotel and restaurant that had become a mecca for influencers far and wide. Even Aimee had to concede that the building's whitewashed concrete walls, archways and palm trees were breathtaking enough to tempt the crankiest of locals into taking a selfie there. But she'd never admit that aloud. She also wouldn't be caught dead at Raes. She knew the exact anxious feeling she'd get the moment she entered. It was the same flush of panic that overcame her when she'd go to the shopping centre up on the Gold Coast and accident-ally walk into General Pants. Loud music and teenagers dressed in weird outfits calling her 'babe'. She didn't belong in General Pants or at Raes.

Aimee was gazing at the hotspot when a guy wearing cream linen everything waltzed out with his two buddies in similar outfits. There was something about Byron Bay that made all visitors coordinate – like the Spice Girls when they'd all wear a slightly different version of the same outfit.

The twenty-something guys basked in the golden hour light and huddled together, wrapping their arms around each other while staring out at the ocean before them, whooping, as if day-drinking and wearing head-to-toe linen and chasing sunsets was the life they were born to live. They looked just like the *Entourage* bros, except all of them were Turtle. There was a white Lexus SUV in the driveway of the restaurant and the first guy slid up onto the hood, reclining across the polished steel while filming himself on his phone. Then a waitress scurried out to the car, holding the wireless EFTPOS machine, and said something about a card being declined.

'Quit judging, Byron Karen,' a girl's voice came from behind Aimee.

Specks of cold water splattered on the side of Aimee's face. She whipped to her right. It was Freya – wet in her bikini.

Aimee closed her eyes, inhaled deeply with a smile and pretended to bask in her new moniker. 'I'm not ashamed of my Byron Karen status. I'm embracing it. Sometimes you really do just need to speak to a manager.'

'Spoken like a true Karen.'

'Ugh.' Aimee stood up on the steps and slung her tan leather satchel across her body. 'I got ambushed by an *actual* Byron Karen today. Tim's mum.'

'Ew.'

'Don't say "ew". It's my new trigger word.'

Freya bent over and whipped her hair forward to vigorously dry it with a blue-and-white striped Turkish towel. 'When are you going to tell me what's actually going on between you and Tim?' Her voice was muffled under the fabric.

Aimee looked out at the hazy afternoon glow that settled over the beach. 'What I've told you is basically it. A time-out over summer. We're just . . . figuring things out. Before we actually get married, we should both feel comfortable that it's what we still want.'

That was the polite version. Toeing the company line. Aimee didn't want to drag her niece into her relationship dramas, so she kept the explanation short and sweet. After all, when the time-out ended and they got back together, she didn't want Freya having any negative feelings towards Tim.

And they *would* get back together . . . wouldn't they? Aimee couldn't help but feel like Tim held all the cards even though she, too, could also decide to end the relationship after the time-out. Still, she knew she never would. Even though she was in stage three of the time-out process. Just like the seven stages of grieving when someone died, Aimee was discovering there was also a step-by-step emotional process to having your fiancé ask for a relationship break. The first stage was complete and utter devastation. The second stage was blaming herself. Lately, she'd been in stage three – a particularly bitter phase where she found herself becoming resentful about all Tim's annoying habits that she'd been tolerating for years. She hoped the time-out would act as a factory-reset on their relationship. And when they got back together, maybe she wouldn't be so annoyed about the grains of beach sand he always brought into their bed sheets. What would stage four bring? She didn't know for sure, but she hoped it involved screaming 'fuck you!' from a rooftop.

Freya bundled her stuff into a red Country Road duffle bag and hooked it over her shoulder. They set off south along the boardwalk, heading up the hill and into the bush of the Cape Byron walking track.

Aimee continued. 'It was Rozzie's idea. The time-out.'

'I actually don't think it's a big deal.' Freya stopped for a moment and turned around to take a photo of the beach at the top of the timber steps. 'It's weird that it came from *Rozzie* – and that his mum is basically suggesting you sleep with other people for a few weeks. But the time-out is normal. You've been together a zillion years and you live in Byron. I'm actually surprised you guys haven't talked about having an open relationship.'

'Are you just baiting me now? I feel like you're baiting me.'

Freya swiped her thumb on the phone screen to review the shots, pressed the button on the side to lock it, then turned around to keep walking. 'Relationships can be whatever you want them to be. There are no rules, Karen.'

Aimee wrapped an arm around her dewy, bouncy almost-adult niece and changed the subject to her run-in with Rozzie at the market. 'I know I shouldn't let her get to me but she just . . . *ugh*. I dunno.'

'What did Tim say?'

'He never wants to say anything bad about his mum. It's always just been him and her. It's annoying because he doesn't *see* what she's trying to do. And then I sound like a nut job when I bring it up.' Even when they were in high school, Rozzie always treated Aimee like she was a bad influence on Tim – as if she was personally responsible for Tim wagging school to go surf and get stoned. Tim flunked tests and assignments while Aimee pretended to breeze by with natural talent. Really, she'd secretly worked harder than she let on. It's almost as if that irritated Rozzie even more. Aimee shuffled her shiny gold Birkenstocks through the light layer of sand that covered the concrete path. 'But, when I cancelled the market stall, we took the furniture back to Rozzie's house and piled it up in her garage again.' She clasped her hands together and smiled. 'She'll be displeased and that makes me happy.'

Freya bopped her hip into Aimee's. 'No antiques sale means no money . . .'

Aimee knew what she was about to say. 'I'll move into Bada Bing's tent before I appear on that reality show.'

They followed a narrow path down to a cliff. When they reached the edge, they stood in silence and looked down at the waves crashing around the rocks like a washing machine. Aimee exhaled, shook her hair back and lifted her chin, as if she was about to say something important. 'I . . . ah . . .'

Freya stifled a laugh. 'Is it bad we think this is so funny?'

'Shhh. I'm being sentimental. Reverent. They would want this.' She grabbed her niece's hand and exhaled. 'The day we scattered the ashes of your mum and nan and pop, at this very spot, it was devastating. The worst day there ever was.'

Freya pushed her lips together, fighting a smile.

'And the first anniversary of their deaths was just as hard. I – a nineteen-year-old – thought it would be a beautiful idea to make you – a one-year-old baby – toss a tiny little handful of ashes that I'd saved.'

'It was very thoughtful of you.'

'Thank you, it was.' Aimee chuckled and tried to regain her serious voice. 'And as you swung your chubby little baby arm up into the air,' she mimicked the action, 'and spread out your teeny sausage fingers – as if you were releasing the world's most beautiful butterfly – the ashes blasted up into the air like confetti.' Her tone dipped. 'And then . . . the breeze picked up. Big time. Almost cyclonic, if I remember correctly. And the fistful of ashes . . .' her shoulders were now shaking and the laughter had started. She was wheezing too much to finish the sentence.

Freya had already dropped to the ground, laughing so hard there was no sound coming out of her mouth.

Aimee bent over and finally shrieked, 'The ashes blew into your mouth!'

This had become something they did whenever Freya visited. When she was a kid, she thought it was hilarious when Aimee told her the story. She'd want to hear it over and over.

Aimee flopped onto the cushy grass and lay with Freya as their chests and bellies settled down. She looked at the way her niece scrunched up her nose when she laughed – the same way her mum did – and she wished she'd gotten to see her grow up every day for the past twenty-one years instead of through photos and memories from visits all jumbled together like a scrappy but beautiful collage. Maybe then she'd be able to step into Freya's life the way her instincts pushed for. As it was, she'd always resisted.

Some other people started to wander over and linger. Aimee craned her neck up to look. Girls in activewear had descended onto the cliff to take photos in the afternoon light. She groaned and turned back to the ocean.

'You know, if Instagram was invented in the olden days, you and Mum totally would've been huge on it,' Freya teased.

Aimee played into it and let out a gasp. 'I don't even know where to *begin* with that. No, I do! The . . . *olden days*?'

'I've seen the photos you and Mum used to take. With the Monaro, at the beach. OG influencers. Two hot chicks in Byron in the 2000s. It's a vibe.'

'Oh, it's a vibe, is it? A *viiiiibe*?'

'A total viiiiibe.'

'Well, I could still become an influencer.' Aimee flicked her hair back, in jest. 'How do I start an Instagram account? Do I have to install some kind of CD-ROM?'

'Stop it. People can hear you.'

'Is there, like, a monthly subscription I have to pay to be a member?'

Freya snapped blades of grass out of the dirt and smiled. 'Why haven't you had a hook-up yet?'

'Ah, strange change of topic, annnd not one I'll be talking about with my niece,' Aimee scoffed, pulling her satchel strap over her head and chucking the bag to her side.

'That's the point of the break. It's what you agreed to. You said Tim's hooking up. If you don't, you're gonna become bitter and resentful. Or . . . *more* bitter and resentful.'

'Don't call me bitter. It makes it sound like I have a dowager's hump.'

Freya sighed. 'I'm worried you're at risk of actually becoming Byron Karen.' Kablamo.

'Whoa.' Aimee looked out at the orange sky over the swirling ocean. 'Way harsh, Tai.'

Freya plucked a dandelion, held it up to her lips by the long thin stem and blew. The breeze blustered the tiny white fluff particles back into her face.

Aimee arched an eyebrow. 'Please tell me that blew into your mouth.'

ELEVEN

'We're in town to go to a permaculture farm.' The young guy was wearing a tie-dye T-shirt and strumming a ukulele while waiting for his order at Charlie's taco truck.

The van was painted green and orange with a big sign on top that read TACOLICIOUS. It was set up in the carpark above Main Beach for the Sunday crowd, where it was every week. The summer holidays were big business.

'We met at an ecstatic dance and voice activation gig,' the perma-culture guy said. He had one of those broad know-it-all accents that kids usually adopted while studying an arts degree at university that their dads paid for. 'It's *conscious clubbing*. If you do it properly, it's like taking MDMA.'

Rob popped up over Charlie's shoulder and shoved her face into the order window.

'We reserve the right to refuse service.' She slammed down the metal roller door.

Aimee ignored the commotion and laid on the black rubber non-slip floor mats of the van. These interactions were not uncommon on the

Sundays they spent selling burritos in the carpark. Particularly over the holiday period. Aimee and Rob always tagged along to help Charlie. Well . . . they didn't exactly *help*. To be accurate, they hung out and drank on the floor of the steaming hot van while judging people. Aimee would always return home smelling like cooked meat and fried onions and Tim would ask why she'd rather do that on a Sunday than go to the beach with him. She refused to read too deeply into it. As Charlie rattled open the door again to serve the conscious clubbers, Rob pumped out three tequila slushies from the frozen daiquiri machine.

'Am I bitter?' Aimee stared mindlessly at the tin ceiling.

Rob handed her a plastic cup. 'Yes, that's why we're friends.'

Aimee tried to fish the straw into her mouth without lifting her head off the floor. 'But . . . am I *unattractively* bitter?'

Rob leant down and kissed her forehead. 'Yes. *That. Is. Why. We're. Friends.*'

The sound of acoustic guitar from a busker in the nearby park drifted into the van and fat beads of condensation started to glide down the sides of the plastic slushie cup Aimee was holding – dripping to her hand, forearm, then slicking off her elbow.

Charlie looked over his shoulder while frying onions. 'Are you still thinking about Tim's mum at the market?' he said over the spatters.

Rob leant her back against the wall and dropped into a squat position on the floor. 'She's got an appointment at the salon this week. Want me to cut her bangs really short, as payback?'

Aimee closed her eyes and shook her head. 'No. Yes. But no. Thanks.' She sipped her drink. 'Maybe just accidentally crimp her fringe.'

'Speaking of hair . . . what's going on with yours?' Rob leant forward and rubbed a chunk of it between her thumb and fingers, assessing it like a scientist studying a strange new substance in the lab.

Aimee jolted her neck away. 'Nothing. I used a little bit of body moisturiser in it because I ran out of hair stuff. About a week ago.'

'What hair stuff?' Rob laughed.

'Product . . . things. And shampoo. Don't look at me like that. Tim already made a comment about it. Jesus. I'm . . . so sick of people judging me. Not you. Just . . . everyone else.'

'Well fuck him,' Rob dismissed, rummaging through her tan handbag with the shaggy leather fringe dangling off it.

Aimee had mixed feelings when Rob spoke about Tim that way. Rob was always on Aimee's side. It was lovely. But sometimes it made her feel like, over the years, she'd somehow slowly tricked her friends into thinking he was always the bad guy.

'Tim has no right commenting about your hair. But, as your hairdresser, *I* have the right to enquire and provide feedback.' She pulled out a hot pink steel can with a pump lid, spurted some of the white cream into her hand and leant back over to lightly massage it through the ends of Aimee's hair.

Aimee reacted like a cat whose owner was trying to clip its claws. Smoke from the grill filled the van and Aimee fanned herself with one of the orange paper menus. 'God, I just feel like such a . . . *loser.*'

'Please. We're the coolest people I know.' Rob flicked her shaggy fringe out of her face and leant back against the wall. 'The Hemsworths *wish* they were us. I mean, look around . . .' She stretched out her arms and scoffed with a little too much confidence. 'We're nearing forty and day-drinking tequila slushies on the floor of a taco truck in Byron Bay.' She paused. Smoke billowed over them and the smug look on her face drooped a little. She stifled a cough. '. . . OK, I just heard myself. Yeah, we're losers.'

Aimee used her mouth to jab the straw into the remaining slush at the bottom of the cup. 'Even *Meredith* is probably doing better than us.'

Charlie called back, 'Meredith *is* actually doing better than us.'

Rob closed her eyes and nodded. 'Business *is* booming for Meredith – ever since she did a tarot card reading for Isla Fisher and Isla posted a video of it on TikTok. She's now doing virtual sessions around the world on Zoom and has a daily segment on *Sunrise.*' She tapped at her phone for a second then held it up to show Meredith's website. 'Psychic to the stars,' read the pink sparkly font over a picture of her posing with a crystal ball that looked like it was taken at one of those shopping centre photoshoot kiosks approximately twenty years ago.

'She's a savvy businesswoman.' Charlie chopped into an iceberg lettuce. 'She was number seven on the annual Byron Bay Power Players List in the newspaper this week.'

Aimee rolled her eyes. 'Yeah, and Bada Bing came in at number one – *again*.'

Rob tapped Aimee's thigh. 'Also, Meredith just bought an Audi. Preowned – from one of those government fleet auctions. Looks real nice.'

Aimee craned her neck up off the floor and squinted. 'Meredith bought an *Audi*?'

Rob nodded, pleased with herself for having gossip. 'She almost ran over me when I was rollerblading.'

Aimee's face was still squished up. 'The woman sells crystals off a fold-up card table on the side of the road.' She thunked her head back down on the floor and felt something wet seep through her hair and onto her scalp. She grimaced but she was too deflated to do anything about it. 'How did I end up a broke, sort-of-engaged, almost-out-of-business bookstore owner – lying on the floor of a taco truck – with less money to my name than a roadside clairvoyant?'

Rob's tone turned pragmatic. 'I can't say for sure. But probably the same way I ended up a broke hairdresser who's lying on the floor of a taco truck with a failed bookstore owner.'

'God.' Aimee stared up at the tin ceiling. 'I am so sick of myself.'

————

Aimee passed the deliveries for the discount pharmacy that were piled up in the hallway and climbed the stained timber stairs to her apartment, the smell of fried food from the taco truck still following her like a cloud. The afternoon sun streamed in through the window at the top platform.

As she reached her door, the rubber tips of her Converses kicked something and she looked down. The carnival clown head sat on the floor with
a piece of paper in its open mouth. Aimee bent down, pulled out the note,
and uncrumpled it. 'Smile. Love you.'

TWELVE

Self-help had become so aggressive. And smug. The smugness wasn't new – it was the reason Aimee didn't stock those kinds of books in her own store. Banning self-help books eliminated a particularly annoying kind of customer and it was a strategy that had been successfully working for her for years. But recent days had raised questions and curiosity. About . . . herself. And . . . *helping* herself. So there she was: in the back of the used bookstore, dragging her finger along a shelf as she studied the hostile titles.

The Life Changing Magic of Not Giving a Fuck

Fuck No!

The Subtle Art of Not Giving a Fuck

Everything Is Fucked

Calm the Fuck Down

Unfuck Yourself

Aimee began to wonder if she should avoid the sweary self-help books. Would they be counterproductive? Sure, she was keen to both unfuck herself *and* calm the fuck down. But, as someone who already didn't give a fuck about a lot of things, perhaps being encouraged to give even fewer fucks wasn't the sagest advice. On the other hand, there were still a number of things she gave way too many fucks about. Can you give a fuck and not give a fuck, simultaneously? Someone should write a self-help book about that. She searched for a title that was more appropriate to her own life. Maybe something like, *Pull Yourself Together, Bitch*.

The shop was so well-stocked with recent titles most customers probably wouldn't have realised it was a *used* bookstore. It made sense. People went to Byron looking to renew themselves. They bought Reese Witherspoon-endorsed and Oprah-approved self-help books at the airport, hoping to kick their bad habits and find their higher selves. Then, after a week, they crapped back off to their toxic lives – leaving in their stuffy Airbnbs the abandoned half-read tomes that eventually made their way to the used bookstore. The idea of buying a second-hand self-help book was almost gross. It had been used by a stranger for somewhat intimate purposes. It was like buying used swimwear.

The store was quiet. Aimee had timed it that way. She'd been lurking at the coffee shop across the street and monitoring the bookshop's entrance to see who was coming and going. She didn't want the town Looney Tunes seeing what she was buying. The last time she had felt this nervous was when she was seventeen and skulking between the chemist, the super-market and the servo, trying to buy condoms for Tim without anyone seeing. When there was a lull at the bookstore, she pounced. She didn't want a repeat of her mission to the crystal store from earlier that morning, where it seemed everyone she'd ever met had suddenly decided they too were in desperate need of crystals.

Pam, the bakery owner who had known Aimee since forever, had accosted her at the counter. 'Well, well! This is the last place I'd expect to find our town curmudgeon.'

Aimee got such a shock at being busted she tripped on the cord of a Himalayan salt lamp and knocked over a giant ornamental Buddha head that was carved out of rose quartz. 'Do people *actually* call me that?' she wondered, jamming the rocks of amethyst and selenite she'd just purchased into her satchel, where they'd remain.

The crystals were a vain attempt at improving her problems. Aimee knew that. And the crystal store *was* the last place anyone would usually find her. In thirty-six years, she'd never once purchased a magical polished rock. Tim used to love that about her. He was the same. In high school, that's what made them so perfect. And in their twenties. They used to laugh at the Byron-ness of Byron. Lately, though, it seemed to be the thing Tim liked least about Aimee. Whenever she made an off-hand joke or snarky comment about the town or the people in it, she could see a flicker in his eyes – like he was choosing not to say what he was really thinking. Instead, he just disconnected completely. She had become aware of these reactions slowly, but could never quite articulate to herself exactly what they meant. It had clicked when they were at the markets a few days earlier and she was making fun of all the collectives and co-ops. 'You just sound *negative*,' he'd finally said. The words had been in her head ever since and she found herself getting wound up about them whenever she had a spare moment. She needed a change. Small. A pivot. Maybe the selenite and amethyst would help.

'They can kinda just mean whatever you want them to mean,' the girl with the wild hair and tattoos at the crystal stall had shrugged when Aimee asked about their specific meanings and how to use them.

In the bookstore, Aimee plucked a well-thumbed copy of Shonda Rhimes' *Year of Yes* off the shelf and added it to the pile she'd already assembled of any book with Brené Brown's name on it. As she lugged her haul up to the counter, she realised how embarrassing it was to be seen desperately bulk-buying enlightenment. Bookstores should put a daily cap on self-help purchases like pharmacies do with pseudoephedrine. She lined up at the counter. There was a customer in front of her. Brent the shopkeeper stopped serving for a moment, leaned to the side, looked to the back of the cramped store and issued a dry statement to himself. 'Wanker.'

Aimee spun around to see who the alleged wanker was. Hot Ew Girl. She was taking photos of herself with a selection of pastel-covered, slim-spined Joan Didion books but ceased the second she and Aimee locked eyes. For a split-second, there was a glint of embarrassment on her face before she smiled and gave a knowing look.

'Aimee . . . right?' She flicked her glance down and set it firmly on the self-help bundle. Brené Brown was at the front of the stack – cover facing out. *Daring Greatly*, the title stated earnestly.

'I own a bookstore,' Aimee blurted out. 'And . . . I'm doing research. For stock. Products. New stock and products. Gotta keep ahead of the market and know what people are buying. Self-help is . . . all the rage right now. So I'm . . .' she fluttered her eyelids and waved a hand in the air as she thought of more words, '. . . researching.' She was mortified and immediately started wondering what sad details Hot Ew Girl already knew about her life, through Tim. She slowly turned back around. The encounter was something she gave far too many fucks about. And she made a mental note to learn the subtle art of not doing so.

THIRTEEN

Electric guitars thrashed as Charlie's band played their surf rock version of The Go-Go's song 'This Town'. Charlie smirked. He thrusted. The crowd drooled.

'Fuck.' Rob sucked on a wedge of lime while looking around at the Music Club crowd. 'They're gonna need squeegees to dry off these seats.'

Aimee screwed up her face. 'OK, that is just unnecessary.'

Just a regular night at the weekly Music Club.

'Bad day?'

'Welp, the first potential buyer came to inspect the store.' Aimee gave a sarcastic thumbs up. 'And then, when I was rollerblading home from work, I almost got *sideswiped* by Meredith's Audi.'

Rob raised her glass and clinked it into Aimee's, welcoming her to the club.

Aimee took a sip. 'But, before all that . . . I was waiting in line at the coffee shop this morning and someone started having a go at me about Freya being on the TV show.'

'Who was it? I want a name!' Rob demanded. She was more than two drinks in and becoming theatrical.

Aimee rolled her eyes. '*Joelle*.'

'Oh, Joelle can go suck it.'

'Joelle is *seventy*.'

Rob raised her eyebrows and doubled down. 'Joelle's hanging out in that big ol' house her husband left her and she's making a mint on the side by renting out the spare bedrooms on Airbnb. Have you *seen* what people can charge for a room up here on Airbnb? That dame's raking in *thousands* over just one weekend. Easy.'

Aimee exhaled and clasped her head in her palms. 'I need to get Freya to quit that stupid show.'

Rob screwed up her face. 'No. Fuck 'em.' Her voice became very no-nonsense. 'This whole argument about what *is* and *isn't* allowed is just ridiculous. Everyone's been happy to make money off this town when it's worked for *them*.' She nodded to the Byron Bay Power Players table down the front, near the stage, where Meredith was sitting with Bada Bing. 'Just remember: Meredith bought an Audi.'

Aimee let out an involuntary laugh.

Rob smirked. 'And, by the looks of it, she also wants Charlie.'

They watched as Meredith seductively chair-danced while maintaining unbroken eye contact with Charlie, who was lapping up the attention on-stage like a really sexy Labrador. Meredith hadn't changed in the years she'd lived in the shire. Mid-fifties, she looked like a rebellious medieval princess who'd just escaped the turret she'd been locked in for centuries. She'd been selling crystals on the side of the road since Aimee was in primary school. Aimee and Fleur used to call her The Witch. When their mum would drive them to school in the morning and the car would pass her, they'd unclip their seatbelts and drop to the floor, screaming, 'The witch!'

'God.' Rob fanned herself with a laminated menu. 'Imagine the things she'd do to Charlie in the back of that Audi.'

'Stop.'

'She wouldn't just be reading his palm, that's for sure,' she stage-whispered out the side of her mouth.

'Nope. Enough.'

Freya bounced up the timber stairs and over to the table, leaning across to playfully muss her aunt's hair. 'Why does Aimee look horrified?'

'She's just being uptight.'

'I'm not being *uptight.*' Aimee's voice went high and strained.

'Wow, you *are* being uptight.' Freya took a sip of her aunt's drink. 'So I guess this isn't a good time to bring up the TV show again . . .'

Aimee closed her eyes and held her palms up, as if to pause time. 'Didn't I shut this down? I remember it clearly. We were drinking Aldi champagne and I'd just been crowned Byron Karen by the internet.'

Rob took a dainty sip of her drink and nodded. 'You did shut it down. It was a very "Byron Karen" thing for you to do.'

Freya cut to the chase. 'Well, they're not taking no for an answer.' She nodded over to the steps. Aimee turned. Her eyes bulged. There he was. The Ferrari Guy.

'Hey, it's the fuckin' hippy from the bookstore.' The guy laughed and held his hands in the air, surrendering, as he made his way over. 'I'm just kidding. I'm sorry. I'm *really* sorry.'

Aimee stared at him.

'I'm Heath, one of the . . . *"showrunners",'* he seemed embarrassed about saying his title and made air-quotes with his fingers, '. . . of the trashfest your niece is on. Isn't that what you called it?' He laughed and clapped a little. No response from Aimee. 'Trashfest? From the protest video. Isn't that the word you used?'

'*Trashbaggery,'* Aimee corrected.

'Even better.' He smiled, almost seeming impressed. 'I was glad to see the temper wasn't just a once-off thing.'

Rob and Freya looked confused at how Heath and Aimee knew each other.

Heath explained. Vaguely. 'We know each other from a little . . . *incident.* At the bookstore. Wires were crossed. But . . . it's in the past.' He rolled up the sleeves of his blue chequered flanno and took a seat on a stool across from Aimee. 'How do we get you on the show?' He slapped his thick right hand on the tabletop.

Aimee exhaled and shook her head. Then she smiled, bemused at the simple thinking of the oafish man in front of her. 'It's really not something I'll consider doing.'

'If I recall correctly, your store is being sold. And Freya told me you could only be won over with money . . .'

Aimee let out an 'ugh' sound and glanced at Freya for a split-second before shutting down the claim. 'Incorrect.'

'We're in Byron, everything's for sale for the right price.' Heath picked up Aimee's glass and tossed back the remaining tequila. 'Ten grand.'

Aimee's eyes shot open. There was less than ten grand sitting in her savings account at that moment, as Narissa from the bank had so helpfully reminded her. Still, she morphed her surprise into a look of disgust.

Heath shrugged. 'Eh, you're right. Ten grand's nothing after tax.' He slapped his palm on the table again. 'Fifteen.' When Aimee didn't jump at it in two seconds, he spun the wheel of fortune again. 'Fine. Twenty. Byron Karen's a hot commodity. Twenty grand won't solve all your problems but, for a few weeks' work, it's worth it.'

Aimee raised an eyebrow. 'You have *thousands* of dollars to throw around for some crappy reality show and yet there's no money to produce great Australian dramas anymore?'

'Relax, Deborah Mailman will be fine.' Heath exhaled and drank whatever was left of Rob's drink. Then he got serious. 'These shows *are* the new great Australian dramas. What's happening here in Byron is *real*. It's emotional. Personal. Yes, there are some girls running around in bikinis. Dickhead guys. But, right now, we've got an iconic Aussie town that's going through a big moment of change. *That's* what the show is. It's a moment in history. Girls in bikinis are just how we get people to care about it.'

Rob interjected. 'You know, I think you almost had her until you said that last sentence.'

The microphone screeched. Everyone in the bar winced and covered their ears. Charlie's band had finished and Bada Bing was fiddling with the microphone. 'Guess Who, Don't Sue: Which big-time movie star has been utilising the services of a local . . . *stimulants* service?'

Rob opened her mouth to yell but Aimee grabbed her arm. 'Don't.'

'You don't know what name I was about to say.'

'Your answer is always Shelley Craft.'

'And one day it will be correct.'

Bada Bing spotted a face in the crowd. 'Oh . . . well, well, well . . .'

Aimee glanced around. 'Is he looking at us?'

'Guess Who, Don't Sue: Which local bookstore owner-turned-viral internet celebrity is now starring in the show she publicly denounced?'

The crowd turned to Aimee.

'That is factually incorrect and I demand a retraction,' she declared, shooting a confident split-second glance at Heath.

The crowd booed. She'd broken the rule. Aimee got to her feet and bounded up to the stage to face the ragtag troupe of town misfits.

'Traitor!' someone called.

Aimee scrunched her face. 'I'm not even on that stupid TV show.'

'Your niece is!'

'That show's the epitome of what's ruining our town,' called another.

'Oh please. This town changed a long time ago. And you're all hypocrites. When the movie theatre premiered that Greta Thunberg documentary, only two people went – and they were both visiting from Melbourne. But tickets to a rerun of *Blade Runner* sold out so fast they had to put on a second screening.'

'Your parents would be disappointed,' Bada Bing sighed.

'Hey,' she warned, her voice low and stern.

'Fleur would've hated her kid doin' this.' Meredith exhaled steam from her vape pen.

Adrenaline shot through Aimee's body and words spat out of her mouth before they even passed through her mind. 'Fuck off, you fuckin' hippies.'

The crowd gasped.

Aimee stood in silence for a second while she recalibrated. 'No,' she corrected herself. 'You're not hippies. You're fake hippies. You're all *fake* hippies.' She walked to the edge of the stage and stared down at them. 'Meredith just bought an Audi.'

Meredith jumped off her stool. 'I also *live* in it!'

'And now she's spruiking herself as a psychic to the stars – the same stars who you all say are ruining this town.' She pointed into the crowd. 'Lenny started a beer company called Byron Bay Brewery and it's not even made in Byron Bay anymore.'

'Boo!' Cynthia cupped her hands to her mouth.

'Oh, shut up, Cynthia, you only moved here in 2009. And stop crapping on about how it's important we all support local business. I see you every morning at Gloria Jean's.' Another face popped out of the crowd. Aimee smiled. 'Ah, Spider. Spider's benefited most from gentrification. You lived illegally in that shack down on Seven Mile Beach for twenty years and then got awarded legal ownership because of a squatters' rights loophole – and *then* you sold it for a million dollars!'

'One-point-two million,' he rebutted. 'And that's why I placed number three on the newspaper's Byron Bay Power Players list.'

The crowd cheered. Aimee yelled over it. 'The Power Players List is just a definitive ranking of Byron Bay Looney Tunes!'

All the Byron Bay Power Players proceeded to boo.

'Don't you boo me!' Aimee pushed her hair out of her face. 'I've given my life to this town.' She pointed at her chest. 'I *am* this town!'

'You *were* this town!' the millionaire squatter yelled.

'Yeah! Don't hate the player, hate the game,' Meredith called.

Aimee shook her head in shock. 'But you're all *complaining* about the game!'

She stared out at the people jeering her and then looked down the back of the room to Rob, Freya and Heath. 'Well . . . You can all watch to see what happens on my new reality show.' She jumped off the stage and her

Converses hit the floor with a thud as the crowd went back to booing. She rushed back over to her table. 'Why aren't you guys moving?' she asked, frantically grabbing her stuff.

Rob clasped her friend's arm. 'Aimee, I love you. But I also don't want Meredith to put a spell on me.'

Aimee leaned in closer. 'Pick up your goddam bag.'

Rob nodded and moved swiftly.

The next band took to the stage and tried to play over the shouts, but the plucky banjo and percussive clickety-clacks of the frottoir were too weak to drown out the chants.

Aimee glared at the Byron Bay Power Players as she stormed down the steps with Rob and Freya in tow. Heath stood against the back wall and watched his new star's performance.

Meredith exhaled steam from her vape pen. 'I shoulda hit you both with my Audi when I had the chance.'

Rob pushed Aimee into the wall and ran ahead. 'I just got chills – get outta my way.'

FOURTEEN

Aimee's body reached the floor of the ocean. Her legs performed frog-like kicks and she manoeuvered her arms and hands like propellers to keep her body from being sucked back up through the water to the surface. Her back grazed the sand. She held her breath and occasionally exhaled a little bit of air from her lungs through her nose, the slow release creating a stream of tiny bubbles that would dance in line above her. It was the only time of the day that she didn't quite feel as sick as she usually did. Not under-the-weather sick. More a feeling in her gut. Like something was wrong or a problem was looming – as if there was an overdue bill that she'd forgotten to pay. And the longer it went unpaid, the more debt it accumulated. She'd been waiting for the day it'd find her. The day she'd have to deal with it. Now her bills were both figurative and literal, with the sale of the store. Signing onto the reality show was a desperate attempt to fix the newest problem in her life, but she couldn't help but think the decision was about to lead to debts of a different kind. Ones she couldn't quite predict, but ones she knew were definitely in the distance – just like when she opened her eyes underwater and could only see a short way in front of her before everything turned into a deep hazy blue. There were things lurking beyond. They just weren't in sight yet.

The ill feeling had grown from what it once was. It was now in every cell – like the vital tissue that connected from the top of her head to the soles of her feet had become infected and went unnoticed and now it had progressed to an almost-irreversible state. Festered. She hated that word. But that's how she felt. Like she needed to be operated on with a fine scalpel that sliced her open and scraped out all the sludge and muck that was building up by the second. Take it all. Wipe it out.

The feeling had gotten worse over summer – from the very moment Tim asked for a time-out and the endless thoughts that followed, looming, like clouds on the edges of her mind. She could assess the shape and colour of the clouds and predict the destruction they'd cause if they floated too close, so she batted them away. She knew the feelings and fears that would rain down once they rolled over. The doubts. Truths. Questions she'd be forced to ask herself about what it was exactly that provoked Tim to request the time-out. *Request*. Ha. Like when you drop off a jacket at the dry cleaner just after midday and then politely request if it can still be ready for same-day pickup. The time-out wasn't a request. It was the final hurdle. Didn't clear it? You lost.

Little bubbles burbled from Aimee's nose as she expelled a tiny spurt of air. With her eyes closed, she couldn't see them dance away out of sight, but she could feel them tickle the top of her lip. Her arms cut through the water, unbreakable blades, moving in time with her froggy kicks.

Sometimes she'd lay awake at night and imagine, in intricate detail, the quiet moments in which he made the decision to ask for the time-out. She wondered how long he'd spent fretting, who he'd spoken to about it – rehearsing the ways he'd bring it up while driving alone in his ute or while out in the ocean, waiting for a wave. Maybe there were multiple scenarios he'd prepared for – trying to forecast and predict potential situations where he could bring it up.

Like when she'd be making a salad for dinner on a Sunday night. Maybe he'd considered that as a good moment. He'd walk in with the grilled fish that he'd picked up down the road and, like every Sunday night, place it on the counter. Only, that Sunday night, he'd place it like he'd never placed it before – too intentionally. 'Hey,' he'd begin, a little jittery, hands by his waist, unsure of whether to slip them inside the pockets of his boardies or place them on his hips. Instead, they'd dangle awkwardly – like the statement 'Hey'. Maybe, in that scenario, he'd thought about asking her on a Sunday night because he knew she wouldn't have to work on the Monday, so that would give her time to deal with it, emotionally. Recover from the blow. Or a Thursday. That was another of the options she'd imagined him tossing up. His reasoning might've been that she could use the Friday to be devastated but then, in theory, be over it by Saturday morning – ready to enjoy the weekend.

She felt silly looking back at all the times she went about her day, in their home, while he sat there – heartbeat getting faster, thoughts racing, thinking: *Just do it. Do it now.* When he finally did do it, it was in the underground carpark at the new Woolworths on Jonson Street. They never really did the grocery shop together – Aimee always just picked up stuff, as needed, on her walk home from work in the afternoons. But that Saturday they'd been out to lunch for his mum's birthday and, on the way home, Aimee made Tim pull into the supermarket. She was in a mood after having to deal with Rozzie's passive-aggressive commentary. She ran into the store while Tim waited in the car with the radio playing. When she came out, holding a navy-blue sleeve of Double Coat Tim Tams, she jumped back in the passenger seat of the ute and, just as the door whacked shut, he switched off the radio and an annoyingly anthemic Mumford & Sons song cut out. That's when he brought it up. While he talked, Aimee looked at the green and black digital clock on the dashboard of the ute. 3.21. She stared at it and didn't reply. Her mind only focused on the number. Twenty-one. Then it ticked over.

A more forceful puff burbled from her nose. Time was running out. One burst left. Then her body would spring up into the open air and she'd swim back to land – the sick feeling getting stronger the further she walked past the sand edges of her life and back into the messy centre.

Bubbles burst in a garbled explosion from Aimee's mouth as she folded her body into a crouch position and her feet pushed with force off the sand, disturbing the muted underwater ambience and shooting her body up towards the rippling sky. Her face shattered the surface.

Gasp.

———

Aimee gasped again. This time, louder. She'd just swung open the front door of her apartment and was standing in the hallway – damp patches of salty water bleeding through her old cut-off denim Levi's from the wet blue swimsuit underneath. Her bag and keys crashed on the floorboards and she whipped off her black Wayfarer sunglasses to get a better look at the destruction inside her home.

Heath turned around from the fridge. 'Oh hey. What's with all the old people furniture?' His rumpled appearance matched his disregard for social graces.

Aimee's carefully displayed clutter had been shoved out of the way and replaced with new haphazardly placed clutter – cameras, cables and big lights on tall stands, all being adjusted by about a half dozen or so TV crew members in all-black outfits. They pecked through her personal space – tossing aside sentimental belongings – like a flock of ibis picking apart a back-alley dumpster. After a few moments of Aimee staring at them, they tossed her expressionless glances – as if to say, 'And?' – before returning to their dumpster dive. *Peck, peck, peck.*

'How did—'

'Freya let us in.' The glass bottles lined up in the fridge door clinked as Heath whacked it closed. 'We just wanted to check things out – see what your place looked like for filming. Do a screen test with you. I've also got your contract.' He pulled the rolled-up papers from the back pocket of his jeans and took a bite out of the end bit of an almost-finished block of cheese. The bent pages flopped onto the table.

Aimee gathered the stuff she'd dropped on the floor and dumped it down on the row of old theatre seats near the door. 'Wait, Freya let you in?

I didn't hear her come in last night and I didn't see her this morning. I was . . . *worried*.' She tiptoed further inside, around her beloved, displaced possessions – a wooden bowl of old billiard balls, several old silver champagne buckets that she'd use as vases or to class-up the Aldi bubbles, and a collection of blue Foo dog statues (she had them before they became cool) – and over to the dining table.

'It's what we discussed. Twenty grand. Six-week commitment but you won't be required every day. You get five grand up front and the rest once you've wrapped your filming commitments.' He rattled off the details with a bored over-familiarity. 'You're not the focus of the show, but you're an active participant and expected to interact with co-stars and attend filmed group events. You don't have to do anything except be yourself and share your life with us for the summer.' He grabbed the pen from behind his ear and held it up with a smile, clearly proud of himself for getting Aimee to do what she'd claimed she never would.

The cocky attempts at charm put Aimee in a bad mood. She flicked her eyes down and then looked back up with a sigh. 'Your fly's undone.'

Heath gave a cursory glimpse. 'It's not undone. It's just broken.'

'It's still down.'

'But not intentionally.'

'Why don't you buy a new pair of jeans?'

'Not necessary.' He shrugged. 'No one ever notices.'

'I noticed.'

'You're the first. And you're always looking for things to judge, so it doesn't count.' He held up the pen again and grinned, leaning in close enough for Aimee to smell his signature scent of cigarette smoke mixed with Joop, which he'd probably bought from the discount pharmacy downstairs.

He hadn't won yet.

'So, you're the . . . *showrunner* . . .' She left Heath and his dangling pen and walked over to the kitchen bench. She pulled a glass out of the cabinet above the sink, twisted the silver faucet and raised her voice over the blast of water splattering from the tap. '. . . does that mean executive producer?'

'Two showrunners, two different jobs. Technically you could call me the production manager,' Heath corrected, popping the last bit of cheese in his mouth. 'Budget, schedules, deadlines . . . finding our all-star cast.' He gestured to Aimee with a grand flourish of his hands. 'That's what I handle. And, technically, you could call Nina the EP – she looks after the stuff that's happening on camera every day, decides what ends up on the show.'

Aimee looked around at the ibis. 'And which one's Nina?'

'None of these idiots,' he laughed, affectionately insulting his rag-tag troupe, who continued to mill about, looking like neglected and apathetic middle children who'd run away from their families to join the circus or a rock band but ended up in this freakshow instead. 'Guys, this is Aimee. Aimee, these are people whose names you don't need to know.' The crew mumbled acknowledgement, clearly accustomed to the vague introductions. 'They're just a few of the weirdos you'll see on set. All up, we've got about fifty here working for us. Lots of producers. Hair, make-up, camos, soundies,' he explained. 'You won't remember them, but that's OK because they'll remember you.'

'Camos?' Aimee shook her head, trying to keep up.

'Cameramen. And soundies – the sound guys, in charge of the microphones. Nina – you'll meet her later, on a shoot. We've got a heap of different things being filmed every day. She's with the kids on bigger shoots at the beach sometimes. Or with Brooke.'

Before Aimee could even ask, Heath already explaining as he scuffed his muddied old Volley sneakers over the hardwood floors to a pile of black bags and tech gear.

'Brooke's a rich lady who wanted her own show . . . And her life is so outrageous that a network thought she should absolutely have one. This whole thing is centred around her move from Sydney to Byron with her husband and her influencer kid, and the influencer kid's influencer mates.'

'That's a lot of influence.' Aimee nodded.

'I guess they're the "brats" in the title . . . *The Brats of Byron Bay*. I dunno.' Heath yanked his silver MacBook out of the rubble and walked back to the table. 'I try not to think too hard about it. And neither should you.' Before he could shoot her that smile and dangle the pen again, she pushed on.

'OK, but . . .' she squinted. 'What is the show actually . . . *about*? Like, the cameras switch on and these people do . . . *what*?'

'Eh. Whatever they want.' Heath shrugged, half-listening while he bent over the table and tapped away on the laptop. 'It's about summer in Byron, rich influencers partying. Brooke's house reno. We're not forcing stuff. Just let life play out and we'll shape it. Brooke and the girls might push for drama, initiate some uncomfortable moments. That's just what they like and what they want the show to be. And, hey, that's good TV. It's up to you how you react. Just remember: the more you resist, the more uncomfortable you make it – and the worse you'll look.'

'I'm not throwing a glass of wine on anyone,' Aimee stated. She didn't watch reality shows, but she knew glasses of wine got thrown. Rob frequently used the GIFs in their texts.

Heath flicked his eyes up from the laptop screen. 'You only throw slime, right?'

Aimee swiftly moved on. 'But what exactly do *I* do?'

'You're the . . . quintessential Byron resident.' Heath launched into his slick car salesman spiel. 'We need you. You're the opposite of Brooke. We didn't anticipate the town backlash to the series – and bringing you in shows the two different worlds. Or the . . . two worlds colliding. But, like I said – don't think about it too much.' He spun the computer around and positioned the screen in front of Aimee. 'Here. This is still rough but it's Brooke's intro for the first episode.' He hit the space bar and a clip started playing. Generic thumpy music blared out of the speakers – the kind that played at runway fashion shows in suburban shopping centres.

'My name's Brooke and I'm the founder of the international children's wear label Tutu Tribe.' Slow motion footage played of a rich-looking woman driving her Mercedes G-Wagon while clutching one of those really big Starbucks cups. Something in Aimee's mind clicked: It was the lady from

Moe's Garage. 'Our clientele includes A-list celebrities like Kate Beckinsale, Victoria Beckham and Nicole Kidman.' Paparazzi photos popped up on the screen, showing the famous women with their kids in the puffy cotton candy-coloured tulle tutus. 'I'm a Boss Bitch.' Cue the overlay footage of Brooke sitting in a white leather chair at a glass desk while pointing at a blank spreadsheet on her computer screen. 'I don't apologise for having goals and achieving them. My standards are high – and I expect everyone else in my life to meet them. Me and my family are trading Sydney for Byron Bay – where I'll be ticking one more goal off my list: renovating a country estate.' The video cut to Brooke in silver strappy stilettos, tailored black leather trousers and a white button-up business shirt with an orange hardhat on. She was holding architectural blueprints rolled up into a tube while walking through dirt and rubble on the farm. 'Am I ready to slow down?' She let out a rehearsed laugh. 'The real question is: Is Byron Bay ready for Brooke?'

Aimee sat stiff and upright in the bentwood chair, her eyebrows raised high, as she tried to think of how to respond. 'Wow. She's . . . confident.'

Heath had already moved on and was fiddling with the laptop again. 'I don't have the video intro for her daughter Bree or her mate Addie. But I do have one of the other girls, Luna.' He hit the space bar.

More cringy reality TV music started playing. This time it was the kind that's used when the 'bad girl' gets introduced on a show – the kind that somehow sounds like a thick, slinky chain dragging along concrete or rattle-snakes being lashed with a leather whip. Lots of slap bass and naughty guitar riffs. Then the voiceover.

'Hey guys, I'm Luna. You probably know me from my podcast Balls Deep, where we go *balls deep* on all issues relating to sex, relationships and taboo subjects that no one else is brave enough to tackle. I'm also a feminist, social activist and avid advocate for women's empowerment.' Luna had big hair and bigger boobs. She seemed like the kind of girl who would've gotten in trouble for bringing her older sister's *Cosmopolitan* magazine to primary school. Footage played of her strutting down a dead-end laneway in a leopard print romper that looked like it was made for a sassy toddler.

'I'm on a mission to reclaim the word *BLEEP*,' a high-pitched noise censored the final word of her sentence. 'Just like reclaiming the word "slut" put the power back in the hands of women, I'm personally campaigning to change the narrative around the insult of *BLEEP*.' The video cut to her driving a convertible. 'I am a *BLEEP*,' she shrugged. 'And I'm proud of it. You don't get to where I wanna go without being a *BLEEP*. All the iconic women throughout history who've inspired me have all been *BLEEP*.' Slo-mo footage played of her punching a boxing bag with big red gloves. 'Take the power back. Put the "U" back in *BLEEP*.'

The look on Aimee's face was the same one she made when she had to scrape soggy vegetable scraps out of the kitchen sink hole with her bare fingers. 'She's . . . also confident?'

Heath waved a hand in the air. 'The bleeped word is *cu—*'

'No, I got it,' Aimee cut him off with a nod.

'You'll meet them all tonight. There's a dinner at Bang Bang.'

Aimee didn't even wait a beat before tossing out her excuse. 'I can't make it, sorry. I've got this . . . class . . . *thing* . . . that I run. It's the last one for the year. I can't cancel.' She had to stop herself from sighing with relief.

'Yeah, I know. Rollerball. Freya told me. She said it finishes by 7pm.' He smirked. 'Dinner's at eight.'

Aimee tried to think of another excuse to squirm out of dinner but came up blank. She looked down at the contract and the dotted line where her signature was supposed to be. One swift flick of the pen could fix her money problems. 'I just don't know what I have to offer on something like this. And . . . *twenty grand*? What's the catch?'

Heath pulled a chair out from the dining table and sat down facing her. 'Getting Byron Karen on *The Brats of Byron Bay* is a slam dunk.'

'But you know I'm not really like that, right? I don't want people thinking I'm *actually* a Byron Karen.'

'Look, the Byron Karen thing is already out there. You can't escape it. You may as well get in on the joke and make something from it. I know you're not really like that. For the show, it's just a hook. After the first episode, it'll be forgotten. It's a gag. The real purpose is to show viewers the other side of this town.'

Aimee grabbed the pen off the table and fiddled with the clickety button on top. She looked around the apartment she'd dreamed of living in all her life – her stuff everywhere, her finance nowhere – and could almost hear the blenders that would soon be roaring inside her old bookstore once it was converted to a juicery. No store, no job. No money, no apartment. Her glance snagged on the carnival clown head that'd she'd left on the floor near the cabinet filled with cassette tapes. Tim's note was still scrunched up in its mouth. She closed her eyes and shook her head, then slapped her palm on the contract to pull it closer. 'I'm gonna get screwed over, I just know it.' She exhaled, giving in and signing the pages anyway. But what choice did she have?

Heath jumped to his feet with a howl and started rubbing Aimee's shoulders like a coach amping up their star athlete. 'You're not gonna get screwed over.' Needless to say, Aimee could not shake the feeling that she was, in fact, going to get screwed over.

She dropped the pen on the contract and stood up from her chair. 'So, what do I need to film?' She stepped awkwardly through the wreckage, closer to the TV gear that was set up to face the couch.

'I thought it might be good to do a screen test today – just to get you feeling comfortable in front of a camera.'

Aimee flopped onto her velvet sofa, sat up straight and adjusted one of the thin navy shoulder straps on her swimsuit. She tossed back her damp, tangled hair and looked into the lens of the chunky black camera that was pointed squarely at her. The lights set up by the crew radiated heat and she squinted while her eyes adjusted to the brightness.

'Sometimes you'll be fitted with a mic pack but, for something like this, today, we can just record you with the boom,' Heath said.

The soundie – standing to the side, behind the camera – held a long black stick overhead. Aimee glanced up at the cylindrical grey microphone attached to the end that dangled above her, just out of shot.

Heath rounded up the rest of the crew and they all meandered behind the camera to face Aimee. 'I'll ask you questions . . . answer 'em. Simple stuff,' Heath called out. 'It'll get you in the flow. We'll record – just in case you say something great we wanna use.' He walked over to a square black box that looked like a mini TV with a screen that showed the footage being filmed in real time.

Aimee sat and watched as Heath and the crew watched her. Not just watched. *Assessed.* She shifted uncomfortably. Heath looked at the screen like it was a weird piece of abstract art in a fancy gallery – crossing his arms, standing back and squinting. He leaned close again, his eyes only an inch away from the screen. Then he screwed up his face. 'Hey, maybe go change your clothes.'

Aimee furrowed her brow.

Heath looked at her blankly and repeated the matter-of-fact demand. 'Your clothes. Maybe go change your clothes.'

'Is my swimsuit not sexy enough for you?' She laughed in disbelief. 'You said girls in bikinis is what gets people interested in this show. But a woman over thirty-five in a bikini needs to cover up? Maybe you should just play a warning before this kind of footage – CAUTION: the following may offend and disgust.'

Heath put a pen behind his ear, cleared his throat, then raised an eyebrow and looked her in the eye with a half-smirk. 'We can see your tits on the monitor.'

Aimee grabbed the mustard yellow velvet cushion from beside her and clutched it in front of her chest.

Heath rubbed his brow. 'With all the lights, your tits are showing through the, ah . . .' he waved a hand at Aimee's chest, '. . . *worn-out Lycra.*'

Aimee took a deep breath and flicked her hair back. 'I'll go grab a shirt.'

Heath avoided looking at Aimee and pulled his phone out of his pocket. 'Actually, I gotta go.' He held up the screen with the time on it. 'The guys will pack up.'

Aimee shot to her feet as he grabbed his stuff. 'I have to get to work anyway.' Her left arm was still holding the cushion to her chest. 'What about the screen-test-thingy?' The crew had already begun rolling up cords and collapsing camera tripods and she followed Heath to the door.

'How about we try to record something later. Down the beach. This weekend.' He gave Aimee a cheeky look over his shoulder and mumbled an aside. *'With a different outfit.'*

She swatted his back and shooed him out into the hall.

'We shoulda filmed ya in front of that Live Nude Girls sign,' he said of the neon strip club memorabilia lighting up the wall in the loungeroom.

'Go. Now.'

Heath jogged down the stairs – pleased with himself yet again – and continued to call out quips as they came to mind. 'And you thought my broken fly was bad!'

FIFTEEN

Instead of sitting passively on the borders of your life, you must make the choice to show up and forge unflinchingly into life's Amazon of emotions like the warrior woman you are.

A podcast by the world's hottest and most annoyingly know-it-all life guru Elowen Wilder was playing over the speakers of The Dream Explosion. Aimee had given up on the accompanying book and decided to cheat with this Greatest Hits version instead – a collection of cherry-picked quotes and motivational nonsense that only inspired involuntary cringing rather than any kind of personal evolution. As she rollerbladed around the store, putting away new stock, a slideshow ran in her head – depicting all the instances she'd hurled judgement and advice just that morning alone. The wise words continued to flow, calm and unhurried, despite the honks and mix-match of music blasting from the cars outside. End-of-day traffic was backed up all the way along the street. Bored backpackers in hi-vis vests – mostly hot British girls with winged eyeliner and acrylic nails, employed by the council for the summer rush – chewed gum and scrolled through their phones while turning their stop/slow signs, lazily allowing a few cars at a time to roll through the intersection down the way. *Thunk, thunk, thunk, thunk, thunk.* The thick hot pink wheels on Aimee's rollerblades rumbled quickly over the gaps in the floorboards. She whizzed over to the counter and tapped a button on the speaker to crank the volume.

Open cardboard boxes were strewn around the shop and mounds of plastic packaging rustled under the breeze of the ceiling fan. Aimee scooped up a bunch of candy-coloured rubber fidgets, clutched them to her chest and rolled over to the other side of the store to stack them on a shelf. The Dream Explosion was once stocked full of beautiful books, but those beautiful books had recently started sharing their shelf space with whimsical toys and weird gadgets – the kind people would use as stocking stuffer gifts or presents for relatives they didn't like.

Book sales had been on a steady decline. A small store in a booming town couldn't slash the prices to match the internet or the big stores that sold books in shopping centres and airports, where most tourists bought their holiday reads. So Aimee had turned to toys and other accessories as a way of bringing in new customers. Turns out, people preferred to buy them on the internet too. She stocked beautiful, handmade timber toys, many from local artists, but the only thing kids were interested in that summer were fidgets – those sensory toys that claimed to boost focus and productivity. They were the new must-have playground collector item, and entire YouTube channels were dedicated to reviewing them. At first, Aimee didn't give in to the trend. But, soon enough, the question was being asked far too often. 'Do you have any fidgets?' mums would desperately enquire on behalf of their kids. 'Where are your fidgets?' Feeling incredibly out of touch, Aimee forced herself to watch a YouTube video of two American tweens with multicoloured hair. They were the Margaret and David of fidget reviewers. She caved in. Of course, by the time she'd started stocking them, a whole new range of fidgets was released. 'They're not the right ones,' little kids would declare to their mothers after Aimee proudly guided them over to the display. Aimee had no idea there was more than just one type of fidget. Now she was stuck with a mountain of outdated fidgets that no one wanted.

Whirling over to a shelf near the display window, she hesitated for a moment and wondered how to arrange the rubbery toys. They were in all different shapes – dinosaurs, cupcakes, shooting stars, flamingos. Years before, when The Dream Explosion first opened, she'd spent an excruciating amount of time tending to her displays like they were a prize-winning garden. Designing them. Curating them. Watching them flourish. She even flew to Sydney to do a 'visual merchandising' course and spent an entire weekend in a function centre, sitting next to an insufferable woman who designed the window displays for regional Just Jeans outlets. Staying up late – fuelled by wine and armed with a hot glue gun – she'd craft large-scale installations out of wire and papier mâché and suspend them from the ceiling with string. She'd been particularly proud of her Harry Potter display, with its giant cardboard lightning bolt. Kids would stop – even at night, when the store was closed – just to look through the windows and point at how they wished their bedrooms looked. The displays were also what every parent wished the school projects – the ones they'd secretly build on behalf of their single-digit aged children – had turned out like. Sometimes mums and dads even offered to buy them – 'name your price,' they'd lean in close, the request sounding more like a demand, as if the cool-looking rocket ship in the window was a rare drug. She'd always just give them away and build another that was more over-the-top and extravagantly imaginative than the one before.

But now, things were different. Even when she could be bothered to carefully organise the fidgets, they'd just be ravaged within minutes by a child who'd then proclaim, 'These are wrong!' *Fucking fidgets*, she thought as she dumped them on the ledge. Abandoning the chore altogether, she began skating laps of the store – rolling clockwise around the timber table in the centre of the room that had the five-level doll house perched on it.

A man walked past the entrance. Seconds later, he backed up to get another look. He crossed his arms, cocked his head and smiled to himself as Aimee continued to whirl around her makeshift rollerdome. She didn't notice the spectator. On about the ninth lap, she whipped off her denim shirt, tossed it onto the counter and adjusted the straps of the white singlet she was wearing underneath. She'd thrown on the outfit and run out the door as soon as Heath and his travelling circus left her apartment. Her hair was down and still a bit wild from her morning swim. Elowen Wilder continued to wistfully preach her scripture over the speaker.

When warrior women resist the opportunities where failure is an option, they also miss out on the opportunity to fly. Fearlessly failing sets you free to soar about the Amazon of life.

The man walked up the two steps into the store and slipped over to the shelf of jumbled fidgets. Aimee only noticed him when she rolled past. 'All good?' she called out, without stopping, giving him the regular amount of attention she'd usually offer to a thirty-something guy in black jeans who was clearly from the city and had probably just wandered into her store to waste time while waiting for a mate to show up at the bar next door.

'Ah, yeah.' He nodded.

She noticed an accent. Maybe Irish.

'. . . Actually, no.'

Aimee pulled a swift 180 spin up near the counter and her hair whipped through the air. With her hands on her hips in an accidental superhero pose, she was now looking at the man across the store. He had the stylishly scruffy appearance of a wolfish shelter dog adopted by a nice family. With shadowy stubble and one eyebrow that looked to have a kinda-permanent arch to it.

He held up a fidget in each hand – one in the shape of a butterfly and the other a cactus. 'What do I do with these?' The eyebrow remained appropriately arched.

Aimee couldn't help but smile at the offbeat image. *Thunk, thunk thunk, thunk thunk.* She rolled over and took the butterfly – holding it with both hands and using her fingers to push the rubbery buttons in and out. They pipped and popped. The guy looked on in silence. She glanced up and noticed the chiselled jaw and the dark, sleepy eyes studying her hands. Then she clocked his black T-shirt stretched across his chest and the way it gripped his shoulders. Painted on, like an Action Man figurine.

'Wait, wait.' He held up a hand. 'Go slower.' He bent at the knees, lowered his face closer to Aimee's hands and watched, intently. He bit his bottom lip.

Aimee made a strange face at the request and slowed down the pipping and popping.

'Hmm. Complicated. Do they come with instructions?' He flicked his dark eyes up at her and she noticed how they sparked the same way moonlight does on the ocean at night. A smirk spread across his face as he let the *Dumb and Dumber* act slip away.

Aimee whacked the butterfly on his chest with a smile. He reached up and grabbed it, letting his hand linger on top of hers for a moment. Was he flirting? Maybe. It had been a while since she'd had a guy flirt with her (the occasional weirdo at Music Club didn't count). Or, more accurately, since she'd been free to flirt back with a guy. A cool, effortless response didn't come naturally to Aimee. Flirting with a guy was supposed to be like Cameron Diaz in early 2000s movies. Carefree. Fun and frothy. Like a can of Sunkist pulled out of an icy Esky on the hottest day of the year, shaken up and then cracked open, fizzing everywhere. Fun and frothy were not qualities Aimee ever felt an affinity with. Her social personality was probably better described as stern and hard-boiled.

As the guy with the painted-on Action Man shirt continued to stare, she went to run a hand through her hair, but it was tangled and messy from her morning swim, and the body moisturiser that she was still using as a make shift leave-in conditioner had added a tactile gunky quality to it. Her fingers got snagged in some knots mid-tousle. She aborted the mission and settled for a casual hair flip before turning to roll away. Then the front wheel on one of her skates wedged into a gap between the floorboards and she tripped, arms flailing, almost demolishing the nearby doll house. The guy moved with swift precision, swooping in front and catching Aimee before the Godzilla-style carnage could play out. Her hands latched onto his shoulders and her face smooshed into the nape of his neck. She could smell his cologne – a smoky swirl of tobacco, spice and vanilla. He stood her upright. Even with the rollerblades on, Aimee was shorter than him. Her hands had moved further up and were linked around the back of his head, touching his unfussy black hair.

'Thanks,' she whispered.

They were standing close. Then Elowen interrupted.

The bravest, purest and most compassionate gift you can bestow upon yourself is cutting the leash on your inner lady lioness and letting yourself be loved.

Aimee snapped back to reality. She found her balance, released the guy from her arms with an awkward laugh and rolled over to the counter to yank the speaker's power cord out of the wall. 'Looking for a Christmas present?' she called back.

'Sure.' He wandered further inside.

'Who are you buying for?'

'A . . . child,' he chirped. It didn't matter how big or buff a guy was, if they were Irish, their voice always sounded like a chirp.

'Yeah . . .' Aimee dragged the word out and waited for more details. 'What do they like?'

He was already distracted. 'Are you a bookstore or a toy store?'

'Bit of both,' Aimee deadpanned.

The guy sorted through a stack of board games before spotting a blue and orange Nerf Blaster hanging on the wall, pre-loaded with foam pallets. 'This'll do.' He grabbed it down.

He moved over to the cash register and placed the toy on the counter. 'I'm Jules.'

Aimee looked up from the shiny bronze till and told him her name. 'That's the display model.' She nodded over to the other Nerf Blasters. 'We've got boxed ones.'

'You should get a drink with me.' He ignored her attempt at polite retail chatter and added the fidget to the counter.

She smiled and held out her arms. 'I'm working.'

'After work.' He looked her in the eyes while tapping his credit card on the PayWave machine.

'That sounds very nice, but . . . I've got some . . . *stuff* on.'

'I gathered that from the rollerblades.' He nodded. 'Only a very busy person would wear rollerblades. Zipping from errand to errand.'

'I'm just getting ready for . . .' She looked over at the crap piled in the corner behind the counter – a basketball, a bucket of chalk and the pair of rollerblades Charlie kept at the store. 'I've got a rollerball class later. In the carpark out back. Then a dinner . . . *thing*.' There were lots of things she'd rather do than go to that dinner *thing*. Like holding the flame of a cigarette lighter to the webbing between her toes.

The back door behind Aimee was open and a dry heat blew on her legs. She'd often spend quiet days in the store leaning on the counter and staring out at those gloriously perfect afternoons – the kind that made you feel like everyone else had amazing plans except you.

'Aimee. Can I give you some advice?' Jules' tone turned serious. He looked thoughtfully up at the ceiling and leant onto the counter as he considered his words. 'Resisting opportunities means you clip the wings off the Amazonian warrior woman who just wants to fly,' he said.

Aimee fought a smile. 'You're very wise.'

'I've got more.' He pinched his chin with his thumb and forefinger. 'Even lady lionesses deserve a break every now and then – otherwise they lose the wings that let them fly ferociously into failure.'

'Sage words.' Aimee played along while internally cursing Elowen Wilder.

Jules walked over to the corner, picked up the basketball and squeezed behind the counter, heading for the back door.

'As I always say, Aimee: A stitch in time . . . gathers no moss.'

'You should do speaking tours.' She nodded.

He lifted the Nerf Blaster and pulled the plastic trigger, popping one of the long, orange foam pellets at her. It flew through the air and bounced off her shoulder. 'Come play with me.' He turned and began walking out to the carpark. 'C'mon, Aimee,' he called over his shoulder. 'You're free to fly.'

———

Aimee sat on a timber shipping pallet while Jules rolled around the concrete in Charlie's rollerblades and used yellow chalk to draw over the faded court lines that were only just visible from the previous week's game.

'This isn't the relaxed drink you had in mind, sorry.' She held a hand over her eyes to block out the glare.

Jules dropped the chalk on the ground and rolled over, reaching into the back pocket of his jeans and pulling out a silver metal flask. 'Isn't it?'

'Now, who seriously carries a flask?'

'I'm Irish.'

'And a stereotype, apparently.'

He took a swig and handed it to her with a wink.

She grabbed it and sipped. Whisky. A good kind. 'So are you staying at one of the hostels down the road?'

A laugh burst out of his mouth. 'You really think I'm a backpacker?' He was genuinely shocked and waited for confirmation. 'I'm not *that* much of a stereotype.'

Aimee raised her hands in surrender.

'So what's got you so blue?' He nudged one of his knees into hers.

'What makes you think I'm blue?' She took another swig.

Jules reached into the chalk bucket next to Aimee and pulled out a powdery pink stick. He used it to draw a tic-tac-toe grid on the concrete at her feet. 'You're living in Byron Bay and spending your days listening to depressing self-help podcasts.' He slashed a cross in the grid.

'Listening to self-help podcasts is actually a very "Byron" thing to do.' She picked up a green piece of chalk from the bucket and drew a nought.

'Ahhh. So you're a stereotype too.' He slashed another cross.

Her turn. 'Today was a one-off. And it'll probably be the last. I just don't know why those self-help ladies insist on referring to themselves as "warriors".' She cringed.

'So you're a cynic?'

'Cynic makes me sound curmudgeonly.' Her unofficial nickname may have been Byron Karen, but he didn't need to know that. 'A cynic hates everything and everyone.'

'And you only hate most things and most people?'

She raised an eyebrow. 'Just the Hemsworths and a few others.'

Jules stifled a laugh. 'Well. That's quite an enemy. What'd Thor do to you? Steal your parking space? Not pick up after his dog? Jump ahead of you at the supermarket check-out?'

Aimee shrugged. 'I don't know how much you know about this town but there's been a lot of changes. Money. Celebrities. Wankers.' She started to laugh at the kind-of-joking-but-not-really declaration she was about to make. 'We're in the grips of The Hemsworth Effect. That's what the papers are calling it.'

He grinned and nodded. 'The self-help podcasts are clearly working.'

'Well, I'm working on acceptance and trust,' she made fun of herself. 'But what I do know for sure is, this town has a way of telling people who don't belong that it's time to go.'

'Do you ever think it's the town's way of telling *you* it's time to go?' He bent down and used the chalk to slash a line through his winning row on the grid.

The playful back-and-forth had cut a little too close to the bone for a second. Aimee changed the subject. 'What do you do?'

'Are you trying to determine if I'm one of the rich and horrible zombies of The Hemsworth Apocalypse?'

Aimee let the question hang in the air.

Jules picked up the flask off the shipping pallet, took a swig and passed it to Aimee. She took a sip and maintained her silence.

'You might not like my job.' He raised his chin and looked at her with pursed lips, pausing for a moment, just long enough to make it uncomfortable. 'I'm here for a TV show.'

Of course he's a zombie of The Hemsworth Apocalypse, Aimee thought.

'Filming around the Gold Coast. But I'm staying at a place down here.'

Aimee rolled her eyes. 'So you're an *actor*?'

Jules pretended to get cocky. 'You don't think I could be an actor?'

Aimee raised an eyebrow while they held each other's gaze.

He paused for a moment and shrugged. 'I do stunts.'

'Stunts?' Aimee laughed.

'I do stunts.' Jules smiled.

'I can't tell if you're messing with me because, honestly, that sounds like a fake job.'

'The only thing here that's fake is this rollerball game you've made up,' Jules teased, looking back at the chalk-outlined court. 'You've explained the rules twice and they were different both times. I don't think *you* even know how to play your ridiculous game.'

'Wait, so you're serious? You . . . do *stunts*?'

Jules let out an exhale, pretending to be disappointed by the disbelief, and rolled back a few metres into the carpark. 'Aimee, I've only told you one lie today . . .' Then with zero warning, he launched into the air – performing a backflip – before landing clean on his rollerblades and holding out his arms to maintain his balance as he glided forward steadily. 'And that lie was about having to buy a kid's Christmas present.' He rolled back over and grabbed the Nerf gun. 'I just told you that so you'd talk to me a little longer.'

Aimee tried to fight the smile that was on her face. 'Oh, I am *well aware* of that lie. Let's just say your acting skills aren't on par with . . . whatever *that* just was.' She waved her hand in the air, referencing the backflip.

'Really? You saw through my acting?' Jules played it up.

'From today's self-help research, I've learnt to speak my truth. And I have to say: Your acting is terrible.'

Jules held up the Nerf Blaster, bopped a foam pellet at her and started skating backwards with a big smile. 'Come get me, warrior woman.'

Just as Aimee went to push herself off the pallet, her hand pressed onto a rubbery pad that popped like bubble wrap underneath her palm. She looked down and smiled. The butterfly. Fucking fidgets.

SIXTEEN

Bang Bang was filled with guys who looked like they drove Jeep Wranglers and girls who looked like they frequently regretted choices made at weekly bottomless brunches. Walking across the polished concrete floor, Aimee anticipated the distinct flush of General Pants anxiety. It could be triggered by several factors – the crowd and the too-loud thumpy music, or even just the flurry of TV producers milling about in their all-black outfits, like sneaky ants frantically streaming out of a dirt mound that had just been smashed by a bratty kid with a baseball bat. But the panic attack didn't seem to kick in.

Something is not right, she thought to herself, quoting Miss Clavel from *Madeline*. She used to run around the house with Fleur, singing the 'Something Is Not Right' song and it was a phrase she still said to herself as an adult. For Aimee, if things seemed right, then something was definitely wrong. She bit her bottom lip and smiled at the taste. *Right. The whisky.* It was probably the shots of smoky single malt she'd slammed back with Jules in the carpark that had calmed her nerves. He'd left just before the kids and Rob and Charlie arrived for rollerball – and with no time to shower after, she ducked home to quickly change before dashing to the restaurant.

Still – even after several shots of whisky from a hot stranger's flask – General Pants anxiety could come on at any moment. She staked out a spot in the back corner and tried to remember if there was any one per cent hydrocortisone cream in her bathroom cabinet, lest she break out in a nervous rash on this excursion and need to do an all-body application when she got home. Usually, in unfamiliar social situations, Aimee would pull out her iPhone and tap her thumbs on the screen, fake-typing a pretend text to someone. But tonight she actually did have someone to message. She scrolled through her recent text threads, clicked Freya's name and punched out an urgent dispatch.

Where the hell are you?

The three floating grey dots appeared in the iMessage feed. Then a reply swooped in.

I've got something else on tonight! You'll be fine! Just don't talk about antiques or Def Leppard xx

Aimee tucked the phone into the back pocket of her skinny jeans. Seconds later, it buzzed again. She pulled it out. Another text from Freya appeared on the home screen.

And don't say the word cassingle

Heath walked over to the shadowy corner of the room Aimee was hiding in. He'd traded the flanno for a stained Harley-Davidson T-shirt with a big faded eagle on the front but kept the same dirty Dunlop Volleys and faded jeans. 'You're wearing a denim jacket in summer,' he observed before leaning in and muttering an aside. '*We definitely won't see your tits in that.*' He held up his hands, expecting to get a swat but it never came.

Instead, Aimee laughed. It was accompanied with a slight eye roll – but, still, a genuine laugh.

'Wow, what's wrong with you?' Heath asked.

'Nothing's *wrong* with me.'

'You're not as wound-up as you usually are.'

'I'm . . . *wound* my usual way.' She turned away slightly, as if Heath was about to somehow find out she'd spent the afternoon flirting with a hot stranger.

'You didn't even screw up your face when I said the word ti—'

She raised her eyebrows and shot him a look.

'There she is! I knew I'd get a reaction,' he teased. 'Oh, come on.' He handed her a glass of Veuve. 'Here's to doin' whatever it takes to pay the bills.' He clinked his green Peroni bottle into her champagne flute.

'What can I say, I'm following the greenlights, like Matthew McConaughey.'

'Jesus.' Heath exhaled. 'Pro tip: Don't say any of that shit near a camera. Australia will hate you.'

Aimee's shoulders slouched and she looked around the hip restaurant, taking in the chaos as the TV crew scurried to finish setting up. 'Is that *other lady* here? The, um . . .' She closed her eyes and clicked her thumb and finger together, trying to think of the words. 'The Boss Bitch lady?'

'Well, well – Byron's newest celebrity,' a clipped British accent cut through the noise before Heath could respond. A woman wearing a she-means-business black blazer appeared beside them. 'Nina, the EP.' She whipped her hand out like a pistol from a holster and locked Aimee's palm in a death grip while staring at her prey. 'You're our fresh meat. Big fan of your work. This is going to be fun,' she said. There was just a hint of a cunning smirk on her face that suggested it would be more fun for her than Aimee.

Heath caught Aimee up to speed. 'Nina's one of the best. We brought her out from the UK just for this show . . . Well, I say *we brought her out*, but . . . it's probably more accurate to say she was *exiled*?' he ribbed.

'Lies and slander,' she snipped, playing up the melodrama. 'It was all a simple misunderstanding.'

Aimee sipped her champagne and half-laughed at what was being said, even though she had no idea what it was all about.

Heath jumped in again. 'The last show Nina produced in the UK ended up getting cancelled after that scandal with the dog and the Marmite,' he said, as if it was a global news event Aimee would be familiar with.

It *was* – but *she* wasn't.

'You know – the dog and the Marmite?' Heath kept waiting for a flash of realisation on her face. When it didn't come, he helpfully added some more context. 'The guy who covered his balls in Marmite and made his mate's dog lick 'em clean.'

Aimee had to stop mid-sip and clutch her chest.

'The official hashtag was *MarMuts*.' Nina proudly swooped a hand up in the air, as if she was announcing the name of a classic Broadway musical.

Aimee's face was scrunched up in disgust.

'They axed the show immediately,' Heath added, kind of in awe of the achievement.

'Oh, it was a lark. Some people just don't get nuance,' Nina dismissed, tossing her sharp black bob back with a laugh. And she was right. In life, there were some people who didn't get the nuance of arthouse theatre. And others who didn't get the nuance of freestyle jazz. Then there were the people who didn't get the nuance of TV stunts involving casual bestiality. 'Since arriving in Australia, I've eaten Vegemite every day in protest!'

'Well, as long as it's only on your toast,' Aimee offered before turning to Heath and changing topics. 'So . . . where did you say that Boss Bitch lady is?'

'Oh, Brooke,' Heath began.

Nina interjected. 'That's what I was coming over to say. She's had an emergency at the farm – a construction problem with her magnesium pool.'

'Relatable.' Aimee nodded.

'So, she can't make it tonight but her daughter Bree's about to arrive.' Nina turned her focus to Heath. 'Can you dash up to the farm? See what's going on and if it'll cock up the filming schedule.'

Heath sank the rest of his beer and held up the empty bottle with a nod to Aimee. 'You'll be fine. There are no dogs or breakfast condiments here.' He broke into a jog as he headed for the door.

'How comforting,' Aimee called, strangely mourning his exit because it left her stuck with a lurking Nina, who possessed the presence of a cartoon villain.

Nina shot Aimee another smirky look and slunk closer with her hands in the pockets of her tailored trousers – pivoting around so they were both looking out at the room. Without prompting, she methodically presented the lay of the land to her new recruit. 'Over there is Addie,' she nodded to a girl with a Kim Kardashian-ish body, wearing a nude-coloured bodycon dress. 'She's a life coach . . . and a fucking idiot.' The quip was tossed out with a knowing look that implied Nina and Aimee were old friends who shared a back catalogue of inside jokes. Nina's laser eyes flicked to another girl. 'And that's Luna – with all the . . . *boobs* and *hair*.'

Aimee looked at the girl spilling out of her white satin corset top and remembered the video Heath had played on his laptop that morning. 'Right, the sex podcaster.'

'Yeah, the girl who thinks she invented feminism and blowjobs. By the way, I've booked you in as a guest on her pod. They record tomorrow.'

Aimee started to babble the beginnings of excuses but Nina cut her off.

'Relax, Aimee – it's just a podcast. There'll be no MarMuts.' She raised an eyebrow and went back to surveying her kingdom. The sneaky ant producers continued to race around the restaurant. They were all wearing headsets identical to the one hooked on Nina's ear. 'They report back and I hear everything.' She tapped the device.

Aimee looked at the other diners. 'Is everyone in here part of the show?'

'No. Just our table over in the corner. The rest are regular diners – nobodies – but we need them to appear in the background . . . it adds buzz. An authentic Byron night out. That's why the producers are going around and getting them to sign release forms.' She paused for a moment and held a finger up to her ear. Her gaze fixed on the entrance as she listened intently.

Then her attention snapped back to Aimee. 'Bree's just arrived outside – she's getting miked up.' The mention of microphones seemed to jog her memory and she leant back to assess Aimee from head-to-toe. Without warning, she lashed out with one of her talons and started fiddling with the lapel mike hooked to the scooping neckline of Aimee's tee that one of the tech guys had fitted when she arrived. Then she glanced up and strained her face. 'Did one of our hair and make-up girls do . . . *this*?' She tugged the ends of Aimee's hair.

Aimee swatted her away and got defensive. 'No, I went for a swim earlier today. You know, I got told about tonight with *very* little warning.'

'Well, I don't know what it is but there's some kind of . . . ugh . . . *gunk* in there.' She reached for a napkin off a nearby table and dramatically wiped her fingers.

'Yeah, I got it,' Aimee said in an impatient sing-song voice.

'Anyway, it's too late to fix now. Bree's about to enter.'

The thumpy music cut out and the murmurs of dinner chat and clinking cutlery suddenly seemed very loud. Nina pulled out her giant iPhone. Her fancy-looking nails tapped away and the light from the screen illuminated her smooth paper-white face in the dark corner of the room. 'We can't have music,' she mindlessly explained. 'It's an absolute nightmare to edit footage with music playing in the background. Now, I'll be hidden away in the kitchen storeroom watching everything unfold on a monitor. I always have a *secret lair* when we do shoots like this.' She looked up from her phone for just a second to give Aimee a playfully evil look. 'You just . . . be you. Chat. Have fun. Ignore the cameras. Get drunk and go on one of your . . . *Hemsworth rants*.' She smirked to herself and then urgently pressed a hand to her ear again. 'Alright, Bree's about to make her entrance.'

Aimee looked over and a pack of crew members crowded the door. Cameras got into position. A boom mike hovered. Then the mood of the entire room changed. A TV scene had begun before anyone even knew it had started. The film crew swarmed backwards up into the restaurant before slowly scattering to reveal Bree, a twenty-something Sportsgirl mannequin in a white linen jumpsuit that was fitted in all the right places and showed off all the right things. She had all the perfect accessories – expensive sandals that were fashionably ugly, one of those tiny Gucci purses on a long gold chain. And a surfy boyfriend. The surfiest of boyfriends: Tim.

'Hot Ew Girl,' Aimee whispered to herself.

Smash.

Her champagne glass had slipped from her hands and shattered on the concrete floor.

SEVENTEEN

'Fuck.' Nina clopped her stilettos out of the puddle like a spooked horse backing away from a barn mouse.

Aimee felt every eyeball in the restaurant lock on her. But the brats and the TV crew and the nobodies were all a blur on the periphery. It was only Bree and Tim she could see clearly – staring at them as they stared back at her for what felt like a full minute before she broke eye contact and pretended to search for napkins. She would definitely need the one per cent hydrocortisone cream after this.

Tim's rubber thongs slapped over the concrete floor and a waiter took over the clean-up of the smashed glass, leaving Aimee no excuse but to stand and watch her fiancé move closer with the girl he was hooking up with for the summer – followed by a TV camera. At some point in the commotion, Nina had scurried back to her lair.

Slap, slap, slap. When Tim wasn't barefoot, he always wore thongs. Along with the jeans and white Quiksilver tee he was wearing that night, it was his version of a nice outfit – his 'going out' outfit. But there was something new Aimee hadn't seen before. On his head. A . . . *fedora.* Tim had never worn a fedora before in his life. He probably didn't even know it was *called* a fedora. Moss green felt. Jaunty. *Annoyingly* jaunty.

'Been trying to get you to try this place forever,' he smirked.

All three of them were now face-to-face and dodging the dustpan brush that was swiping around their feet. Aimee looked at the floor and forced a laugh. 'And I've quickly realised why I avoided it for so long.'

'Aimee, I'm Bree.' The Hot Ew Girl smiled, and leant forward to kiss Aimee on the cheek. 'We met on—'

'The roof . . . the roof.' Aimee strained a smile and tapped a finger on the side of her head. 'I remember.'

'What are you—' Tim had started to ask about Aimee's presence when Bree cut him off with a shriek.

'Oh my god,' Bree laughed. '*You're* Freya's aunt? Byron Karen? From the videos?' She placed both palms on her forehead. Bree was warmer and more easygoing than the stick figure Aimee had created in her head after their brief rooftop and bookstore interactions. 'I had no idea that was you! I mean, I'd seen the video and Freya said it was her aunt . . . but I didn't put two-and-two together . . . we'd only met so briefly on the roof – and the Byron Karen footage was so grainy. I knew we were getting Byron Karen on the show but . . .' she trailed off. 'We *love* Freya!'

Aimee noticed the confused look on Tim's face. 'Freya's on the show, too,' she attempted to explain the bizarre turn of events in a single sentence. 'And now . . . so am I.'

Tim shuffled on the spot and squished his eyes shut. 'Wait . . . you—'

'It's too complicated to explain right now,' Aimee said.

Tim gave her a weird smile. 'Why didn't you tell me?'

'Time-out. No contact,' she said, with just a little too much zing. Still, there were worse things she could've said. Like, *Nice hat. You look ridiculous*. The tension was broken when a waiter scooted up and handed her an elegant flute of fizzing champagne to replace the one she'd dropped.

Tim took the moment to recalibrate. 'Bree's on the show and asked me to come tonight.' It was clear he was kind of embarrassed. And he should've been. He was wearing a fedora. 'So Freya's in town?'

'Yeah, and she's . . . one of the . . . *brats*. Brats? Do I call you guys that?' Aimee looked at Bree with a laugh for clarification before returning her attention to Tim. 'She's one of *the brats of Byron Bay*. She's staying with me for the summer.'

'Wow.' Tim nodded.

It was around then that Aimee noticed the two TV cameras hovering around, filming the awkwardness, and she looked almost tearfully thankful when a junior producer rushed over to direct the trio to their seats at the dining table. Aimee sat down, physically relieved, as if she'd just been winched out of a natural disaster. But when she looked up, Tim and Hot Ew Girl were sitting directly across from her. She'd been plunged back into the eye of the storm. It was just the three of them – producers were still wrangling the rest of the cast. Not quite ready to continue the small talk, Aimee shuffled her chair back and forth – pretending as if she was trying to find a comfortable distance between her body and the dining table. The squeaks provided a jarring soundtrack in the quiet restaurant.

'Bree's a jewellery designer,' Tim took a random stab at chit-chat.

Aimee looked up from her pretend chair issue and used one hand to scoop her hair back behind one ear. 'Oh wow!' she said, with the same over-the-top enthusiasm she'd usually use when replying to little kids in the store who said they wanted to be fairy princesses. *Dial it down, like, thirteen notches*, she imagined Rob whispering to her. 'There's the markets – every weekend . . . They hire out stalls. You should check it out – if you're looking for a place to sell.'

'Oh, nice!' Bree smiled and licked some satay sauce off her thumb after reaching for one of the chicken skewers in the middle of the table. 'Above Main Beach, yeah? I checked them out the other week – they're awesome. I wish we could sell there but I'm technically *not allowed*.' She waved her hands in the air like it was all a big drama. 'We sell through our online store and we actually just signed a deal with David Jones to be the exclusive retail stockist.' She tried to play it down like it was no big deal. 'But that's all still very hush-hush . . . it only happened a few days ago.'

Tim jumped in. 'Bree actually started the brand when she was living in Bali. Then one of her necklaces got used on a . . . um . . . what was the TV show?'

'*Emily in Paris*,' Bree said. 'The brand kinda blew up on Insta first. Then Pat Field, the costume designer for *Emily in Paris* – she's awesome . . . she also did *Sex and the City*. Anyway, she saw it and DM'd and asked if she could use one of our pieces.' Bree placed a hand on her smooth, tanned chest and fiddled with a brushed gold crescent moon on a thin chain. 'It's our signature piece – called The Stevie. Named after Stevie Nicks.'

'Well . . . congratulations!' Aimee went to say something else but got distracted when she noticed the two cameras hovering around – one behind her and another behind Tim and Bree.

'You get used to it,' Bree assured her of the TV crew. 'They're always filming. You won't notice them after a while.'

'What's the name of your brand?' Aimee asked.

'Lola. I've just always loved the name. It kinda encapsulates my aesthetic and sensibility. I'm actually helping Tim come up with names for the new bar.'

Aimee stared blankly. 'Isn't it just called . . . Byron Boards?' she deadpanned.

Bree laughed and used a fork to slide the chicken off her skewer.

'That'd be too confusing.' Tim shrugged.

'We came up with *lots* of options.' Bree set down her fork and picked up her phone. 'OK, so these were some of the top picks . . .' She cleared her throat and read from a list on the Notes app. 'Elk Social Club. The Merchant's Secret. Cloak and Swagger. The Neighbourhood Speakeasy Project.' Bree laughed at that last one. 'Um . . . Workman's Canteen. Annnnd . . . Buffalo Barn.'

Aimee had to consciously control her face to not look like someone had just cut in front of her at the post office.

'I still kinda like The Factory.' Tim swigged his Corona.

Oh, Jesus, Aimee thought. *Here we go.*

'You know – like Warhol's Factory? That's what he called his loft in New York where he made all his art and everyone partied.'

Along with fedoras and trendy podcasts about start-up culture, Tim had also recently discovered Andy Warhol. And because it was new to him, he thought it was new to everyone else. One time, Aimee walked up behind him on the couch and saw he was googling genuine Warhol prints for sale at New York auction houses. He didn't seem to realise that even a used tissue of Warhol's would be worth millions. That moment – Tim naively browsing to purchase a Warhol – made her judge him so much that she just wished she'd walked in on him watching porn instead. In social situations, he relished the opportunity to wedge a Warhol mention into whatever conversation he was having. *You didn't discover Andy Warhol!* she wanted to yell sometimes. And then she'd feel mean for thinking it and do something overly nice for him.

'I like the one we chose,' Bree said, still scrolling through the notes on her phone.

'Which one did you choose?' Aimee asked.

'Harley, Hawk and Co.' Tim nodded, clearly proud.

Aimee let out an involuntary scoff. 'Who the hell are Harley and Hawk?'

Tim looked down at the table and used a hand to turn his beer bottle in place. 'They're just cool names, Aimee.' He glanced back up. And there it was. The look in his eyes again. The one that flickered whenever she mocked something.

The chair next to Aimee squeaked back and a girl flopped beside her. Others followed as the producers got the rest of the cast into position at the table.

Aimee turned slightly to her right and glanced at the Kim Kardashian-ish girl who Nina had pointed out.

'Hey babe, I'm Addie,' the girl said, without looking away from her phone screen that she was using as a makeshift mirror to check her make-up. She stayed focused on the screen – even when Aimee introduced herself – stretching her thick red lips out to assess her chunky white veneers that practically glowed in the dark. Even though they were pristine, she wedged one of her long, red acrylic nails between the gaps, just to make sure they were spotless. 'Whose mum are you?'

Aimee didn't have the energy to correct her. 'Freya's.'

'Ohhh, we *love* Freya. She said you're cool.'

Aimee hated herself for feeling mildly validated.

'This summer's big for me,' Addie said. 'It's the first since my BBL infection.'

Aimee's blank expression said it all.

'Brazilian Butt Lift surgery.' Addie locked her iPhone screen and chucked it on the table. Its white leather case had brown smudge marks on it from make-up and tan. 'They lipo fat from your stomach and then put it in your butt to make it bigger and rounder.'

Aimee didn't realise she was grimacing, but she was. 'Why would you do that?'

Addie ignored the question and continued regaling her dinner companion with the ins and outs of her botched butt lift. 'I got it done last year just before summer, but then it got infected and the incisions around my cheeks kept leaking gross yellow fluid – which is normal for the first two weeks but this kept going for, like, two months. And then a massive lump formed.'

'That's . . .'

'Not a vibe,' Addie finished Aimee's sentence.

'It is certainly not.'

'Normally, you're not allowed to sit on your butt for two weeks post-op, which was fine because I'd accounted for that. But, with the infection, I couldn't sit all summer.' Addie picked up her phone again and the acrylic nails click-clacked over the glass screen as she started scrolling through her photo gallery. 'And obviously I couldn't go to the beach – because of the leakage and the weird lump. But everything's fine now and my ass looks amazing. So this summer's really special for me.' She shoved her phone in Aimee's face to show a graphic photo of the leaking butt cheeks and rogue lump – all held together with black stitches and taped-on gauze.

Aimee shrieked and everyone in the restaurant turned. Her eyes flicked across the table to look at Tim but his chair was empty. She whipped her head around to see where he'd gone and saw his jaunty green fedora bobbing out the door while he talked on the phone.

'He had to go.' Bree waved a hand in the air. 'He got a call. Probably better. We can have more fun.' She lifted up her really big, salty-rimmed margarita glass with a laugh and took a sip while giving Aimee a cheeky look, like they were gal pals out on the town.

Addie shoved her phone back in front of Aimee and scrolled through the catalogue of before-and-after images. 'Anyway, it's kinda what inspired me to become a life coach,' she said. 'I was already modelling and influencing and that was my income, but the more I documented my journey with the BBL infection, it just really resonated with people. I started off just doing these motivational quotes I'd write and post but now I have clients who I guide. I wanna enrol in a psychology degree but I don't wanna have to spend, like, three years doing it – so I'm looking into some online weekend courses instead.'

The *ting ting ting* of silver cutlery tapping a wine glass interrupted the conversation and Luna, the podcaster from the video Heath had played for Aimee that morning, stood up to address the table. Aimee sighed with relief.

'Guys, as you all probably know, I have my own line of sex toys launching soon. And . . . I thought we'd do something *a little bit fun* tonight . . .' She put on a funny voice and shimmied her shoulders. 'A little bit *cheeky*. A little bit *naughty*.' Looking around the room with a grin, she pulled a large straw beach bag out from under the table. 'You guys are gonna be the first to try the LeVibe!' She pulled one of the white square boxes out of the straw bag and hoisted it above her head with a squeal. The label featured a photo of a pastel pink C-shaped device.

Aimee sunk low in her chair, and dreamt of a more innocent time, not long ago, when all she had to do was passively listen to a girl describing her butt infection.

The boxes were getting passed around the table as Luna continued her speech. 'This is my patented, clinically-tested remote control vibrator that not only *guarantees* an orgasm – but also creates an intimate two-way experience for couples to enjoy in even the most public of settings, thanks to the phone app that connects with Bluetooth. The person controlling the app can activate a suction function, control the vibrations and make it move in a *come-hither* motion.' She used a finger to demonstrate the movement of that last feature. 'It can also vibrate to the beat of a song if you sync it to your Spotify.' Her voice then dipped down into a smooth cheesy saleswoman tone, '*So you can DJ your way to an orgasm.*' She laughed at herself and played up to the phone Addie was using to film the antics. 'Ladies, tonight your mission is to insert the vibrator while the guys control the vibration patterns and pulse strengths with the app.'

Aimee looked around the table. Two guys. No way in hell she'd be letting them DJ her orgasm.

Addie pulled the vibrator out of its box, ran her finger over the smooth rubber coating and tapped a nail on the rose gold metal accents. 'I'll be ba-ack!' she sang as she stood up and trotted her stilettos across the concrete towards the bathroom. The random guy she'd brought with her to the dinner carefully studied the instructions on the packaging and pulled out his phone to download the app.

'Aimee, have you met Kai?' Bree smiled, pointing to the guy who came with Addie. He had a swoopy fringe, was wearing denim overalls – and was way too distracted with the app to meet new people. 'He's a little too keen for tonight's experiment,' Bree teased, before pointing down to the other guy next to Luna. 'And that's Bodhi.' He had one of those intentionally bad haircuts that didn't look like it was cut quite right.

'We're @ThoseTwoVanGuys on Instagram.' Kai looked up from his phone.

'You know how some people flip houses? They flip campervans,' Luna explained. 'And Bodhi's also a comedian.'

'I'm @GourmetChikoRoll on TikTok.' Bodhi nodded. 'I do a lot of those "relatable" skit videos. And sometimes I film myself doing random acts of kindness for people in need. Like, last weekend, I was in Sydney, so I went to the Woolworths at Westfield Bondi Junction and found this hot blonde yoga mum – paid for her groceries and carried them back to her Range Rover. She was super grateful. People get off on that kind of good Samaritan shit.'

Aimee's mind was still stuck back on van flipping. 'Cool.' She took a deep breath in before turning her attention to Kai. 'And . . . do you also film yourself helping hot yoga mums in need?'

'Nah, the viral content is all Bodhi. Before we started flipping vans together, I spent six months as a deckhand on a billionaire's superyacht. It was fucking insane. This bitch ate duck three meals a day. And she only wore Swarovski crystal-encrusted kaftans. One day, it was really windy, and heaps of the crystals blew off. I got the dustpan, swept them up and sold them for $15,000.'

Before Aimee even had a chance to feel pangs of resentment about the van guy's accidental windfall of cash, Luna interrupted.

'Babe, check out your LeVibe,' she encouraged Aimee. Unsure of what to do, Aimee grabbed the parcel that had been placed in front of her and pretended to read the description on the back, but the vibrator busted out of the bottom and dropped into her lap. She picked it up between her thumb and index finger and dangled it in the air.

'Fuck,' Luna said. 'Was that package already open? I'm so sorry, hon. That must be the one I already tested.'

'Ugh!' Aimee's fingers sprang apart and the vibrator dropped into the share-plate of fried rice.

'It's OK, I washed it,' Luna assured her and passed a new box across the table. 'Aimee, you didn't come with a guy tonight, so you can control your own – or you can try DJing?'

'Oh, no thank you.' Aimee shifted in her seat.

'C'mon, I'll show you how – what's your favourite song?'

'Anything by Sheryl Crow, really—' Aimee cut herself off and shook her head. 'I'm totally fine just sitting this one out.'

The cameramen swirled around to get the perfect angles.

'Well,' Bree raised an eyebrow and gave Aimee a mischievous look, 'I'm also by myself.'

'You can control each other's!' Luna cheered.

Aimee took the pink vibrator out of its box and tucked it into her satchel. 'You girls go ahead. I'll just be on standby in case anyone's vagina catches fire.'

'Oh my god, you're such a mum!' Luna laughed.

When Addie returned from the bathroom, Kai leant over, kissed her on the cheek and tapped madly on his phone to control the app. She let out a squeal and slapped him.

'Is that a positive review?' Luna called out across the table.

'Let's just say it's working.' Addie covered her face with a hand as the others whooped.

Bodhi wrapped an arm around Luna and rubbed his face into her neck. 'Babe, go put yours in. I wanna program the vibrations to "Boom! Shake the Room" and film it for a funny video.' He held up his phone with a grin.

Aimee's bag was still on her lap, so she leant down to stow it – and possibly her entire body – under the table. Doubled over, she caught the faint smell of something exotic but also familiar. It took her a moment to place it. Then she remembered. Jules. The smoky swirl of sweet and spicy she'd smelt on his neck when she tripped and fell into him. It must've rubbed off on her clothes and skin a little bit. She closed her eyes and inhaled until the scent was lost. When she sat back up, the others were distracted with their apps. Bree gave her a smile and winked.

EIGHTEEN

'Hey guys, welcome to another episode of the Balls Deep podcast where we get raw, uncut and brutally honest about all the things other people are too embarrassed to talk about,' Luna said into a microphone perched on a white washed coffee table. 'Today, I'm joined by two of my co-stars from *The Brats of Byron Bay*. Obviously you guys know life coach Addie . . .'

'Hey babe.' Addie leant forward into her mic on the other side of the table.

Both girls were sitting cross-legged on the jute rug in the living room of the Airbnb they were sharing for the summer and speaking with 'podcast voice' – that strange phenomenon where anyone who ever went on a podcast felt the need to lower their tone and talk with a confident, almost smug, smoothness that indicated they were wise, considered and earthy. The camera crew crouched down around them.

Luna continued her introduction. 'My other guest is someone who you guys might know as Byron Karen – but her real name is Aimee McDonald. She runs an ice-cream shop here in Byron and she's also the mum of one of our other co-stars – Freya.'

Aimee leaned closer to her microphone and hesitated for a second, tossing up which piece of incorrect information to address first before just giving up completely. 'Hi.'

'Aimee, I only met you last night at a dinner party but I feel like I've known you for, like, a thousand years.'

'Well, your vibrator's been in my fried rice, so I feel like I also know you quite well. You should swing by my *ice-cream* shop some time.'

'Oh my god, you guys, the vibrators!' Luna launched into an explanation for the listeners about the X-rated dinner party challenge. 'OK, be brutally honest. Last night was an opportunity for you guys to road test my upcoming vibrator, the LeVibe. What did you think?'

Aimee zoned out for a second and wondered why Addie kept calling it 'the LeVibe'. Wasn't 'le' supposed to be French for 'the'? Then she busted herself. It was the exact kind of observation Tim would've hated.

Addie was off and running with a personal anecdote, revealing everything as if she was a guest on one of those nineties tabloid talk shows like *Jenny Jones*. 'As you guys know, I've spoken openly about how the BBL infection changed my life, iverricobly,' she said, mispronouncing the word irrevocably. 'Particularly when it came to sex. Obviously, having intense surgery in an area like that means you have to be careful not to expose it to vigorous activity – and, on top of that, the infection just made it even more sensitive and extended the recovery time.' Luna reached across the table to grab Addie's hand. 'The leakages made me really self-conscious about my body and I didn't feel sexy for a long time. And that's when I really got into self-love and experimenting with different toys. It also made me rethink and appreciate my sexuality and be more proud of it – which is why I felt so comfortable inserting the vibrator at the restaurant last night and letting Kai control it in front of everyone.'

'Yassss! Babe, I love that for you.' Luna high-fived Addie. 'And, hey, we all saw what happened after Kai started controlling it on the app. Or . . . more accurately, we *heard* what happened after Kai started controlling it.'

Addie shrieked and leant across to slap Luna on the arm. 'Bitch, you did not!'

'Bitch, we did!' Luna laughed. 'It got so intense you had to go hide out in the bathroom for, like, twenty minutes! And while you were in there, Kai was at the dining table working that app *hard*.' Luna raced to talk over Addie. 'And, you didn't realise this at the time, but we actually sent one of the TV camera guys into the bathroom to capture any sounds that might've been coming out of your stall. I've got the audio off the producers and I'm gonna play it right now.' Luna hit a button on the podcasting equipment and the sound of porn star sex noises blasted into everyone's headphones.

As the audio played, Luna methodically went through the talking points scribbled down on her notepad while Addie looked up at the ceiling and smiled at the sound of her own quivers. Aimee avoided eye contact and tried to zone out from the hell she'd been parachuted into by glancing around the luxe Airbnb, admiring its commitment to the nautical theme with countless statement lanterns and boat oars and orange life buoys.

The moans got louder in Aimee's ear. It was Meg Ryan-in-a-deli kinda stuff. She doubled down on the Shaynna Blaze interior design observations. It may have looked like a display home when the girls first moved in, but they'd since made their mark. Shoes were scattered throughout the house and items of tangled clothing had been flung onto surfaces so random it made you think, 'How did *that* get *there?*' When Aimee had first arrived and walked past the kitchen, she noticed the mounds of plastic bags and takeaway food containers piling up on the timber benchtop. The living room seemed to be the only area that looked the way it should – with all the debris excavated out of the way for the guests and TV cameras. Looking around, Aimee became so focused on the unnecessary abundance of wicker baskets that she didn't even realise the moaning had stopped until Luna's smooth podcast voice purred through the micro-phone and into her ears.

'So . . .'

Aimee snapped back to attention and realised Luna was talking to her.

'Did you use the LeVibe when you got home?' Luna smirked.

'It was 10.30pm when I got home,' Aimee replied. 'I ate an entire tub of Magnum ice-cream and watched YouTube compilation videos of chiropractors cracking people's backs until I fell asleep.'

'Well, just to explain for listeners – you didn't have a partner at last night's dinner. And . . . Aimee, I want to remind you . . . this is a safe space for us to talk about anything. The more open and vulnerable we are, the more it helps our listeners . . . I wanna address this diplomatically and I don't want you to feel uncomfortable. But, basically, after you left, we kicked on to a bar and Bree told us the back story about how the guy she brought to dinner is actually your fiancé and that you guys are on a break over summer where you both can basically just fuck whoever you want.'

Aimee sat still. The sound of her breathing into the microphone became amplified in her headphones.

'Babe, this is so cool what you're doing – and it's something that a whole lot of women *wish* they could do but no one ever talks about it. It's the unvarnished truth of long-term relationships. That's why it's so important that you speak your truth about it. It's what this podcast is all about: raw, uncut and brutally honest.'

'Well . . .' Aimee ventured, glancing up at one of the cameras that had moved around the coffee table to zoom in on her face. 'The situation is a little more complex than what you described. But yes, we're on a time-out . . . after being together for about twenty years, I should say. We're engaged. But, after being together for so long without ever taking a break, we thought it was important that we take some time apart just to really make sure getting married is . . .' she raised her shoulders and tried to wrap up her explanation, '. . . what we both actually want.'

Addie jumped. 'But if one of you doesn't want to get married, will you stay together anyway?'

Before Aimee could answer, Luna fired another question. 'And you guys haven't fucked anyone else before?'

Aimee paused. The sound of silence hissed through her headphones. 'We've been together since high school. Year twelve – that's when we started dating.'

'And you haven't fucked anyone else in your life?' Luna repeated her question.

Images flashed into Aimee's mind of being younger with Tim and laying in the back of his ute on long afternoons at deserted beaches along the coast. Carefree. The days of having sex because they wanted to. Sex for fun instead of obligation. Back when they were obsessed with each other and would make up lies to get out of other people's plans – just so they could spend every second together. Now Aimee lied about having plans just to get out of sex with Tim. Well, that wasn't entirely accurate. Tim had stopped initiating it a while ago.

'We've . . . only been with each other. Yes,' Aimee confirmed, unsure of where this interrogation was heading and how much detail to give away.

'Fuck,' Addie sighed.

'Fuck.' Luna nodded.

Aimee waited for the moment to pass.

Luna didn't let it. 'So I was talking to Bree, who's hooking up with Tim – your fiancé – and she said that *he* said he hadn't had sex in about a year and that *she* was the first to, kind of, break his dry spell.'

Aimee's first instinct was to flip the coffee table and march down to Tim's surf store. She waited a beat. 'Um . . .'

Luna didn't wait for a response. 'Had you guys not had sex for a year?'

'Well, I haven't kept a . . . *sex diary* . . .'

Luna continued relentlessly on her line of questioning and fired a follow-up like she was Leigh Sales. 'But for the purpose of clarity, what would a ballpark figure be?'

'I don't know. I don't know.' Aimee pushed her hair back and tried to let out a laugh to hide her feelings. 'Maybe a year. Maybe six months.

If you're with someone for two decades . . . surprise! You don't have sex much. God, if you're with someone *two years* you don't have sex much after that.'

Luna attempted a diplomatic tone. 'Neither of us have been with someone for two years, so we can't talk to that point. Bodhi and I have been hooking up for a few weeks but we're keeping things relaxed – it's *our version* of an open relationship. We can fuck other people but we need to tell each other first. Obviously it's different to *your* situation – our relationship is still new and fun and we're *choosing* to be open. *Your* time-out is kind of a last ditch effort and there's now a ticking clock on your relationship.'

Aimee felt like she was being blasted in the face with a tsunami of home truths she didn't ask for.

Luna continued. 'What I really wanna drill down on and unpack is what it must be like to see a younger woman with your fiancé when you've basically given permission for him to fuck her.'

The cameraman hunched down onto his knees and focused on Aimee. She hesitated again and inhaled the too-sweet scent of the big vanilla candle that was burning nearby, racking her brain for all the other possible details Tim might've let slip to Bree, who could in turn have told X-rated Leigh Sales. 'Part of the rules of our time-out are that we can have . . . hook-ups . . . with other people over summer. And, I guess we don't *need* to tell each other about those hook-ups. We're allowed to . . . *explore. Explore* is probably the right word.'

Addie raised her eyebrows. 'Have you fucked anyone yet?'

'I . . . have not.'

'Aimee, I'm a truth-teller.' Addie squinted and perched her elbow on the coffee table, relishing the opportunity to put her life coach skills to use. 'I'm a straight-shooter and I call out bullshit when I see it. Babe, can I tell you the truth?' She didn't wait for Aimee's response. 'I'm gonna tell you the truth. You need to fuck someone.'

Aimee had no words. But apparently Addie still did. 'Tim's fucking Bree. You need to fuck someone too.'

Luna piled on. 'Or start slow, with the LeVibe. Begin your self-love journey and reclaim your sexuality, like Addie did. You gotta build your confidence.'

Aimee shifted uncomfortably and grabbed the underside of her legs, feeling the indentions left on her skin by the big knots on the jute rug.

Luna leant over and grabbed her hand. 'OK, babe. I can see you're feeling weird about this and I don't want you to feel like you're under attack, you know what I mean? This podcast is about owning who you are and being fearless. My life is an open book for my listeners – I put myself on the line every time I turn on the microphone. I talk the talk and I walk the walk – and, to show you that you're not alone, I'm gonna tell you guys a story that happened to me last night.' She let go of Aimee's hand, pulled her wild blonde-ish hair over one shoulder and sat up straight at the microphone. 'You know Bodhi – from last night's dinner? Well, we'd been playing with the LeVibe during dinner, obviously. And, when we went home, we were fooling around and he wanted to put it in my ass. And so he did and then we started playing with the vibration patterns on the app. Anyway, after we fucked and we both came, I was on all fours and he went to take the LeVibe out of my ass, and then . . .'

Addie covered her face. 'Stop. Stop. Oh my god.'

'Wait! Wait!' Luna shrieked. 'So I'm on all fours and he slowly pulls it out and . . . I feel it slide out. Or . . . at least I think I feel *it* slide out. And then he makes . . . a *noise*.'

'Oh my god. Oh my god.' Addie closed her eyes and held her hands up.

'And then I feel him jump off the bed and, like, *scamper* to the bathroom. And I'm still in doggy and then . . .'

'I can't! Babe, I can't!' Addie screamed.

Luna tried to compose herself by taking some deep breaths. 'And then I look down and . . .' She put her forehead on the table and let out a scream. 'Look, you get the picture. *You get the picture.*'

Addie flopped on the floor. 'I. Would. Die.'

Aimee couldn't hide her bemused expression. And when Luna looked over with tears running down her face from laughing so hard, she knew she wasn't giving the desired reaction. 'I don't get it,' she admitted with an apologetic cringe. 'What happened?'

This made Addie howl louder.

'Oh my god, *bless*. Bless!' Luna wiped her cheek with one hand and looked at Aimee like she was a naïve child. 'I shit the bed. I literally shit the bed.'

———

I shit the bed. I literally shit the bed. I shit the bed. I literally shit the bed. I shit the bed. I literally shit the bed.

Rob played and rewound Luna's confession from the podcast repeatedly over the Bluetooth speaker at The Dream Explosion the next day. She flopped her body over the store counter and wheezed. Aimee was ignoring her – walking around the shop, putting away new stock and tidying the displays that had been torn apart in the lead-up to Christmas. A conservative-looking mother appeared in the doorway with her young son just as Rob hit play on the audio again. The mum promptly turned around and stormed out.

Aimee shot Rob a look.

'Hey, if you wanna come into The Dream Explosion, you gotta be prepared to *get raw, uncut and brutally honest*.' Rob picked up a piece of the chicken katsu roll she'd brought them both for lunch from that wanky new sushi joint Aimee had been complaining about.

'It's as if Luna was drawing parallels between *my* relationship time-out and *her* shitting the bed. They are two *very* different things!' Aimee said, just as another mother appeared in the doorway.

Rob stood up straight and crossed her arms. 'Aimee, that was very unprofessional,' she mock reprimanded.

The disapproving woman vacated the store and Aimee threw a fidget at her friend. Rob dodged to the side and snapped the toy between her hands.

'Hey!' She inspected the three-pronged device closely. 'What's this?'

'It's a fidget.'

Rob started to spin it between her fingers. 'But it doesn't have little pushy-poppy buttons on it like the *other* fidgets.'

'That's because it's not a *pop-it fidget*. It is a *fidget spinner*.'

'There are different *kinds* of fidgets?' Rob threw her hands in the air. 'Since when were there different kinds of fidgets?'

'Apparently since forever, I've just discovered. And now I'm playing catch-up.' She whipped her head to the side and her voice went up real high. 'Did you know there's a seven-year-old on Instagram who's made *millions* selling fidgets? Her parents quit their jobs and now work for her. *She* pays *their* income. Trixie May. That's her name. *Trixie May*.'

Rob put her hands on her hips and shook her head in mock fury. 'That little bitch.'

Aimee returned to her restocking. 'I shouldn't have let you go to the sushi train. Sushi trains always put you in a silly mood.'

Rob picked up a set of bamboo chopsticks and theatrically snapped them apart. 'Those girls completely blime-fibeb you,' she declared.

Aimee scrunched up her face. 'Huh?'

'They *blindsided* you. On these reality shows, people are always being blindsided with a scandal. Except, because their lip filler hinders their ability to enunciate, they always accidentally pronounce it as *blime-fibe*. You were blime-fibeb!'

'I *was* fucking blime-fibeb!'

'Why the hell is Tim going around telling people you guys haven't had sex in a year?'

'Ah, *thank you!*' Aimee violently arranged a family of stuffed bears on a shelf.

'And why didn't he tell you that Hot Ew Girl was a reality TV star? Or that *he* was appearing on the show?'

Aimee continued the massacre of the stuffed bear family.

'Sweetie, don't take it out on the bears.' Rob waved her chopsticks in the air.

Aimee walked over to the counter and shoved a piece of sushi in her mouth. 'He's technically not part of the show – Hot Ew Girl just dragged him there. Besides, I can't exactly blame him,' she conceded. 'I hadn't told him me and Freya signed on.'

'That's very level-headed of you. Brené Brown would be proud.' Rob flicked her hair. 'But he still shouldn't be telling people about your sex life. And those bitches telling you on the podcast that he's fucking the Hot Ew Girl?! I mean, yes, we *assumed* they're fucking. But you don't need to be ambushed with it on a podcast and then get forced into justifying your *own* sex life.' She pointed her chopsticks in Aimee's face. 'They were metaphorically shitting in your bed.'

Aimee started to laugh and pushed the chopsticks away.

'Maybe we can pay them to shit in Tim's bed. Or his fedora.'

Aimee groaned. 'That fucking fedora.'

'Ooh! Business idea! We could pimp out Luna's services on Airtasker for people who wanna get revenge on their ex!'

Aimee shook her head with a smile. 'Jesus. The things these girls share about themselves, without even giving it a second thought. "Everything's content", Luna kept saying afterwards. "Babe, babe – loosen up, everything's content." I'm sorry, but no. Not everything's content. Some things you should just keep to yourself.'

Rob had picked up her phone and was scrolling through Addie's Instagram. 'I'm just so fascinated. On one hand, I don't relate at all to these kids and they irritate me immensely. But at the same time, I'm so intrigued. I never thought I'd be so invested in a random girl's Brazilian butt lift infection. It's like a circus but all the clowns are wearing thong-back bikinis.'

'They're all so sex-positive, I can't stand it,' Aimee said, joking but also kinda not.

'I know.' Rob frowned. 'Why can't they subconsciously associate sex with shame and chronic self-loathing, like the rest of us?'

'I swear to god, I felt like they were just seconds away from calling me frigid. I started having PTSD flashbacks to primary school.'

'I think being called frigid is the one insult from primary school that would still kill me as an adult. In grade three, a rumour started going around that this girl, Gabby Hayworth, was frigid. I just remember watching it unfold at little lunch and thinking, "Well, of course Gabby's frigid – she's nine."'

'I *hope* Gabby was frigid.' Aimee shoved a hunk of sushi in her mouth.

'But . . . can I ask a question?' Rob scrunched her nose and grimaced as if she was about to yank off a Band-Aid.

Aimee sighed and put her hand on top of Rob's. 'Yes, I will get Luna to give you a LeVibe.'

'Can I ask another question?' She paused. 'Are you gonna fuck someone new?'

Aimee fluttered her eyelids and exhaled. 'I mean, if Bodhi isn't still traumatised after his recent experience with Luna, then, sure, I guess I could try him,' she deadpanned.

Rob started playing the Balls Deep audio again. 'Shit the bed,' she snorted. 'That's such a good TV catchphrase. I mean, I still love, "I'll have *that*, with cheese" . . . but I might also steal, "Shit the bed".'

Aimee's phone buzzed. A text from Jules.

Spotted in the wild. Want me to throw a chickpea patty at him?

There was a picture attached. Aimee clicked it to enlarge. A fuzzy photo of some guy in a trucker's hat and sunnies waiting in line at a coffee shop. He towered over everyone else. Aimee looked closer and realised who it was. A Hemsworth. Not Chris. But one of the brothers. A laugh burst out of her mouth and Rob looked up.

Aimee stumbled for a second. 'Just scrolling through Addie's Insta,' she dismissed.

'It's gold,' Rob declared, already familiar with it. 'Her half-baked moti-vational quote memes are next-level. My favourite is: There's no "I" in "relationship" but there is "us" in "me". I'm screenprinting that on a T-shirt.' She clocked the time on her phone and gasped. 'Shit the bed – I gotta get back to the salon.' After flipping shut the clacky plastic lid on the sushi tray, she grabbed her fringed leather handbag, and her brown leather boots banged across the hardwood floors. 'Goodbye, my beautiful, frigid friend.'

Aimee's phone vibrated again. She read the message on the home screen.

Does patty-ing a Hemsworth get me a date?

She stared at it and her senses sparked. The taste of the whisky. The sweet, smoky cologne. The shoulders. She was standing in the same part of the store where she'd tripped over her rollerblades and Jules scooped her up.

'Aimee!' a voice came from behind.

It was familiar. Aimee locked her phone and spun around – as if she'd been busted doing something she shouldn't.

'It's Bre—'

'I remember,' Aimee cut off the Hot Ew Girl before sliding her hands in the back pockets of her jeans with a laugh to try to seem breezier than she was.

Bree seemed different to how she was at the dinner party. Still cool and warm but it was as if she was holding something back. Like she was nervous to be there. 'I just wanted to come by. I didn't want to say this the other night because of the cameras and the other girls. And . . .' She shook her head and laughed. 'Look, I just . . . really feel like I should say that I didn't know it was *you* who was joining the show.' She scrunched up her face. 'Sorry, what I mean is . . . I've obviously been seeing Tim casually . . . and, when I got told Byron Karen was joining the show, I genuinely didn't know it was *you* – Tim's fiancée. No one did – not even Nina or Heath.

And I know it must be weird and awkward . . . but I want you to feel comfortable. And . . .' She tucked a hand into her tiny black leather Gucci purse with the big gold logo on it. 'I just wanted to give you this.' Her hand popped out of the purse and out came the thin chain of a gold necklace. She held it up.

Aimee recognised the brushed gold crescent moon.

'It's our signature piece I told you about. The Stevie.' Bree walked closer and handed Aimee the necklace. 'Just a token. To make things less weird. Hopefully?'

'Um . . .' Aimee said, reaching out to accept the gift. 'Look, you really didn't—'

'I know . . .'

'But it's lovely. Beautiful.' Aimee admired it before looking up at Bree. 'Thank you.' *Ugh*, she thought. *Now the Hot Ew Girl is trying to humanise herself.*

'And I heard you on the Balls Deep podcast.' Bree smiled.

'Oh Jesus,' Aimee groaned.

'You handled it all really well. Luna and Addie can be *a lot*.'

'What? Nooo. They're both so timid,' Aimee joked.

They smiled and stared at the ground.

'I rinsed the cups!' Bree broke the silence.

'Huh?'

'The KeepCups. I washed them straight away. I'm OCD about it now.' Bree adjusted the gold chain of the purse that was slung over one shoulder. 'Anyway . . . I gotta get back to filming. I'll tell Tim you said hi.' She turned to walk out the door.

'Actually, don't . . .' Aimee called out.

Bree turned back to face Aimee.

'Maybe don't tell him I say hi. Not because I don't want to say hi. But . . . maybe just don't tell him that we spoke. We're not meant to be communicating – me and him. I don't want him to think . . . I don't know . . .' Aimee gave up trying to explain.

Bree nodded and disappeared into the sunlight and foot traffic, leaving Aimee standing alone in the middle of her store – holding the necklace gifted to her by her fiancé's new younger girlfriend. Then her phone buzzed. She looked at the home screen.

Patty-ing a Hemsworth absolutely has to get me a date.

NINETEEN

It was one of Aimee's least-favourite places.

'Apparently we might see a Damon or an Efron here.' Jules held up his phone to show a list of Google search results about The General Store cafe. 'Admit it: you're addicted to the razzle dazzle of celebrity. That's why you suggested it.'

One of the trendiest eateries in town, it featured regularly in Instagram posts and tabloid articles on the *Daily Mail*. All the wait staff who worked there looked earthy and like they lived in hollowed-out tree trunks. It was healthy. Organic. Pure. The kind of place that made people feel nourished the very second they set foot inside – as if a few sips of a green juice could reverse a lifetime of booze, fried food and regretful sex.

'Busted,' Aimee joked as she sat down at the table Jules was at. He'd arrived before her and she almost didn't see him in his sunnies and cap, hidden on the side patio. She took off the denim shirt she was wearing over a white singlet and fanned herself with a menu to blow away the humidity that clouded the tiny outdoor space as a summer afternoon storm gathered over Byron. 'I actually hate it here,' she confessed, a little too loudly, and a nearby waitress couldn't help but glance over. 'But everyone who comes to Byron is obsessed with this place and . . . I thought you might like it.' That wasn't the only reason she'd chosen it. No one she knew went there – and it wasn't in the town centre, so the chances of being spotted were minimal.

Why did she feel like she was doing something she shouldn't? It's not like she was breaking the rules – in fact, she was doing exactly what Tim *wanted* her to do. She just didn't want to be talked about by the town Looney Tunes. Also, if it ended up being a terrible date, at least the memory wouldn't ruin a cafe she actually *liked* going to.

'Well, I have in fact been here already. Annnd . . .' Jules scrunched his face, searching for the words. '. . . I just don't know why they need to serve everything with sprouts.'

'I know!' Aimee's eyes shot wide open and the metal cutlery bucket clanged as she slapped her palms on the reclaimed timber table. For the first time in a long time, she felt seen. All because of unnecessary sprouts.

'It's like, "We get it. Your restaurant is healthy".' Jules matched her excitement.

'And giant mushrooms. Huge. The kind that mice use as umbrellas in cartoons.'

'Big mushrooms freak me out. Also, why is it so hard to find a good cafe that just serves *normal* white bread? Toasted sourdough cuts my mouth!'

Aimee tapped his wrist and leant in. 'Sometimes, if I'm feeling down, me and my friend Rob come here for coffee just so we can sit near the counter and eavesdrop on annoyed out-of-towners trying to order bacon.'

Jules shot Aimee a mischievous look. 'How about we blow this sprout farm and go find somewhere that has normal food?'

Aimee pressed a fingertip on her phone screen to check the time. It was almost 3pm. 'Most places usually close around now before dinner.' She glanced up at the flaking white ceiling, thinking about other cafes in town.

Jules smirked. 'Let's just go to yours.'

———

Oil spattered as Jules slapped strips of bacon down in a frying pan. He moved around Aimee's kitchen, opening drawers and cupboards, as if it was his own. And, when he'd open a drawer or cupboard, he'd find what he needed, *then close it*. Aimee noticed this and had to stop herself from standing there, admiring it, slack-jawed. Tim never closed cupboards. Sometimes it was like he just walked around the house, opening cupboards for fun. Even cupboards that contained nothing of relevance to him. If it had a door, Tim would open it and leave it open.

Jules glanced over at Aimee, who was watching him from across the room. 'Close your eyes,' he said, tossing a tea towel over his shoulder.

She gave him a weird look before submitting with a laugh. 'Okaaay.'

He'd taken his black leather boots off and his bare soles padded and skimmed across the floorboards. Aimee could feel him moving closer. The energy around her body changed. A moment later, she could feel his face close to hers and the air exhaling from his nose onto her chest. Her heart started racing and she became self-conscious about whether her own breathing was too loud and what to do with her lips – purse them, open them a little, bite the bottom one? Then she sensed movement – arms lifting up and around her – and felt the coolness of a thin metal chain drape onto her neck.

Aimee's eyes shot open. They were level with Jules', only centimetres away. His arms were still around her neck and he smiled while he fiddled with the clasp on the chain. Aimee reached up to touch what she knew was dangling on her chest – the brushed gold crescent moon.

'It fell out of your bag when you were looking for your keys,' he said.

When they'd arrived at Aimee's apartment, she was digging through her satchel to find the house keys – pulling out her phone and wallet and hand sanitiser and receipts – when it all went crashing to the floor. She'd shoved Bree's necklace in there when she was closing up the store to go meet Jules.

Then he smiled and turned back to his frying bacon. The metal tongs clanged as he snapped them in the air with a grin. Aimee realised she'd been standing still with her palm on the crescent moon for an odd amount of time and moved over to the rack of cassette tapes that ran along the back wall. Music. They needed music. She caught her face in a nearby mirror and tried to shake off the mix of perplexed disappointment that was splashed across it. Her finger dragged along the scuffed plastic spines of the cases, stopping occasionally when one sparked a memory. Blondie's *Eat to the Beat*. INXS, *Kick*. The soundtrack to *Saturday Night Fever*. Hundreds of cassettes that had been collected by Aimee and Fleur to play in the Monaro.

What started as a sorta-joke blew into a serious hobby – cruising up and down the coast on a Saturday, stopping at suburban garage sales they'd circled in the newspaper. It was the early 2000s. CDs had taken over, MP3s were the next hot thing and everyone had been holding onto their old cassettes for way too long. Sometimes Aimee and Fleur would strike gold and find entire racks of cassette tapes being sold for five bucks for the lot. Sitting in her apartment that was clouding up with the smell of bacon grease, Aimee studied the music library to find the perfect soundtrack. A blank spine stood out from the others – the words 'Fleur + Aimee's Perfect Playlist' was scribbled on it in black felt pen. Sometimes, they'd record mix tapes off the radio – or off other cassettes, with a double-decked stereo. She plucked it off the shelf, slid the cassette out of its case, clicked open the tape deck on the stereo and slotted it in. A big chunky plastic button with the 'play' logo on it gave a satisfying *click* as Aimee pressed it. The tape started blaring in the middle of a song. It hadn't been rewound. Only a second had to pass before Aimee realised what track it was: The B-52's, 'Rock Lobster'.

Jules laughed and slammed his head along to the rapid-fire ting-tongs. 'You know, you just don't hear enough cowbell in music these days.'

Aimee climbed up off the hardwood floors. 'Some may judge, but this is a classic.'

'Oh, I know.' He used a plastic spatula to shuffle fried eggs and bacon out of different pans, stacking them on top of the toasted white bread. 'B-52's.'

Aimee stood up straight and cocked her head.

Jules went on to one-up himself. 'I was kinda hoping you'd choose New Kids on the Block, "Hangin' Tough".' He smirked as Aimee squinted at him. 'When you went to the bathroom before, I snooped through your collection. Very impressive. *Bizarre* . . .' he paused to squirt barbeque sauce on the sandwiches, '. . . but impressive.' He placed the final slices of toasted bread on top of the two mountains of fat and grease. 'Rock Lobster' was fading out and Cindy Wilson was rattling the windows with her Yoko Ono-ish squeaks and squeals. Jules picked up one of the sandwiches and walked over to Aimee. There was a moment of silence when the song finished before two quick hits of the snare drum thumped through the speakers and the keyboard intro of Talking Heads' 'This Must Be the Place' floated through the living room. Raindrops started to tap on the old pub's corrugated iron roof. Jules stood close. The humidity and the heat from the stove had made him sweat through his faded black shirt and Aimee noticed the skin on his neck glimmer in the light. The sweat had also stirred up the scent of his smoky cologne and it was mixing with the smell of fried bacon. Under normal circumstances, it would be a repulsive combination but, on that afternoon, in Aimee's apartment, with a hot Irishman serving her carbohydrates to a soundtrack of the Talking Heads, it was the sexiest thing she'd experienced in a while.

She stared into his moody black eyes as he moved closer and she was finally able to put her finger on the thing she liked most about him. It had been on her mind since the afternoon they spent out the back of the store. At first she thought it was his big chest and shoulders. Maybe his smile or voice. But it wasn't any of those things. He had a way of existing in the world with a natural confidence. He was so easy and sure. Aimee always wondered what it would be like to feel so comfortable.

Jules held the sandwich up between them, then started to lean in slightly. Aimee wasn't sure if he was waiting for her to bite the sandwich or to meet him half way for a kiss. The cogs in her brain turned and she scolded herself for being such an idiot. *He asked you on a date and invited himself back to your house. He's not just here for a fucking sandwich.* So she leant in. And as she jolted forward, the delightful trills of Talking Heads cut to the pre-programmed beats and filthy hook of 2 Live Crew's 'Me So Horny'. Jules' hand shot up and smashed the sandwich into Aimee's face as he snorted at the abrupt soundtrack change. She let out a noise that was muffled by the bread.

'I'm sorry!' He laughed, turning to grab a tea towel from the kitchen. 'I was not expecting . . . *that*.' He pointed at the stereo. 'That is a song I have not heard in *quite* a while.'

Aimee squinted to stop the barbeque sauce from getting in her eyes and grabbed the towel from him. 'It's a mix tape,' she explained in a flat voice, as Jules walked over to wipe her face for her. 'Some of the songs have been . . . taped over with . . . other songs. Years ago. I can't remember that one being on there.'

There were three knocks at the door. Aimee took the towel and finished wiping away the rest of the sauce and grease as she walked towards the door, making a pained face to herself while her back was turned. A quick look through the peephole worsened her distress. She opened the door a crack and peered through the gap only to find Heath's face also pressed in the tight space. She sputtered and pulled back.

'I swung by the bookstore but that backpacker said you'd left for the day,' Heath said.

'Her name's Courtney. She's British and she's lived here for three years,' Aimee said, already fed up.

'Did you ever think that maybe your finances are so bad because it's mid-afternoon on a weekday and you're at home frying bacon?'

Aimee opened the door just enough to squeeze her body out into the hall and closed it behind her, shooting Heath a look when she turned back around to face him.

'C'mon, I'm only joking.' He flashed his smile and leant back against the wall.

'You can't just always say that after making a rude remark and think it stops you from being an asshole.'

'I love it when you bite back. That's who I wanna see on camera.' Water dripped off the tips of his hair and his wet T-shirt clung to his dad-bod.

Aimee was barefoot and she felt her soles squelch in the slippery mess Heath had dragged in on his shoes.

'Are you OK?' he asked.

'On a scale of one to MarMuts?'

'You're annoyed . . .' he stated.

'I *am* annoyed!' Her voice went up and she quickly restrained it so Jules didn't hear.

'Why are you annoyed?' Heath raised his voice to match and smirked a little at the repetition.

'You told me, *you won't be the focus of this show,* and, suddenly, I'm surrounded by vibrators and I've got two twelve-year-olds in my face asking detailed questions about my sex life with my fiancé, who – surprise! – is also on this show and sleeping with one of the other twelve-year-olds! Meanwhile, you've fallen off the face of the fucking earth and I'm looking like a goddam idiot with cameras pointed at me. It sure as hell feels like I'm the focus of this stupid fucking show.'

Heath took a breath and spoke calmly. 'I heard about what happened at the dinner. You, Tim . . . Bree. That's why I'm here – I just wanted to check in. Obviously that was a surprise to everyone.'

'A reality TV producer's wet dream, I'm sure.'

'And I didn't know the girls were gonna ask you all that stuff on the podcast.'

'I was blime-fibeb!'

'You were *what?*' Heath spat.

Aimee shook her head and avoided an explanation. 'I felt completely ambushed.' She shot him a look.

Heath squinted. 'Are you wearing Bree's necklace?'

Aimee's hand grasped at her chest, and her forehead wrinkled as she stumbled over her words. 'She gave it to me. It's . . . never mind.'

Heath laughed. 'That's kinda fucked up.'

'Do you *need* me for something right now?' She furrowed her brow in an attempt to maintain her annoyance.

'Just looking after my star talent,' Heath teased. 'Also, I need you to meet Brooke. On camera. She wants you to come to her farm tomorrow.'

'So . . . I'm being *summoned*? You know, you could've just texted me that.'

'What can I say, I'm a hands-on producer.'

'Yeah, you're a real *auteur*.' Aimee rolled her eyes and turned to open the door again – sliding through the crack and swiftly pressing it shut behind her so Heath couldn't see inside.

'Can I have some bacon?' he called from the hallway. 'And why are you playing "Me So Horny"?'

'Goodbye,' she said in a raised voice then listened for the thuds of Heath's shoes banging down the steps until they faded out. Now it was just her and Jules. And 2 Live Crew. She turned around to find Jules sitting on the kitchen bench with barbeque sauce on his face.

'It's *so good*!' He wiped his mouth and leapt onto the floorboards with a bang.

It was then Aimee noticed he'd put his boots back on. They thumped over to her.

'I gotta run.' He held up his phone, as if to signal a text message or call had come through while she was out in the hallway.

Aimee didn't know whether to blame Heath or 2 Live Crew for ruining her moment with Jules. For a second, she thought about rewinding the tape to Talking Heads in a desperate bid to recreate the almost-kiss. The rain had stopped pounding down but the drainpipes gurgled as water ran off the roof. Aimee slid her hands into her back pockets and moved away from the door so Jules could leave.

'Your sandwich is on the bench.' He shot her a cheeky smile as he turned the knob. 'I added sprouts to it when you weren't looking.'

He turned in the doorway to look back. And just when she thought it was all over . . .

'Can we do this again?' he asked. 'Maybe this weekend?'

'Sure. Ah . . .' Aimee shook her head, remembering the farm she'd just been summoned to. 'Not *this* weekend. But . . .' She tried to think.

'How about I just swing by the store again.' He smiled and continued to jog down the stairs.

She nodded and closed the door. Standing alone in her apartment, she began to walk over to the greasy sandwich that was waiting for her. Then she changed direction and veered over to the stereo. She reached down and clicked the rewind button.

TWENTY

Aimee had problems. So did Brooke.

'We're being fined for demolishing a historic milk shed,' she said in a *we-all-know-what-that's-like* kind of tone.

She was driving around her under-construction estate in a pastel pink Mini Moke electric buggy and gripping one of those really big Starbucks cups. Trailing behind were two other matching pink Mokes with the TV crew aboard. All up, the fleet cost about $140,000. How did Aimee know that? Because Brooke proudly declared it. Actually, no. That wasn't fair. The price did come up naturally in conversation. After leaving Aimee and the crew waiting outside in the sun for twenty minutes, Brooke finally emerged from the house and, spotting the red Monaro across the lawn, observed, 'Ugh, whose car is *that?*' That's when she gestured to her Moke fleet and mentioned the cost in the same way other new car owners might say, 'It even has those reverse beepy sensor things!' It was obvious when Aimee arrived at the farm that Brooke had no idea they'd actually met briefly a few days earlier at the mechanic. Aimee didn't bother bringing it up. Instead, she just white-knuckled the pink railing of the Moke and wondered where the hell the crazy rich lady got a Starbucks from when the nearest one was an hour away on the Gold Coast.

'You didn't know it was heritage listed?' Aimee asked about the destruction of the historic milk shed while squinting out at the glare.

'No, we did,' Brooke chirped. 'But it looked horrendous and we needed the space to build the additional master suite.'

The TV crews continued to speed behind them in their Mokes to document the grand tour and Aimee tried to stop looking directly at the GoPro camera attached to the dashboard in front of her. Brooke seemed to be in her element, spouting random facts and costs about her new pet project as they came to mind. 'We're trying to source a flock of peacocks.' The estate sprawled over a few hectares and Brooke had made it her personal mission to utilise every inch of the space. There was the main house and then paths that led to different zones around the sprawling property. 'Excuse the mess over there,' she sighed, apologetic and embarrassed. 'I'm excavating a lake.' The chic blazer that was caped over her shoulders picked up in the breeze as she rounded a bend. When she zipped past a newly-built weatherboard barn, she just waved her hand vaguely and stared ahead. 'That's where bad ideas go to die,' she snipped. The big sliding doors on the front were wide open and Aimee glimpsed inside as the Moke whirled by. She couldn't help but scrunch her face up at the sight: Rows of DVD vending machines.

Brooke was one of those women who smelt like the David Jones perfume department at all times. Her blowout managed to remain in place while whizzing around on the buggy and her white tailored trousers were pristine, even after being toured through a rural construction zone. She was older than Aimee – probably late forties – but didn't look it. Aimee squinted at Brooke's side profile, trying to spot a single wrinkle or flyaway in the sunlight. It was impossible. Brooke shimmered, like diamonds being tossed into a waterfall of champagne. Frivolously decadent.

'The renovation has been such a headache,' Brooke said. 'I've lost an entire week thanks to an LED strip-light fuck-up in my walk-in closet.' She paused for just a second, as if to leave space for Aimee to gasp and sympathetically enquire about how she was coping. Aimee didn't, but that did not stop Brooke from regaling her with the ins and outs of the strip-light fuck-up. 'Anyway, I walk in with the cameras for the big reveal and my closet is just radiating with this *blinding* fluorescent glow – like it's the deli aisle at Coles.' She exhaled her frustration. 'Heath told me about your situation with your . . . house . . . or . . . store. Ugh. You're so lucky you don't own.'

Aimee had to use all her willpower to not grab the steering wheel aggressively and veer the buggy into the lake Brooke was excavating. She wished her biggest problem was an LED strip-light fuck-up. 'Is Heath here?' Her voice went a little too high and sharp.

'No, I think he's down at the beach with the crew I sent. I told them I want moody footage of waves rolling into shore so we can cut to it during dramatic and emotional moments, like on *Big Little Lies*.'

The cart returned to the farmhouse and Brooke led the way across a limestone path while a cameraman ran ahead to capture their entrance through the folding glass doors. Original features inside the house had been kept: century-old stone walls, wide, rustic timber floorboards, some old light fixtures. But the rest of it had been overhauled. Gutted. It had that renovation smell of fresh paint and new cabinetry.

Aimee looked around and admired the whole space, taking hesitant steps further inside like a cat that had just been let out of its carrier after arriving at the home of its new family. 'The original beams.' She looked up at the ceiling. 'Beautiful.'

'Oh, no – they're not *technically* the originals. The originals were century-old pine and looked horrendous so I replaced them with these reclaimed cedar beams from an old house in Tasmania. They were original to *that* house, though.'

Aimee had quickly picked up from the grand tour that Brooke deemed a lot of things 'horrendous'. It was one of her favourite words. Looking around, she wondered what other parts of the historic home Brooke might tear out and toss aside. Aimee imagined what Brooke would think if she ever went to her apartment. *It's like a junk yard!* she'd exclaim, before finding a way to segue into how much she pays for the independent garbage collection service she probably contracts. The thought was almost more depressing than the calculations Aimee had done during the grand tour – $140,000 for three Mokes equalled about three years of income from the bookstore. Brooke picked up her iPhone off the thick Carrara marble kitchen benchtop and started tapping away. Notification pings filled her locked home screen and Aimee could see Brooke's finger gliding through them.

'We've gone global,' Brooke declared. She held up the screen to show a news story on UK tabloid website *The Sun*.

Aimee squinted to read the headline: *Reality star's humiliating sex fail.* It was an article breathlessly re-telling the harrowing tale of how Luna shat the bed.

'We got amazing coverage after that podcast. All the Australian outlets ran with it.' Her French bulldog named Chicken scurried over and its claws clicked across the floor. She made a fuss but refused to touch it. 'I heard you on the pod! The girls are wild!' She leant on the marble bench and softened her voice to appear compassionate. 'I also heard about your situation. With your fiancé. And . . . Bree.'

Aimee waited to see where the comment was going.

'Aimee, I don't want that to make it weird for us.' Then she winked.

How to respond? Aimee had no idea. Particularly now that the cameramen surrounded them. She was always surprised at how easy it was to forget they were around. One second, the crew seemed distracted and bored – the next, they were recording every single second of a sensitive conversation you'd just been ambushed with. She could almost feel their lenses zooming in on her face. There was a pause and she didn't move – as if she was trying to ward off predators in the jungle who were looking for their next meal.

Brooke placed her manicured hand on top of Aimee's. 'And can I just say, we *love* Freya. What a great girl. She's just fit right in with everyone. She stays over here if the girls have been filming late – in the guest villas I just showed you.' It was clear on the unofficial golf cart tour that the guest villas were Brooke's pride and joy. 'We feel like she's part of the family. Her and Bree get on like sisters.'

'She's amazing.' Aimee nodded.

'I'm so jealous. I wish Bree was like Freya when she was twenty-one.' She let out an exasperated sigh and the silver band of her big diamond ring tapped the marble as she slapped her hand on the bench. 'At twenty-one, Bree was trouble. TROUBLE.'

Aimee wondered if it would be rude to ask what kind of trouble but, before she could even fully consider it, Brooke was already providing in-depth details.

'Partying, drinking, drugs. Not the bad kind – just a bit of cocaine,' she assured. 'I put my foot down. I told her she was going to rehab. I wanted to nip that in the butt,' she said with a click of her fingers, not realising the correct word was 'bud'. 'But the only way we could get her in one was if it were in Bali. So, we did it.' She put her hands up in the air and closed her eyes. 'I wouldn't admit it to many people, Aimee. I know, it's crazy, but . . . you do anything for your kids when they're in that kind of trouble.'

Almost instinctually, Aimee's eyes flicked into the lens of the camera over Brooke's shoulder, as if it were a rude stranger trying to eavesdrop on some juicy gossip at a coffee shop. The cameraman waved an arm in the air – warning Aimee not to look down the lens. It caught Brooke's attention.

'Oh!' She laughed and reached out one of her elegant arms to tap Aimee on the wrist. 'It's fine! None of this is a secret. Fuck, it's a reality show! Anyway, it's a positive story! It was in rehab that she learnt how to make jewellery. And when she got out, she stayed in Bali a while, selling her stuff in local markets. Cool people started buying it, the brand got big. And that's when she moved home. The business was blowing up. I told her to come back to Australia, use my warehouse and team. And . . . there you have it: Everything works out in the end.'

While Brooke talked, Aimee tried to push down her jealousy by focusing on thoughts about how Brooke got her creamy café latte-coloured skin to be so pore-free.

'I think Freya will learn a lot from Bree.' Brooke gave Aimee a knowing smile.

Good god, let's hope not, Aimee thought. 'She's just graduated uni,' she said. 'Now she's just trying to decide what she wants to do.'

'Well, I think the photography thing will definitely work out for her.'

'Photography thing?' Aimee responded, a little too sharply.

'She's really into her photography.' Brooke's acrylic thumbnail tapped the iPhone screen as she scrolled through Instagram.

'Well, yeah. But . . . that's not what she went to uni for. That's just a hobby.' Freya was always taking pictures on her phone. Sometimes she'd text some to Aimee or show her if they were hanging out. But she'd never said anything about wanting it to be a job.

'She seems pretty serious about it. She's applied for a few jobs. And she's really good. Her portfolio's amazing.'

Aimee's brow furrowed. She fiddled with the microphone pack that had been attached to the back pocket of her jeans.

'This is just her professional Instagram – the portfolio's even better.' Brooke passed her phone across the bench. 'Tea?' She widened her eyes at a kettle that looked more like an expensive art installation than a kitchen appliance.

'Sure.' Aimee looked mindlessly at the grid. Photos of the ocean and architecture and cool old cars parked in dodgy streets. She pretended like she was familiar with it, even though she'd never seen it in her life. Freya's personal Insta? Yes. But not her apparently secret professional Insta. Well, not so secret. It had nearly ten thousand followers. Aimee made a mental note of the Insta handle to find it later. 'Yeah. She's very good. It just . . . worries me.' She shrugged. 'Everyone reckons they can be a photographer these days. Anyway. She's twenty-one next week. That's really young. She's got time.'

A newspaper rustled and the energy in the room shifted as a guy walked in. The cameramen took a few steps back and adjusted their positions while the boom mic stretched up to arch over them all. Brooke looked to her side. 'Babe, this is Aimee – Freya's aunt. Aimee – my husband Rich.'

Aimee looked over, cocked her head and squinted. There was something about him. Was he familiar? Or maybe it was just because he wasn't what Aimee imagined Brooke's husband to look like. In her mind, she'd pictured one of those businessy guys who magically gets even more attractive and charming as he ages. One of those CEOs who works sixteen hours a day but still manages to do marathons every weekend for weird charities no one has ever heard of. Rich wasn't *unattractive*. He was just . . . blah. Practical and unremarkable. Like brown leather shoes. 'Hi,' Aimee said over the sound of the kettle that had reached a boil. 'I'm sorry, have we met before?'

Rich formed a pout with his lips as he squinted and assessed Aimee. 'Hmmm . . . Don't think so.'

Brooke interrupted. 'Babe, did you contact the palm farm and reschedule?'

Rich took a deep breath. 'I didn't reschedule it – I cancelled it. It's impossible and we're not paying more fines.'

With a sigh and a wave of her hand, Brooke gave Aimee the brief explanation. 'I wanted a fully-grown palm tree for inside the house, which meant we'd have to cut a hole in the roof and crane it in, then cover the hole with a raised glass dome. I just don't know why it's so hard.' Brooke turned her bemused gaze to Aimee, as if they both had an in-joke about how clueless Rich was. 'I have a whole Pinterest board of pictures that prove it can be done.' She handed over a stylish white mug of black tea.

'That's a $900 dollar cup of tea you're drinking.' Rich raised his eyebrows.

Aimee felt the sting of the comment. It then became clear the barb was aimed at Brooke, who again offered an explanation about her husband as if he wasn't in the room.

'We're not tea drinkers,' Brooke said.

'This is the one and only time that ridiculous kettle has been used,' Rich added from the sidelines.

'We're more of a coffee household,' Brooke continued. 'Coffee, coffee, coffee. But that's what the La Marzocco is for.' She gestured to a fancy-looking silver coffee machine. 'So, yes, Rich is correct: This is actually the first time I've used the kettle.' She turned to offer a condescending comment to her husband in a sing-song voice. 'Very observant, darling!'

'You're *drinking* money.' Rich nodded to Aimee, intending for it to be a joke but failing the execution. It just made the interaction more uncomfortable.

'Look at it!' Brooke pointed to the kettle with both hands, like a TV game-show girl gesturing to a prize. 'It's stunning. *Stunning*. And we need a kettle for when friends like Aimee come around!' She winked at Aimee, who was also exclusively a coffee drinker but sipped her tea anyway. 'And we can't spend all that money on a beautiful kitchen only to ruin it with an ugly kettle that doesn't match.'

They continued to bicker – sort of playfully, sort of not. Aimee slid her phone out of her back pocket and pretended to reply to a text while meandering from the kitchen into the open-plan living area. The cameramen stayed filming the kettle debacle, which was just as well because, if they'd followed Aimee, they would've busted her scrolling through Instagram – searching for Freya's secret photography account. Was it secret? Aimee didn't know about it, so it felt like a secret. She tried to remember the handle. *Found it*. Warm, faded, hazy coloured tiles flashed by as she thumbed down through her niece's feed. Beautiful pictures, with captions like 'Day for it!' and 'Beauty and the beach'. Just like all the other beautiful pictures you'd find on Instagram. A text notification swooped down from the top of the screen and Jules' name appeared in bold.

JULES
Attachment (1)

It startled Aimee for a second. Mainly because she worried about touching the wrong thing on the screen and accidentally 'liking' one of Freya's photos. The Insta account Aimee used was an anonymous one, but she still liked to lurk with caution. She used her thumb to carefully tap the text and it opened to the messaging app. It was a shirtless selfie of Jules on the beach. Aimee clicked the photo open and enlarged it to look at the buff hairy chest at the bottom of the frame. She usually hated men who took selfies, but Jules was making a goofy face which, in her mind, made it less wanky. What was she supposed to reply? Maybe she didn't have to reply. It's not like he asked a question. She paused for a second and then started tapping the keys.

Nice!

Backspace, backspace, backspace.

Handsome, sir!

Backspace, backspace, backspace.

Ugh, she thought to herself. *Handsome, sir?* She sounded like Jane Austen's lame younger sister. She thought hard for a moment, now aware that Jules had probably seen the floating grey dots pop up in the chat each time she'd tried to type. *Just reply. Write anything. ANYTHING.*

Day for it!

Aimee hit the send button and then promptly cringed at herself. She locked the phone and walked further into the living area. On a lounge chair rested one of the annoying $4,650 Louis Vuitton 'Byron Bay' handbags Aimee had seen around. Of course Brooke owned one. For a second, she gleefully willed one of those knock-off designer handbag companies to make an identical one with the name of a less glamorous-sounding beach emblazoned across it. COOLANGATTA. Then she wandered over to the Christmas trees. Plural. There were three in total. A cluster of Christmas trees in the living area. All varying in size but all huge. Aimee could tell by the fresh smell that they were real and they looked like they'd been decorated by one of those professional companies. Cobalt blue kugels with an aged, flaked patina dangled from all the branches.

'Aren't they special?' Brooke appeared by Aimee's side. 'Antiques. From Paris.' She reached out and tugged one of the baubles off the tip of a branch. 'Here, take one.'

Aimee resisted but Brooke grabbed her hand and placed it delicately in her palm like it was an injured bird.

'C'mon.' Brooke turned to walk down the hallway. 'Let me show you my walk-in Coles deli.'

TWENTY-ONE

'We had to move further down the beach because of the booing,' Heath said.

Aimee used a hand to block out the afternoon glare and looked at him, standing behind the camera gear as the crew fussed around her and set up the new filming location, away from the Main Beach park where protesters had gathered again with megaphones and signs. One of the tech girls on the TV crew ran a mic cord down Aimee's singlet and popped it out near the waistband of her jeans.

'Did we have to do this on a Sunday?' Aimee wriggled and looked around self-consciously to see if the protesters had followed.

'Do people not boo on weekdays?' Heath laughed. He was standing behind the camera and looking in his little monitor to check the shot.

'I just think maybe we could've avoided the weekend crowds. You know, lay low.'

'The show must go on. Besides, it adds drama. Tension! Greed! All the elements of a great story.'

'Wow, I didn't realise *The Brats of Byron Bay* had such Shakespearean undertones,' Aimee deadpanned.

'We're Australia's answer to prestige television.' Heath grinned, mocking his own program. He took a pair of headphones off one of the soundies and squinted up at the sky while listening. 'You can still faintly hear the booing – but, with the waves, it all kinda mixes in.'

One of the hair and make-up girls quickly flicked a brush over Aimee's face and tried to tame the flyaways in the breeze.

Aimee clicked her fingers at Heath to get his attention. 'So . . . what do I need to do here?'

'Just answer the questions. Simple. They're just about you and your life.'

'Yeah, but what kind of questions?'

'Oh, you know, really deep stuff. Like, *if you were a Spice Girl, which one would you be?* And, *what do you think clouds taste like?*'

'*What do I think clouds taste like?*' She shot him a look. 'Is it just *impossible* for you to ever give a serious answer?'

Heath rolled up the papers he was looking at, tucked them into his back pocket and walked over to Aimee. 'Look.' He knelt down in the sand and put his pen behind an ear. 'I know you're nervous about this stuff,' he rushed to continue his sentence as Aimee opened her mouth to interrupt, 'and you're allowed to be nervous. No one expects you to know how all this works. That's why I'm doing this interview with you instead of one of the regular producers.'

Aimee interjected. 'And who *are* the other producers? Everyone just wears black and I can't tell who's a producer and who's not. And they all have clipboards and look at me like they know my secrets.'

Heath sighed and entertained the slight derailment to his moment of kindness. 'There's lots of producers. Date producers, event producers, storyline producers – and a house producer who stays with Luna and Addie at the Airbnb they're living in for the summer. Lots. They're all guns at what they do but they can be a bit . . . *dog with a bone*. Instead of throwing you in the deep end with them, I wanted to do this first interview myself. Give it the sensitivity it needs. Any more questions?'

Aimee raised an eyebrow. 'You? Sensitive?'

Heath swiped his pen out from behind his ear. 'Is it just *impossible* for you to give a serious answer?' He smiled like he'd just won a prize for that quip and stood up. 'Oh, and some of the questions will be about your personal life. Can you handle it?'

Aimee rolled her eyes. 'Are you forgetting the podcast inquest about my sex life?'

'I'll start off slow . . .' He walked back behind the camera.

'OK, Tracy Grimshaw.'

'Just remember,' he called out. 'State the question in your answer, like I showed you earlier. If I ask you, *What's your favourite ice-cream flavour?* You reply, *My favourite ice-cream flavour is . . .*'

'I know, I know,' Aimee replied, trying to mask her sudden pang of nerves with mild irritation.

'Alrighty,' Heath yelled. 'We good to go?'

The camera and sound guys both gave a thumbs up.

'We're good to go,' Heath declared.

Then one of the crew waved his hand in the air at Heath and pointed to something.

'Ah, fuck,' Heath said. 'We are *not* good to go. Hold up.'

A guy in all-black jogged over with an orange Esky and plonked it down in the sand next to Aimee. He flipped the lid off it and propped up all the bottles inside. Aimee cocked her head and read the label. 'CocoRama,' she said aloud.

'They're a sponsor,' Heath said. 'It's a coconut water.'

The crew member arranging the Esky handed her a bottle.

'No, I'm OK,' Aimee declined.

Heath laughed. 'No, you've gotta *hold* it. It's part of the sponsorship.'

'So I'm a coconut water spokesperson now?'

'It's just part of the show. All you have to do is hold it . . . But if you wanna crack one open to sip from it mid-interview and then say something like, "Mmmm moist!" then I won't stop you,' he laughed.

The hair and make-up lady ran over to quickly pull some strands of hair out of Aimee's face as the guy finished styling the Esky. Then she started dabbing on more products around the eyes and cheeks.

Aimee winced. 'Is something wrong?'

'Just some rough spots, darl,' the woman in her fifties said. 'I know what it's like – happens to me, too.'

Aimee cringed a little. *Does she think we're the same age?*

'I do all the girls' faces in the morning and they barely need a thing. Especially that daughter of the rich lady.'

'Ah, yeah,' Aimee mumbled.

'The girl glows. Golden. Like caramel dripped over a lightbulb.'

'Poetic,' Aimee replied. '*And* a fire hazard.'

Heath clapped his hands three times. 'C'mon people, we good to go?' Everyone ran out of shot. 'Alrighty, we're good to go . . . *again.*' Heath cleared his throat and crossed his arms. 'OK, Aimee – let's ease into it. Tell me about yourself: name, where you live, how long you've lived here . . .'

'Ah. My name's Aimee . . . I'm thirty-six – and I've lived in Byron my whole life. I was born here. And I've owned a bookstore in town for about eighteen years.'

'What was it like growing up in Byron?'

'Hmmm . . . different—'

'State the question in the answer,' Heath gently reminded.

Aimee closed her eyes and shook her head quickly to reset. 'Right, sorry. Ah . . . Growing up in Byron was different to how it is now. It wasn't trendy. Well, it was but it wasn't. There weren't lots of celebrities or huge mansions. But it was the beginning of that whole enlightenment craze. Late nineties, early 2000s. New people started coming. And I remember some locals blamed the Madonna *Ray of Light* album because that's around the time she got really into Kabbalah and yoga. Anyway, the town was still very different to how it is now.'

'And what was your family like?'

'They . . . Sorry,' Aimee corrected herself, remembering to state the question. 'My family were good. Close. Me and my sister, Fleur – who's Freya's mum. And our mum and dad owned an antiques store for years. And that became *my* store – the bookstore. The Dream Explosion. I took it over when they passed away.'

'Does Fleur still live in Byron with you?'

'Ah, no . . .' Aimee swapped the CocoRama bottle to her opposite hand. 'No, she actually passed away too. With my parents.' She paused and scrunched up her face a little. 'I'm not sure how much of this stuff you wanna go into?'

'We can stop if you—'

'No it's fine,' she brushed it off, again trying to appear breezier on camera than she actually was. 'It was a long time ago. I just . . . didn't know if it was what you wanted me to talk about.'

'Whatever you feel comfortable with.' Heath gave her a nod.

'Well, I was in my last year of high school. Fleur was twenty-one and had just given birth to Freya about a month or two before the accident. Tim and I had been dating a little while and he had a surfing comp up on the Gold Coast, so I went with him. He had surf comps all the time – Perth, Geelong . . . one in Bali. He was in talks with Billabong to sponsor and go pro – all that stuff. So I went away a lot with him. And for the store, my parents would go off antiquing – driving around . . . going to estate sales, auctions, garage sales. They'd drive all around – up and down the coast, country towns. Anyway, while I was with Tim at the comp, Fleur went with my parents on one of their trips.' Aimee paused. 'Ah.' She coughed and looked away. She dug a fingernail into the pad of her thumb and tried not to cry. 'And . . . that's when there was a car . . . thing. Accident.' She looked down and felt a tear dripping from her right eye. Then she saw it hit the sand.

'Guys, I reckon that's enough,' Heath directed the crew.

Aimee looked up quickly and nudged the corners of her eyes with her thumbs. 'No, I'm fine.' She cleared her throat. 'I'm fine,' she said again, unconvincingly. 'We can keep going. I'm all good.'

Heath looked around the beach. 'Nah, no more today. We got what we needed.'

Aimee wiped her eyes again and shook her head. 'I thought I'd be fine talking about that. I wanted to explain it so Freya wouldn't have to do it on the show later.'

Heath walked over.

'Sorry.' She looked out at the waves and forced a laugh. 'That was probably not what you were wanting. It doesn't really fit in with . . . *babes and bikinis*. Did you need me to say something else? I can give a . . . *less maudlin* answer.'

'Nah. These guys are already packing up.' Heath nodded at the crew, who were winding their cords and clacking down equipment like a travelling circus about to head to their next town. 'We're losing light anyway. The sun's going down. Wanna go for a walk instead?'

'A walk?' Aimee laughed, a little stunned. 'What for?'

'I thought we could recreate that opening scene from *Grease* with Danny and Sandy on the beach,' Heath gave a mock reply before letting out a laugh. 'C'mon.' He nodded down to the water. 'Just come for a walk.'

———

The waves rolled in and skimmed up the shore, wiping out the abandoned sandcastles and big pointless holes that had been dug by little kids throughout the day. *Clack, clack, clack.* Sandals were whacked together to get rid of every last pesky grain of sand and towels flopped in the breeze as people shook them out before heading back up into town before the light disappeared completely.

'You know, I'm disappointed you're not actually a true Karen.' Heath lightly kicked some water over at Aimee with his foot. They'd both rolled their jeans up and were walking through the shallows down the length of the beach.

'Well, never meet your heroes.' She laughed and splashed some water back.

'It's why we booked you on the show in the first place. I should sue you for breach of contract. We ordered a Karen!' He committed to the joke. 'Legally I should be allowed to get that old lady on the make-up team to cut your hair into one of those short Karen bobs with the choppy highlights.'

'Ugh, *her*,' Aimee groaned.

'Oh, the only reason you don't like her is because she didn't say your skin was like the other girls,' Heath teased.

'The woman thinks I'm the same age as her!'

Heath let out a big laugh and kicked the water. 'Hey,' he said, switching to a slightly more serious tone, 'I didn't know your history when we got you to do the show – but what I said to you that night at the pub was true. I wanna tell a real story about life here. Yours is a real story.' He looked over at Aimee. 'You OK with your interview being included?'

Aimee held her hair behind an ear to stop the breeze from blowing it around and thought for a second. 'Yeah,' she said, a little hesitantly before nodding more decisively. 'Yeah. It's what happened. And with Freya on the show, I'd rather explain it up front than have her put on the spot.'

They both did a little jump to stop a particularly vigorous wave from getting more than just their shins wet.

'What happened with Freya? After the accident? If you don't mind me—'

'No, it's fine,' Aimee said. 'Her dad moved with his family soon after. Sydney. He was young . . . they both were – him and Fleur. Twenty-one. It was hard. Him moving away with Freya made it harder. I was a mess. I was dealing with everything. And I'd just graduated. I didn't even have plans figured out for after high school. It was just gonna be travelling with Tim. Surf comps and travel. But I couldn't go after everything that happened. Mum and Dad's landlord at the antique store, he was very nice . . . let me take a few months while I figured out what to do. Then . . . I sold all the furniture and changed it to the bookstore.'

Heath widened his eyes and exhaled. 'Wow,' was all he could say.

'Anyway, what about you?' Aimee tried to change the tone. 'Was your childhood dream to make shows about hot girls shitting in beds?'

'Please don't disparage my art.' Heath pretended to be offended for a second. 'Nah. Look. This . . . was certainly not the plan. I'd always done TV – documentaries. Spent most of the '90s living between South Africa and London. I was twenty-two, twenty-three when I went there. It was around the end of Apartheid, so I was filming a lot for that – a doco and stuff for BBC. The landmines in Angola – I was there filming when Princess Diana walked through that active field. Other stuff . . .' He bent over to scoop his hand through the water.

In her head, Aimee tried to do the math and figure out how old Heath was. She hadn't been able to tell exactly. But the life history pointed to fifty.

'Then life happened,' Heath continued. 'Got married. Had a kid . . .'

The child revelation caused a huge smile to flash across Aimee's face.

'Don't look so shocked,' Heath said.

'I'm not! I just . . . did not expect that.' She shook her head slowly as she adjusted to the new perception of Heath. 'What's the kid's name?'

'Sadie. Ten. She's perfect.'

'Sadie,' Aimee repeated. 'Great name.'

'Thank you.' Heath proudly accepted the compliment. 'Though all credit for that goes to my ex.' He gave Aimee the shorthand version with a wave of his hand. 'We split, shortly after Sadie was born. And that, my friend, is how I wound up making shows about hot girls and their beds.'

Aimee laughed.

'Reality TV pays a hell of a lot more than docos.' He shrugged. 'Can I give you a little piece of advice?'

Aimee tried to think of something sarcastic to respond with, but nothing came. 'Sure.'

'Don't resist. With the show. When you're around the brats and Brooke – they're performing for the camera. They want attention. They'll do anything to make a moment. Usually it's something awkward or dramatic. So don't resist it. Resisting will just make it worse. It's like a snake – the more you struggle, the more it tightens its grip. Just surrender.'

All the colour was almost gone from the sky. Looking up, Aimee nodded, thinking about what Heath had just said.

'Lemonade,' she eventually replied.

'Lemonade?'

Aimee smiled and kicked a little splash of water at Heath. 'I think clouds would taste like lemonade.'

TWENTY-TWO

There was a takeaway coffee cup in each of Aimee's hands. One empty. The other full of milky liquid that had gone cold. Aimee plonked both cups on the grass where she was sitting in the park above Main Beach and pulled out her phone to check the time. Then her thumb tapped open the real estate app. She refreshed the recent search results. It was something that she'd been doing so frequently that the actions had become mindless. The results never changed. There was nothing. Nothing suitable, at least. There were shops that were nice but far too expensive. Shops that were terrible and still far too expensive. And shops that were so decrepit they were probably actually illegal to inhabit . . . while still being far too expensive. Her thumbs flicked the property app closed and automatically tapped on the Instagram icon. Aimee had a secret Instagram profile that she used exclusively to lurk and judge. Lurk, lurk, lurk. Always lurking, always judging. There was no bio or profile pic – just the standard grey cartoon head avatar. Her handle was a jumble of letters and numbers – probably just an auto-generated one. She'd been following Freya's personal account for years – not because she thought Freya needed to be monitored, she just wanted to see as much of her niece's life as she could. And she didn't ever tell Freya because she didn't want Freya to feel like she couldn't be herself – no one wants their aunt following them on Instagram.

Aimee searched for Freya's professional photography Instagram and scrolled through the grid again. Nothing new had been posted since she stalked it the previous night, so she went to a different profile she'd been lurking on a lot lately: Bree's. Of course, Aimee had found Bree's profile after meeting her with Tim at the *Brats* dinner. The flush of shame and pettiness that erupted in her body every time she flicked open the profile wasn't enough to make her stop. She clicked on Insta Stories and the first clip to play showed Bree and Brooke in the G-Wagon – with Freya leaning between them from the back seat. A Kanye West song played and the words 'that Gold Coast life with these absolute 10s' were written in cursive over the top.

'Scoping out your competition?' a clipped British voice came from above.

Aimee locked her phone screen frantically. 'Nina . . . I didn't see you there . . .' She twisted her body to look up at her. 'I'm waiting for Freya, she's late . . . I thought I'd just . . .' She exhaled as her mind caught up. 'I thought I'd just check their social accounts to see where they are.' Ten points for quick-ish thinking. The delivery? Not so strong.

Nina smirked at the excuse behind her dark sunglasses. Her silence made Aimee scramble to fill it.

'Not out filming today? I mean . . . *Do* you go out while they're filming stuff? I'm still not sure what an EP does.'

'Oh, just dealing with yet another high-octane drama,' Nina issued a dry response. 'We were supposed to be filming with Addie and Luna but one of them decided to put on fake eyelashes.' She let out a big sigh. 'The lashes were so long they were literally casting a shadow across her entire face. We've had to pause everything while the make-up crew deals with it.' Nina seemed more amused than irritated with the inconvenient delay. 'Anyway, Freya's up on the Gold Coast with Brooke and Bree. A crew went up with them for the day . . . Though it looks like you figured that out all on your own.' She raised an eyebrow and smiled. 'They'll be caught in traffic.

Our crew said the main road back into town had been shut off temporarily while another production films this afternoon – that Netflix show . . . *Oceans of Angels*. The one with all the cocks – have you seen it?'

Aimee shrugged. 'I'm . . . familiar with it.'

'People will watch anything these days as long as there's hot people fucking in it.' Nina let out a laugh as she tilted her head and lit a cigarette. '*Says the old bat making a show about hot idiots twatting around Byron for the summer.*' She exhaled smoke to the side and half-heartedly corrected herself. 'Well, not *your* girl. Or . . . *you*.' Nina turned her attention across the path and gave a nod at something in the distance. 'Here she is,' she declared with a firm wave.

Aimee whipped around and saw Freya running across the grass.

'Well, I'm off to deal with my eyelash drama.' Nina strode away.

'Sorry!' Freya ran over the grass above Main Beach. 'Just got back from Surfers.'

Aimee stood up and handed her the cup. 'It might be cold, sorry.' She brushed the grass off the seat of her jeans and they set off down the footpath. 'What was happening up on the Gold Coast?'

'Oh nothing.' Freya scrunched her nose. 'Brooke and Bree were just going shopping and they asked if I wanted to go. Brooke said you came to the farm yesterday.'

'Yeah, it's nice. Could use some peacocks, though.'

The joke went over Freya's head as she adjusted the long gold chain hanging off her shoulder. It caught Aimee's attention. Her eyes traced it down to Freya's hip where a tiny black bag was bouncing. It was the same one Bree had at the Bang Bang dinner. Aimee could tell by the gold metal Gucci logo on the front.

'Is it weird for you?' Freya bopped a hip into her aunt's side.

The question threw Aimee for a second.

'We haven't had a chance to really talk properly about . . . *everything*.'

'Ahhh, yes. *Everything*.' Aimee dragged out the word dramatically before taking a serious tone. 'Look, I know that no one else is brave enough to say it, but I will: I think Leah on *Home and Away* is secretly an anti-vaxxer and I don't know why the writers are ignoring it as a storyline.'

Freya groaned. 'Sorry, I've never owned a TV so I don't know what you're talking about.'

'Way—'

'Way harsh, Tai,' Freya cut her off with a smile.

'OK. You can't say I'm old and then quote *Clueless*. I introduced you to that cinematic masterpiece.'

'I didn't *say* you're old. I merely *insinuated* you're old,' Freya said with an exaggerated air of superiority before jumping back to her initial question. 'Seriously though. Tim and Bree. Is it weird me hanging out with Bree for the show?'

'Look,' Aimee sighed. 'No one saw this coming. Not even Meredith the roadside clairvoyant to the stars predicted it. And if we're gonna blame someone, it may as well be Meredith.'

'Sometimes, if we're filming late, me and the other girls just sleep there and I kinda keep forgetting about the whole . . . *Tim thing*.'

Thoughts flooded Aimee's mind. The Tim stuff didn't even place at the top of the list. Freya was right – they hadn't had a chance to talk about everything that happened at the Bang Bang dinner party because Freya was never at Aimee's apartment, where she was supposed to be living for the summer. She'd say she was staying out late filming but Aimee would wake up during the night and find the guest room empty. Freya had told her she was crashing at Brooke's some nights. *It's just easier after a few drinks*, she reasoned. Aimee always trod carefully around this stuff. One thing she feared most was the day she'd have a fight with Freya after trying to behave like a mum.

Aimee wrapped an arm around her niece as they kept walking along. 'I mean. Yes. It's weird. There's no way it wouldn't be weird. But . . . that's not your fault. That's just the situation. As long as you feel comfortable . . .'

Their shoes scratched along the sand that covered the footpath and the sound of a guitar being played drifted down from the busker performing ahead.

'Ugh, "Wonderwall".' Aimee cringed at the song.

'She doesn't say anything about you,' Freya said. 'Bree. And if she did, I'd tell her to stop. And I'd tell you.'

Aimee kissed the side of Freya's face and then tugged the long gold chain hanging from her shoulder. 'This is new.'

'Yeah. I got in up—' Freya pointed.

'Surfers,' Aimee finished the sentence. 'Did Brooke buy it for you?' She bristled at herself.

Freya rolled her eyes. 'Stop it, Byron Karen.'

'I didn't mean it like that.' Aimee tried to lighten the mood. 'Something more important: What are we doing for your twenty-first? I thought we could do something at our place? Low-key. Or we can go out somewhere – the Palace Hotel? You, me and Rob and Charlie? Some of your friends or people from the show?'

Freya made an awkward face. 'Actually . . . Brooke's asked if she can throw a party at her place. She said it'll be good for the show. Bigger space. More people.'

'Oh,' Aimee said, more stunned than she intended. She shook her head and adjusted to the news.

'That's OK, right?' Freya said.

'Um . . . yeah – no, cool . . . that's fun.' Aimee didn't think it was cool or fun. She held her hair to stop the wind throwing it around. 'It's just . . . I thought we were gonna do something, *just us* . . . you know?'

'Well, of course we'll do something *just us*.' Freya laughed to ease the weirdness.

'OK.' Aimee nodded. 'But . . . Brooke's party . . . only do it if that's what *you wanna* do . . . don't feel pressured to do it just for the show. Like . . . did Brooke suggest it to you *on camera*? Because that would've been a bit weird – of course you would've felt like you *had* to say yes.'

Freya shot her aunt a look. 'She didn't ask me on camera.'

'Alright.' Aimee pulled back from the topic. 'Just . . . if you change your mind and you don't wanna do it, let me know and I can have a quiet word with Heath.'

Freya chose not to reply and Aimee realised she might've overstepped the boundaries she'd been trying so hard not to cross. Still, that didn't stop her from finding another one to jump over.

'When I was at the farm, Brooke said she saw your photography portfolio. She said it was great. I didn't know you were so serious about photography.' Aimee forced an upbeat tone.

'Well, you like to rant about how, these days, everyone thinks they can be a photographer . . .'

It was true. And the rants did tend to escalate during peak holiday periods. Ever since Brooke told her about Freya's portfolio the previous day, Aimee had spent a lot of time combing her mind, trying to remember if she'd let loose with one of the rants around Freya since she'd arrived. Turns out she had.

'I would never mean that about *you*,' Aimee said. 'I'd love to see your portfolio.'

Freya nodded. 'Smile.'

'I'm not cranky—'

'No. *Smile.*' Freya's chest lifted slightly as she pulled her shoulders back and her walk turned into a refined stride.

Aimee squinted. Then she heard the rapid-fire *snap snap snap* of a camera. She looked ahead and saw a man in dark clothes crouched down with a long black lens the length of his forearm.

'We've been getting papped the past few days since the show started getting written about in the tabloids.' Freya picked up the pace and turned her head slightly to Aimee as she talked, making sure to flash a relaxed smile for the camera.

We've been getting papped?

In the tabloids?

It was the first time Aimee had ever heard someone in real life say something like that.

As Freya walked ahead, Aimee noticed the new expensive-looking black sandals her niece was wearing. It was all she could focus on for a moment.

Then Freya turned and laughed. 'Why are you walking weird?'

Aimee snapped back to reality. 'I'm just trying to walk *normally* but . . . now you're making me think about it and I don't know how to walk anymore.' She tried to catch up. 'Wait,' she whisper-shouted, 'am I moving my arms weird?'

TWENTY-THREE

'You're worried she's trying to steal your niece?' Rob popped a square of chocolate in her mouth and leant on the counter at The Dream Explosion.

'No, that makes me sound crazy,' Aimee said. 'But, also . . . Yes, I think she's trying to steal my niece.'

They were pillaging the chocolate from a cardboard Advent calendar that had a big picture of a cartoon Santa head on it. Christmas was just days away, but the calendar was brand new and they were making up for lost time.

'How much do we know about her? You just can't trust people these days. Remember when I got Dirty Johned?'

'You didn't get Dirty Johned. You just dated a guy who did F45.'

'Which he kept secret. And then one morning he tricked me into going to breakfast but it was a trap and I ended up in a gym. You never really know someone until it's too late.' Rob held up her phone to show Aimee. 'Are these the ones?' A pair of weird-looking black sandals was on the screen. They looked like the new ones Freya was wearing at the beach the previous day.

Aimee squinted and leaned closer. Chanel. She saw the price. *Three thousand and seventy dollars? And they're so—*'

'Ugly. I know. They look like chemist shoes. And I want them. Do you think Brooke can buy me a pair too? I'm joking but, also, not really.'

'I don't know for sure if Brooke bought them for her. Or the bag. How much did you say it was?'

Rob switched internet tabs on her phone and held it up to show a picture of the tiny black purse. 'Gucci. Sixteen hundred.'

Aimee exhaled. 'Freya's not that kind of girl. She's not into those designer brands. I mean . . . even if she was, she couldn't afford it. She's still young. And I know these other girls from the TV show are only twenty-four or twenty-five . . . but that's a big difference in your twenties. Their lives are *very different* to Freya's.'

'Look, Freya's just having fun. If anyone her age got offered money to be on a TV show over summer, they'd take it. She can handle herself, just let her be.' Rob tried to calm Aimee down, unsuccessfully, then clicked her fingers as she remembered something. 'Hey, how did the big beach interview go with the TV hotshot? Did you tell him everything? Bare your soul? Reveal your *deep dark secret*?'

Aimee rolled her eyes and laughed, tossing back another chocolate. 'What's my *deep dark secret*?'

'That you want Toni Collette to re-form her band and release a second album.' Rob's eyes widened as she awaited the reaction she knew was coming.

'Hey! Toni Collette & The Finish was a great band! That album isn't talked about enough.' Aimee held her hand to her chest.

'I agree!' Rob laughed, satisfied with the pay-off of her provocation. 'You know I watch the YouTube video of them performing at the 2007 Live Earth concert on repeat. Toni really loved that xylophone, didn't she?' *Gasp!* She grabbed Aimee's wrist. 'We should get Toni Collette & The Finish to re-form and play at your wedding.' Before she could even laugh at herself, she winced at the clumsy mention of the on-hold special day.

Aimee didn't react – instead, she completely ignored the wedding reference and picked up her satchel to rifle through it with purpose. 'Also . . . Brooke gave me . . . *this*.' She pulled out the antique kugel. Her fingers pinched the brass ring attached to the top and it dangled in the air, the light flicking off the worn patina.

Rob cringed. 'An antique butt plug?'

'An antique *kugel*.'

'What is with this family giving you stuff? First that crappy necklace – which I hope you haven't been wearing . . . it'll probably turn your skin green.'

'That's just one of the many reasons I'm not wearing it,' Aimee muttered.

'And now this?' Rob tapped her thumbs over the phone screen. 'Annn-tique kooo-gels,' she dragged out the words as she said them aloud and googled. '$1,200 on eBay. Wanna sell it?'

Aimee ignored Rob's enterprising spirit. 'Freya's been sleeping at the farm. And now the gifts. All that stuff's annoying but . . . it's the party that's just . . . *bugging* me.' She placed one of the small square chocolates between her front teeth and bit down, snapping it in half. 'Why the hell is this woman throwing a twenty-first party for a girl she barely knows? And why didn't she tell me about it when we were chatting at the farm? I liter-ally told her Freya's turning twenty-one next week.'

Rob winced. 'Do you think she only decided to throw the party *after* you told her?'

Aimee put her head down on the counter. 'I just want to sleep and wake up three months from now.'

Rob pressed her thumbs on the back of the calendar. The perforated edges around one of the slots busted open and a chocolate popped out. 'She's an asshole.'

'That's the thing, though. I don't know if she *is* an asshole.'

'The woman's excavating her own lake. She's an asshole.' Rob picked up her phone and pulled up Brooke's Instagram. The grid was filled with photos of Brooke wearing OTT designer outfits while standing amongst the rubble of her under-construction estate. Snaps of her French bulldog Chicken in equally inappropriate locations also featured heavily. 'FYI.' Rob held up the phone to show Aimee a Boomerang of Freya with Brooke and

Bree at Gucci. *Scroll, scroll, scroll.* A picture of Brooke posing in front of the Byron Bay lighthouse. The caption: 'Scouting locations!'

Aimee groaned. 'I've got to go pose with them in front of that stupid lighthouse tomorrow. They're doing a promo photoshoot for the show.'

Rob continued to trawl Brooke's Instagram. She pointed out all the photos of her driving around Byron in her G-Wagon while sipping from her really big cardboard Starbucks cups. 'There's not even a Starbucks in Byron Bay. Where the hell is she getting these cups from?'

'There are lots of questions about this lady. The mysterious Starbucks cups are just one.'

'I can't stand these people. Her husband's bankrolling her ridiculous life and she gets to run around building lakes and buying expensive ugly shoes and stealing people's nieces and pretending she's a businesswoman. She's an asshole.'

'Well . . . maybe not quite an asshole,' Aimee said. 'What's an insult that's just one step below an asshole?'

'Hmmm.' Rob scrunched up her face as she tried to think of an appropriate jibe.. 'She's a . . . cooter-weasel.'

Aimee shook her head with a laugh. 'I don't even know what that is.'

'I just made it up,' Rob conceded.

'Fine, Brooke's a cooter-weasel.'

A cough came from out of sight – down near the entrance. Aimee looked up, Rob spun around. Brooke was standing in the doorway. Her troupe of sneaky ants crowded around her and blocked the outside sunlight from cracking through. The two cameras poking over her shoulder had a clean aim on their targets and the boom mike reaching through the door hovered high up to the ceiling, settling above the room. A frenzied explosion of colour burst around Brooke's face – pink and purple and blue tulle shooting out in all different directions, spangled with sequins and stars and tiny plastic jewels.

'Hi. Aimee . . . I just . . . I thought I'd drop by and show you some of my tutus.' She closed her eyes and shook her head a little as she tried to decide what to say. In that moment, Brooke was no longer just the ridiculous cari-cature who drove a pink Moke and tore down heritage-listed buildings. 'I thought I'd see if you'd want to stock some in the store.'

Aimee and Rob stared at her with wide eyes. Busted. So busted. The smell of Brooke's expensive spicy floral perfume filled the store.

'Maybe another time.' Brooke and the crew disappeared as swiftly as they'd appeared – the bustling outside world sucking them back out like water through a sink-hole.

Rob turned back to face Aimee and let out a deflated sigh. 'Shit the bed.'

Aimee raised her eyebrows. Her forehead crinkled in disappointment at herself. 'I know. We're the assholes.'

'No.' Rob held up the hollow, ravaged cardboard calendar. 'We're out of chocolate.'

Aimee exhaled. 'Shit the bed.'

TWENTY-FOUR

The iconic white lighthouse on Cape Byron was both the most beautiful and most irritating place in the world. Aimee stood back and studied it while waiting for the photoshoot to begin. She wondered if, when resident keepers were manning the lighthouse at the turn of the nineteenth century, they ever stared out into the bleak darkness and imagined a time, just decades into the future, when hot young people would use the iconic structure as a prop while taking photos of themselves in activewear. Sunset at the lighthouse was peak hour for selfies. So, obviously, many people were perturbed when, on the afternoon of the TV show's photoshoot, they were blocked from entering the area by metal barricade fencing around the perimeter. Aimee considered lying at the edge of the hill and letting gravity roll her body down into the ocean.

All the different producers were running around and talking into headsets while the rest of the crew tinkered with equipment. Aimee watched on as the brats were all being positioned around the base of the lighthouse in strappy white tops and floaty dresses. The cast was told to dress in white. Aimee looked at the girls. And then she looked down at her own outfit – a white linen shirt and linen pants. She felt like their grandmother.

A young producer walked up to her. 'Turn around.' She held a bulldog clip in the air.

When Aimee spun, the producer grabbed a fistful of the linen shirt and clipped it.

'It'll stop your outfit from looking so . . . *billowy*.'

Billowy. That's how everyone wants to be told they look just moments before being photographed. Aimee had already been dreading the entire day. It'd be the first time seeing Brooke since the incident at the store. She'd been thinking about it ever since it happened and there were even one or two times when she went to text an apology but she wasn't sure what to say – or even what Brooke had actually heard.

The photographer looked over at Aimee's adjustment. 'It's still not great but it's better than before.'

Nina weighed in. 'Jesus Christ, Aimee!' she chortled. 'There's so much excess fabric we could use it to make a condom to put over the lighthouse!'

Unnecessary, Aimee thought.

Freya was positioned alongside the other girls, down the end. She looked over at her aunt to make sure she was OK. Aimee smiled and tried to seem more relaxed than she was.

The bulldog clip chick grabbed Aimee by the wrist and positioned her on the end, next to Freya, who playfully grabbed her aunt's hand. She lifted up her phone to take a photo of them together.

Aimee saw the screen had a big diagonal crack shattered across it. 'Your poor phone!'

Freya pretended to sob. 'I dropped it getting out of the car yesterday.'

'Positions!' the photographer gave a final warning and a producer waved a hand over at Brooke's G-Wagon.

The car door opened. *Slap, slap*. Brooke's straw-fringed sandals flung out onto the bitumen. She was wearing a dress like Bree's – ethereal and floaty and fitted just enough in the right places to not warrant bulldog clips. A producer took the Starbucks cup from Brooke's hand and guided her to the opposite end of the line before arranging her limbs. Brooke whispered in the producer's ear and the message was quickly relayed to the photographer who didn't wait a second before yelling at the group.

'You and you. Switch.' He was talking about Freya and Bree.

The girls traded cautious looks before swapping spots. That's when Aimee found herself spooning Bree. Even under the orange glare of the setting sun, Aimee could feel a particular chill being blown her way from Brooke.

'Sorry about Mum,' Bree whispered over her shoulder.

Stop giving me reasons not to hate you, Aimee thought. Her insides twisted at the thought of Bree – and now Tim – knowing about the incident at the store. She leaned in. 'I like your dress.'

Bree didn't break her gaze from the camera and continued to angle her head in weird ways. 'Thanks! It's cottagecore.'

Aimee had no idea what that meant and made a mental note to google it later.

'Embody the graceful posture of a dancer but look at me with the determined eyes of a hunter!' The photographer started yelling out instructions that were vague and specific all at once. Aimee just did what she did in all photos: smile without showing her teeth while secretly wanting to die. With the coordinating white outfits and everyone lined up in front of the ocean, the group looked like Britney Spears and her backup dancers in the video clip for 'Sometimes'.

She was already embarrassed. Then her face dropped.

The photographer snapped his fingers at Aimee without pulling his face away from the camera. 'You're scowling.'

It took a moment for her to take her eyes off the distraction: Tim. Walking up to the photoshoot. In a white linen shirt and blue linen shorts. She couldn't help but feel Bree's energy pep up at the sight of him, mainly because it was in stark contrast to her own reaction.

'Did you know he was coming?' Bree whispered out the side of her mouth to Aimee.

Heath was dealing with other crew members near a monitor with Nina but glanced over to see what was happening.

Brooke called out without breaking her pose. 'I thought he should be in some shots. You can never have too many options.'

Even though it was a photoshoot, the TV crew was still there filming and the slight tension caused the cameras to move with a little more precision. The photographer walked over to Brooke. They whispered. He returned to his spot. And then came the vague but specific direction. '*You* with *them*.' He pointed his finger from Tim to Aimee and Bree.

Of course. Aimee heard Heath's voice in her head. *Don't resist. It makes it worse.* She looked around to spot him but couldn't.

Tim did what he was told. As his rubber thongs clacked over, Aimee tried to laugh off the weirdness. She could tell he felt just as ridiculous, in his linen shorts and shirt that were absolutely purchased purely for this occasion. He nodded at her with a smile and he squeezed into his spot – between his fiancée and the woman he was dating for the summer.

'That's new. The outfit,' Aimee whispered.

'Yeah.' He let out a shy laugh. 'Brooke called at the last minute and just said to wear white linen. I didn't have anything so I went to a store on Jonson Street on my way here. They said the navy shorts would look less wanky. I still feel like an idiot.' He tugged down the bottom of the shirt, which was blowing in the wind.

'It looks really nice,' Aimee said, her tone a tad unconvincing.

Bree piped up. 'It does.'

Tim rolled his eyes at the attention.

The TV cameras loomed and the photographer snapped away.

'I didn't know what this was,' he whispered to Aimee. 'I didn't know it was a . . . photo thing.'

The photographer clicked his fingers at the odd trio. 'Closer. Squeeze together.'

Aimee and Bree both leaned into Tim.

'Lean. *Lean*. Leaaaan,' the photographer continued to instruct.

All three of their faces were almost touching and the fronts and backs of their bodies were pressed together. Aimee could smell Tim. He'd had a post-surf shower. Pre-shower, he smelt like a mix of sunscreen, pineapple surfboard wax and the ocean. Post-surf shower, he smelt like Dove soap. For some reason he insisted on only using a bar of Dove in the shower. He had since high school. Aimee could also smell Bree. It was one of those sweet, sugary, fruity perfumes that was familiar to anyone who'd passed a twenty-something girl walking down the street with her friends on a Saturday night out.

The photographer offered more feedback. 'Closer! I want you all basic-ally dry-humping each other.' He stalked around in his black skinny jeans and combat boots. Then he stood on a milk crate before jumping off and crouching down on the concrete. After a few more uncomfortable minutes, he pulled the camera away from his face. 'Break!'

The girls unfroze from their poses and the photographer strutted over to Aimee and Tim. He looked down at the screen on his camera and toggled through a slideshow of images with his thumb. Brooke's straw-fringed shoes slapped over the cement to join them.

The photographer sighed. 'I think I've got all the shots I can take with the guy.' He nodded at Tim. 'The blue shorts just look out of place when everyone else is in all white.'

'Yeah . . . I didn't know what this was for.' Tim scratched his head and half-heartedly provided an excuse.

Brooke interjected. 'We can just shoot him from the waist up.'

The photographer showed her the screen on the camera and flicked through the gallery. 'Already have. This afternoon light is precious and I'd rather just get the shots with the girls while we can.'

Heath walked up behind them and heard the end of the conversation. 'Even without the shorts, it's weird with just one guy in the shot,' he jumped in. 'Especially if Rich isn't in it.'

Brooke was quick to shoot back. 'Rich won't be appearing much on the show – so it's not really relevant to have him in the photos.'

'Well neither is Tim, so it probably makes sense for none of the guys to be in it,' Heath said. 'We've taken some waist-up shots with Tim. Sounds like we got all we need with him. I'll get the girls back while the light's still good.' He clapped his hands three times and the crew scrambled. As he turned to walk away, he glanced over at Aimee and they locked eyes for a second. She gave a little nod to say thanks.

Tim exhaled and unbuttoned his shirt a little. 'I'm gonna run down to the beach before it gets dark.'

Aimee teased him. 'Really? I'm sure we could find someone with white pants who you could swap with.'

'Nope. Surf emergency,' he laughed. It was something silly he and Aimee said to each other when Tim wanted to get down to the beach. 'Catch ya.' He winked and jogged off, throwing a hand up in the air to wave at Bree, who was getting her make-up re-touched at a nearby tent.

There was a pang in Aimee's chest as she watched him run into the glare – getting smaller and fuzzier until he was out of sight. It was only when she took a deep breath that she realised how tense she'd been during the whole interaction. Her mind had been flooded by a swirl of nostalgia. Nostalgia was seductive and cruel. It put a sunny haze over memories and made them seem cosier than they were. Blemishes were blurred and the details flaked by age. Were you truly happy in that memory? Was it as romantic as it appeared years later? And did you only yearn for it once life got harder and you wanted to escape back to a time when your new problems didn't exist? The sudden stress of all her worlds colliding at the photoshoot also hadn't helped. It was that latter concern that made Aimee feel slightly relieved to see Tim eject himself from the situation. Still, she couldn't help but wonder when she'd be standing that close to him again. The soapy smell of the Dove bar disappeared in the blustery sea breeze. Tim's quick escape also meant Aimee was left standing alone at the base of the lighthouse with Brooke, who was lingering nearby.

'Nice dress,' Aimee said.

'Thanks, it's cottagecore,' Brooke snipped.

Aimee nodded. 'Thought so.' She looked around. One of the TV cameramen and a sound guy had hung back and were trying to shoot the conversation without looking too obvious about it. They failed. 'Hey . . . So, I'm not sure what you heard yesterday—'

'You called me a C-word,' Brooke snipped.

Aimee glanced at the camera over Brooke's shoulder. 'No.' Her voice went high as she squinted and cocked her head, trying to negotiate this bizarre turn. 'No, not *the* C-word.'

'Aimee, I heard it with my own two ears and we caught it on camera – you called me a C-word.'

'No . . . no, see – when you say that I called you a C-word, it makes it sound like I called you *the* C-word.'

'Aimee, all I know is you called me a C-word. And all the best reality shows have a C-word scandal each year. So, you've just given *The Brats of Byron Bay* its *own* C-word scandal.'

Aimee tried hard to not get tangled up in whatever psychotic mind game Brooke was trying to play. She closed her eyes and grabbed her face for a second as she searched for the right words. 'My friend Rob and I were hyped up on Advent calendar chocolate and talking rubbish. We were being silly. Childish. It was all just . . . stupid. I'm sorry.'

Brooke went silent and took a sip from her really big Starbucks cup that a producer had returned to her grip.

'And I'd love to stock your tutus in the store. You know . . . if you'd still be keen to. I think they're beautiful.'

Brooke tapped the French-tipped nail of her right forefinger on the plastic lid of the cup. 'Well. That's very kind of you, Aimee. I'll have a courier deliver them tomorrow. I'd do it myself but I'm very busy excavating my lake.' She took a sip and turned south to look at the ocean rolling in along Tallow Beach.

'Great. I know exactly where I'll put them.' Aimee reached into the pocket of her linen pants. 'Also, this is silly. But . . . there are these toys called fidgets. We sell them at the store. There was this one in the shape of a peacock. I thought of you.'

Brooke turned to look. 'What do you do with it?'

'You press the buttons in and out.'

'That's it?'

'Yeah,' Aimee said in a flat tone. 'They're big online. Kids go nuts for them. Anyway.' She held it out and the purple silicone looked like grape bubblegum against the grey cement.

Brooke's tanned, manicured hand took hold. Aimee turned to walk away.

'I'll see you at the Christmas party,' Brooke said.

Aimee stopped.

'We're having a Christmas party at the farm. For the TV show, obviously. But you and your friend should come.'

Aimee smiled and nodded.

'Turn around,' Brooke instructed, walking closer to fiddle with the back of Aimee's shirt. 'You don't need this.' She released the mound of fabric from the bulldog clip.

Aimee spun back to face her, just as the wind picked up.

Brooke squinted and assessed again. 'Actually, you do. It's . . . *billowy.*'

TWENTY-FIVE

A relentless honk blared around Aimee's bedroom. *Gasp.* She shot upright. The sun was pouring in. Her hand fumbled around on the bedside table before it eventually landed on the phone. She picked it up and squinted at the screen. Just after nine. She must've forgotten to set an alarm. The phone remained in front of her face as she stared while swiping her thumb, waiting for the automatic facial recognition to do its job and unlock. It didn't. Rude. This had started happening every morning – the phone deeming Aimee completely unrecognisable thanks to under-eye bags, sheet crease marks and a deep wrinkle across her forehead that, upon waking, made her face look as if it had been folded in half like a piece of paper. She made a mental note to google prescription retinol. It was a mental note she made every morning. The honking hadn't stopped. In fact, it had gotten worse and become so irritating that it probably brought out more wrinkles. Then the phone started buzzing. Aimee jolted and it fell into a tangle of cream bed sheets. Heath's name appeared on the screen. She considered ignoring it, but now her ringtone – Ace of Base's 'The Sign' – was blaring over the top of the honking and it was all becoming way too much to handle in the morning.

'What?' she answered.

'What's that noise?'

'The sound of summer in paradise.'

'Why would anyone wanna live here?' Heath laughed.

'I've been thinking the same thing. What do you want?'

'Not a morning person?' Heath teased.

'Ugh. I hate people who ask that. Nobody's truly a morning person. It all depends on what you consider "morning" to be. People who ask that question usually get up at 5am – and then pose the question to people who've just woken up at a normal time. No one wants to be chipper as soon as they've woken up! How would 5am-ers feel if someone who gets up at 4am ran into their bedroom and started asking condescending questions the very second they opened their eyes? They'd be annoyed. Which, by their standards, would technically make them not a morning person.'

There was silence on the other end of the line.

'Hello?' Aimee asked.

'Oh, you're done. Sorry, I put the phone down while you were ranting. Anyway, I didn't get an answer to my question. So you're not a morning person?'

Aimee flopped on the bed and crawled under the covers to escape the honking. 'What do you want?'

'A friend can't call another friend to chat? Shoot the breeze? Chew the fat? Confabulate?'

'We're not friends. I'm hanging up now.'

'Alright,' Heath gave in. 'I'm just calling to coordinate some schedules. Brooke's sending a shipment of tutus to your store today and the team wanna be there to film it and do a quick on-camera chat with you about it.'

'Oh, you make it sound so innocent.' Aimee wrapped a pillow around her head to block the noise. 'We both know it's not just gonna be a quick breezy chat.'

Heath laughed. 'Aimee. What'd I tell you about resisting? It just makes it worse. You're on the show, a misunderstanding happened between you and Brooke. Just explain your side. Simple. Don't make it harder than it needs to be.'

'Fine,' Aimee muttered as she got up to walk out to the living room. Her hair was sticking out at weird angles and her eyes still hadn't quite adjusted to the daylight. 'I'm already going to be getting tortured at the store today anyway – the real estate agency is sending a guy to bolt one of those really big FOR SALE signs to the roof. Bring on the tutus and the cameras! Hey, isn't this the job of a junior producer to be calling the cast about minor scheduling issues?'

'Well, there was something else I was gonna warn you about . . .'

Aimee walked into the kitchen and screamed.

'Annnd I think you just found it . . .'

Standing naked at her kitchen sink was one of the @ThoseTwoVanGuys. Or, more accurately, @OneNakedVanGuy. He had the body of a twenty-something who worked out hard but partied harder. Muscly-ish, but could use a two-week detox. Glazed in sweat. There were tattoos on body parts Aimee wished she'd never seen. He grabbed a tea towel and half-tried to cover himself, unfussed.

'Heath,' Aimee said sternly into the phone, making another mental note to burn the tea towel later.

'Have fun!' He swiftly hung up.

Aimee looked around the apartment in frustration and noticed they weren't alone. Of course. There was a camera crew.

'Sorry, Freya's mum,' the smiling van guy said.

Aimee closed her eyes and backed up against the fridge as something dawned on her. 'Please, oh god, tell me you and Freya didn't . . .'

The bathroom door swung open.

'Oh, shit,' a naked Charlie exclaimed. He reached back to grab a towel and wrapped it around himself before walking out into the kitchen.

Aimee squinted and waved her finger back and forth between the boys. 'You two?'

Charlie smiled. 'Us twoooo?' he repeated, playfully making his friend work for an explanation.

'Wait.' Aimee turned to the naked van guy. 'Aren't you with . . .?'

'Luna, yeah,' he finished the sentence. 'I'm Bodhi – from dinner the other night. @GourmetChikoRoll, remember?'

'Yeah. Yeah.' Aimee scratched her head, trying to restrain her annoyance. 'It's all coming back . . . so *vividly*.' Her tone changed as she had a sudden realisation. 'Wait, so you and Luna are?'

'Oh, we're open.' Bodhi nodded enthusiastically. 'Open relationship.'

'Right, right. I remember. She told me all about it.' Aimee looked around at the cameras.

'Yeah, kinda like your situation with your husband,' Bodhi added.

'Well . . . it's a little different.' Aimee cocked her head and furrowed her brow again. 'Wait. And . . . you're . . .' She pointed at Charlie then back to Bodhi.

'Bi.' Bodhi nodded enthusiastically again.

'Wonderful . . . look at all the fun you get to have.' Aimee tried to breezily conclude the awkward chat. She looked over at Charlie, who was grinning at his friend's discomfort. It was only then she realised the honking hadn't stopped. 'What the fuck is that fucking noise?' She screwed up her face and shuffled to the big wall of windows that looked out over the street.

Her red Monaro was parked below. Freya was hanging out the driver's window and upped the honking at the sight of her aunt. Then she reached inside and flicked the dial on the stereo. Def Leppard's 'Pour Some Sugar on Me' blasted out. The volume got louder.

Aimee cracked a smile. 'I hate you!'

'It's all fixed, rev head!' Freya started doing the Marcia Brady thumb dance.

'I really hate you!' Aimee laughed.

'Not a morning person, huh?' Freya teased.

'I have a naked van guy in my kitchen!'

'I know.' Freya scrunched up her nose. 'You thought I hooked up with him, didn't you?'

Aimee raised her brow and nodded, her face awash with a weird mix of disgust and relief.

———

Not enough time had passed for Aimee's folded forehead crease to go away. The questions weren't helping.

'How do you feel about spending Christmas with your fiancé and the girl he's dating?' a junior-looking producer asked.

Aimee used her thumb to click up the blade of her Stanley knife and sliced open the top of a stock box resting on the store counter. The sudden release of the cardboard flaps unleashed a mass of pink tulle that sprung out like a really flamboyant jack in the box. She ignored the camera that was focused on her face – and the rest of the crew that crowded around it. *Don't resist – it just makes it worse.* Heath's words were in her head. 'Well, we're not seeing each other over Christmas. That's the point.' Aimee tried to smile while unpacking Brooke's tutu delivery. There were different shades of pinks and purples and peaches. Sequins and sparkles. Aimee carefully pulled the outfits out and held them up to admire.

'But you're both now involved with the show, how does it make you feel? Knowing they're together? It must be hard . . .' the producer probed, attempting to sound like a sympathetic gal pal.

Aimee clipped one of the tutus to a coat hanger. 'Fine.' She shrugged.

The producer winced. 'Remember,' she whispered before a high-pitched drilling noise ripped through the entire store and everyone flinched. 'Remember!' she yelled over it. 'State the question *in* your answer! When you answer the questions in these interviews, just pretend like you're explaining it to me like I'm an idiot!'

Pretend you're an idiot? Aimee thought sarcastically. She exhaled. 'I feel fine about both Tim and I being on the show—'

'Wait till the drilling's—'

The whirling cut to a halt.

'OK, say it again,' the producer instructed.

Aimee tried hard not to look annoyed. She saw the FOR SALE sign being dragged up onto the roof when she first arrived at the store for the day and it was about three times the size of what she'd thought it'd be. It even featured annoying 3D animations of what the new space and additional apartments could look like. FOR SAAAAALE the red block letters screamed, basically advertising Aimee's failure. 'I feel fine about both Tim and I being on the show,' Aimee said, looking at the producer, who nodded with wide eyes and enthusiastically signalled for her to keep talking. 'It's not what we planned but . . . he's my fiancé, not my *mortal enemy*.' She scoffed a little. 'And we're on a mini break, so he's allowed to see Bree, who's lovely.' It was true. Bree *was* lovely. It made her even more annoying. If she was awful, then Aimee wouldn't have to be polite and everyone would understand why she didn't like her. But Bree wasn't awful. She was nice. And not even in a fake way. She was warm and easygoing and respectful of the time-out situation. If Aimee let slip one bad word, then *she'd* look like the crazy one. To everyone else, hating Bree would be like hating Reese Witherspoon. It just wouldn't make sense. Even if Reese was fucking your fiancé.

'Didn't she give you one of her necklaces?' The producer flicked her eyes to Aimee's neck. 'How come you're not wearing it?'

Aimee looked like she'd just been spritzed in the face with vinegar. 'Ah . . . well . . . I . . . went for a swim this morning.' She nodded, composing her reaction. 'I went for a swim. Didn't wanna lose it. It's very special.'

The producer dug more. 'You guys were super close yesterday at the photoshoot. You, Tim and Bree. Your bodies were touching. What did you feel when that was happening?'

'It was nice being next to Tim at the lighthouse photoshoot.' Aimee made a conscious effort not to cringe at herself for having to repeat the lame questions in her answers. 'It's the closest we've been – physically – since before the time-out.' Aimee didn't mention the thing about Tim smelling like the Dove soap bar.

'Describe what it was like being sandwiched between Tim and Bree. Do you like Bree?'

'Bree understands the situation we're in and . . . we all get on really well.'

The store phone started to ring. Aimee jumped at the opportunity to get out of the punishing interview and answered it before it could ring a second time. 'Ah, yes. That was me – calling about the refurbished iPhone.' She leant over to click at her laptop and a website for a business called GoodAzNew appeared on the screen in shockingly bright red font. It was one of those tech stores that refurbished old government computers and iPhones and sold them for cheap. 'So . . . it's less than two years old and no scratches? And it . . . works? Sorry, I know that's stupid to ask. But, it's a gift for a twenty-one-year-old. So . . . It's got everything on it that a twenty-one-year-old would want?' Aimee looked out the side of her eye at the camera and turned to face the wall. 'Great. I'll pick it up myself.' She hung up, satisfied with her find. Slightly happier than how she woke up. Until . . .

'So you were saying you all get on really well. You, Tim and Bree,' the producer commented.

'Um.' Aimee paused.

The drilling on the roof began again. Aimee tried not to smile at the interruption. 'We should probably just wait a minute till he's done.' She pointed up to the ceiling before turning away and picking up her phone, opening a text to Freya.

Hey kiddo, don't wanna be a nag but

Backspace, backspace, backspace.

Hey hey, was just worried last night when I didn't hear you come home and

Backspace, backspace, backspace.

Oh hi! I meant to ask earlier . . . are you gonna be out again tonight? I haven't seen you at home lately! xx

Aimee sent the message and then kept fake-tapping on her screen, to avoid returning to the TV crew. The three grey dots appeared under her text to Freya and then a reply whooshed in.

Heyyy I thiiink I'll be out with some people at a thing but I'm not sure yet sry . . . I'll txt if I know!

'So you and Tim and Bree are all getting on well?' The producer pushed the question again, the moment the drilling stopped.

'That is . . . what I said.' Aimee spun around and nodded. 'Tim and I messaged after the photoshoot yesterday. We agreed we're both involved in some parts of this show and sometimes we're going to run into each other. It's no big deal. We all *get on well.*'

'Except for you and Brooke,' the producer added, trying to edge Aimee into saying something negative.

'Me and Brooke get on fine,' Aimee tried to dodge the drama. 'That's why she sent these tutus.'

'Why'd you call her a C-word?'

Aimee stuttered for a second. 'I didn't call her a *C-word.*' Ugh. Aimee had been replaying that moment over and over in her head since it happened. Brooke's face as she stood in the doorway – she looked truly hurt. Surely she wasn't just hamming it up for the cameras. Aimee hadn't slept since. It's probably why she forgot to set an alarm for that morning to go for an early swim. She'd been distracted by it – combing through the scene, second by second. Trying to remember the volume at which her and Rob were talking – and imagining if it could realistically be heard from the store entrance. She already knew Brooke heard part of it. But all of it? And how much did the cameras film? She'd never admit this but, after Brooke left that day, Aimee waited until the shop was empty and then she recorded herself on her phone – vaguely repeating what she could remember of the incriminating conversation – and then let it play out on the counter while she stood in the doorway to see if it could be heard. The answer?

'You called Brooke a C-word. When she came to the store the other day, she walked in, you called her a C-word, and she left really upset.'

Aimee closed her eyes and shook her head quickly. 'You weren't even here.' She gestured at the plain-Jane producer girl who looked just like every other person in the crew.

'We've got it on tape. The cameras were with Brooke when she walked in on you, here at the store. You said something about her husband making all her money and then you called her a C-word.'

'Would you stop saying that?'

'Aimee, we've all watched the footage several times and we can hear pretty clearly that you called Brooke a C-word.'

Aimee was starting to get frustrated. 'I know what you're doing,' she snapped. 'You're trying to make it sound like I called Brooke *the* C-word and that's simply not true. I didn't call Brooke the C-word. Jesus. If I *really* thought Brooke was a C-word then I'd just come out and say *I think Brooke is a C-word.*' Then her face dropped. 'No!' She waved a finger at the camera and looked directly in the lens. 'Don't you dare use that.'

The producer furrowed her brow in faux-confusion. 'Aimee, we're just asking you simple questions.'

'Oh, that's not *all* you're doing.' Aimee rolled her eyes. 'I know how this stuff works.' She squeezed out from behind the counter and walked across the shop to hang the tutus. 'I know it's all edited to make people look bad. And . . . You're gonna edit that last bit to make it sound like I said *I think Brooke is a C-word.*' She winced and scrunched her hands into fists around the tutu. 'Dammit! I did it again! And this time I said it angrily! This is such a trap.'

The producer stayed behind the cameraman and the soundie, who'd turned to follow Aimee. 'Aimee, no one's trying to trap you. I just thought you'd like right of reply – to give some context on why you called Brooke a C-word.'

Aimee's attention had shifted from the brazen entrapment to something outside the shop's door. She was staring across the road. The camera lens popped over her shoulder to catch a glimpse. A new sign was being attached to the front of Tim's surf store.

HARLEY, HAWK & CO had been scorched onto a big piece of timber in black old-timey saloon-style font.

'You didn't seem to like the new name of the bar when Tim and Bree told you about it over dinner. Can you tell me why you hate it?' the producer asked softly.

'I didn't say I hate it.'

The plain Jane producer girl started talking in her gal pal voice again. 'Are you feeling a little bit like your fiancé has replaced you with Bree? My boss Nina said she saw you down at the beach and you were stalking Bree's Insta. What made you do that?'

Aimee inhaled. 'Alright, I think you've got enough for today.'

'But we've still—'

'You've got enough for today.' Aimee widened her eyes.

The plain Jane producer scrunched up her nose and gave a fake smile. 'Alrighty, I think we've got everything for today,' she told Aimee before instructing her crew to ship out. 'Guys, let's get outta here and give the office a call. They might need us down at the beach.' She clipped some papers to her clipboard. 'Aimee you did so well today! You're my favourite to work with. I tell everyone!'

'Oh, you're my favourite too,' Aimee replied, equally insincere.

A few moments later, they were all gone. Aimee walked towards the back of the store and leant on the counter. She took a deep breath in and blew it out through her mouth.

'You've got a fiancé?' a voice came from behind.

The Irish accent gave him away. Aimee whipped around to see Jules standing at the back screen door.

The drilling screeched again.

TWENTY-SIX

The front doors of the Monaro were wide open. The paper floor mats were still on the floor after Freya picked it up from the mechanic and they crinkled under Aimee and Jules' feet as they sat staring at the back wall of the bookstore in the carpark. Aimee switched on the ignition to fire up the air-con. The engine coughed, rattled and settled to an idle, just as the Def Leppard tape in the cassette player started playing automatically.

'So you're a TV star?' Jules said.

Aimee dropped her head on the wheel and let out an 'ugh' sound.

Jules laughed at Aimee's irritation. 'It's kinda funny, considering you talk so much about hating celebrities and how they've changed the town.'

'It's what I just told you. A TV show's in town . . . my niece got roped in, then *I* got roped in. And I hate it and it sucks but it is what it is.'

'You've explained the TV show more than you've explained the fact you have a fiancé.'

'We're on a time-out and . . . I got roped in and it sucks but it is what it is?' Aimee cringed, repeating her previous answer while scrunching up her face.

'Does he know you and I have been hanging out?'

'No. But he's hanging out with other people too. That's the deal.'

'Well . . . if you know *he's* hanging out with people, why doesn't he know *you're* hanging out with people?'

'Because . . .' She turned the volume down a little. 'I kinda just . . . *forgot.*' She clasped her face in her hands.

'You forgot you had a fiancé?' Jules ribbed her a little.

'No, no – that sounds ridiculous. I just . . . I guess, in the moment, I was so overwhelmed with the idea of hanging around a guy who wasn't my fiancé and worried about how to do that . . . that I just . . . kinda . . . *forgot I had a fiancé.*' She gave up explaining and collapsed on the steering wheel. She couldn't even remember if the thought of Tim had crossed her mind during the times she'd spent with Jules. It seemed impossible. She felt like she'd been thinking of Tim obsessively since the time-out had started. Maybe it was more like when you forget someone's birthday – you know it's there, you know it's coming up, but then other things happen and all of a sudden you've missed it. Jules had become the *other thing.*

He laughed, sort of. 'Ouch.' He sucked in some air. 'Should I feel sorry for him?'

'I know. It must seem like I was *lying* or keeping a secret. I hope you don't think I was trying to *trick* you or something.' Aimee fiddled with the air-con vents, which seemed to just be blowing out hot steam. Did she even need to explain all this to Jules? They'd only technically been out on one date. Maybe this was why she'd been so hesitant to lock in a second – so she didn't have to have the very conversation she was having right now.

Jules looked around the car, placed a hand on the side of her neck and looked into her eyes. 'Aimee. I'm hurt and disgusted. You're a terrible person. And if you ever want me to forgive you, I demand you ditch work right now and take me for a spin in your eighties teen boy car.' A smile crept across his face.

Aimee knew she should stay at the store. She looked at Jules' steely blue eyes and his half-smile. Then she glanced at the old-school clock on the dash. Just after midday.

Jules raised an eyebrow. 'Ditch work or I'll go tell that mean little producer that you called Brooke a C-word.'

Aimee laughed and rolled her eyes. Mid-roll, she sensed him lean forward across the centre console. Then his lips were on hers. She froze. After years of kissing the same man, the simple act suddenly felt so different in a way she'd never expected. He bit her bottom lip and sucked it just a little. Had Tim ever done that? She liked it. Her ears pricked at the little breaths and noises she was making involuntarily. Did she ever make them when Tim kissed her? Kissing Jules was like diving into crystal blue water without testing it with your toes first. It looks incredible but your body still seizes up as you jump off the rocks, preparing just in case for it to be freezing. *Splash!* Then? Every muscle relaxing. The water even warmer than you hoped it would be.

A few seconds later, his jeans scratched against the vinyl passenger seat as he shifted his body weight back down.

Aimee sat still for a moment. Then she glanced up at Jules. The car jolted slightly as she pulled the gear stick into reverse.

———

The Monaro roared down Bangalow Road, heading towards the hinterland. The Def Leppard tape was still playing out of the tinny old speakers.

Jules pointed ahead. 'Just keep following this road.'

'You know, it's a lot easier to drive somewhere if you just tell me where I'm going,' she teased.

'Ah, a back-seat driver.' He smiled and placed an elbow on the ledge of the open window.

'You're not a back-seat driver if you're the one *actually* driving.'

'It's a surprise. I wanna show you somewhere.'

'I've lived here my entire life. There's nowhere that could surprise me.'

'OK, TV star.'

Aimee laughed. The breeze was blowing in and she pushed her hair out of her face. One of the paddocks they were driving past had just been mowed and the smell of fresh-cut grass drifted through the car.

'Can I ask what happens after this time-out?' Jules asked.

It took Aimee a second to get comfortable with the sudden change of topic. 'Um . . . We decide if we wanna go through with the wedding.' She shrugged, breaking her eyes away from the road to give Jules a quick glance. He looked good in her car. And she liked the way she looked in the mirrored lenses of his aviator sunnies.

'If one of you doesn't wanna get married, will you break up?'

'Well, we *are* getting back together after the time-out.' Aimee heard herself. It felt like the wrong answer on so many levels. The truth was, she didn't want to get married. She knew that deep down. Did that mean Tim would want to split for good? This is the point in the anxiety spiral where Aimee always felt like taking a really long nap.

'Then what's the point of the time-out if breaking up isn't an option?'

'To decide what we want. Tim's the one who wants to get married. I've never really been big on marriage.'

'Kids?'

Aimee exhaled. 'Um . . . we've talked about it over the years. I thought neither of us were really fussed about it. Or . . . it's never really been something I felt I absolutely needed to do. But over the last year or two, Tim's started to want it. Or to think about it. I guess? Marriage and kids.'

'And you definitely don't want it?'

'We've been together so long . . . to me it just felt like it didn't mean anything if we got married or not.'

'So if it doesn't matter, why not just do it?'

Aimee laughed. 'I don't just wanna do it for the sake of doing it. I feel like I should . . . *want* it. I should *really* want to do it. The same with a kid.'

The spangly opening riff to 'Hysteria' began to play and Joe Elliott sang the opening lines.

Jules went to talk, then hesitated. Aimee glanced over. He went ahead and said his initial thought. 'If you're really honest with yourself, do you see you two staying together at the end of this break?'

Aimee pursed her lips and stared at the mountains in the distance. The greens and blues in the summer around Byron almost looked like a cartoon. She hadn't let herself truly consider the harsh reality of what might happen at the end of the time-out. She just kept assuming things would go back to how they were and they'd continue on with their life: Tim occasionally bringing up the topic of marriage and kids and Aimee snaking out of giving a definitive answer. Jules reached over and grabbed her thigh. His hand was big and callused and made Aimee feel delightfully tiny.

The chorus was building up over the stereo and Aimee's mind started to wander. It was lazy afternoons like this when she used to drive around with Fleur listening to the eighties glam rock song on repeat.

'OK, you've asked all about me and I've told you way too much,' she said. 'Now I get to ask about you.'

Jules straightened up in his seat. 'What do you want to know?' He smiled innocently.

'Well.' She thought. 'Who *are* you?'

'You're a terrible interviewer,' he teased.

She slapped his chest with a laugh.

'I'm a free spirit,' he mocked. 'The transient way of life is what brought me to Byron. I felt it in my soul. And I think Byron feels the same way about me. I don't know if you know this, but, the town has a way of telling you when it's time to go.' He smiled at his own joke.

Aimee rolled her eyes and played along. 'Oh yeah, so it's the town's *energy* that attracted you, right?'

'Correct. Yes. Well, that and TV stars like yourself.' He waited a second and then finally gave a serious answer. 'I was born in Ireland but I haven't lived there for a while. Annnd . . . I got a job here for summer.'

'Well, I know *that* part! Where do you usually live?'

'Hmmm . . . lots of places. Mostly the US in recent years. I go every-where. Depends on the work, you know?' His hand was still on Aimee's thigh and he tapped it along to the rhythm of the music. 'Are you happy together?'

A moment passed and Aimee realised she had forgotten to breathe. Was she happy with Tim? That was another thing she hadn't really thought about. She didn't feel happy most of the time but that wasn't necessarily related to being with Tim. She didn't believe anyone was truly happy. The afternoon sun flicked through the passing trees and lit up Jules' face. She looked over and watched him – at ease and comfortable, even during an awkward conversation about relationship troubles. He raised his chin and smirked. Then his expression changed completely.

'Aimee!'

An old white Toyota HiAce van covered in spray paint graffiti rolled through a stop sign at an intersection, swerved in front of the Monaro and slammed on its brakes. Aimee screamed. In a nanosecond, Jules lunged over, glanced up at the oncoming lane, used the palm of one hand to spin the steering wheel away from his body until it locked, and ripped up the handbrake with his other hand. The Holden spun a full 180 degrees and parked – almost perfectly – in the oncoming lane. Aimee's hands were frozen in the air. It happened so fast she couldn't even remember if there was a screech or a bang. She felt something drip down her chin and raised a hand to touch it. It felt wet. Then she looked at her hand and saw a little bit of blood. The van had disappeared, heading west towards Nimbin – the weed capital of Australia. The person driving the van was probably already stoned. In the Monaro, Jules was still leaning over the centre console with a hand on the wheel. His smoky cologne mixed with the smell of burnt rubber.

Aimee looked in the side mirror. No traffic coming up behind them. She snatched off her seatbelt, opened the door and staggered to the front of the car, placing two hands on the hood. She tried to catch her breath. The motor was still running and the metal vibrated under her hands. She became hyper aware of every nerve in her body. Through the open windows, the finals bars of 'Hysteria' faded out.

TWENTY-SEVEN

Aimee was seated on the end of a bed in a caravan. She was still in shock after the near-accident and Jules had driven the rest of the way. She didn't ask questions when he pulled off the road and followed a dirt track onto a property and down near a field, where the van was parked under a tree. From the black T-shirts and jeans spilling out of the open suitcase on the floor, she'd assumed he was living there. He was crouched on the floor, at her feet, holding her hands. She'd just finished telling him about her family.

He broke the silence. 'Now I feel bad about making fun of your sister's car.'

Aimee laughed through a sob and flicked her eyes up at the tin-panelled ceiling. She tossed her hair and looked out the trailer door to a lush green field that swooped down to an old fig tree. Sunlight flashed through the open door and the slits of the metal venetian blinds on the windows.

Jules locked his fingers in between Aimee's.

'That really sucks, Aimee.' He looked at the side of her face as she focused on the fig tree. The graze on her chin looked like it was still bleeding a little. 'I'm sorry . . . It sucks so much that I don't even know how else to describe it. It just . . . sucks.'

'That's all I want people to say.' Aimee shook her head and looked down. 'It's one of those things where people try to say too much about it but none of it's quite right and then they just keep talking and saying *more* stuff. Even after eighteen years. Especially with people in town – people who knew my family. The only way to describe it is: it sucks.' She looked around the room and sniffed. 'So. You made fun of my car. Can I make fun of your caravan?'

Jules got to his feet. 'You TV stars are *so demanding*.' He walked over to the kitchenette, ran a paper towel under some water from the tap and came back to kneel in front of Aimee. 'Here.' He wrapped the paper around his thumb and dabbed the graze on her chin. His other hand caressed the side of her neck. They looked into each other's eyes. It was that time in the afternoon where everything's quiet and still and the lighting's so perfect you wish you could press pause.

Who was this guy? The question still hadn't really been answered. A part of Aimee didn't even want to know. Don't ask, don't tell. She felt like she'd already told him too much. It was as if the knock to the head in the car accident had sobered her up and she was starting to see part of her life clearly. As far as she knew, he was just a hot guy in town for work. He was a fling. If she found out any more, it would make him real. There'd be investment and feelings she'd have to deal with. She didn't expect anything of him and that's how she wanted it to stay. But there was one feeling she couldn't bat away. She wanted him to like her. It was ridiculous. He was interested. Clearly. That's why he asked for her number and suggested a date and invited himself back to her house. It's why he walked into her store and pretended to have a child he was buying presents for. It's why he fidgeted with her fidget. OK, that sounded unintentionally dirty. Let's rephrase: It's why he fiddled with her fidg—

Ugh, no scratch that.

'You're always thinking,' Jules whispered.

Aimee snapped back to reality.

'I can see it. In your eyes. You're always thinking.'

Aimee tried to laugh off the observation.

He crouched down on his knees and looked up at her sitting on the edge of the bed. 'You gotta stop thinking so much. Gotta let go.'

Aimee wrapped her hands around the back of his head, leant down and kissed him. When she pulled back and opened her eyes, she ran her fingers through the sides of his hair. 'So. You still haven't explained the caravan.'

'Well, a caravan in a rolling field on the outskirts of Byron Bay. It's the dream, eh?'

Aimee looked out the open door. 'Ah, yes. *Very* transient.'

'Lenny Kravitz lives in a trailer in the Bahamas.'

'If it's good enough for Lenny.'

'The production's filming on the Gold Coast – but I wanted to stay out of town, down here. Found this place online.' He shrugged. 'Don't need much. Keep it simple. An Airbnb wouldn't be better than this.'

'And how often do you have to go up to film. *Film*? Is that right?' She covered her face. 'I'm sorry. *Stuntman . . .*' She winced at herself as she gave in and admitted: 'I still don't exactly know what you do.'

'We're both finding out things about each other today.' He smiled. 'So . . . why'd you call that Brooke lady a C-word?'

She slapped his chest. 'God. That *stupid show*. I'm so embarrassed.'

'Why?'

'It's just so ridiculous. I hate that you even know I'm involved. It is not a reflection on me, I swear.'

Jules laughed at how defensive she was being. 'What's it called?'

'The name of the show? I'm not telling you! You'll google it. And *watch clips.*' She cringed like she'd just stubbed her toe. 'Oh god, there are gonna be clips on the internet.'

Her reaction was compounded with the realisation that the videos would appear right up there on internet search pages alongside the Byron Karen articles. What if he found those too? No one in their right mind would fuck Byron Karen. This was even more of a reason to keep Jules as a fling – separate from her disastrous real world. She made a mental note to research how to wipe your digital footprint. 'It's just something I have to do for the next few weeks,' she said of the show. 'And after that, it's finished. Until then, the less I have to talk about it and think about it, the better.'

'I get the feeling you don't wanna talk about it?' he teased.

Desperate to avoid any more questions that would reveal too much about *The Brats of Byron Bay*, she flipped the conversation onto him. 'Tell me about *your* stupid show.'

'I'm not telling you about *my* stupid show,' he mock-protested. 'You didn't tell me about *your* stupid show.'

'OK, well what does a stuntman *do*?'

His voice turned serious and his eyes became moody. 'We're real-life superheroes.'

Aimee groaned.

'OK, serious answer,' he laughed. 'It's just something I got into. Always trained hard and loved cars and bikes. There was a natural skill. Moved to LA and bummed around for a while before a job came up looking for a stand-in for minor stunt work. Then I got addicted to it. Fell in with that crowd and specialised in different skills. It's fun. Hard work. But fun.'

Something clicked in Aimee's mind. 'Is that how you knew what to do with the car? Just before – how you . . . did the *tricky thing* with the steering wheel and . . . all your other action movie moves?' She laughed.

'Yes, that's how I knew to do *the tricky thing with the steering wheel*.' He paused and then flicked his eyes at her. 'You think it's a stupid job, don't you.' He grinned like he'd just caught her out.

'I don't!' Her voice went high-pitched. 'I really don't. I like anyone who works hard at a skill like that. I like people who are good at what they do.' She really did. Aimee didn't have a certain type of guy she was attracted to. The thing she found sexiest about someone was seeing them in their element, doing what they do best. It's why she loved watching Tim surf when they first started dating.

'But . . .' Jules said, 'I bet *my* stupid show is stupider than *your* stupid show.'

Aimee flicked her eyes up at the ceiling and a smile sparked across her face.

'What?'

'Can we make a pact?'

'Does whoever lose have to get naked?'

'It's a *pact*. Not a *bet*.'

'Well the person who breaks the pact can get naked.'

Aimee playfully ignored the flirting and proposed her idea. 'The pact: We don't talk about either of our stupid shows.' It was an easy way to hide the parts of her life she didn't want him to know about. This fling could be something that was just hers. With no one's judgements. A place she could escape her real life.

'Hmmm.' Jules smiled and pretended to think before straightening his back to get close enough to kiss her.

It was as if the car accident had made every inch of Aimee's body feel more alive. The lightest touch of Jules' lips on hers felt like something she'd never experienced before. And with that kiss, the deal was sealed on their own little world away from reality.

When he sat back down, Aimee nodded over to her bag. It was sitting on a green vinyl-covered bench seat where the built-in dining table was. 'I've got some aspirin in my bag.'

While Jules turned to grab it, Aimee looked around the trailer. Lots of stainless steel and laminated surfaces. Some tins of tomatoes and tuna were on the counter. Packets of pasta and rice. A big tub of protein powder. Eggs. Loose papers spread around with locations and times on them. Down the end was a beautiful chest of drawers. Aimee got up and walked over.

Jules was flicking through her bag to find the aspirin. He looked up and saw her at the chest. 'I found that on the side of the road. I thought it looked special.'

Aimee ran her finger along the golden cedar timber top and traced the crack that ran down the length of it. The bronze keyholes on the drawers were tarnished. One of the bottom knobs was missing. 'It's beautiful.'

'Ah. Aimee?'

She turned around.

Jules was sitting on the bed and pulled a box out of her satchel. 'What's a . . .' he squinted at the packaging before sounding out the word emblazoned on it, '*LeVibe*?'

Aimee closed her eyes and smacked her forehead. The vibrator was still in there from when Luna handed them out at the dinner. 'It's just . . .' She walked over to grab it but Jules pulled it away.

He laid back on the bed, stretched out and held the box far away, grinning like a dog who knew he was about to be let inside the house. His black tee had pulled up to show his perfect-but-not-too-perfect ab definition and the scruffy patch of hair between his belly button and belt buckle. Aimee jumped on top of him and straddled his waist, desperately trying to grab the LeVibe.

Jules craned his neck to read the box. 'The LeVibe is a *dual-satisfaction* pleasure device that not only *guarantees* an orgasm but also brings the male into the woman's *mind-blowing* experience.' His Irish accent had come out strong. It was boyish and a cute contrast to the barrel-chested, bulging bicepped man who'd just saved Aimee's car from being totalled. '*DJ your way to an orgasm?* It syncs to your Spotify!'

Aimee swiped at the box with her hand but Jules was too quick. She covered her face. 'It's from one of the girls on the show. She's releasing a line of sex toys and she gave them to us to try out.'

Jules examined the box. 'It hasn't been opened.'

'No, it has not.'

'Aimee. Don't be rude to your friend. You have to try it.' He ripped off the cardboard top and pulled out the vibrator. 'It says it comes already charged *and* there's an app to control it. You know, they make orgasms so convenient these days,' he joked. 'Get my phone.' He scooped his left forearm under Aimee's lower back and swiftly sat up so they were face-to-face. Aimee's legs flung around his back and her hands were linked behind his neck. He kissed her.

'Hey,' he whispered. 'This place. Was it a surprise?'

Aimee smiled and grabbed his ears. 'I'll get your phone.'

TWENTY-EIGHT

Rob's boots banged over the floorboards at the Palace Hotel and annoyed everyone trying to enjoy the Rufus Wainwright cover being performed by the folksy band onstage.

'I have news,' she declared, hopping onto a stool at the back table Aimee had snagged. She sipped the margarita that was awaiting her, looked up and saw Aimee's face. 'Ouch, what happened to your chin?' Then she let out a gasp. Everyone turned to look. 'Did Meredith hit you with her pre-owned Audi?'

It had been a few days since the almost-accident but the chin graze was still hanging around. Aimee covered it with a hand and shushed Rob. 'Your news?'

'Well, it's not really *my* news. It's just . . . *the* news.' She unlocked her phone and pulled up a website. 'I was cutting someone's hair at the salon and I looked down and saw them reading the *Daily Mail*.' She got distracted looking at the homepage. 'Oh my god. They've got a story saying Shelley Craft is selling another house she's renovated in town. Can we go to the inspection? I want you to take a photo of me in her bed.' She crossed her arms, closed her eyes, and leant back in her chair as if she'd been put to rest in a crypt.

Aimee raised her eyebrows, waiting for her friend to get to the point. Rob exhumed herself and flicked her thumbs over the screen . . . then paused. She looked up and squinted at Aimee. 'How many drinks have you had?'

'One . . .'

Rob pushed her margarita across the table. 'Here. Drink mine really fast before you read this.'

Aimee grabbed the phone out of her friend's hand. The big splashy story at the top of the *Daily Mail* homepage was filled with a collage of photos and an unnecessarily long headline that screamed:

Controversial Byron Bay reality star SHOCKS in risqué bikini while HUMPING embattled footy champ on family beach as CHILDREN WATCH – and angry locals who called for the show to be CANCELLED are left FUMING . . . SEE THE PHOTOS! (Warning: Graphic)

With all the photos and the capitalisation of random words, it took a moment for Aimee to take it all in. The biggest picture in the middle showed a girl in a racy pink bikini straddling a guy in boardshorts on Main Beach. Then Aimee saw the little photos around it. Her eyes zoned in on one of her and Freya walking along the beach just days earlier, when they got stalked by that paparazzi photographer. Then she realised the rest of the photos were just Freya. Aimee dropped the phone on the table.

The microphone screeched and the grating voice of Bada Bing blared over the speakers. 'Guess Who, Don't Sue: Which newly-minted reality TV star is secretly dating a hunky celebrity?'

Rob grimaced. 'Ew. Bada Bing just said the word "hunky".'

Aimee didn't bother getting up from the table to argue. She just yelled out from the back of the room. 'Old news, Bada Bing!' She held up Rob's phone with the story still lit up on the screen. 'Ya got scooped!'

The Byron Bay Power Players were sitting at a table down the front, near the stage, and led the booing.

'That ain't the full story, Byron Karen,' Bada Bing shot back. Then he joined in the booing.

Aimee called out over the noise. 'Also, you shouldn't say the word "hunky"! It's weird!'

Rob sat back and assessed her friend. 'What's wrong with you? You'd usually have marched up on stage by now and had hot chips thrown at you.'

'I'm not letting the town Looney Tunes wind me up.' She took a sip from Rob's margarita.

'Wow. You've changed. I kinda hate it. And does this mean you don't care about the Freya photos?'

'Are they that bad?' She picked up the phone again and clicked on the story. 'Oh my god.'

'You just saw the GIF of them humping, didn't you?'

'I'm horrified.' She zoomed in. 'Who is this . . . *guy*?'

'Some football player who cheated on his pregnant wife and then got kicked off his team after failing a drug test.'

Aimee's eyes clocked something across the room. 'Oh no.'

'I know. He's not even that cute. If you're gonna date a philandering junkie, at least choose a cute one.'

Aimee shook her head. 'No. Over at the stairs.'

Rob turned around. Brooke was standing at the top of the platform, wearing three-quarter tailored black trousers, a white silk top and a black blazer caped over her shoulders. She was also clutching a glass of red wine with one of her talons.

'Ugh,' Rob said. 'I hate people who cape their blazers over their shoulders. It's like they're saying they're too good for sleeves.'

Brooke locked eyes on them. Then her stilettos started clicking over the hardwood floors. The booing had faded and some young guy in high-waisted wool trousers and a white singlet was playing an accordion. 'Ladies!' Brooke sang as she approached the table before perching her silver Miu Miu handbag on a spare stool. She rested an elbow on the round bar table and immediately recoiled when she realised it was wet. 'Freya said this is where you'd be tonight . . . so, I thought I'd join.' Her voice went up at the end like her appearance was a surprise to be cherished.

'It's Christmas Eve,' Aimee said. 'I thought you'd be busy preparing for the party tomorrow.'

Brooke sighed. 'The team's been working on it all week. I just needed to . . . *get out*.' She pressed her fingers on the sides of her head.

Rob sat back and enjoyed the awkwardness for a second before raising a hand to introduce herself. 'I'm—'

'Rob,' Brooke cut her off. 'I know.' She looked at Aimee and squinted. 'What happened to your chin?'

Rob interjected. 'She got hit by a clairvoyant in an Audi.'

'I . . . tripped . . . while unpacking stock.'

The accordion wailed around the pub.

Brooke looked at the table and saw the humping GIF still playing on Aimee's phone. She tapped the glass screen with her French-tipped fingernail. 'Ah. Now *that's* great media coverage.'

Rob jumped off her stool. 'We need drinks. I think Aimee's about to have a conniption.'

Aimee looked at the GIF again and exhaled.

'He's a great guy.' Brooke took a seat, not quite comprehending Aimee's concern. 'Just another failed footballer. But . . . nice enough. Big on the social scene.'

'You've met him?'

'Well, he *is* her boyfriend.'

Aimee dismissed her with a shake of the head. 'She's been in town a few weeks. This guy is not a boyfriend.'

'Well, he came with her from Sydney.' A moment passed before Brooke cocked her head and smirked. 'Didn't you know Freya had a boyfriend?' There was way too much delight in her tone.

Aimee muttered half-formed words and tried to hide her surprise by taking a fake sip from the empty margarita glass that was still on the table.

Rob returned with shots. Aimee grabbed one and downed it.

———

Forty minutes later

Charlie's band was on stage, playing a cover of the Madonna song 'Beautiful Stranger'. Empty glasses crowded the table. Brooke raised her arms above her head and writhed to the music while Aimee got progressively more irritated about Freya's secret boyfriend with each drink. And Rob? She'd stolen Brooke's blazer and was wearing it caped over her own shoulders.

There was something else on Aimee's mind. 'I'm sorry again about . . . *you know*.' She looked at Brooke.

'About what?' Brooke laughed.

'About me calling you a cooter-weasel,' Rob blurted. 'I'm sorry, too.'

'Ugh, forget about it!' Brooke shrieked. 'It's perfect for the show. The C-word scandal can be arced over a whole episode – maybe even a week. The shot of me walking into the store and hearing it would be a great cliffhanger. *Definitely* one for the promo.'

Aimee resisted the urge to pounce on Brooke's determined use of the phrase 'C-word scandal'. 'But, I just want you to know I don't, *we* don't think those things about you.' She looked in Brooke's eyes with a sincere nod.

'Aimee, really. It's fine.' Brooke picked up her phone to swipe away some notifications that had lit up the screen. 'First impressions mean nothing. When I met you I thought you were a pissed off little wet cat.' She put the phone down and there was silence for a moment as Aimee's brow furrowed slightly and Rob tried not to spit out her drink. 'Oh, I don't think that *anymore*,' Brooke added. 'That's my point! . . . But,' her tone became a little less flippant and surprisingly sincere, 'You should really know Rich didn't make our money.'

Aimee and Rob gave each other guilty looks.

'But anyway!' Brooke's tone spiked with frivolity again. 'We have a show to produce. We need the drama. It's the Christmas party tomorrow. Get drunk and call me a cunt, I don't care. Just make sure the cameras are rolling when you do it.'

Aimee didn't quite know how to reply. 'Everything's content,' she sarcastically quoted Luna. As she went to clear away some of the empty margarita glasses, she accidentally knocked over the glass of red wine. Merlot-hued liquid sploshed through the air and down the front of Brooke's white silk shirt. Then the glass smashed on the timber floor. Everyone in the pub turned to look.

Aimee froze. 'I am . . . *so sorry.*'

'Oh, Aimee – relax!' Brooke laughed as she grabbed some napkins out of the silver box dispenser on the table. 'My god! You look like you're terrified I'm about to scratch your eyes out! It's just a shirt I threw on – it's a stain, who cares!' Aimee and Rob shared a split-second glance of relief and surprise.

Brooke slapped her palms on the table. 'Right. I'm exhausted from TV cameras and party planning and conference calling with my business team about optimising the customer experience for our high-profile clients.'

Just when you thought Brooke could finally be relatable, she had to go and say something like that. Aimee was almost in awe of how she made selling tutus sound like a military mission.

Brooke looked around the bar. 'Aimee. You need to have at least *one* hook-up on this time-out.' She pointed down to the Power Players' table. 'What about that guy?'

Aimee grimaced. 'Spider?'

Rob embarked on a brief explanation of Spider for Brooke's benefit while whipping her loose sleeves to the music. 'He's a professional squatter and just one of many locals Aimee has recently become enemies with. He's also missing a thumb.'

Aimee tried to shut it down. 'Music Club is not prime scouting ground for hook-ups. Just ask Rob.'

Rob hung her head and exhaled. 'A few weeks ago, I *may* have hooked up with a weird dad wearing a beige polo.'

Brooke clarified. 'Hooked up, as in: fucked?'

Rob nodded. 'He was gross. More gross than that guy I dated who was obsessed with his camera drone.'

Aimee choked on her drink. 'Ugh, drone guy! Drone guy was the worst.'

'Wherever he went, he'd insist on showing everyone the videos he filmed with his drone,' Rob said.

'So many swooping shots over oceans and forests and suburban streets at sunset,' Aimee wistfully recalled.

'Remember when he kept trying to take Tim on a drone date?' Rob put on a dumb bro voice. '"Dude. Have you ever flown a drone? You *gotta* come one day and fly the drone. It's *all about* the drone."'

Brooke laughed hysterically and sipped her margarita. 'I don't know what that means.'

———

One hour later

Aimee sat at the table alone. She picked up her phone and scrolled through the humping article again. Rob was getting more drinks and Brooke had gone to the bathroom. She felt two arms wrap around her from behind and she knew who it was, even before she saw the braided string wrist bracelets and felt the mop of curly hair rub into the nape of her neck. Charlie.

'Is that porn?' He saw the GIF over Aimee's shoulder.

'Almost.'

He grabbed the phone. 'Whoa! Freya . . .'

'Do I need to say something to her?' Aimee fixed her hair as Charlie sat down. 'I know it's trendy to be all *sex-positive* but what if a future employer sees this?' She banged two fingers on the phone screen.

Charlie laughed and covered his face with his hands.

'I'm serious!' She slapped his chest. 'Am I supposed to stop it? Do I call her dad? When I called him when she first arrived, he was just . . . *barely* interested – said she was doing her own thing for the summer. Do I step in? She's meant to be staying in our apartment but I never see her. I have to stop myself from calling her every night to make sure she's OK.'

Charlie waved it off. 'Sometimes I hear her come in late. And then she leaves early.'

'Over the years I've just always been very cautious about not being *over-bearing* with her. I've never wanted her to think that I'm trying to *mother* her. I'm thirty-six. If Fleur was still alive she'd only be forty. It's only four years difference, but right now it seems like *a lot* more.' She picked up one of the damp cardboard drink coasters with the green and gold VB beer logo on it and tapped the edge on the table.

'She's twenty-one and in Byron for the summer. She's staying out late. Partying. Hanging with people.' Charlie leaned over the table and got in Aimee's face. '*Hooking up*.'

Aimee pushed him away and cringed before something sparked in her mind. 'Question for you: You hook up *a lot*.'

'Thank you.' Charlie smiled.

'Do you ever . . . *catch feelings*?'

Charlie made an 'eh' face and shrugged.

'Never?'

'Depends. Most people are really annoying once you start talking to them.'

'But do you find yourself *wanting* to spend more time with someone you've just started hooking up with?'

'Sure! If all we've been doing is fucking and I haven't found out they're annoying yet.'

Aimee gave up. 'Are you saying @OneNakedVanGuy isn't going to be the man who makes you settle down?' she teased as Charlie started to laugh. 'Because, Charles, I think you're writing him off – I attended that *Brats* dinner with him and he was just a fountain of wisdom. Really – the conversation was electric. Just this pitter-patter of dialogue skipping out of his mouth, like a Truman Capote character.'

'Case in point: Most people are best for simply hooking up with, *not dating*. Now, question for you . . .'

'Lay it on me.'

'Who are you hooking up with?'

Aimee stuttered for a moment.

'I knew it, I knew it.' He poked her.

She whacked his hands away. 'It's just . . . very new. You're the only person I've mentioned it to – and that's only because I'm drunk and I needed advice.'

'I'm at your service.' Charlie sat up straight. 'Wait . . . so you have feelings for him?'

'No, no, that's not what I meant.' Aimee quickly shut that down. Did she mean it? It was probably just the tequila.

'Who's the guy?'

'Just . . . someone. A random guy. Well, not a *random* guy. A guy who came into the store. We started talking and it just kinda happened?'

'Photos!' Charlie demanded.

'No, no photos – I haven't got any and he doesn't use social media.' That was only partly a lie. Jules had said he wasn't online, but Aimee did have one photo – the beach selfie he'd texted her. She found herself staring at it sometimes – clicking it open when she was bored at work or frustrated after searching the real estate listings for the seventh time in an hour.

'Dick pics?'

'Not *everyone* sends dick pics.'

'Well then describe it to me. Paint the picture!'

Aimee shook her head with a chuckle. 'Calm down, it's not like that big one from the show you and Rob are obsessed with. The . . . one that's getting *think pieces* written about it.'

Charlie squinted. 'So it's small?'

'I didn't say it was *small*—'

'Who's bigger: New Guy or Tim?'

Aimee hesitated for a second. 'Ummm . . .' her voice went high.

Charlie made a face. 'Ooh, sorry to hear.'

'I didn't say anything!'

Charlie delighted in getting his friend muddled up. And she eventually gave in.

'It wasn't as big as Tim's,' she whispered.

'Interesting, interesting.' Charlie stroked his chin. 'Who's more buff?'

'Oh, New Guy,' Aimee responded immediately. 'Tim's lean. New Guy is *buff*.'

Charlie slapped the table conclusively. 'Oh, well it all makes sense. This always happens. It's a thing. The big muscle guys have tiny ones while the skinny guys have whoppers. There's memes about it.'

'Only memes? Why not think pieces?' Aimee eye-rolled at the logic.

'Well, that guy in those racy photos with Freya is buff,' Charlie laughed.

'Ew. I don't want to think about that.' Aimee held her hands up. Her spurt of playfulness drooped at the thought of Freya and her headline-making activities.

'I was doing a lot worse things when I was twenty-one.' Charlie tried to downplay it.

'Oh god. Don't tell me that. I can just imagine – and it *terrifies* me.' She reached over and grabbed his scruffy hair. They were both glazed with sweat from drinking in the humidity. 'Just . . . why hasn't she told me about the boyfriend?'

Charlie took a sip of Aimee's drink. He looked up and squinted. 'What happened to your chin?'

Aimee paused. The microphone screeched. A familiar melodic mumble rumbled through the speakers.

Rob appeared on stage, with the blazer still caped over her shoulders. Then . . . Brooke. There were now two voices, humming the same off-key riff. It was an AC/DC duel.

Aimee was thunderstruck.

TWENTY-NINE

The sun hadn't come up but the lamps that lit the discount chemist's awning signs glared into Aimee's bedroom window. She stared at the ceiling and watched the fan spinning. With a frustrated exhale, she reached over to grab her phone off the bedside table and squinted at the harsh brightness when the screen activated.

4:07
Saturday, 25 December

ApplePay notification bubbles were still on the phone screen from the pub. Last purchase?

Palace Hotel
$51.90
2 hours ago

She kicked off her blue linen bedspread and cream sheets, sat up and swung her legs over the edge of the bed. Her eyes weren't bleary.

She concluded she was still drunk and would pay the price later – even after consuming The Bomb. She stood up and walked to her wardrobe, pulling out a perfectly gift-wrapped rectangular box. Brown stock paper. Metallic gold ribbon. She padded out into the living room. That blue early morning hue glowed through all the windows along the wall that overlooked the street. Charlie's bedroom door was closed. Freya's was open. Aimee walked past the dining table and towering cabinet of cassettes and stood in the doorway of Freya's room. Bed untouched. The hospital corners of the moss green waffle-weave blanket were still folded the way Aimee did them the previous morning – the same way her mum used to do for her and Fleur. She placed the gift on the end of the bed. Out in the living room, she perched cross-legged on one end of the peacock blue couch and held one of the thick down-filled velvet cushions to her chest – her arms slowly sinking into it as she hugged it tighter. The Christmas tree she had put up with Rob and Charlie was in the corner, decorated with a chaotic jumble of lost-and-found ornaments. She swiped open her phone and went to text Freya.

Heyo!

Backspace, backspace, backspace.

Just checking in :)

Backspace, backspace, backspace.

WHERE THE HELL ARE YOU?!

Backspace, backspace, backspace.

Aimee paused.

Just let me know you're OK?

Aimee's finger lingered over the 'send' button. Then the message disappeared and the phone started buzzing – the Ace of Base ringtone blaring in the darkness. It was an incoming call. One name was at the top of the screen in white font: HEATH. Aimee silenced the Swedish pop novelty ringtone and then froze. Should she let it ring out or just reject it? If she rejected it, it'd be obvious she saw the call and chose not to answer it. Better to let it ring out. Then she looked up at the open bedroom door and the bed that hadn't been slept in. She rushed to answer the call but, just as her thumb tapped the screen, the buzzing stopped and Heath's name disappeared. Her unsent text to Freya returned to the screen: *Just let me know you're OK?*

Knock, knock, knock. Knuckles tapped on the front door.

Aimee shot up from the couch and her bare feet skimmed across the floorboards as she darted over to the front door. She leant in close to peer through the peephole then jolted back, pausing for a second. Her heart started to race.

'I know you're home,' came Heath's voice through the timber.

Aimee flicked the deadlock, snatched at the brass knob and swung open the door so fast it didn't even make its usual creaking sound.

'Is Freya OK?' She squinted at the hallway light blasted into the apartment.

Heath looked at her like she was ridiculous for asking. 'Why wouldn't Freya be OK?'

Turning on her heels and walking back into the living room, Aimee held a palm to her forehead. 'You call me at 4am and then knock on my door. Of course I'm gonna think something's wrong with Freya.'

'Something—'

Aimee frantically spun around, pointed over at Charlie's closed bedroom door with one hand and placed an index finger to her lips with the other, miming *shush*.

'Something *is* wrong,' Heath whispered.

She walked right up to him and placed her hands firmly on his shoulders. 'Heath, I really need to know: is Freya OK?' she said slowly.

'I just told you she's OK.'

'No, you didn't tell me she's OK – you actually just mocked my question.'

'I didn't mock anything. And if I was gonna mock something, it'd be your Ace of Base ringtone.'

Aimee shot him a look and walked to the couch. Heath laughed at the reaction.

'Why are you here?' She cut to the chase while flopping her tired body down onto the velvet cushions.

'I need your help.' He leant on the back of the sofa and stared down at Aimee.

'And I need you not to be here.' She hugged a pillow and turned to her side.

'It's something only *you* can help with.'

'At four in the morning?' She rolled onto her back and furrowed her brow. 'On Christmas day?'

'Yep. It's important. I wouldn't be asking otherwise.' There was a sincerity in his eyes.

Aimee sighed. 'What do I need to do?'

'Thank you. C'mon.' Heath turned to walk towards the door.

Aimee whisper-screamed across the room. 'Hey! . . . Hey!' She sprung off the couch and quickly tiptoed over. 'You need me to go *outside*?'

'Yeah . . . What's the problem?'

Aimee looked down at her pyjamas – long blue cotton pants and a white singlet – then looked up, waiting for him to grasp her point. He didn't. 'I'm gonna need to change.' She spelled it out.

'What's wrong with what you're wearing?'

'They're *pyjamas*.'

'Well, they look just like your normal clothes. I mean . . . they've even got food stains on them.' He pointed.

Aimee whacked his hand away and let out an irritated huff. 'Just . . . give me a minute.'

'There's no time.' Heath headed for the door and plucked Aimee's house keys out of the deadlock.

'You know, I could've changed clothes by now.'

'You should've thought of that before you started arguing.' He playfully grabbed her by the hand. 'C'mon.'

She reluctantly followed.

————

Aimee stood on the footpath with her arms crossed.

'There's an emergency at my store?' She raised an eyebrow as Heath used her keys to unlock the glossy red door of The Dream Explosion. Her mood was sour. Heath refused to give her more details on the walk over and a group of drunk backpackers who were still out partying had whooped when she walked by in her pyjamas. It was way too early.

'The emergency isn't here.' Heath looked over his shoulder with a smile. '. . . But the *solution* is.' The door pressed open. He disappeared inside.

Aimee rushed in behind to disable the alarm that would start sounding after ten seconds. While she was punching the rubber digits on the wall-mounted pad, she heard a loud thud and then a grunt. Then the sound of boxes falling. She used her free hand to flick the nearby light switch and found Heath half-attempting to re-stack a pile of books he'd tripped over.

'Just leave it,' she sighed.

'What's the most expensive thing you have?' Heath started looking around the store, kind of frantically – as if it were a bank and he only had a few minutes to steal everything and make a getaway before the cops showed up. 'I need the perfect Christmas present.'

'For *who*?' Aimee placed her head down on the counter and closed her eyes.

Heath moved over to the fidgets. 'What the fuck are these?' He picked up one in the shape of a red apple and inspected it for a second before tossing it back on the shelf. With Aimee clearly unamused, he walked over and leant on the counter. 'My Christmas presents to my daughter haven't arrived in time. My ex texted me last night, but I was asleep and only saw it when I woke up to go to the bathroom. I need to get something down to Sydney today.'

Aimee yawned and lifted her head. 'How are you gonna get it down to Sydney today?'

'I booked a flight. Six-thirty. I've gotta be at Ballina airport in . . .' He checked his phone for the time. 'Fuck. I gotta be there in fifty minutes.'

Aimee's irritation with Heath evaporated a little. 'That's . . . very sweet. *Surprisingly* sweet.'

Heath shrugged. 'You do what you gotta do. There's no way Sadie's not getting her Christmas presents from me today.'

The earnestness jabbed Aimee in the heart. Her face softened as she looked at Heath. He broke eye contact and looked at the ground.

'Freya's OK.' He eventually said.

'Huh?' Aimee jolted at the sudden change of topic.

'Freya's OK.' He leant on the counter. 'She's a smart girl.'

Aimee exhaled and tried to untangle all the thoughts that had knotted up in her head about her niece. 'Do I need to worry about the other girls?'

'Freya's not like them.' Heath smiled. 'And why are you so concerned about the others? They're harmless. Ish. Harmless-ish.'

Aimee thought for a moment. There were too many reasons to list. Then she glimpsed the clock above the entrance. 'OK, your fifty-minute count-down is ticking fast.'

Heath sprung away from the counter and marched around the store. 'Give me your expert opinion,' he instructed.

Aimee pushed her hair back. 'She's ten, right? Sadie?'

'Ten,' he confirmed. 'Or eight. Maybe thirteen.'

Aimee gave him a look.

'I'm kidding, she's ten. And she likes dolls. It's all about dolls.'

An idea sparked across Aimee's face. She walked around the counter and over to the big round display table in the middle of the store, where the five-level doll house was. 'Ta-da.' She gestured at the mini-terrace – with its chimney and pastel pink walls and green ivy vine painted up the side wall. It was handmade by a local woodworker.

Heath spun around and bent at the knees to inspect it. 'I know millionaires who don't have houses this nice.'

'She'll love it.' Aimee traced the roof with a finger.

'Yeah. She will.' Heath looked up at her. 'Thank you.'

He stood upright and walked over to the counter while Aimee closed the front of the wooden mini-mansion and clicked shut the gold latches on the side.

'Do you want me to wrap it?' She carried it over.

'Nah, no time. I'll just fix you up and take it like that.' He pulled out his Visa.

'Oh, don't worry about it.' She placed the gift near the register. 'The EFTPOS machine needs to be started up. It'll take forever. Just . . . take it.'

Heath picked up the house and rested it on a hip. It was the length of his torso. 'I'll fix you up when I get back,' he assured.

'Whenever.' Aimee shrugged, not fussed.

They stood awkwardly in the store as the street outside became more clear.

'I'll be down in Sydney for the night, so I won't be with the crew for Brooke's party.' Heath's phone buzzed and he glanced at the screen. 'Jetstar check-in reminder.' He held it up.

'You better go,' Aimee said.

He nodded and turned to walk away.

'Good luck. The present is perfect.' She went to turn the lights off and re-set the alarm.

Just as he was walking out the door, Heath stopped and ducked over to the corner display window to grab something. He held up a small green container of slime and kept walking. 'Now it's perfect.'

THIRTY

The faded red Monaro pulled up on a patch of lawn off the long driveway at Brooke's. A canopy of lights twinkled in the distance, up near the house.

'Wait up,' Aimee told Charlie and Rob, before anyone could open a door. She grabbed a packet of Nurofen out of the centre console, popped two of the red gel capsules, and swigged from her bottle of Gatorade. After Heath's early-morning wake-up call, she hadn't been able to get back to sleep and she'd been feeling the effects all day. The morning was spent laying in the sun at the beach, waiting for Freya. The plan was tentative, but eventually cancelled when Freya texted to say she was caught up with stuff for the show. Aimee could feel a slight sting on her flesh from being in the sun too long. The afternoon was wasted away, with hours lost to almost-texting Jules and then wimping out. As she gulped the Gatorade, she looked at the clock on the car's dash. A few minutes before 8pm. They were about an hour late – just the way she had planned it. She didn't want to arrive on time and then get stuck making meaningless small talk.

Rob opened her door and then slid her seat forward for Charlie to get out of the coupe's back seat. 'I still can't believe how *not* hungover I am.' She slammed the door.

The sound of gravel crunched under their shoes as they made the trek up towards the blur of lights near the house. Aimee looked over and saw Rob's white T-shirt. It had a slogan screen-printed on it in big black letters that was more than familiar:

THERE'S NO 'I' IN 'RELATIONSHIP' BUT THERE IS 'US' IN 'ME'

Aimee came to a halt. '*Roberta.*'

Rob grinned like a toddler who'd just been caught stealing from the cookie jar. She stretched out the front of the shirt to show it off. 'It's cottagecore.'

'I still don't understand what cottagecore is but I know it's not *that*.'

Rob skipped ahead. 'I know. I googled it and I still don't get it. I think it's just slang for "slutty pilgrim".'

Charlie ran after her. 'It's super quiet here.' They all became aware the only noise was the crunchy gravel and the cicadas.

Aimee caught up. 'They can't play music while they're filming.'

'So we're hanging out in silence all night?' Rob said.

Charlie laughed and slapped Rob's arm. 'Maybe you and Brooke can duet again.'

'Oh, we're now best friends.' Rob flicked her hair. 'I'm trading you in, Aimee. It's all about Roberta and Brooke. That uptight dame is the Christine McVie to my Stevie Nicks.'

'Are Tim and the Hot Ew Girl gonna be here tonight?' Charlie asked.

'Well, the Hot Ew Girl is Brooke's daughter Bree, so yes. And Tim and I texted this morning . . . he's coming.'

'That's weird,' Rob said. 'You guys had your makeshift Christmas before the time-out because you weren't gonna see each other all summer.'

'Thank you for the recap – I remember.'

'It's probably a good thing. Can you imagine if the TV crew wanted to film you guys giving each other presents this morning? And then you'd have to tell the camera that, instead of gifts, you guys just went halves on a Roomba.'

Charlie laughed. 'You guys really *have* been together for twenty years. If you don't get back together, who gets custody of the Roomba? Do you have Monday to Friday and he gets it on the weekends?'

Rob stacked on. 'And if you stay single, are you worried about the Roomba attacking you in your sleep?'

'Well, *now* I am,' Aimee deadpanned. 'And then it'll hoover up my remains and I'll become an urban myth: the sad, single lady who got eaten by her Roomba.'

They reached the top of the driveway and stood on the edge of the lawn behind the house. The place looked like a Donna Hay cookbook. Old farm-house tables were positioned on the lush grass – some of them draped with stylishly rustic linens in faded blues and neutrals. Mismatched bentwood chairs were scattered around. Cane lanterns and thick cream candles lit up the space. Lots of artfully assembled grazing platters with cheeses and nuts and grapes and weird fruit pastes. Big silver antique ice buckets were filled with bottles of champagne and placed everywhere like they were bouquets of flowers. Real champagne. Not the Aldi stuff.

'Are we allowed to drink those or are they just decorative?' Rob said.

In their jeans, the three of them did not look like they belonged in a Donna Hay cookbook. At best, they looked like they belonged in one of those free recipe catalogues you pick up at the Woolworths checkout.

Aimee gave one final briefing. 'Just remember: Cameras are everywhere. Be careful what you say. And only refer to Bree by her real name – not Hot Ew Girl.'

'Ladies!' Brooke walked over, barefoot, in a floaty floral dress with a fedora on her head, even though the sun had gone down. Her look for the evening was the same as the decor: highly-curated effortless. A cameraman and soundie were in tow.

Rob stepped forward and kissed both Brooke's cheeks. 'That dress is stunning! *Very* cottagecore.'

'The place looks great,' Aimee said.

Brooke waved away the compliments. 'No, no, it's all very thrown together. I'm embarrassed – I wanted the flock of peacocks to have arrived for the party.'

Rob nodded. 'Look, I didn't wanna say anything – but that is *exactly* what's missing.'

Brooke stepped back and looked at the trio. She cocked her head and her voice went high. 'Did you guys get the Pinterest link?'

They all turned to each other. No one ventured a reply.

'For tonight. The Pinterest board. I told Bree to send it to you.' Brooke closed her eyes and shook her head. 'It's not your fault. It's just for functions, the Pinterest board provides a selection of sample colours that make up the aesthetic of the evening. Photos of decor and atmosphere inspiration. It's so guests can coordinate with the colours and everyone looks good in photos.'

The trio of uncoordinated misfits stood in silence.

'Is that a *thing*?' Rob said.

Brooke threw her hands in the air. 'It's fine.' It clearly wasn't. She led them into the crowd. All the other women looked like Brooke and Bree – carefully groomed to appear relaxed and thrown together. 'Help yourself to drinks . . . The girls are around.' She looked through the glass French doors that were folded open and led into the house. Rich was in the kitchen. She called his name and waved him over. He wandered out, barefoot – but not stylishly barefoot like his wife. His hair looked like he'd just woken up and he was dressed like a dad walking down to the corner shop to pick up the morning newspaper. Brooke barely tried to hide her irritation and spoke about him like he wasn't standing next to her. 'He still needs to have a shower and change into the outfit that's laid out on the bed.'

Aimee tried breaking the tension and introduced Rob and Charlie. They just stood in wide-eyed silence, making it even more awkward. The cameraman captured it all.

Brooke interrupted. 'Aimee, Freya was looking for you. You also need to be mic'd up. And I need to go chat with the production crew. Rich, show these two around – they won't need to be mic'd.' She floated off across the deck and the cameraman followed.

Aimee looked around the landscaped yard but couldn't see Freya. Then two hands mussed her hair from behind and wrapped around her waist.

'Thank youuuuu. I ducked home before and found the present on my bed.'

Aimee turned around just in time to see a pained look on Freya's face, and the TV camera over her shoulder.

'Can I tell you something?' Her voice was strained. 'I feel like a dick . . . I actually went and bought a new phone the day *after* the lighthouse photo- shoot.' She hammed up the distress to show how sorry she was. 'I feel like an idiot. I had no idea you were gonna buy one. And I can't return mine – I've already set it up.' She looked down and shook her head as she rattled on. 'And I also needed one with a better camera and more storage anyway.' She held up her shiny, gigantic new phone. 'This one's 256GB . . . the one you got's only 64GB. Is there any way you can return yours and get your money back? Or maybe *you* need a new phone?'

Aimee made a bunch of faces and weird noises and swatted her hands in the air to make it seem like she was totally fine with it. She said she could totally return it, even though she knew she couldn't. She had no idea about gigabytes or the differences between the two phones. All she knew was she felt pathetic for even having tried to impress her niece. While she was attempting to be chill and breezy, she noticed Freya was wearing cut-off denim shorts and an old faded blue men's Ralph Lauren shirt – sleeves rolled, half tucked in. French tucked. She'd learnt that phrase from the episodes of *Queer Eye* Rob had made them all watch on Netflix. Aimee wondered if the shirt belonged to the secret boyfriend.

'I'm taking photos tonight for Brooke. She's projecting them up over there as a *slideshow thing*.' Freya nodded to a big cream sheet of fabric tied to the branches of an old jacaranda tree. It rippled in the breeze while images of guests beamed up from one of those small wireless Bluetooth projectors. Freya had used that retro filter that adds a digital timestamp in the margins and makes the photos look old school. 'Here . . . let's take one.' She cuddled up to Aimee, stretched an arm out to position the phone in front of them and used her finger to hit the capture button repeatedly.

Aimee squinted at the flickering screen. 'Did we get one?'

'Heaps. Always need options.' Freya scrolled through a few of the frames as a tech guy from the crew appeared next to them. 'I gotta go get some other people.' Freya planted a kiss on Aimee's cheek and bounced off. 'And thank you again!' she called back, leaving the cameraman with her aunt.

Aimee looked around the garden – mainly to avoid eye contact with the cameraman and the tech guy, who'd already started running a cord down the back of her shirt and connecting the black power pack to the waist-band of her jeans. At night, you couldn't tell the sprawling property was still under construction or that, at the bottom of the slope, a kilometres-long lake was in the process of being excavated. She felt a nudge on her shoulder. Tim: holding a beer in one hand and a glass of champagne in the other. He was wearing an outfit that matched the decor.

He held out the flute and smirked. 'You look like you need it.'

'And you look like you got the Pinterest link.' She reached out to take the drink and glimpsed his hand. On his finger was a silver ring with a round piece of turquoise on top. Tim wasn't the kind of guy who wore jewellery. In fact, he used to make it quite clear how much he hated it. In the 2000s, when they were teenagers and it became cool for guys to wear those white puka shell necklaces and silver metal dog tags, Tim resisted. No rings or adornments of any kind were allowed as gifts for any birthdays or Christmases or anniversaries when they were dating.

'Did you have lunch at your mum's?' Aimee asked.

'Yeah, the usual: Relatives. Mum's alternative therapy mates. It was fine. Only, this year I couldn't piss off at the end of the day and go home to our place.' He laughed.

Aimee squinted. 'Am I an asshole for saying I'm glad I got to miss it this year?'

Tim pursed his lips and shrugged. 'Am I an asshole for saying I'm jealous?'

A breeze picked up and Aimee turned into it, clocking the hovering camera and cringing to herself. She'd forgotten it was there. A series of short sharp buzzes vibrated in the back pocket of her jeans. She pulled out her phone and glanced at the screen. A text from Jules. 'Sorry.' She flicked her eyes up at Tim.

'No, no,' he rushed to say. 'Do what you need to do.' He looked around the yard and waited for Aimee to finish.

Happy Christmas. Can't wait to see you again x

Then another message appeared *DJ your way to an orgasm*, it read, and there was a link to a Spotify playlist Jules had made: AIMEE'S LEVIBE JAMS. A quick scroll revealed it was a jumbled mix of tacky hyper-sexual novelty rap. She let out a delighted burst of laughter that immediately drew the attention of her fiancé – the look on his face was almost confused, like he hadn't heard that noise come out of her before. She calmly locked her phone before he could ask any questions. All the candles and cane lanterns were making the air hotter than it already was. She adjusted a shoulder strap on her white tank top and looked at the turquoise ring on her fiancé's finger again. Her stare lingered.

Tim followed her eyeline, flicking his gaze to the jewellery. He got embarrassed and swapped his beer to the opposite hand so he could slide the bejewelled finger into the pocket of his jeans. 'It was a gift. From today. I felt like I *had* to put it on.'

Aimee had to try hard not to ask who it was from – even though she already knew. She recognised it from the Lola online store. Of course she'd stalked the website as soon as she got home after meeting Bree at the dinner. Then she caught herself making a face. She always thought she was good at hiding her reactions, but she wasn't. She attempted to defuse it. 'It's nice. It matches the turquoise pendant necklace I'm gonna buy you,' she joked.

Tim groaned and resisted a smile.

'It also matches the fedora.' Aimee nodded at his head before looking out across the yard. She noticed the rest of the TV crew, dressed in all-black outfits and doing their best to be everywhere while also not being noticed. They were paying particular attention to one table. Aimee squinted. Brooke flurried past, as if she was on her way to deal with some kind of grazing platter emergency. Aimee stuck a hand out to get her attention. 'Is that Meredith?'

Brooke stopped. 'The hippy? Yes! I met her last night when we were at the pub. Told her she should come and do readings at the party.' Then she tapped Aimee's wrist and altered her tone, as if she were about to divulge a secret no one knew. 'She's *Isla Fisher's* psychic.' A moment later, she'd grabbed Aimee and Tim by the hands and was dragging them across the lawn. 'Oh, Aimee, Tim told me you have a bunch of old antiques you're trying to get rid of.'

'Um . . . well, I was *thinking* of selling them, but . . .'

'How much do you want for the lot?'

'But you haven't seen them.'

'I'll buy the lot, take what I need, then dump the rest. You'll get paid anyway.'

'I'm just . . . not really wanting to sell them anymore.'

'Fine, what pieces do you *wanna* get rid of?'

Tim looked over at Aimee. 'Just show her some of the pics you took at the market stall.'

Aimee didn't know how to respond.

Tim gave her a look like she was being rude. 'Just show her the pics. You don't need to keep *everything*.'

Aimee pulled her phone out of her back pocket and scrolled through the photo gallery.

Brooke leant over and glimpsed an image of some big green enamel factory dome light shades and grabbed the phone to look. 'Now *they* are something I'd buy. How many?'

Aimee closed her eyes and tried to remember. 'A dozen. *About* a dozen. Maybe.' She exhaled.

Brooke clicked her long acrylic nail on the screen. 'We could use them for the lights in the barn.'

Aimee looked up and saw Meredith in her element, holding court. She glanced up from her deck of tarot cards. 'Oh, hey Byron Karen.' The camos and soundies edged back to widen the circle.

'Aimee next!' Brooke insisted, shoving her down in a chair at the table.

'Yes! Aimee next!' another voice cheered. It was familiar. Aimee glanced around and saw who it was: Bree. Meredith was just wrapping up with her. Crystals were being rearranged. Cards were being shuffled. Tim pulled a chair over and sat down.

'Let's do aura readings!' Brooke clapped. 'I got told I'm orange: creative and passionate.'

'I got yellow,' Bree said. 'Positive, optimistic.'

Of course you are, Aimee thought. *It's easy to be positive and optimistic when you're twenty-five.* Then her mind flashed back to when *she* was twenty-five. Was she ever positive and optimistic? At twenty-five, she'd owned the store for the better part of a decade and was just getting acclimated with small business debt. She couldn't remember ever being positive and optimistic. Surly and pessimistic, though, were more than familiar feelings.

Bree looked up and teased Tim about his potential aura reading. 'I think your colour will be . . . *black.*' She scrunched her nose up and looked at Aimee to share the laugh.

Cameramen bustled. One crouched down. Another stood. A boom mic hovered.

Aimee raised an eyebrow at Meredith. 'Weren't you protesting this reality show?'

'Yep. But then that crazy rich lady paid me to come here and be on it.' Meredith nodded over at Brooke. She sat back and used one of the tiny knives to scoop a hunk of brie onto a cracker, followed by a mountain of quince paste. 'Alright. A reminder: these are just snap readings. I can complete your reading if you book a full session – simply go to Mystique-Meredith.com and confirm an appointment through the online portal.

Or you can DM me on Instagram or TikTok.' She sat back, locked her eyes on Tim for several minutes and mindlessly picked nuts off the grazing platter. 'Blue. You're *clouded* with blue. It's like someone dipped a big paint-brush in blue watercolours and splashed it all around you. Dripping. You're *dripping* in blue. Blue means you're an empath. Emotionally sensitive. Care a lot about others.'

Aimee caught herself making a face again – the same face she usually reserved for green-flavoured Clinkers. Then she felt guilty. Of course Tim was emotionally sensitive. Sometimes. Maybe. When he wasn't busy leaving all the kitchen cupboards open for no reason. Was it bad she was so disgusted by someone pointing out a nice quality in her fiancé? Or maybe that was a natural reaction to have – especially when you've reached that stage in your relationship where, instead of buying romantic Christmas gifts, you just go halfsies on a Roomba. Aimee got so distracted trying not to make her green Clinker face that she didn't realise Tim's aura reading had ended and Meredith had moved on to studying her. She exhaled and used both hands to push her hair back.

'Wooft.' Meredith sighed. 'Murky. Like a swamp. A murky swamp colour. Greys and browns. You're anchored by negativity.'

'Well—' Aimee stumbled but Meredith powered on.

'Pessimistic. Glass half-empty. Kinda selfish. It's blocking your energy flow.'

Aimee looked around. 'Maybe it's just the lack of lighting out here.'

'It's not the lighting. There aren't enough selenite crystals in the world to cleanse that filthy aura.'

Aimee blinked and resisted the overwhelming urge to pick up the tiny silver cheese knife and use it as a weapon. People who call you negative are the worst because the moment you scrunch up your face and deny it, they point and say, 'See! You're being negative!' What a trap.

Meredith wrapped up a wedge of blue vein cheese in one of Brooke's rustic linen napkins and threw it in the Coles reusable shopping tote she used as a handbag. 'Oh, also. You've had sex.'

Brooke and Bree guffawed. Cameramen moved swiftly to capture Aimee's humiliation from multiple angles. Aimee closed her eyes and shook her head fast, like a cartoon character who'd just been whacked with a giant mallet.

Tim jolted. 'You've had sex?'

Meredith popped a grape in her mouth. 'She's had sex.'

Aimee picked her jaw up off the lawn. 'Well, I think you need to cleanse your crystals, because . . . it seems you're a little bit misguided tonight. On *a lot of* things.'

Meredith sighed. 'There's that trademark pessimism again. And my crystals are fine. You've had sex.'

Brooke trotted over and hugged Aimee from behind while cheering.

'Would you please stop saying that?' Aimee squeezed out of the embrace.

Meredith shrugged. 'If you keep having sex, your aura might change to a nicer colour.'

A rowdy table nearby started calling for Brooke to bring Meredith over. They wanted to experience the joyful enlightenment Aimee had just bathed in. 'We're coming!' Brooke helped Meredith up from her seat.

Aimee excused herself to find the bathroom.

Porta-a-loos were not something Brooke would ever install on her property. And allowing the guests of a moderate-sized outdoor party to use the bathrooms *inside* her home was also something that would never happen. Brooke's solution? She had a Guest Rest Centre built. That was its official name. There was a carved wooden sign and everything. It was basically a public toilet block but with marble tiles and bronze faucets and Aesop products and enclosed rooms instead of stalls. Of course, it was built out of sight – away from the party – at the end of a pathway and behind a canopy of jasmine. Thousands of the white buds had burst open like little stars and the warm night coaxed out their sweetness. Aimee stopped for a moment and inhaled – a moment of peace, away from the TV crew who didn't notice her escape and who'd probably be annoyed to find out she'd unplugged her microphone cord from the power pack on her waistband.

She noticed the weatherboard barn nearby – newly built, painted white with navy trim, lights on. The one she'd spotted when Brooke was giving her the tour of the property. 'Where dreams go to die,' Brooke had sighed when the golf cart whizzed past it. The one Brooke was now wanting to put Aimee's green vintage factory lamps in.

Aimee followed the path towards it and heard the sound of cricket playing on a TV. She was a little curious, but mostly just looking for any excuse to delay her return to the party. The big timber doors were rolled open. She kept walking inside and suddenly became aware of the echoes being made from her boots on the cement floor. The jasmine perfume had been replaced by the stink of marijuana. Brooke's husband Rich was sitting on a tan leather couch and smoking a joint in front of the big plasma screen that was mounted to the wall. He turned around, sucked back on the white rolled-up paper and held it up, offering Aimee a puff.

She shook her head.

He looked her up and down and blew out a cloud of smoke. 'You didn't get the Pinterest link.'

Aimee looked at the slob in front of her. 'Neither did you.'

'You're Freya's mum?'

Aimee looked around. 'What's with the vending machines?' There were twelve – organised in two rows along one wall.

'My empire.' Rich started to laugh. 'DVD rental vending machines. Open twenty-four hours, seven days a week. The 7-Eleven of movies.' *Inhale.* 'Then Netflix came to Australia.' *Exhale.* 'And fucked me.' He swigged his beer. 'You know how much one DVD vending machine costs?'

Aimee didn't answer.

'Twenty grand. And I bought twenty of 'em.' He burst into a fit of giggles. 'Half . . . a million . . . dollars.'

Aimee's eyes were getting dry from the smoke and Rich was clearly stoned. 'Well, I'm gonna go—'

'We had to move back in with Brooke's parents. Sold off whatever machines we could for a couple grand. Brooke took the cash and started making her tutu*things*.' He flicked the butt on the ground. His tone had turned distinctly bitter. 'Millions of people wanna buy some fuckin' ugly dress for their baby from a stranger on the internet just because some celebrities told them to? Who knew.' He burped, then looked over to Aimee. 'Brooke told me about you and your boyfriend.'

'Fiancé.'

'And . . . *Bree*.' Another burst of giggles bubbled up from his chest. He reined it in. 'That's fucked up.' He kicked back on the couch again. 'You shouldn't worry,' he dismissed. 'Bree's an entitled little brat.'

Aimee pursed her lips and turned to walk out.

'That Christmas decoration Brooke gave you?' Rich's voice echoed around the barn.

Aimee stopped.

'It's not from France. It's from Target.'

————

Aimee walked back into the Donna Hay wonderland. Charlie and Rob scurried out of the house, through the folding glass doors and over to Aimee.

'Did you get it?' Charlie asked Aimee.

Aimee furrowed her brow and took a step back to assess her friends. 'What is *that*?'

Charlie and Rob were both holding the really big Starbucks cups that Brooke always carried.

Rob cackled. 'We went through her kitchen and found a whole drawer full of them. The woman buys the empty cups and then fills them with her own coffee! She drinks fake Starbucks!'

Aimee shushed them.

'Here, we got you one, too.' Rob held out one of the cardboard cups. 'We filled them with champagne.'

Charlie nudged Rob. 'The other thing,' he said out of the corner of his mouth.

'Oh yeah. Did you get it?'

'Get *what?*' Aimee was becoming frustrated.

'The text. Charlie sent you a video.'

Aimee reached behind to slide her phone out of her back pocket but it wasn't there. Then she remembered. 'Brooke has my phone. She was looking at pictures of the antiques earlier.'

'Eek.' Charlie's face dropped.

'Fuck.' The colour drained from Rob's.

A microphone screeched. 'Guess Who, Don't Sue,' Brooke's voice boomed through the yard over a speaker.

'Where the hell did she get a microphone?' Charlie said.

Everyone looked around and saw Brooke standing on a chair near the jacaranda. The TV crew moved like undercover army operatives around the yard to secure the best positions to film what was about to happen. Brooke's lookalike friends gathered. Aimee, Rob and Charlie hung back and watched on.

'This is a fun game I learned at Music Club last night,' Brooke began. 'I give you hints on a rumour and you speculate who it's about.'

Laughs and murmurs came from the crowd. Aimee tried to spot Freya but couldn't.

'Which *Brats of Byron Bay* co-star is involved in a cheating scandal?' Brooke smirked, leaving a pause for guesses that never came. 'It's a hard one,' she teased.

Aimee shot Charlie a look and leaned in close. 'Is this about you hooking up with Luna's boyfriend? That . . . *van guy?*' she whispered hastily.

'I really wish it was,' Charlie winced.

Brooke's voice interrupted. 'Maybe this next clue will be easier: Which *Brats of Byron Bay* co-star has been dubbed a *dud root?*'

Murmur, murmur.

Cough.

'Another hint?' Brooke asked the crowd. She was having fun, toying with the pin on the grenade she was about to hurl.

Rob grabbed Aimee's arm. 'We should probably leave now.'

'Which bogan hairdresser secretly fucked my husband?' Brooke tapped her phone screen.

The photos being projected onto the big white sheet switched to video footage. It was the clip of Rob kissing the weird dad in the beige polo shirt at Music Club.

Rob leant closer to Aimee. 'Remember how you thought there was something familiar about Rich?'

Everyone at the party turned to look at the trio. Cameras swung around and zoned in.

Aimee, Rob and Charlie stood still. Holding their really big Starbucks cups.

———

Producer: Tell us what you're feeling, Brooke.

Brooke: I feel hurt, betrayed. By all three of them – Rich and Rob but also Aimee. The fact they were all keeping this secret behind my back. This . . . *cheating scandal*. I'm blindsided. Absolutely blindsided. Us girls were supposed to be best friends. This totally breaks the girl code. Y'know, last night at the pub, Aimee threw a glass of wine at me?

———

Producer: Rich, why did you cheat on your wife?

Rich: Get that fuckin' camera outta my fuckin' face.

———

Producer: Rob, what made you blow up Brooke's life like this?

Rob: Yes! I did it! I made out with that weird guy in the beige polo! Australia, meet your new reality TV villain! I'll have *that* with cheese!

———

Producer 1: Aimee! Stop running, Aimee!

Aimee: No comment!

Producer 2: I'll cut her off round the other side.

Producer 1: We just wanna give you the chance to tell your side of the story, Aimee! If you don't, Australia will assume the worst about you. I'm giving you an opportunity to come out on top!

Producer 2: Aimee!

Aimee: Aaargh! Where the fuck did you come from?!

Producer 2: Put the keys away, Aimee – no, no! Get out of the car.

Producer 1: Has she locked the door?

Producer 2: Film her through the window before she drives awa—

Cameraman: Aargh! My fucking foot! That bitch ran over my fucking foot!

Producer 1: You'll have to talk some time, Aimee!

Producer 2: Aimee!

THIRTY-ONE

*Oooh, yeah . . . I can feel it . . . Crunchies. Lotsa little crunchy bits –
right in there. OK, breathe in . . . out . . .*

Crack

Ooh, there it is. Yeah . . . Breathe in . . . Deep one in . . . And out . . .

Crack

*Yeah, there it is. There it is. Alright. That was a big one. OK again . . .
In . . . Out . . . Let it go, let it go . . .*

. . .

Nope. It's not gonna go. It's deep. Deep in there.

Aimee was laying in bed and had commenced her nightly routine: watching
YouTube videos of chiropractors cracking people's backs. They usually

calmed her down and sent her off to sleep but, that night, they weren't working. She felt sick after the Christmas party drama and just wanted to pass out and escape it. It wasn't Rob's fault. It was all Rich. Aimee played it back in her head – the weird interaction with Rich in the barn and Brooke exposing her own marriage troubles in front of a bunch of TV cameras. She couldn't help but remember Brooke at the pub, the previous night, begging for the confection of drama at the party. Surely she didn't mean *this* kind of drama. Rob was certain Brooke actually loved it – 'it's exactly what she wants for the show,' she'd said cynically as they sped away. It's why she played into the drama when producers cornered her for a piece-to-camera interview as they all tried to escape. 'Can you imagine if I get edited as the villain?' She was more excited than concerned, high on the adrenaline of the night and whatever was in her Starbucks cup.

Aimee looked over at the bedside table and picked up the kugel Brooke had given her. Pinching the gold metal clasp between her thumb and finger, she held it up and let it dangle. The glow of the street lights shining through the windows sparked on the decoration's chipped metallic paint. Why would Brooke lie about it being an antique? Aimee dropped her arm down beside the bed and let it go – *bop, bop, bop* across the floorboards.

She slid the MacBook Air off her lap and reached for her phone. The home screen lit up.

11:13
Saturday, 25 December

She unlocked it and opened Instagram. Lurk, lurk, lurk. Always lurking, always watching. She searched for Brooke and scrolled. The photos of Chicken and the selfies in the G-Wagon were all familiar. But she hadn't noticed the lack of Rich before. She found one photo and tapped on it. Brooke was in a white bikini and gold stilettos on a yacht. Rich was in boardies, holding a bundled-up blue and white towel in front of his stomach. 'Hello, lover,' read the caption. Aimee looked at the date. It was posted about two years before. She clicked on the search button to look up another profile: Bree.

She tapped on one of the most recent posts: A selfie of Bree in her white cottagecore dress at the lighthouse photoshoot, overlooking the ocean. The caption: 'Lyrics from Van Morrison's "Into The Mystic".'

Aimee groaned – mostly at Bree, but also at herself for somehow winding up in a one-sided feud with a twenty-five-year-old. She clicked on the latest photo, posted a few hours earlier. A picture of Bree at the Christmas party – walking away from the camera but turning her head over her shoulder just enough to make eye contact with the lens. The caption: Chow chow xx. Aimee took a screenshot, then texted it to Rob, with a question:

Does she mean . . . Ciao ciao??

A reply immediately whooshed back.

I'm screenprinting this on another T-shirt xx

Aimee typed again. Even though Rob had laughed off the events of the night, Aimee wasn't entirely sure how to handle it.

Are you sure you're feeling OK? I can come over if you wanna talk?

The three grey dots floated, followed by a swift response.

I'm fiiiine. Thrilled to be involved in Australia's next great cheating scandal x

A series of smirking emojis followed.

Back on Bree's Insta grid, Aimee noticed there was a second photo in the most recent post. She swiped right and almost dropped the phone on her face. A picture of Bree with Tim. She was posing with a hand on her hip. He looked awkward and reluctant. Aimee's thumb tapped the screen and a tag appeared over Tim – *@harleyhawkco*. There was a moment of confusion. Then Aimee tapped the handle, opening up a whole new world exposing Tim's secret online identity.

OK, that was a touch dramatic. The only posts on the grid were five photos of the under-construction rooftop bar. Tim was never good at taking pictures and this profile exemplified that. Still, she couldn't help but roll her eyes. Why the hell did Tim need to be on Instagram? She knew who would've talked him into it. Clicks and cracks from the chiropractor video were still popping out of the laptop speaker. Aimee shook her head at her own behaviour and sighed. Then she opened the Safari app on her phone and went to Google. She tapped away on the screen's keyboard.

How to change my aura

Backspace, backspace, backspace.

Negative qualities of blue auras

Backspace, backspace, backspace.

Are people with yellow auras annoying?

Backspace, backspace, backspace.

Successful people with brown auras

Before she could hit the search button, the phone buzzed and a text message bubble swooped in at the top of the screen. Heath.

Heard about tonight. You OK?

She opened the message. The three grey floating dots danced. He was typing something else. Then they disappeared. Aimee's phone started buzzing. A call? Usually, her automatic response would be to reject it. But that's how a person with a brown aura would respond.

'What's with you and late-night phone calls?' she answered.

'It's before twelve – that's hardly late-night,' Heath laughed down the line. 'Heard we got ourselves a cheating scandal.'

'Look, I've seen all of Nina's missed calls – I'm not in the mood to be berated right now for leaving the party.'

'No, no, no,' Heath talked over her. 'I'm just checking in. Yes, I heard what happened. I told you . . . Brooke will do anything for the camera.'

'Would she really do *this* just for the camera?'

'Well, she pressed play on the video,' he muttered. 'And hooked it up to a projector.'

Aimee hit the space bar on the laptop to pause the chiropractor video, put Heath on loudspeaker and placed the phone on her chest so she could pick her nail cuticles. 'Well, everything's content,' she sighed sarcastically.

'Sorry I wasn't there. I'm flying back from Sydney tomorrow.'

Aimee didn't respond. Her mind was still replaying what had happened at the party.

'And just remember,' Heath sensed her concern, 'big chunk of cash for six weeks' work.'

The statement was meant to pep Aimee's spirits but all it did was make her wonder if the drama was really worth it.

'Alrighty,' he said. 'Night.'

She locked the phone, put it on the bedside table and slid the laptop onto her stomach. Squiggling her finger on the grey mousepad, she clicked the cursor into the YouTube search bar and tapped on the keyboard. *Heath Jacobs documentary*, she typed. Thumbnails of clips appeared – old footage of things he'd filmed in Africa. One about landmines in Angola.

A BBC report covering the end of Apartheid in the early nineties. Her phone buzzed. A text from Heath. She unlocked it and found a picture of Sadie in front of the doll house. *You made someone very happy today*, the message read. Aimee put the phone down and looked back at the laptop screen, spotting one particular thumbnail titled, 'Hope inside the murder capital'. She clicked. When it started to play, she toggled the arrows on the keyboard to skip through. Then Heath appeared on camera, walking down a dirt road. He was younger – fitter, no grey hair. The video description listed the doco as being produced in the early 2000s. He was wearing khaki chinos with a white shirt tucked in. Corrugated iron shacks lined the streets.

'*This* is Nyanga. Just kilometres outside Cape Town and only a few minutes' drive from million dollar compounds where royalty and Europe's elite come to indulge the senses, lies this shanty town that has become the murder capital of South Africa. It's where more than 260 locals are murdered each year.' Some small, smiling kids in old clothes started to kick around a soccer ball behind Heath. 'With both unemployment and crime rates at an all-time high – and five slayings a week being carried out on these dirt streets – we go inside to find out what it's like growing up in the danger zone . . . and the community school program that's helping children find a way out.'

Aimee heard a key clink into the lock on the front door to the apartment. It opened and shut. She paused the video and closed the lid, moving the laptop to the bedside table. A few seconds later, her bedroom door creaked. Freya crawled into bed and hugged her.

'Heard about the party,' Freya said. 'I'd left to pick up a mate just before it happened. You and Rob OK?'

'Oh . . . It was a *viiibe*,' Aimee replied.

'You're not using that word right.' Freya laughed. She was still wearing the baggy blue shirt.

'Hey . . .' Aimee ventured a thought and then paused. 'The guy. The footy player.'

Freya groaned and clasped her face.

'Hey, hey.' Aimee nudged her. She'd been trying to find an appropriate time to ask her niece about it. The guy. The photos. 'I wanna know.'

'I was hoping you wouldn't bring it up.'

'Well, I'm bringing it up. Who is he?' What she really meant was, *Why didn't you tell me?*

'He's just a guy I've been seeing from Sydney.'

'And he's been here the whole time with you?'

'He came later.' Freya tried to skirt around it. 'It's nothing serious. I came up here for the holidays. Then he had mates coming up, so he came with them. It wasn't a planned *thing*.'

'OK, and the *story*? The news article?' She avoided the words *humping photos*.

'You saw the paparazzi photographer that was following us the other day at the beach. And the stories they've been writing about the show and the other girls. I guess they just busted me and Jax at the beach and snuck some pics.'

'So his name is . . . *Jax*?'

'Why do you say it like that?' Freya sighed.

'Say it like what?' Aimee's voice went high-pitched.

'You know how you said it.' Freya laughed before doing an amped-up imitation of her aunt. '*Oh . . . Jaaaax*.'

Aimee fluttered her eyes and pretended like she hadn't just been busted.

'It's short for Jackson,' Freya said.

'And it's spelled with an "x"?' Aimee cringed. 'In my mind, it's spelled with an "x" – like a *Home and Away* character.'

'That's enough, Byron Karen,' Freya dismissed. 'And . . . yes. That's how it's spelled. Any more questions?'

'Kiddo, I have *so many* questions.'

'I'm tired.' Freya snuggled further into the bed.

Aimee gazed at her effortlessly gorgeous niece and wondered if she'd ruin the moment by pressing for more.

'Whatchu watching?' Freya nodded to the laptop.

'Just chiropractor videos.'

Freya closed her eyes and started to doze. 'Knew it.'

THIRTY-TWO

Jules stood naked on the beach.

'Don't leave me hangin'.' He put his hands on his hips and smirked.

'You're doing a good job of that yourself,' Aimee said before cringing at herself – partly because of her lame reply but also because she was standing there, covered up in her swimsuit, while a hot guy had stripped off and was waiting for her to follow.

Usually, Sundays were reserved for taco truck hangs with Rob and Charlie, but Aimee couldn't deal with the Boxing Day crowds after the previous night's Christmas party drama. She'd been replaying Brooke's *Current Affair*-style gotcha exposé on her brown shoe of a husband in her mind, and she needed to escape everyone. Rob was hungover and had abandoned the taco truck, too.

Aimee hadn't told anyone where she was spending the day. When Charlie brought her breakfast quesadillas in bed, he'd vaguely asked about her plans and she'd frozen up.

'If you're going to the beach, I can meet you there later if you're still around,' he'd said.

'Um . . . nah, I think I'm just gonna get some air.' She shrugged. 'Then come back to bed.'

It was the only time she could ever recall lying to Charlie. Well, along with telling him she didn't have a photo of Jules. Not that she meant to lie. It was just weird. She didn't know how to explain the whole Jules thing. She hadn't told anyone. It almost felt . . . silly. Girlish. And maybe it was. Still, when she woke up, there was only one person she wanted to be around.

'You told me you wanted to go somewhere you wouldn't run into a single soul.' Jules held out his hands and walked around proudly. He was partly right. Aimee had told him she needed to get away from everyone and avoid the Boxing Day crowds – go somewhere, just the two of them. Preferably near a beach. She was more than capable of picking an adequate location that matched the criteria, but Jules got a thrill out of trying to find at least one place she didn't know about. The remote beach he'd taken her to was south of Byron and required an almost-hour long drive through a rainforest on an unsealed dirt road to get to. Had he succeeded? Aimee let him think so.

'It is a hot day, my friend – and that Irish skin is going to *burn,*' she said. 'Have you put sunscreen on your . . . areas?' *Jesus Christ*, she thought to herself. *Why bring up dick sunburn?* She was never good at flirting.

Jules reached for his phone and, a few seconds later, music started playing.

Aimee closed her eyes and laughed. She knew instantly what the awful song was: 2 Live Crew's 'Me So Horny'. 'We really need to revise the LeVibe Spotify playlist,' she said.

'You're right. Not enough novelty rap.' He gave her a cheeky wink and then took off across the sand, running into the water. It was a reminder of how fit *he* was and how unfit *she* felt. She knew she wasn't *actually* unfit. But the pressure of being naked on a beach with a hot guy brought out her biggest fear: That she would eventually get to an age where her butt looked like a sliding pancake. Fine, it wasn't legitimately her biggest fear, but it *was* a scary thing to think about.

Feeling her cheeks start to burn, she reached down to look for the sunscreen amongst all their stuff and the touch of her hand woke up her iPhone screen. There was an Instagram notification.

HarleyHawkCo is going live

Aimee couldn't help but roll her eyes and open it up. While scrolling/lurking in bed the previous night, she'd decided to follow Tim's new account after stumbling across it. She was his fiancée – of course she was allowed to follow him! The fact it was with her secret anonymous account was simply a detail she chose not to analyse too deeply.

The Insta video played and the sound of an acoustic guitar blared out of the speaker as Aimee watched footage of a busker perform a Jack Johnson song. *Ugh, Tim*, she thought. *Nobody wants to watch that*. Then she twinged at herself for being so judgy. In the bottom corner of the screen she could see that she was the only person viewing it. Ick. What a sobering moment. Had she really become *that* person? Stalking her partner on a fake Insta account. Just as she was about to swipe away the video, the busker disappeared and the camera flipped around. Tim was holding it up high, filming himself and Bree laying on the grass with beers. He leant in and gave her a quick kiss. Then the video ended.

'Aimee!' Jules yelled out from the water, his voice echoing up the deserted coast.

She whipped around and watched as he whooped and dived under a wave. Then she pulled the navy Lycra straps off her shoulders, let her swimsuit fall to the sand, and ran in.

THIRTY-THREE

'Did you see Nicole Kidman's in town?' Rob was sitting on the counter at
The Dream Explosion, eating sushi with one hand and scrolling through
her phone with the other. She held the screen up to show Aimee a tabloid
news story.

Aimee was distracted by the potential buyers the real estate agency had
brought in to tour around the building. All men. About five of them. Clearly
from capital cities, holidaying in the area over summer, who saw the big
FOR SALE sign bolted onto the awning that touted commercial development potential. They all ignored Aimee and she ignored them. But she
felt like she knew them well. They looked like all the other businessmen
who jetted into town for a mixture of work and holidays – swapping their
suits for trendy short-and-shirt combos with boat shoes that their wives
had picked up for them. No one who actually lived near a beach wore
boat shoes.

Rob was still stuck on the Nicole news and quoted directly from the
report. 'The A-lister flew into Sydney with Keith and they spent a week at
their historic mansion in the Southern Highlands before catching a private
jet to Byron Bay where Nicole is set to begin production on a new movie.'

She held up the phone again to show Aimee a picture of the country estate – an English-style sandstone manor, probably built in the early 1900s. It even had a turret. 'Nuff said. Their creepy old mansion looks haunted. Don't you think it looks haunted?'

Aimee pushed the screen out of her face.

'Could you imagine the pressure you'd feel if you were the ghost in charge of haunting Nicole Kidman's house?' Rob inhaled and shook her head. 'I wouldn't be able to handle it – being Nicole Kidman's ghost. I'd get way too excited if I drifted into one of the bathrooms and found Keith flat-ironing his hair. Nope. I'd have to trade mansions with another ghost and just haunt regular people.'

Aimee's phone buzzed. She picked it up, read the text on the home screen and interrupted Rob's musings about Nicole Kidman's ghost. 'Ugh,' her face drooped at the subject matter, '. . . Brooke just texted.'

'Who?'

'Brooke.'

'Use her real name.'

Aimee sighed. 'The crazy bitch with the lake.'

'Thank you. And what does the crazy bitch with the lake want?'

Aimee made a bemused face and exhaled as she quoted the message from the phone screen. *'I'm inviting Rob to make amends.* She wants you to come to Freya's twenty-first party. It's crazy. Isn't she mad? Not at you, but at Rich. This woman is supposed to be heartbroken about her husband cheating on her, and yet it seems like she's more focused on creating TV moments.'

'Well, it sounds like typical behaviour for crazy bitches with lakes.'

Aimee scrunched her face up and slowly ventured an awkward request. 'Am I a crappy friend if I ask you to come?'

'I'd rather be Nicole Kidman's ghost.'

'I thought you enjoyed the drama?' Aimee forced a peppy tone, knowing it was a losing battle. 'On the drive home from the Christmas party, you kept improvising straight-to-camera monologues as the show's new villain.'

Rob smiled. 'I *do* make an excellent villain.' She let out a giggle before her tone snapped back. 'Look, it was amusing in the moment. But what if she pulls more of that shit on us? I have no doubt she jumped at the chance to perform that cheating scandal stunt for the TV cameras – and that's what worries me. The crazy bitch with the lake is crazy by name and crazy by nature. Besides, she called me a bogan hairdresser. That's offensive. Almost more offensive than when Bada Bing calls me "sir".'

'She shouldn't have done that. That was horrible. Rich is the asshole.'

'Does the crazy bitch with the lake know that?'

'Well, this is actually a follow-up text.' Aimee tapped the phone screen with a fingernail. 'She called this morning to ask if we're coming – and informed me that she and Rich are now on *a summer time-out*.' She gave Rob a can-you-believe-it? look.

Rob let out a low, evil-ish laugh.

Aimee continued with an impression of the phone conversation. *'This is the reset I need! And I have Rob to thank!'*

Rob sighed. 'I wasn't going to tell you this, but she did send flowers to the salon yesterday with a card, apologising. I *may* have marched them out to the back alley and thrown them in the dumpster.'

Aimee stifled a laugh and relayed the rest of the phone call. *'A summer time-out! Now me and Rich are just like you and Tim!* Jesus. I don't even wanna be me and Tim. Crazy bitch with the lake.' She winced and looked over at the door to make sure they weren't busted by a lurking camera crew again. 'And unfortunately, I'm . . . *contracted* . . . to these . . . *idiots*.' She ran both hands through her hair and exhaled. 'Can I get out of it? The show? Like, legally?'

Rob jumped off the counter and leant on it to face Aimee. 'No. And even if you *could* quit, you shouldn't. These morons are paying you. Take their money.'

'I feel like she's holding Freya's twenty-first birthday hostage. Like, after what happened at the Christmas party, why would she still *insist* on throwing it? I dunno. Is there a chance we're overthinking it? Heath says to just take it as it comes – not react.'

'Oh, *Heath*.' Rob dragged out the name for dramatic effect. 'I thought you hated him.'

'I never said I *hated* him.'

'You literally slimed his Porsche.'

'Technically not true. It was my landlord's Porsche,' Aimee said, slightly pleased with herself.

'You said if he was a cartoon character he'd have stink lines drawn around him.'

The businessmen looked over.

'Well,' Aimee said, leaning across the counter and lowering her voice, 'that was very immature of me.'

'Whatever. I ain't goin' to the party. It's not even Freya's real twenty-first. She probably hates all those idiots. She's smarter than them.'

'Well, she's still going to be there, which means *I* have to as well. And while I really *don't* wanna go . . .' Aimee paused. 'This sounds stupid . . . but I feel like it's the only way I'm going to get to see Freya and celebrate. She's always out doing things with the show and with friends . . . Charlie says he hears her coming in late. We've barely hung out since she's been living with me and I've actually started to get paranoid that she just might not *like* me that much right now.'

'Hey.' Rob grabbed her friend by the hands.

'I'm fine.' Aimee tried to compose herself. 'Ugh, that's so crazy and pathetic.'

'She *adores* you.'

'I know, I know.' Aimee sighed.

'She's just . . . going through that party stage. Just graduated uni, no commitments, in a cool new place with fun new people.' Rob looked around at the annoying rich property developers poking through the store, then raised her chin and smirked at her friend. 'I will go to the party on one condition.'

'I'll show you where the weird DVD vending machine graveyard is?'

'Tempting . . . but I have one more condition: I will only go if you *assure* me we'll get sent the Pinterest link this time.'

Aimee grabbed her friend's hands and nodded assurance. 'I've already got the Pinterest link.'

'Cause I don't wanna be *humiliated* like last time, OK?' Her voice went high-pitched and silly. 'I wanna match the Donna Hay tablecloths, like everyone else.' A reminder notification pinged on her phone. 'Shit the bed, I gotta go – Tim's mum is coming in for an appointment. She said she has a *special occasion* or something.'

'Probably Tim and Bree's wedding,' Aimee deadpanned while tapping away on her own phone. 'There – the link is sent. You can now match the tablecloths.'

Rob's phone pinged again as she raced out of the store and squeezed by one of the businessmen who was blocking the entrance. 'Ooh, hey, you guys should probably know,' she slapped a palm on his chest, 'this store is haunted – like Nicole Kidman's house.'

The confused men looked at each other and Rob gave a triumphant thumbs-up from the footpath outside. Aimee forced a smile at the potential buyers and tried not to show her disdain for their unemotional assessment of her building. Shifting her attention back to the Excel spreadsheet that she'd been tinkering with since the morning, she toggled with the arrow keys on the keyboard and zoned out. None of it made sense anymore. It was all just numbers. Who cared? The store was shutting anyway. Then she felt the mood shift in the room and all the businessmen became slightly awkward. Aimee looked over to the entrance and saw why: there was a witchy-looking woman hovering in the doorway.

'Hi Meredith,' Aimee called out. 'You here to tell me who I've been having sex with?' She winced a little when the buyers turned.

'Relax, Byron Karen. Not everything's a fight.'

'I'm not *fighting*.'

Meredith poked around a shelf with her veiny white hands. 'What's this?' She held up one of the rubber fidgets. It was in the shape of a flower.

'It's a fidget.'

'I thought you sold books?'

Aimee impatiently changed the subject. 'Do you need something?'

'No, but you do.' Meredith's crafty handmade shoes clicked over the floorboards as she walked up to the counter, her gnarled fingers popping the rubber buttons on the toy.

'Fine, just a second.' Aimee straightened her hair and stood upright. 'OK, I'm ready to be publicly humiliated again.'

'You say I embarrassed you the other night – but I only told you *part* of what I saw and felt in your aura reading. I thought maybe you'd want me to tell you the rest privately.'

'How considerate of you,' Aimee muttered.

Meredith sighed. 'You need a change. A big one. If you don't change, you're gonna . . . get all sick and stuff. I can sense it already. You need to get over whatever it is that's making you so *angry*.'

Aimee pretended to study her Excel spreadsheet.

'Not everyone's out to get you, Aimee.' Meredith looked over at the businessmen. Then she pulled a cardboard rectangle out of her pocket and slid it across the counter.

'Here . . .'

Aimee squinted at the colourful and intricately sketched image of two homeless people shivering in the snow. A stained-glass church window glowed behind them. It took a second for her to realise it was one of Meredith's tarot cards.

'After I read your aura and you walked away, I went to shuffle my deck of cards and this one jumped out on the table. It's the Five Of Pentacles card. You're out in the cold and struggling. There's light behind you . . . but you're so caught up in your own sadness that you can't even see it. Help is there. You just gotta ask for it.'

Aimee stared at the card and cleared her throat. 'Is that all?'

'Can I keep this?' Meredith held up the fidget.

'Sure.'

Meredith looked down at the toy and started popping the silicone buttons in and out.

'Hey Meredith?' Aimee asked.

'Yeah?'

'Get your Audi out of my loading zone.'

THIRTY-FOUR

A tattered, coffee-stained copy of the *Byron Times* had been left on the table at Raes that Aimee was sitting at. Rozzie glared up from the ad for her health clinic that appeared on the back page.

A waitress appeared. 'Drink to start?'

'Definitely.' Aimee tapped her phone screen to wake it up. It was 12.17pm. 'But . . . I'll just wait for my friend first.'

The waitress scrunched her face and leant forward, like she was about to deliver some bad news. 'Just a reminder we have another party booked for your table at one o'clock, so you'll have to be done by about 12.50. It's hectic every day over the holidays.'

'Oh . . . ah . . . sure. No worries.' Aimee glanced quickly around the bustling outdoor area. It was only a Tuesday but, in summer, restaurants everywhere in town felt like a Saturday.

'It's only because we had to squeeze you in.' The waitress nodded, like it was a grand favour.

'Got it,' Aimee replied, flipping over the newspaper to stop Rozzie's eyes death-staring her. 'We'll be done by then.' She flicked through the paper and half-read the stories until the waitress disappeared.

Monster surge in great white sharks with seventeen predators tagged in three days

Line in the sand: Crackdown on crack after substance spike in Byron waterways

Namaste, no pay in Bay: Byron sea-change boom leads to yoga teacher glut

There was a two-page spread about another reality show coming to film in town – *Buying Byron*, a show about rich people buying up all the real estate in Byron. Down one side of the story was a dedicated 'Your Say' column, where cranky locals on the street gave their disapproving opinions about the show. Aimee rustled the pages and flipped the paper over to reveal the front page. The headline was in giant bold font.

BYRON'S BIGGEST BRAT: *Dodgiest driver named and shamed*

About six photos were collaged together to show Brooke's black G-Wagon parked illegally in various loading zones, up on footpaths, across driveways and in whatever other random spaces she could find. One photo showed the car on a median strip. There was also a photo of Brooke walking around the streets in a particularly expensive outfit and the newspaper had done a price breakdown of each item, superimposing price tags over each piece of designer gear. There was the acid green $3,850 Balenciaga handbag that looked like an accessory for trendy aliens. The $500 matching Yeezy slides. A watch worth an estimated $43,800. And what the newspaper claimed was $800 worth of linen, bringing the ensemble's total cost – helpfully calculated and printed in a big cartoon money bag – to $48,950. Aimee whispered aloud the kicker that appeared under the headline – *lifestyles of the rich and clueless*. There was only one thing to do. She whipped out her phone and hovered it high above the page to snap a photo and text to Rob. But before she could click the capture button, it vibrated in her hands. Aimee quickly tapped the notification on the screen, thinking it was a message from Freya. But it was from Heath:

Checking in. Feeling OK about tonight? I'll be in the office, suffering in spreadsheet budget hell. Nina will be there.

This was followed up with two emojis: A piece of toast and a dog.

That's supposed to be a MarMut. There's no Vegemite emoji . . .

Before Aimee could roll her eyes, Freya arrived.

'Sorry I'm late. I overslept.' She slumped on the table for dramatic effect. Her hair was messy. Black Wayfarers on. She looked up and smiled. 'I'm surprised you picked this place. You hate it.'

'I don't *hate* it,' Aimee replied. It was a total lie.

'You hate it,' Freya laughed.

Aimee reached under the table to pull something out of her satchel. 'Be that as it may, I wanted to do something special.' She sat back up. A white glossy box with a thick pink ribbon tied around it was in her lap. She placed it on top of the dodgy driver newspaper exposé and smiled. 'Happy birthday.'

Freya, still slumped on the table, pretended to be embarrassed and Aimee reached over to rustle her hair. She tugged at the ribbon, lifted the top off the box and pulled open a layer of pink tissue paper. Placed inside was a beautiful black analogue camera with zoom lens. NIKON was spelled out in white letters on the front and a thin red stripe was down one side.

'It's a Nikon F3. From 1980,' Aimee rushed to explain. 'I looked on some photography blogs and they said this was one of the most sought-after vintage cameras. It's a classic. There's a thread on Reddit just dedicated to the F3.'

Freya picked it up and wrapped the well-worn black leather strap around her hands.

'Apparently it takes amazing photos.' Aimee paused while Freya looked at it. 'There's some rolls of film in there too. I don't know if you know how to use an analogue camera, but you can google it. There are heaps of YouTube videos. I thought it'd be good for you to have one – if you're pursuing professional photography work next year.' She paused and watched Freya assessing it. 'I saw – at the Christmas party, with the photos you took – the ones projected on that big sheet, you'd put that old-school camera filter effect on them, so . . .' She trailed off.

'It's very cool.' Freya kept looking at it and rotating it in her hands. She wasn't disappointed. But she also wasn't clamouring to go use it immediately.

'Yeah?' Aimee's voice went a little high.

'Yeah. I love it. Thank—'

'So sorry to rush . . .' The waitress leaned in and winced, while whipping out a ratty little notebook from her back pocket that was covered in scrawled orders and reservation names. 'You guys might not have time to do food before the next booking arrives.' She looked at her Apple watch. 'You could still do drinks?'

Freya put the camera back in the box and scrunched the tissue paper around it haphazardly. 'That's OK.' She pointed to Aimee. '. . . I'll just have what you're having.'

Aimee widened her eyes, put on the spot. 'Oh, um. I haven't ordered. Ah . . .' She picked up the narrow menu and flipped it over repeatedly, trying to find the drinks section, before just giving up. 'Just . . . two glasses of . . . like a . . . rosé? Yeah?' She scrunched up her nose and nodded at Freya. 'Like, a dry rosé?'

'Hmmm, I'm not a big fan of rosé,' Freya said. 'I might go with a negroni.'

'Oh, I'll have one too. Done.' Aimee gathered up the menus off the table and handed them to the waitress. 'Good choice.'

A group of young guys had sat down at the next table and were filming themselves clinking tequila shot glasses.

'Hey . . .' Freya ventured. 'Are you feeling OK about tonight?'

'The party? Yeah!' Aimee tried to act breezy. 'I spoke to Rob. Everything's fine. Brooke texted and made sure we were both coming. She was very insistent that everything's fine.'

Freya picked up the glass carafe and trickled some water into a glass. 'I don't want you to feel awkward. Or be uncomfortable.'

Aimee held up the newspaper to show the exposé about Brooke's terrible parking. 'This is on the front page of newspapers all over town today. There is *no way* we're not coming tonight.'

Freya looked down. 'Well, it's totally fine if you guys change your mind.'

The tequila boys downed more shots and slammed the tiny glasses on the table, whooping.

Aimee leaned in to talk over the noise. 'It's your twenty-first party! I'm not missing that!'

Freya let out a sort-of laugh. 'But it's not *really* my twenty-first party. It's more just an excuse for Brooke to have a party so there's something to film for the TV show. I don't even really know anyone other than the girls.'

'Is everything OK with the girls?' Aimee sat up a little straighter, catching herself digging.

'Yeah, but we can just do our own thing another night.'

Aimee scrunched her face, then glanced over at the rowdy boys to make it seem like that's what was troubling her. 'Just . . . um.' She shook her head and tried to think of words that wouldn't seem naggy or clingy. 'Is it . . . that you don't *want* me there?'

The waitress returned with the negronis and placed them on the table, spilling a little of Aimee's over the rim.

Freya's face became concerned and she rushed to answer her aunt but waited for the girl to finish mopping up the red liquid.

'I got it, I got it.' Aimee ended up grabbing a wad of napkins and dabbing the puddle.

'No, not at all. That's not it.' Freya leaned over the table when they were alone again. 'Come. I want you to. I've just been worried about you with the Tim and Bree thing—'

'I told you I'm fine with that.' Aimee tried to be breezy again.

'And after the Christmas party stuff with Brooke, I just . . . didn't want you to feel like you had to come and suffer for me.'

Aimee took a breath. 'So, you're *OK* with me coming?'

'Yes! Come.' Freya laughed.

Aimee gave her niece an unsure look. 'Okaaay.' She ended the discussion and sipped her negroni, still feeling like she hadn't quite got to the truth.

'How is it?' Freya looked at the drink.

'Oh it's terrible,' Aimee laughed. 'We're basically having rocket fuel for breakfast.'

———

'I'm just walking in the door now.' Aimee held the phone to her ear as she clomped up the steps to her apartment. A beach towel – looking wet and heavy – was draped over a shoulder. She used her free hand to push her aviator sunnies on top of her tangled hair, still damp and stringy from an afternoon swim. She squinted while her eyes adjusted to the dim hallway after being outside in the glare all afternoon. 'I'll pick you up at six-ish. No. Do not ask Brooke to sign your newspaper. I will lock you in the car, Roberta.'

She hung up and rummaged through her bag for the house keys and they jingled as she yanked them out. Before she could slide them into the lock, her thighs banged into something and the top half of her body jolted forward. She looked down and cocked her head. A piece of furniture had been dumped right in front of the door. Then a smile flashed across her face. It was the old chest of drawers from Jules' caravan – the one with the missing knob, that he found on the side of the road. A green Post-it was stuck to the top with a message scrawled on it: 'Late Xmas present'. There was also a white sealed envelope resting on top of the golden, cracked timber top. Aimee nudged the side of the chest over with her hip so she could open the door, snapped up the letter and walked inside. The envelope and phone were in one hand and she used the other to chuck her bag on the couch.

She walked over to the stereo. 'Aimee & Fleur's Perfect Mix Tape' was still in the cassette slot from the first time Jules came over. *Click*. Aimee pressed the rewind button to bypass 2 Live Crew, listened to the high-pitched squeal for a few seconds, and then hit the play button at whatever random spot it had landed on. Talking Heads, just as she'd hoped. The middle part of 'This Must Be the Place' filled the apartment. She shoved her little finger through a gap in the side of the envelope, tore open the top, and pulled out the letter. As soon as she unfolded the paper, she knew it wasn't from Jules. It was Tim's writing. Messy and scratchy. It hadn't changed since high school.

Aimee. Been thinking . . . It's really important we do this time-out properly. I won't be at Freya's party. I'm gonna stop coming to the TV stuff. I think maybe we should talk about extending the time-out a bit.

The beats of the song kept bopping. The synth trilled along. Aimee pursed her lips and dug her thumbnails into the tips of her forefingers but her eyes still welled up. Rage bubbled inside her stomach and she needed to find a way to release it immediately from her body. She picked up the phone that was resting beside her and felt the weight in her palm. Then she swung her arm back and pelted it at the wall.

THIRTY-FIVE

'Whoa,' Rob said.

'I know.' Aimee stood next to her on the outskirts of Brooke's lawn. Same location as the Christmas party. Completely different Pinterest board.

'So much—'

'Macramé.'

'Yeah.'

Mismatched Persian rugs were layered in crisscross patterns over the yard with the Brats and about twenty other random girls all gathered in the middle – sitting on tan leather Moroccan pouffes around really low timber coffee tables. Fairy lights twinkled overhead and Aimee could tell they weren't the same ones used for the Christmas party. Reusing Christmas fairy lights at a birthday party? That would just be embarrassing. A warm breeze picked up and nudged around the dozens of different sized balloons, all in coordinating shades of blush, pink and bronze, that were gathered in one of those big garland arrangements – the kind you'd always see on Instagram at baby showers and weddings. It swooped across the yard.

And the macramé. So much macramé. Macramé wall hangings. Banners. Table runners. Outfits.

Even after consulting the Pinterest link, Aimee and Rob still looked out of place. They'd worn white and cream and tan but, somehow, they didn't quite match the whites and creams and tans of the décor.

Freya walked up with two glasses of champagne. She was wearing a white linen jumpsuit with a V-neckline that dipped down low and showed off her bronzed summer skin. 'You guys okaaay?' she asked with a nervous laugh and handed over the flutes.

Rob kissed Freya on the cheek. 'We're macra-mézing.'

Freya looked around at the event and seemed a little embarrassed. 'I know. It's a bit ridiculous.' Then she spotted Aimee's phone. 'You switched to the new one!'

Aimee stumbled over her words for a second. She hadn't told Rob about Tim's letter or how its contents led to the complete destruction of an electrical appliance and part of her living room wall. 'Oh. Yeah. My old phone smashed today. Like yours did – on the cement. Cracked. It's why we're a bit late, sorry. It took me ages to set this up.' She nodded to the new phone. 'I'm still not sure I've done it properly.' A logical explanation, but Aimee didn't sound convincing. It was probably the almost-silent atmosphere at the party that added to the awkwardness.

'Well, Brooke's insisted on waiting until you guys got here to kick things off,' Freya said before cracking a smile. 'And, because we can't have any music, I'm sorry to say you won't be allowed to serenade me with a Jet cover, as promised.'

'Rob's here.' Aimee raised an eyebrow. 'We can go acapella.'

'Ooh, can't do that either,' Freya said with mock disappointment. 'The production still needs to pay fees for licensing, even if the song's sung acapella. All the budget was spent securing Byron Karen, which leaves no room for Australian rock hits of yore.'

Aimee pretended to be offended and playfully grabbed her niece's arm, holding it up as if it were evidence. 'Don't think I haven't noticed that you're still wearing this old green Jet concert wristband!' The tattered neon paper contrasted against Freya's thin tanned wrist, even in the dimly lit backyard. Aimee had noticed she'd been wearing it ever since she found it in the Monaro. 'You're basically a card-carrying Jet fan!'

'I'm wearing it *ironically*,' Freya protested.

Aimee got distracted by the guys from the TV crew, who were trudging over with cords dangling from their hands. 'Ugh, I forgot,' she started assessing her outfit, 'I need to get mic'd up.' Before she could even finish the sentence, the crew had arrived and, with zero greetings, started tugging at her clothing.

Freya slipped away again and wandered deeper into the Moroccan fantasy world. 'Have fun, you two cold hard bitches!' she yelled back, crowbarring in one final Jet taunt.

'Rude!' Rob called back.

Aimee had zoned out. *This isn't her*, she thought while looking around at Freya's OTT party, filled with strangers. Then she froze for a moment. All the talk of Jet made her mind flash back to seeing the band at the Palace Hotel – twenty-one years ago, on Fleur's own twenty-first birthday.

'Back at the scene of the crime,' a British accent snipped out of view.

Even after only a handful of meetings, Aimee could recognise Nina's voice. Something about it sounded gleefully ominous. Aimee tried to twist her ahead around to spot her but was restricted by the tech guys who were still fitting her.

'You must be the *bogan hairdresser*.' Nina introduced herself to Rob. 'We didn't meet the other night but I watched it all from my lair.'

'Ohhh . . . you're MarMuts!' Rob clapped. 'Aimee told me. I'm a big fan of your work.'

'The feeling's mutual.' Nina waved over one of the cameras that was lingering nearby along with that plain Jane producer girl whose name Aimee still hadn't learnt.

'You've probably got time for a quick on-the-fly chat before things kick into gear,' Nina instructed before striding off over the grass.

'Aimee! I've missed our chats!' The producer girl switched on her fake gal pal voice and lunged in for a hug. 'I've been thinking about you all day.

It must be so hard. What's going through your mind after reading Tim's letter?'

The question slapped Aimee in the face.

'What letter?' Rob whispered, as she shuffled to the side, out of shot.

'We heard Bree talking about it on the phone to Tim when she was getting her hair and make-up done for tonight,' the producer said softly, as if trying to feign concern. 'What was in the letter?'

Aimee was quiet for a moment, self-conscious about the camera, which remained very still, as if she wouldn't notice its presence. 'What did *Bree* say about it?' she asked the producer.

'I really can't remember word for word.' The producer shrugged before switching on her gal pal voice again. 'But maybe you'll feel better if you talk it out. It must be so hard. What emotions are you feeling right now?'

'Was she talking about it on camera?' Aimee looked beyond the crew and tried to spot Bree but couldn't see her amongst all the other girls dressed like macramé wall hangings.

'Well, *everything's* filmed.'

'Can I see it?'

'Ooh, sorry babe.' The producer scrunched up her nose. 'You know I can't show you stuff like that.'

'Well, I guess I can't comment on it.' Aimee tried to beat the producer at her own game.

'You seem angry at Bree for talking about the letter. If she was here right now, what would you say to her?'

Aimee looked down and took a deep breath.

Rob called out from off-camera. 'You OK?'

'Hello?' Brooke's voice was amplified over a PA system. She tapped the microphone with a finger to get everyone's attention and the TV crew scurried to their positions.

'I can keep chatting to you later about it babe,' the producer promised Aimee, as if she was being selflessly helpful, before turning away to talk into her sneaky headset.

Brooke continued. 'I just wanted to welcome everyone and thank you all for coming to celebrate Freya's twenty-first. She's quickly become a big part of all our lives after fate *whisked* her in at the beginning of the summer. But it's probably better if we get her aunt up to say a few words.'

Aimee looked around hesitantly. 'Ah . . .'

'Just a few words,' Brooke said, staring at her over the crowd and waving her down.

Rob scrambled to grab her friend's champagne glass and bag. 'Maybe just do a dramatic reading of "Cold Hard Bitch"?'

With a deep breath, Aimee walked across the grass and up to the stage, while Brooke held out the mic until she arrived to grab it. Looking out at the strange girls in strappy white tops, sitting on Moroccan pouffes, Aimee raced to think of something nice to say that wouldn't make her look unprepared but also wouldn't be so gushingly sentimental that it would embarrass Freya. 'This summer has been . . . quite . . . irregular? Maybe that's not the right word. It's been weird. But Freya showing up was the best surprise. She's my only niece. And I love her. And . . .' she looked over the crowd at Freya, 'I'm so glad I get to spend your twenty-first with you. Happy birthday.' She handed the microphone over to Brooke and prepared to dash back to her spot with Rob. In her hasty exit from the stage, she got whacked in the face by an arrangement of dried palm fronds.

'Beautiful, beautiful,' Brooke cooed into the microphone before smiling at Freya in the crowd. 'Now, don't worry, Freya – I'm not forcing you to make a speech.' She let out a fake-ish laugh and then dropped into a considered, wistful tone. 'I just wanted to say that this summer has been so special for all of us. It's something we couldn't have planned. You've been like another daughter to me. And ever since you showed me your photography portfolio and talked about what kind of work you want to do next year, I was impressed by your skill and talent. I think you've found what you're supposed to do with your life and I love nothing more than seeing people thrive in their passions. Now, it's only something small, but . . .' she paused for dramatic effect, 'I thought it was about time you got yourself a real camera.'

She reached down and lifted a black camera bag up in the air. 'I called my friend at an ad agency in Sydney and he said, right now, the industry standard is the Nikon Z 7II. Which is perfect, because . . .' She waited a beat to build anticipation again, then spoke slower and closer to the microphone, as if she was announcing the Best Picture winner at the Oscars. 'I want to commission *you* to shoot the next print and online campaign for Tutu Tribe!' She let out a shriek and jumped up and down on the spot as the other girls clapped.

'Didn't you already buy Freya a Nikon?' Rob whispered.

Aimee's eyes followed Freya as she walked up on the stage to hug Brooke. She looked slightly embarrassed. But also kinda happy. 'I did.' Aimee stared ahead. 'Just . . . not that one.'

'And . . . And . . .' Brooke waited for her guests to settle. 'Doing that kind of work requires more than just a good camera. You'll also need to edit. Which is why you're also getting a new MacBook Pro!' She shrieked again and clapped. 'It comes with the latest version of Photoshop and . . . well . . . a whole bunch of other stuff that I know nothing about but *you* will. And . . . now, now . . . there's just one other, teeny-tiny little thing. You've been talking about doing a master's in photography next year. I know you've applied and you're waiting for everything to be confirmed, but in that camera bag, you'll also find a cheque that will cover the *whole two semesters* of tuition fees.'

Freya's jaw basically hit the floor. But not harder than Aimee's. It was this last gift that caused her to wipe away a tear that was forming in the corner of her eye. She could feel it building and she nudged it just before it glided down.

Rob leaned in. 'I saw her G-Wagon in the garage. Want me to drive it into the lake?'

———

Inside Brooke's kitchen, Aimee and Rob sat at the Carrara marble island bench in silence, sipping champagne from Starbucks cups while the party whirled on outside.

'That kettle is fucking ridiculous,' Rob mumbled, glaring at the over-priced appliance.

Freya ran in. Her bag was on one of the timber bar stools. She dipped a hand in and pulled out her car keys.

'I just gotta run out for a minute,' she said, clearly unaware of her aunt's disappointment. 'I'll be back.'

Aimee went to open her mouth but Freya cut her off.

'I haven't been drinking. I knew I'd have to pick someone up – I'm drinking when I come back.'

'That's not what I was going to say – I *know* you wouldn't do that,' Aimee said. 'But it's your birthday party, should you be leaving?'

'I have to pick someone up to *come to the party*,' Freya replied, a little frustrated with having to explain herself. 'Everyone else has been drinking and can't drive.'

'Well, *I* can pick them up,' Aimee insisted, pushing her chair back to go find her keys. 'You stay – you shouldn't have to leave your own party—'

'Aimee! Stop *trying* so fucking hard!' Freya snapped.

Aimee felt a pang in her chest and an immediate sickness in her stomach. Like her body had just smacked down on cement. The only other time she'd ever felt that way was in the Woolworths carpark when Tim had asked for the time-out.

'Ugh, sorry – but . . .' Freya exhaled loudly and avoided eye contact. 'I'll talk to you later.' Her tan sandals clacked over Brooke's expensive reclaimed hardwood floors.

'You'll probably get home well after me, so just remember to take The Bomb before you go to bed,' Aimee said firmly. It was the first time Freya had ever spoken to her like that. It was the exact tone – and that specific *look* that her niece had shot her – that Aimee had spent years trying to avoid.

Rob waited a beat before breaking the silence. 'Do you wanna talk about *that* outburst, or would you rather tell me about Tim's letter?'

'Can we talk about literally anything else?'

'OK.' Rob paused. 'Would you rather fuck a guy who drives a Kia Picanto or a guy who drives a Nissan Cube?'

Aimee ignored the joke and shook her head. She wasn't quite ready to fume about the letter or Freya but there was someone else she'd been waiting to explode about. 'It was like she was hosting the grand finale of one of those TV talent shows and she just kept handing out prizes,' she said of Brooke's Oprah-style birthday giveaway. Then she fiddled with her microphone pack that she'd ripped off and placed on the benchtop – double-checking that the power switch was turned off.

Rob sighed. 'I know. I was half-expecting her to give Freya an overseas holiday to Phuket and a Suzuki Vitara.'

'It was inappropriate, right?'

Rob jumped off the stool. 'Let's just go. It's weird us being here. We came, you gave a speech. Freya won't care.'

'Well, *Freya's* not even here.' Aimee got to her feet and swung her satchel strap across her limp, defeated body. Rob wrapped an arm around her. Holding their Starbucks cups, they slipped out the folding glass doors and into the yard. The cameras were distracted, filming everyone at their really small tables while the @ThoseTwoVanGuys performed some kind of skit. Aimee and Rob were just about to exit Morocco . . . and that's when they heard the crying.

'Freya's mum!' a voice sobbed.

Aimee and Rob turned. Sitting on the ledge of the patio was Luna. Upset and clearly drunk. She got to her feet and trudged over.

'I don't know how you've fucking done it,' she sniffed.

Aimee and Rob looked at each other, trying to figure out where the interaction was going.

'You and Tim and Bree with your open relationship make it look so easy. How are you so cool with him fucking other people?'

Aimee didn't have the energy to nit-pick the details over what exactly her relationship was but that was OK because Luna still had things to muse about.

'Me and Bodhi have been trying an open arrangement – but with *rules*. We're supposed to tell each other *before* we hook up with someone. Not just go around fucking people in secret and hiding it from each other.'

Aimee wrapped an arm around Luna to stop her from swaying. 'Well, is that what Bodhi's been doing?' she asked, immediately regretting getting involved.

'He's been fucking *everyone*.'

Aimee and Rob shared a nervous glance. They both knew about Charlie hooking up with Bodhi but did Luna know? And did she know they were friends with Charlie? Neither wanted to experience another *Brats of Byron Bay* cheating scandal..

'He gave me *chlamydia*.' Luna raised her eyebrows. 'And . . . I'm open and positive about STIs – they're a part of an active sex life. But it pisses me off that I probably only got it because *he* was breaking the rules. I just . . .' she started to slur, 'I'm so blime-fibeb! You know, I shat the bed in front of him! During sex! That kind of intimate experience binds two people together.'

'That's one way of putting it.' Rob stroked Luna's hair.

'Baaaaabe! Baaabe!' A nasal voice interrupted from across the yard. 'Are you okaaaay?' Addie stumbled over. Well, it was more a limp. When she finally reached the trio, she wrapped an arm around Aimee's other shoulder and leant on her for support.

'Hon, you said you were gonna go to the hospital,' Luna whined.

'I found some codeine in Brooke's pantry and mixed it with champagne, so the pain should start to go away soon,' Addie said, her eyes welling as if she was in extreme physical discomfort.

'Why do you need to go to hospital?' Aimee took a serious tone.

'I'm not going to hospital!' Addie grunted.

'Her Brazilian butt lift is infected again,' Luna said urgently. 'Babe, you can't keep ignoring it.'

'I am not losing another summer to a BBL infection!' Addie screamed.

Aimee looked down at her thigh. She felt a damp patch. 'I think something's spilled on my jeans . . .'

'Sorry babe, the BBL lesions have started to weep through my dress.'

Aimee looked at Rob square in the eyes. 'Kill me. Kill me now and toss my body in Brooke's lake.'

'It's fine.' Addie waved away Aimee's concerns. 'Right now it's just a clear pus. The yellow pus comes a few days into the infection.'

'Well, I think you both maybe need to sit down and have a sip of water,' Aimee said, too distracted by her own issues and pus-stained white jeans to deal with what would inevitably become another podcast episode.

'I can't sit!' Addie screamed. 'My butt cheeks could permanently dent!'

'Let's find some food,' Rob suggested, leading them across the yard to the weird tiny tables near the stage. Aimee followed, lugging both Luna and Addie whose arms were wrapped around her neck. But before they could dump her off . . .

'Hi . . . hi . . . me again. Sorry,' Brooke said into the microphone. 'I know this night's not about me but we just received some good news and I wanted to share it.'

Aimee and Rob paused and looked up at the stage.

'As you all know, we moved to Byron to start a new chapter and expand Tutu Tribe. We've been searching for a space here to make it our official HQ. I have looked at *a lot* of properties. None of them were perfect. None!' She paused to laugh. 'But . . . I finally found *the* place. It wasn't for sale, but, when I saw it, I knew *I had to have it*. I made an offer – and, apparently, the owner couldn't refuse. They just confirmed a few moments ago and accepted. Tutu Tribe's permanent HQ is now in the garage on Jonson Street! Formerly known as Barber Rob's!'

The cameramen turned and swooped in closer to Rob and Aimee.

'I am driving that fucking crazy bitch's G-Wagon into her fucking lake.' Rob dropped her handbag on the lawn.

'Hey!' Aimee yelled over the crowd. It was like a growl, deep from her chest. It even startled Rob and caused her to stay put while her friend marched up to the base of the stage, making the drunk twins Luna and Addie – who were still draped on each of Aimee's shoulders – hobble quickly to keep up.

'What the hell is your problem, lady?' She looked up at Brooke with squinted eyes. 'I know this is the moment on a reality show where I'm supposed to . . . I don't know . . . *pull your hair,* or call you a MarMut.'

Brooke let out a high-pitched laugh. 'What's a MarMut?' she said into the microphone while looking around, bemused. The crowd laughed along with her. Then Brooke's tone took a turn. 'I wouldn't act so superior if I were you, Aimee. Let's not forget how you called me a C-word.' She held out her arms as the crowd gasped.

'I called you *a* C-word, not *the* C-word,' Aimee tried to correct over the murmurs.

Brooke was already on a roll. 'And then, after the C-word scandal, you tried to glass me!'

Aimee's face scrunched up. 'When did I try to *glass* you?'

'At the pub. After you called me a C-word, I thoughtfully went to meet you at the pub to make amends but you threw a glass of red wine at me!'

Like a slow motion replay, Aimee remembered the night where Brooke got drunk with her and Rob and the moment she'd accidentally knocked over a glass on the table. 'Nope, not what happened,' Aimee snipped. 'There were no glassings.'

Then Brooke reached behind the stage and pulled out the white silk shirt she'd been wearing that night. The red wine stain was still splashed across it.

'Did you seriously have that on standby as a prop?' Aimee furrowed her brow.

'See? Exhibit A!' Brooke held up the damaged shirt. 'I'm the victim of a brazen glassing attack.'

The gloves were off. And Aimee's temper cracked like the glass of wine she did or didn't throw.

'OK! All right! You know what? If that's the reaction you're looking for, Brooke, then . . . *fine*. Fine! You've got it! You're seeking some kind of petty revenge against my friend to get ratings for this heinous show – all because your beige polo-wearing husband couldn't bear to spend another night listening to you crap on about how perfect you are. Well guess what, Brooke? You're *not* perfect. I *know* you're not perfect. I know those decorations on your Christmas trees inside aren't from France.' Aimee raised her voice louder to address the crowd. 'Did you all know that? She tells everyone they're from France but they're actually from Target! Your doink of a husband told me that when he was getting stoned in the back shed during the Christmas party. Oh!' Aimee let out a laugh as she thought of another barb and straightened her back that was starting to tire under the body-weight of Luna and Addie. 'And she drinks fake Starbucks! Those really big Starbucks cups you see her with? She buys them empty and then just fills them up with her own coffee at home! *Fake Starbucks*! There's not even a fucking Starbucks in Byron Ba—'

Splat!

Luna heaved and projectile vomited all down Aimee's top.

Splat! . . . Again.

Addie chundered down Aimee's side, adding to the pus-stain. Turns out codeine and champagne don't mix.

Just as Brooke's high-pitched laugh started to cackle out through the microphone speakers, it was drowned out by an electric guitar riff that tore through the backyard. It was so loud it almost seemed like it was coming from a live band. For a second, Aimee thought Charlie was playing, until she remembered he had a gig in Kingscliff that night. The drums kicked in and the thumps made the windows on Brooke's house start to shake. Everyone looked up and saw Rob standing on the patio, with her phone plugged into the sound equipment. She picked up one of the spare microphones. That's when Aimee recognised the song: Jet, 'Cold Hard Bitch'.

'You can't use the footage if there's a song playing!' Rob yelled. 'Now, I didn't get this hooked up fast enough so, Aimee, I'm sorry but they can still probably use all that stuff you said just before about Brooke's fake Starbucks and her boring husband. But if there's anything else you wanna say, do it now!'

THIRTY-SIX

'We should've taken her micro-dog Chicken and held it hostage.' Rob held the phone to her ear and paced around the living room in the open-air loft that looked down over her salon. The big metal roller door of the garage that opened out to Jonson Street was pulled up and midnight revellers walked by, bouncing from different clubs and bars – the thrumming optimism of a good night out at odds with the panic-stricken frenzy that jittered inside.

'Just keep calling and we'll figure this out.' Aimee took a sip of tequila from one of the many Starbucks cups Rob had stolen from Brooke's place. 'She can't just *buy* your building.'

'Why not? Yours is being sold without warning.'

Aimee paused. 'That is true.'

'I've been calling that fucking rat of a landlord since we left the party and he's refusing to answer,' Rob said before glancing at Aimee. 'You *should've* thrown a wine glass at her.'

'If the TV cameras weren't there, I *would've* thrown a wine glass at her.' Aimee pushed a hand through her hair.

'Well, I appreciate what you *did* say. It was very classy. Elegant, even.'

Aimee rejected Rob's facetiousness. 'I hysterically exposed a woman for drinking fake Starbucks and then got double-vommed on.' Aimee tugged at the Kylie Minogue tour merch T-shirt Rob had given her to change into. 'There was nothing elegant about it.'

Rob hung up the phone. 'Aimee, don't sell yourself short. You also told her rich friends that she shops at Target. Ooh! And you even got a jab in about the beige polo-wearing husband. And all in a rather succinct way. It was impressive how it all just spilled out of you like that. Public rants are your talent. You know, you probably absorbed the skill from falling asleep to all those old episodes of *Becker*.'

Aimee flopped her body onto the floor dramatically. 'Please stop quoting my rant back to me. I'll have to re-live it enough when the footage airs.'

Rob poured more tequila into their Starbucks cups. 'If the only positive thing to come out of this is that you get turned into a meme again, it will have all been worth it.' The temporary spark of glee that came from imagining Aimee's supercharged viral stardom fizzed out quickly and Rob tossed back her drink. 'We need to go somewhere.'

Aimee sat back up. 'Where?'

'Anywhere. We need to stay out all night and toast our final days in Byron. Admit it: the countdown's on. We're just moments away from having to move out to *Casino*.' Rob stuck her tongue out and shuddered.

'Well, we've probably missed our window for that,' Aimee said sarcastically. 'Narissa says Ballina has become just as expensive as Byron – so Casino's probably boomed by now as well.'

'Fuck.' Rob threw her head back before making an aside. 'Also, it's *Nichelle* . . . But, fuck!'

The Fleetwood Mac song 'Gypsy' played over the speaker system and echoed off the polished concrete floors and brick walls. Rob stared up at the exposed metal air vents attached to the ceiling and sighed. 'That fucking crazy bitch with the fucking lake.'

'Has your landlord texted back?'

'No. And I've left so many voicemails his inbox is now jammed up. It seems that, after ruining my life completely, he decided to fall off the face of the earth. I can't get another shop like this. You've seen how expensive other spaces are right now. There's nowhere else to go.'

Aimee lay flat on the floor and felt the cool cement touch the backs of her arms. She was defeated and exhausted by the issues that just kept mounting. All summer, as each problem sprang up out of nowhere, her secret first thought was always: When are the adults going to step in and handle this? But there were no adults waiting on the sidelines. Aimee was the adult. She wondered if adults ever got to an age where they actually felt like one. 'It's my fault. I did this stupid show. Without me, this wouldn't have happened.'

'Look, our buildings getting sold would've happened eventually,' Rob said. 'Suddenly, every day around here has become a fun new surprise, waiting to see what else in your life is going to get fucked up.'

Aimee sighed. 'Tim wants to extend the time-out.'

Rob's face looked pained. 'What?' She was as blime-fibeb by the news as Aimee was.

'That's what that letter was. The one Bree was caught on camera talking about. Tim wrote me a note saying he wants to extend the time-out. Do it "properly" this time – not see each other or talk.'

'Sweetie.' Rob paced over and dropped to the floor to hug her friend. 'I'm so sorry. I'm so sorry you've been holding onto that while all this other stuff is going on. It just . . . sucks.'

'It really sucks.'

'It *fucking* sucks. What are you feeling? Tell me as much or as little as you want.'

'Thanks. Look, it's heartbreaking. Devastating. Completely and utterly soul-destroying. Maybe it has just shocked me more than anything. It's like waiting to find out a diagnosis for a terminal disease: Your engagement *might* be over and *you* might be the problem.'

Rob took a deep breath. 'Well . . . Tim's not the only one who's making the decision.'

'Yeah, but . . . why does it feel like he is?'

Rob sat up. 'What do you want? What do *you* want?'

Aimee stared into her Starbucks cup. 'God, I just don't know anymore.'

Rob used a knuckle to nudge up Aimee's chin so she could look her in the eye. 'Do you still wanna be with Tim? Because it's *so* OK if you don't.'

Aimee paused for a moment. 'I don't wanna talk about this anymore.'

Rob's phone vibrated on the floor and the screen lit up.

Aimee looked over. 'Landlord?' She was almost thankful for the subject change.

Rob got to her feet and grabbed her long leopard print jacket that she insisted on wearing everywhere, even in summer. 'Nah.' She plucked up her keys.

'Is Charlie here? I thought he had a gig in Kingscliff?'

'It's just a delivery.'

'Pizza?'

Rob flitted down the spiral metal stairs. 'Sure,' she called back, her voice high-pitched and playfully deceiving.

'Well, is it?' Aimee clambered up off the floor and followed her down the winding steps.

Rob pretended to get melodramatic. 'Aimee, I'm too overwhelmed to answer your questions right now.'

'Roberta.'

Rob reached the bottom floor and turned around to look up at her friend. 'Aimee. You're my best friend and, right now, we're both in crisis. Tonight, we are going out. We are going to drink too much tequila. Dance. *Not* hook up with weird dads in beige polo shirts. And we're also going to indulge in the cocaine that I've just ordered.' She spun around and headed for the big metal door on the back wall.

Aimee took a beat. Then ran after her. 'No. Absolutely not. *Ab-so-lute-ly not.*'

'Well, the delivery is already here.' Rob pushed the door open and skipped out into the laneway.

'How do you even get cocaine delivered?' Aimee whisper-screamed.

'Some Melbourne girls were in the salon and talking about a dial-a-dealer they're getting their coke from for the weekend.' She gave Aimee a sly look over her shoulder. 'I may have requested the contact.'

'And what? You really just shared your personal address with an anonymous drug dealer?'

'Aimee, don't be ridiculous – that would be dangerous. I gave them the address of the Meals on Wheels kitchen down the alleyway.' She ran ahead to the taillights in the driveway.

This was not Aimee's world. She tolerated Tim's weed habit through high school and into his twenties – but he only ever occasionally smoked now. The strongest thing she'd ever consumed was The Bomb after a night of tequila. She'd never done cocaine in her life. Not that she was judgmental about it – it just wasn't something she'd ever gotten around to doing . . . like Pilates. It wasn't something Rob did either, though she was never shy about telling stories from her party girl days living in New York and London. The main reason Aimee'd never tried it was because she always had a gut feeling that the *one* time she decided to experiment with drugs, she'd get the bad batch and wind up in hospital. Then the town Looney Tunes would give quotes to the local newspaper, saying things like, 'She kept her habit hidden well – but, then again, most junkies do. She seemed so innocent, running that bookstore. I guess you never really know someone.'

Aimee jogged after her friend, who came to a sudden halt a few metres away from the driver's side window.

Rob turned back towards Aimee. She looked sick.

The yellow glow from a streetlamp flooded through the windscreen of the car and Aimee squinted to see better. She would've recognised that wild golden hair anywhere.

THIRTY-SEVEN

'I am so mad. I am *so mad*. I'm not even angry. There is a difference between mad and angry. Jesus, no word describes how angry I am. Furious. Livid. I'm beyond all of it. I could *throttle* you, Freya.' Aimee paced around Rob's living room. Her breathing was loud and her hands jittered like they were trying to expel the fury that was raging inside her.

Freya sobbed. She tried speaking up but Aimee cut her off.

'I have stood back and not interfered and not nagged you at all, the whole time you've been staying with me – and all you have done is *lie*. From the very first day. You didn't tell me you were on the TV show. You didn't tell me you had a boyfriend – and I had to find out in *the news* . . . with a really inappropriate GIF. Seriously, what if a future employer sees that humping GIF?' She shook her head quickly and got back on track. 'And then I had to find out through Brooke that the boyfriend actually came with you from Sydney. Brooke. Your new best friend, Brooke.' She paced. 'How does Brooke know more about you than I do? Did you know she's just bought Rob's garage? And she's kicking her out in some kind of . . . petty, made-for-TV, revenge scheme.'

Freya furrowed her brow and looked over at Rob, who'd just come out of the kitchen and handed her a glass of water. A slideshow of the few cute and innocent moments Aimee had shared with Freya over summer played in her head and she got angrier knowing that underneath it all, Freya had been tricking her.

'You haven't wanted to see me the entire time you've been here and . . . whatever, that's fine, Freya . . .' She changed tack because the thought was making her upset. 'You've treated me like I'm an *idiot*. Like I'm foolish. It is *so* disrespectful. And trying to keep me at arms-length from your life – telling me it's because you're worried about my feelings with Brooke and Bree and Tim when really you just wanted to sneak around. That's manipulative. You *manipulated* my feelings. And it hurts because I have gone out of my way – and *against* my own better judgement – to give you respect and treat you like an adult.' Aimee stood above Freya, who was still dressed in her outfit from the birthday party with her shimmery make-up. '*Stop trying so fucking hard,*' she repeated Freya's words back to her – the ones she spat at Aimee during the party. 'Stop trying so fucking hard? Clearly I didn't try fucking hard enough! I'm fucking *furious* that I didn't try harder! I should have kept trying until you hated me because I'd rather you hate me than you be in this mess.' Her hands were shaking and she was starting to sob. Rob reached out but Aimee pulled away. 'Are the other girls doing this too? Luna? And, that one with the butt infection?'

'It's just me,' Freya sniffed. 'No one knows about it.'

A thought sparked in Aimee's mind. 'What about Bree? Brooke told me she was in rehab. Is she involved? Did she get you into this?'

'She went to rehab ages ago and it wasn't like she had a serious problem.'

'Unlike this,' Aimee shot back. '*This* is a serious problem. And I don't care that you've said you don't *use* drugs yourself.'

'You're just mad about Bree and Brooke and how much time I've spent with them,' Freya said, a flicker of defensiveness seeping through the shame and upset.

It was a slap to the face for Aimee. Her eyes locked on the green paper wristband strapped around Freya's wrist and she nodded at it. 'This is *very* different to how your mum spent *her* twenty-first.'

Freya winced like she'd just been stung.

Aimee regretted her words instantly but she'd come too far. She crossed her arms. 'I need to know exactly how this happened. And I don't want the cute skimmed-over version like you've been giving me for everything else over the past few weeks. You tell me *everything.*'

Freya tried to take a deep breath but she was still trembling from crying. Rob sat down on the couch and wrapped an arm around her.

'It started in Sydney. It wasn't a planned thing,' Freya began. 'Just with friends. We'd go out and one person would want a bag and I knew someone who could get it, so I'd organise it. And then another person would want something, so I'd get it for them. And then *their* friends would know I could get some, so they'd ask. And Jaxon, my boyfriend . . . he thought we could make some money doing it – because we were already getting it for friends anyway. People would pass the mobile number around to each other . . . They'd text what they wanted and where they'd be. We'd deliver it. It just kind of became . . . a *thing.* And then Jax had the idea to come do it in Byron over summer because it'd be full of people from Sydney and Melbourne and Brisbane and everyone partying.'

'Well, this is where it ends – *tonight.* Do you hear me? Because I don't think you realise how serious this is.'

'It's not that easy.'

'Just stop doing it.'

'I have too much that I still need to sell.'

'Throw it out.'

'It's worth too much. I can't afford to.'

'I don't care,' Aimee said with a shocked laugh. 'This is dangerous and *idiotic.* You're not putting yourself at risk for . . . A thousand dollars? Two thousand dollars?'

Freya looked down and paused. 'Thirty thousand.'

Aimee dropped to the floor. 'Jesus Christ, Freya. I'm gonna be sick.'

'That's street value – it sounds worse than it is. It's only, like, a hundred bags.'

'Oh. *Only* a hundred bags.'

'Well, *you guys* were buying one.'

Aimee squinted and tried to think of a response. She hadn't anticipated that fact being thrown in her face. 'That is completely different.'

Rob interjected. 'Can I still get my bag, or?'

Aimee shot her a look.

Rob backed down. 'Not the right time. Got it.'

Aimee turned to Freya. 'Where did you even get it from?'

'Jaxon. He organised it.'

'And where's Jaxon now?'

Freya eyes started to well up again and her breathing got heavy. 'We had a fight and he flew back to Sydney and now I've gotta deliver it myself while also doing the show – and the pap photographers are following all of us and it's just become a mess. And I haven't been able to tell anyone. Most of the bags are for New Year's and I've got to film that night. Jax was going to do the deliveries but now I have to and I don't know how I'm going to.'

Aimee exhaled and pushed her hair back. She'd been trying to avoid this moment all throughout Freya's life. She snapped into mum-mode.

'You will *not* be selling anymore. Not even *one* drop off – do you hear me?' She pointed a finger and her voice became sharp and stern. 'I'll be checking with Heath *every day* to see when and where you're supposed to be filming. If I text you or call, you respond immediately. And you won't be spending the night at Brooke's anymore. From now on, you sleep in your own room at *my* house.'

'What about the rest?' Freya looked helplessly at her aunt.

Aimee knew it all came down to her. 'I will fix it.'

————

3.26am

The headlights of the Monaro lit up the dirt trail as it rolled, a little reck-lessly, down into a field. No other lights from houses or street lamps could be seen. The location was clearly remote, but the car moved forward with certainty – as if it were being pulled towards its destination with a magnet. No music was playing on the stereo. Silence. Just Aimee driving into the darkness. She couldn't stay at home. Her thoughts had become too big. The only way to escape them was to move forward – focusing only on the few metres she could see in front of her. Stone-faced. If she started showing emotion, she wouldn't be able to stop. The Monaro rolled into a clearing and pulled up in a worn-down patch of grass, the handbrake creaking as Aimee yanked it up and switched off the ignition. She burst out of the car and ran towards the caravan on the edge of the field. Her palms banged on the cold metal door.

'What's wrong?' Jules answered, bleary-eyed and stunned.

'Everything.'

Jules' face creased with concern and he grabbed her by the waist. 'Tell me.'

'No.' Aimee popped up on her toes to gain an inch of height and kissed him. She drank him in like she'd just woken up from a twelve-hour nap in the desert. When she eventually pulled back, she ran her palms over his bare chest and looked at his dark steely eyes.

This was one of those moments she'd usually go swimming. Even at night. There was something about black water. It could be scary. But it could also be the one place you could hide and escape all the problems trying to grab at your ankles. With Jules, Aimee had found somewhere else to dive.

THIRTY-EIGHT

The time on the Monaro's old dashboard analogue clock was 6.07 when it rolled up the hill towards the Cape Byron lighthouse. Morning joggers were out. Young hot people took photos in activewear. Aimee and Freya sat in silence, their bodies bouncing and swaying as the tyres rolled up the ascent. There'd been no real talking since the previous night – just a lot of stomping and huffing from Aimee. And when Freya had tried to switch on the stereo after they jumped in the car that morning, Aimee made a point of swiftly switching it off. They'd left Rob's salon late and only had a few hours between getting home and leaving again to make it on time to Addie's 'letting go' ceremony at dawn. Aimee hadn't slept. After her secret midnight runaway to Jules, she snuck back in just before Freya got up. An early morning with a wannabe Instagram guru was the last thing Aimee needed. The walls and ceiling of her mind had closed in and the only thing she could think about was how to rank all her problems in order of most concerning to least concerning – a difficult task when they were all equally catastrophically concerning.

1. Freya being a secret drug dealer
2. Her long-term relationship being on a prolonged hiatus

3. Her store closing, leaving her unemployed
4. Her best friend losing her store and home because of Aimee being involved in the TV show

Somewhere in that list, she'd have to fit in the issue of helping her niece get rid of 100 bags of an illegal substance while also recouping thirty-thousand dollars. *Thirty-thousand dollars.* Aimee had never even had that much money in her savings account.

'Where'd you go last night?' Freya mumbled – testing to see if she could get a non-pissed off response.

Aimee turned slightly and looked like she'd just been asked the most inconvenient question. 'I didn't go *anywhere.*'

'I heard the front door close. At like *3am.*'

Aimee hesitated. 'It must've been Charlie,' she huffed.

It wasn't Charlie.

'He's still in Kingscliff.' Freya looked out the window.

Fuck.

Loose stones on the bitumen crunched under the wheels when the car pulled into a parking space near the lighthouse. Freya jumped out before Aimee could switch off the engine and just as the passenger door slammed, Aimee's phone rang. A random number. She answered. Her tone changed from unsure to familiar. Then her voice switched to frustration.

'Jesus Christ,' she groaned, whipping off her sunglasses and using her spare hand to rub her face. She hadn't bothered trying to use make-up to disguise the bags under her eyes and the morning forehead crease wasn't disappearing anytime soon. 'What if I pay more? I can't afford to pay more but what if I could? – I don't know – you tell me.'

Freya tapped on Aimee's window with her knuckle. Aimee squinted and waved her away.

'Don't we have an agreement? Like, I agree to not burn down your property and you agree to not ruin my life?' She paused. 'When did you want this to happen?' Aimee thunked her head on the rubber steering wheel.

'That's only in a few weeks. That's not enough time. There will never be enough time but that's *really* not enough time.'

Freya's knuckle tapped again. Aimee gave her an irritated look.

'We're late.' Freya's voice was muffled through the glass.

'Can I call you back?' Aimee blurted into the phone. 'I'll call you back soon. An hour. Just . . . don't do anything until I've called back.' Aimee hung up and stared ahead at the green grass that crept to the edge of the cliff and clashed against the blue sky. Her breaths were getting louder. The morning sun belted down onto the car and she could feel beads of sweat dripping down her body from under her arms.

'They're waving us over,' Freya's faint voice called again.

'I'm coming,' Aimee snapped. She grabbed her sunnies, ripped off her seatbelt, got out and slammed the door.

Freya blocked the glare with a hand and assessed her aunt. 'Where's your thing for the ceremony?'

'What *thing*?'

'The . . . *thing*. Addie said everyone needs to bring a personal object.'

Aimee made a face and huffed. She yanked open the car door and flopped inside with a sigh, picking up her satchel and rummaging through it. Wallet, gum, pen, water bottle, old receipts. Nothing. She chucked it across to the floor of the passenger side and looked around. The neon blues and oranges on the cover of the Def Leppard cassette caught Aimee's eye from the centre console and she snatched it.

By the time she slammed the car door and turned around from fiddling with the key in the lock, Freya had started running over to a producer with a clipboard. Aimee shuffled along in a daze, looking at her niece from behind. She started thinking about an article she'd once read in the waiting room of a doctor's office – *That's Life!* or one of those other rags that pay weirdos $50 for their ridiculous real-world stories. A woman had lost her cat, only to have it returned soon after. Then years later, when it died, she found out it wasn't her cat after all – it just *looked* identical. In hindsight, there were little signs – like the way the cat rejected the certain brand of food it once loved and how it no longer let people touch its chest. But the woman wanted so desperately to believe her cat had returned home, she just overlooked all the other stuff. Aimee watched her niece walk round the bend and disappear from sight, feeling a little like that woman from the article. This wasn't the Freya she once knew.

The producer waited until Aimee was near and then paced ahead, leading the way around the lighthouse, down the steps and along the path to a grassy patch on a cliff overlooking the ocean. Everyone was sitting in a circle and waiting. They all picked at acai bowls and looked over at Aimee, who had both arms raised in the air while one of the guys in the crew attached a microphone to her white singlet – running the cord under her top and attaching it to a pack in her back pocket. Aimee heard the chatter come to a swift hush. She knew what they would've been talking about – her blazing on-camera takedown of Brooke and the fake Starbucks. One of the Brats had probably filmed it on their phone and played it on repeat for everyone to giggle at before she arrived at the lighthouse. Her mind had been so caught up on Freya that she'd almost forgotten about the public meltdown – she'd even forgotten to rank it in her list of Really Big Problems. While her stomach panged at the memory, it was now the phone call in the car that was distracting her (add *that* to the list, too). Still, she avoided eye contact with Brooke and tried to suppress the urge to charge directly at her.

Tears started to flood her eyes and she blinked them away. Heath was with a cameraman nearby and looked over, but Aimee pretended not to see him. Just one friendly smile from someone would've broken her completely. She didn't want to melt down on camera. Not again. There was already too much to suppress. It was bad enough she was contractually obligated to mingle with these people just hours after what had happened at the twenty-first, let alone everything that unfolded afterwards. She looked at the grass as she walked over to join the circle and sat down next to Freya on one of the navy striped Turkish towels that had been laid out. Addie – who tried airing out her BBL infection with a pair of flowy harem pants – stood on a boulder at the edge of the cliff. The braided leather band tied around her head stopped the wind from whipping around her blonde hair. Her eyes were closed and she was leading the others in a breathing exercise. *Deep breath in . . . one, two, three, four, five. Hold. And exhale . . . one, two, three, four, five.*

The ocean below the cliff rumbled and Aimee could picture what it looked like even without seeing it. Choppy swirls of blue crashing, whipping up white froth that sprayed and slapped the snaggy rocks. Wild and dangerous. Aimee and Fleur used to call those patches of ocean 'the washing machine'. Cameramen circled around the group of ladies and hung low like seagulls – ready to swoop in on whatever scraps of trash caught their attention.

Addie exhaled and opened her eyes with a smile. She had that 'no make-up' look – the kind that required multiple products and special practice to achieve. 'Welcome.' Her tone had dropped into 'podcast voice'. 'I want to thank everyone for being a part of today's resurfacing ceremony. With New Year's just a few days away, it's important we stop, reflect . . . and really analyse the people we *were* coming into this year – and who we *are*, walking out of it.' She looked around the group, her eyes lingering on Aimee a little longer than anyone else. 'The bond we've all formed over this summer is unbreakable. We've shared memories, joy, sadness . . . *boyfriends.*' Her eyes settled on Aimee again. 'Wherever we go in the new year, we'll always be united by this summer we spent together. And it's wild to realise that, whatever happens, your next move has been influenced a little bit by the people you're sitting next to, right now. That's the push and pull of the universe's energy.'

Aimee was too wound up and emotional to think cynical thoughts about all the Insta-psychology Addie was bestowing on them.

'I've asked you all to bring an item of significance. It can be something that represents your past or symbolises a lesson you've learnt. I'm going to go around the circle and, as you place your item in this calico bag, I want you to tell the group what your object is and what it means. I'll start.'

She held up what looked like a few thin red scraps of fabric. 'This is an old bikini from before I got the Brazilian butt lift. It represents the bravery, courage and determination it takes to evolve. And even though my body has started attacking itself again with another BBL infection, I have faith that this too shall pass. No regrets.'

Aimee stared past Addie and out at the sky. It was perfectly blue. She wished it was a gross overcast day, because then it would match her mood. She jabbed her fingernails into her thumbs.

Addie clamoured down from her rock and placed the red bikini in the bag before limping over to Luna, who raised a smooth, pink, rubber-coated vibrator. 'This is the LeVibe that I used that night with Kai when I shit the bed. Telling that story on the podcast made headlines around the world and led to the vibrator selling out. It means a lot because it represents the success that can come from being your authentic self – raw, uncut and brutally honest.'

How does one follow that up? Addie walked over to Bree.

'This is the block of surf wax Tim used on the boards when he was teaching me to surf,' Bree said, her eyes flicking over at Aimee with a guilty look, as if she was only just realising in the moment that maybe she should've brought another item. 'It smells like pineapple.' She quickly popped it in the bag.

Addie moved on to Brooke, whose bejewelled Camilla kaftan – with its clashy print of leopard spots and zebra stripes and wild flowers – fluttered in the breeze as she held up a jagged stone. 'This is from the rubble of the heritage-listed milk shed I was fined for demolishing. For me, it symbolises the strength it takes to follow your gut and fight for what you want. Living with no regrets.' The rock dropped into the bag and Addie jolted slightly at the weight.

Freya lifted a bundled-up men's shirt. It was the blue button-up one she was wearing at the Christmas party. 'Ah,' she shook her head a little and looked down at her feet. 'This is a reminder of . . . mistakes.'

Aimee was still staring out at the sky and didn't realise it was her turn. It was only when Addie appeared in front of her and blocked the view that she snapped back to attention. She sniffed and wiped her nose. 'Um . . . This means a lot.' She placed the cassette in the bag and tried to deliver her spiel in a matter-of-fact way. 'It symbolises me and my sister – Freya's mum. And I think about both of them every time I play it.' A tear slid out from under the left lens of her aviator sunnies and down her cheek just as Addie turned away.

'For this ritual,' Addie said, stepping back up on her rock, 'I want everyone to tap into the person they are in this very moment. There is no yesterday. There is no tomorrow. There is just now. Repeat after me . . .'

She guided everyone, phrase by phrase.

I will not dwell on mistakes or memories from my past.

I will not stop reaching once I have achieved my goals.

I will keep moving forward.

Addie closed her eyes and inhaled deeply, tilting her face up to the sun. And then she tossed the calico bag of items off the cliff.

Aimee screamed and shot to her feet.

THIRTY-NINE

Cardboard boxes were piled up around Aimee's living room and she marched around – feet stomping on the floorboards – gathering books, cassettes and clothes. There was a knock at the door and she dumped a stack of tapes into a box on the way to answer it – their old plastic rectangular cases clacking together. When she grabbed the knob and ripped the door open, Heath was leaning against the wall in the hallway. She barely glanced at him before whipping around and marching away. There was still a chance that if she took a moment to look him in the eye and he did or said something nice, she'd just crumble. There was no time to crumble. Too much needed to be done. Besides, she was angry and wanted someone to blame.

Heath shuffled in. 'You stormed off.'

'I'm sure it was great TV.'

'Nah. Storm-offs aren't as dramatic as they used to be,' he tried to lighten the mood. 'They happen too often . . . lose their punch. You shoulda thrown one of the acai bowls at her. That would've been good TV.'

Aimee continued to mill about. She wasn't in the mood for the peppy back-and-forth their conversations usually descended into. Heath stood back and watched.

'You're moving?' he asked, trying to make sense of what he saw.

'I'm being kicked out.' She pulled apart the pages of an old edition of the *Byron Times* and used the sheets of newspaper to wrap up some framed photos. 'Landlord called this morning – just before that ridiculous resurfacing stunt. He can make more money if he puts the apartment on Airbnb. So, I'm out.'

Heath looked around the room. 'You only left the lighthouse twenty minutes ago, how'd you get all these boxes?'

'The discount pharmacy downstairs. They had a stock delivery last night. It's the only time I've ever been glad to live above it.'

'Where you gonna go?'

'I'll probably just end up sharing a tent with Bada Bing.' Sarcastic, yes. But really, what were her options?

'Can you and Tim find a place nearby?'

'Tim extended the time-out,' she replied in a matter-of-fact way. 'Or at least he wants to *talk* about extending the time-out. Which is impossible because he also said we need to have no contact for the rest of the *current* time-out . . . so, I don't know how or when an extension will be decided.'

'Aimee.' Heath walked closer but she backed away and raised her hands.

'No, don't be nice to me. Don't *you* be nice to me,' she said with bite, sniffing her nose and wiping her eyes, which were beginning to well up again. The only way to barricade the emotional landslide that threated to fall was to be angry.

Heath ignored the digs and swipes and patiently waited for the others that were obviously about to come his way as Aimee's packing became more furious.

'I don't know what my life is gonna look like a few weeks from now. No home. No store. Maybe no relationship. Freya.'

Heath furrowed his brow. 'Why, what happened with Freya?'

Aimee bypassed the question and barrelled on, her rant accelerating into hysterical. 'I gotta say, I blame you a little bit. I really do. You and this *stupid* show.'

Heath didn't say anything.

'If this show didn't exist then Bree wouldn't be seeing Tim. And Brooke wouldn't have bought Rob's garage. *I* wouldn't have wound up at a protest about the show and become Byron Karen – and then *you* wouldn't have recruited me to appear on it.' She pulled plates out of the kitchen cupboard, one by one, and slammed them down on the benchtop. 'Take the show away, none of that stuff would've happened. Freya wouldn't have had an excuse to be out all night. And . . . well . . . The bookstore still would've been sold – I can't blame you for that. Or maybe I *can* blame you for that. Gimme a minute . . .' She took a moment and thought aloud. 'If this show didn't exist, you wouldn't have come to Byron Bay and you wouldn't have been in the store and called me a fucking hippy – and then *I* wouldn't have been provoked to slime the landlord's Porsche, thinking it was yours. If that sliming didn't happen, maybe I could've convinced her not to sell – or talked her into giving me more time while I found a new place.' She let out a frustrated laugh. 'See? All of this can be blamed on you. *You.* Always making out like things are no big deal. *The more you resist, the worse you look.* Well, Heath, I didn't resist and I still got fucked. Every which way. And you saying *those girls* were nothing to worry about. Like Freya was perfectly fine.'

'Aimee, has something happened with Freya?'

'And that's what kills me. That those girls weren't the problem I thought they were going to be for Freya. They were just problems in every other way . . . but not for Freya.' The flatware clinked and clanked as she piled it up. 'Ooh, I got another one,' she said a little viciously. 'If this show didn't exist, then that idiot with the infected butt wouldn't have thrown one of the only memories I have of my dead sister off a fucking cliff.' She knocked a plate and it smashed on the floor. 'God dammit!' She slapped her hands on the benchtop then furiously picked up two more plates and smashed them down with the other shattered one. As the tears began to stream, she dropped to her knees and started picking up the shards of white ceramic.

Heath walked closer. His dirty Dunlop Volleys came into Aimee's sight. They squelched. Then a droplet of water splashed onto the floor amongst the fragments.

Aimee flicked her eyes up and saw he was soaked.

Heath reached into the back pocket of his old jeans and pulled out the Def Leppard cassette. The gesture stunned Aimee and she took a moment to process it. It might've been the nicest thing that someone had ever done for her. Looking up, she could see tiny bubbles of condensation had started to fog up the inside of the case after being plucked from the water and shoved inside Heath's warm, damp jeans. There were no words to say. Aimee stood up, grabbed the front of Heath's wet flanno and kissed him.

———

The sheer white curtains fluttered and sunlight flickered across the bed where Aimee and Heath were lying, twisted in the sheets. The cardboard boxes were still strewn around the apartment, but for a moment, the chaos had come to a standstill.

Aimee slapped her forehead and laughed.

'What was the word?' Heath asked.

'*Oafish*. I thought you were oafish.'

Heath reached over to the bedside table to grab his phone. 'Look, I just wanna establish a clear definition of the word *oafish*.'

While he jabbed a fingertip at the screen and typed the word into Google, Aimee watched with a smile on her face. The fan spinning overhead tickled her skin and she stretched out.

'Rough or clumsy and unintelligent.' He let out a throaty laugh and clicked on another link. 'Merriam-Webster defines "oafish" as "not having or showing an ability to absorb ideas readily".'

Aimee let out a shriek and covered her mouth. 'I didn't necessarily use the word with *those* definitions in mind. I just meant . . .'

'The broken fly on my jeans?'

'Mostly the attitude. You're very sure of yourself. When I first met you, I thought it was cockiness.'

Heath made a face.

'Look, you came into my store and called me a fucking hippy!' Her voice went high-pitched as she playfully defended her point. She looked around the room. 'Anyway. What did you think of me?'

'Shrill,' he shot back.

Aimee's eyes bulged.

'I'm teasing, I'm teasing.' He had one arm wrapped around her and he pulled her in to kiss the top of her head.

'I liked you. You're also very sure of yourself. You know what you want, but I think you probably pull back, right when you should be reaching out to grab it.'

The sound of cars motoring past puttered through the open window.

Aimee exhaled. 'This is not how I thought my life would be.'

'How'd you think it was gonna be?'

'I don't even know anymore.' She looked up at the cracks in the ceiling and thought for a few moments. 'Everything's a mess. I have nothing. I have less than nothing. There's nowhere else to turn.'

'Well. You're being given an opportunity to make a change. Store. House. Tim . . .'

The mention of Tim's name made Aimee zone out for a second and she realised she was lying naked in their bed with another guy. They'd had that crappy old mattress for over a decade and it was only the two of them who'd been on it. With Jules, she'd only hooked up with him at his caravan and she reasoned in her head that that's how it should remain. No new guys in the bed she shares with her fiancé – even if said fiancé declared a time-out with approved hook-ups. She'd never even planned on hooking up with anyone during the time-out, anyway. And the 'No Fucking in the Apartment' rule was just one she made after sleeping with Jules as a way to keep things separate. Jules was a fling. The Don't Ask Don't Tell pact they'd agreed to about the TV shows they were working on meant they could just be with each other – without the outside noise. When Aimee was with Jules, it was like her real life didn't exist – the one with a failing business and a tumultuous engagement and a horrid TV show that was further destroying everything. And Freya.

Aimee wouldn't tell Heath about Freya either, but he knew about everything else. He'd also seen Aimee at her worst. Her ranting, angriest, most emotional worst. And he hadn't batted an eyelid.

It was then Aimee realised she was now sleeping with two guys. They couldn't be more different. And she was a different person around each of them. The Aimee with Heath was different to the Aimee with Jules. She liked both guys. Or maybe it was that she just liked who she was able to be when she was with them. One offered escape. The other offered acceptance. Both were secret. Aimee wondered if it was wrong to keep it that way. Then she stretched out in bed – her bare thighs skimming over the crisp cotton – and, for the first time since Tim left, noticed there was no sand in the sheets.

Heath cleared his throat. 'But, what would I know? I'm just a rough, clumsy, unintelligent oaf.'

'I watched your documentaries,' Aimee said. 'Or . . . clips from them. They were on YouTube.'

Heath covered his face with his hands and groaned.

Aimee propped her body up on one elbow and placed a hand on his chest. She was surprised by his embarrassment. 'They were good. They were *really* good.'

'Eh. Long time ago.'

'I was impressed. Why don't you go back to docos? You're better than this *reality stuff*.'

He shrugged. Aimee's face hovered above his and he used a finger to push a wisp of her hair back. 'Sometimes you gotta learn to let go of the plan.'

FORTY

'This is so rock 'n' roll, I can't stand it.' Rob swung her boots up on the dashboard of the Monaro.

'This is beyond rock 'n' roll.' Aimee kept her eyes ahead and focused on the road. 'It's fucking crazy.' The white glow of passing streetlights flashed by and she had butterflies in her stomach. Not the good kind. Her hands were shaking, as if she was about to walk into an exam for a subject she knew nothing about. They'd been jittering like that all day. She sniffed a few times, then squinted. An orange ember glowed in her peripheral vision. Her brow furrowed. 'Are you *smoking*?' She turned to Rob. 'You don't *smoke*.'

'I thought I'd try it now we're drug barons.' Rob grinned as she exhaled. 'Want one?'

Aimee swatted away the pack her friend was holding up. 'Stop calling us *drug barons*.'

'Villainesses?'

'We're doing this so Freya doesn't have to,' Aimee said, firm. 'We're getting her money back. That's it.'

Rob blew smoke out the passenger window. 'Is she at Brooke's ritzy New Year's party? I'm guessing we didn't receive an invite or a Pinterest link.'

'Yes. And Heath is keeping tabs on her whereabouts.'

'You told him?'

'No. Not about the drugs. Just . . . I said she was running around and staying out too late and not telling me. Which is true. The girl is only twenty-one. I should've been tougher from the beginning.'

'There's no way you could've known,' Rob said. 'And for what it's worth, I think it's cool what you're doing.'

Aimee shook her head, almost in disbelief at what was unfolding. 'It's a lot of things, but cool is not one of them. What else was I supposed to do? Thirty-thousand dollars. *Thirty-fucking-thousand-dollars.*'

'It's a lot of money.' Rob nodded.

'It's obscene. We're practically twice her age. I've never had thirty-thousand dollars.'

'I've never had thirty-thousand dollars, either.'

'I know you've never had thirty-thousand dollars. *Who* has thirty-thousand dollars?'

Rob looked out the window at the obnoxiously renovated and newly-built houses in the neighborhood they were driving through. 'The people around *here* probably have thirty-thousand dollars.'

'Just . . . the *ignorance* for her to start doing something like this – as if it's nothing. As if it's something *everyone* does.'

'It's actually more common than you think. The *Daily Mail* is always writing about a new Sydney influencer who's in court for dial-a-dealing,' Rob said with bizarre pep.

Aimee looked at her, horrified. 'Why the fuck would you tell me that? That is the *worst* thing you could tell me right now.'

'Oh, that's different. That's Sydney. And those situations are large-scale operations. We're tossing out a few bags to rich idiots on holiday for one night. You know, I was looking at the tiny zip lock baggies before – so boring and ugly. We should've gone to that new bespoke paper store in town and bought fancy tiny envelopes to put the baggies in – glam up the drug trade a little.'

Aimee rolled her eyes and kept driving. 'I thought she was so much better than those other girls,' she said after a pause. 'I was so judgy . . . thinking *they'd* be the ones dragging her down.'

'Would you rather she have a butt infection?' Rob tried to lighten the mood.

'I just keep thinking about what Brooke told me – about Bree going to rehab. In Bali. For drugs.' Aimee flicked her eyes over to Rob and then back onto the road. 'Brooke told me that when I first met her. Now I can't help but think . . . is Freya using them too? Not just selling them? I know she said she doesn't, but it wouldn't be the first thing she's lied to me about.'

Rob sighed and shrugged. 'She's probably tried it?' She looked at Aimee as if she didn't want to deliver the hard truth. 'I know you don't wanna hear that but it's a fact. You'd be lying to yourself if you didn't just accept that she's probably tried stuff before. And that's fine. Most kids do. If it was a problem, you'd probably know by now.'

'Jesus.' Aimee shook her head.

'How did Brooke react? You know . . . when she found out about Bree's problems?'

Aimee paused. The passing streetlights flashed through the windows and lit up her face in jolts. She thought back to what Brooke had told her in the kitchen that morning. 'She said . . . you do whatever you need to do for your kid.'

A beat passed as they both let Brooke's words settle.

'Well . . .' Rob looked over at her friend. 'Freya is lucky that she has you to help her. I know she's grateful beyond words.'

'She should be more than grateful. What choice did I have? She had no other option, which meant *I* had no other option.' She nodded at her phone. 'Can you text Heath for me? Just ask him if Freya's at the party. I want to make sure.' Then she had a sharp realisation, just as her friend picked up the phone: What if Rob saw the recent messages between Aimee and Heath and sensed they'd slept together? She wasn't ready to have that conversation.

'OH. MY. GOD.'

Fuck.

'Whose almost-peen is this?' Rob flipped the phone screen around.

Aimee almost drove into one of the fancy letterboxes. On the screen was a photo of a man's toned torso – rippling abs and angular hip bones with a trail of scruff that led from the bellybutton down to . . . the area that was strategically cropped out of the picture. She knew whose almost-peen it was. And it wasn't Heath's.

'You had a new message when I unlocked the phone, so I read it!' Rob leant away to evade Aimee's grabbing hand. 'Who's . . . *Jules*?'

'He's . . .' Aimee fluttered her eyelids and reluctantly tried to answer the question.

'The guy you told Charlie you're hooking up with?' Rob said with glee.

Aimee almost nosedived the car into another letterbox. 'I *knew* he'd tell you!'

'Of course he told me!'

'I'm gonna beat him with his own guitar!' Aimee exaggerated.

'Well, even with the threat of a throttling, he'd still rather be here than at that Ballina New Year's gig. You know, I think he almost cried when he realised he was gonna miss out on our secret mission. I would too. This is the coolest thing we've ever done.'

'What did he tell you about *my romantic situation*?'

'Ugh, Aimee. *Romantic situation*? You make it sound so unsexy.' Rob cringed. 'He wanted to see if I knew any more details, which I didn't. And please note,' she sat up straight, 'I was very well-behaved after finding out that information and I didn't probe you at all. I was being *respect-ful*.' She held up the screen again with a wide smile and pointed at the picture.

Aimee grabbed it. 'Yeah, *real* respectful,' she deadpanned. 'It's Jules. Just . . . Jules.' She batted away the conversation with a hand.

'Well, I do have to say, I was a little hurt you didn't tell me.' She hammed up her upset but Aimee knew there was a kernel of truth to it.

'I didn't *not* tell you intentionally.' She reached over and affectionately squeezed the back of her friend's neck. 'It's just . . . I was . . . I dunno. I was a lot of things. Embarrassed. Nervous. Scared if I talked about it that it would become something it shouldn't be . . . or that I'd jinx it and it'd go away. I've been with the same guy for twenty years! Talking about hook-ups isn't something I'm used to!'

'Are you saying you're not the kind of girl who shits the bed and broadcasts it on a podcast?'

They shared a knowing smile at the in-joke.

'Well, to make it up to me,' Rob said, 'can I see a face?'

'I don't wanna say anything more,' Aimee tried to end the chat. 'Because there's really nothing more to say.'

'I've almost seen his penis. Show me his face.'

'It's just a hook-up. It came out of nowhere and . . . at the end of the time-out, it'll disappear again.' It was all true-ish. What Aimee had with Jules was just hook-ups in a caravan. Nothing more. He was just an escape – someone who didn't know about her problems. Someone who, without knowing much about her, made her feel more excited than she'd felt in twenty years.

Something buzzed on the plastic of the centre console and Aimee was grateful for the interjection.

'Ooh, we got another one!' Rob held up the Nokia that Freya had given them.

It was one of those basic mobile phones you can buy from the cigarette counter at Coles – clunky, and with an old-timey keypad. It received all the text orders and addresses. Freya told them to just drop off the orders to the addresses as people texted them in. The simple instruction made it sound so innocent – which is partly how Aimee convinced herself to do it. She was just dropping stuff off to strangers . . . and getting paid with wads of cash. It was easy enough.

'I've always wanted a burner phone,' Rob said. 'Mainly just so I could talk about *having* a burner phone.'

'Am I still going the right way?'

Rob flicked the cigarette butt out the window and inspected Google Maps on her iPhone. They'd headed south out of Byron and were cruising around the streets of Broken Head. 'Keep going straight about a hundred metres. I searched the address on Street View and the house has a big white concrete fence with black bars.'

Aimee had been assessing the addresses as they were texted in – making sure there weren't any properties she recognised. Freya had said the orders they received were all from out-of-towners – people there on holiday – but Aimee wanted to make sure. At least with the fancier homes, she was sure they definitely wouldn't know anyone inside them.

'A lot of these houses are almost as ridiculous as Byron Bay West-field,' Rob said, referring to Chris Hemsworth's sprawling white concrete compound.

Aimee kept squinting at the numbers on the letterboxes that slowly rolled by. Rob held her hand up when she saw the big white concrete fence and started texting the owner to come outside and collect. Aimee pressed her foot on the brake and the Monaro came to a stop.

'Hey . . .' Rob reached over with one hand and squeezed the back of Aimee's neck. '. . . Don't let it change the way you think of her.'

Aimee paused for a second and stared up at the big white house. It was one of those mansions that was so expensive it actually looked ugly from the outside because the owners had to design it with huge fences and no front windows to ensure their privacy. It was basically a million-dollar shipping container.

The phone buzzed. 'Come inside,' Rob read.

Aimee scrunched up her face. 'Like . . . *in there?* Absolutely not. Tell him to come out here.'

'Sent.' Rob clicked her seatbelt off.

'Is he coming out here?'

'No, I told him to open the gate – I wanna go *inside*.' She shot Aimee a mischievous look, jumped out of the car and whacked closed the door.

Aimee killed the engine, grabbed her stuff and paced up the Pebble Tec driveway after her. She'd rather skid *down* the Pebble Tec driveway on her bare knees than be doing what she was about to. They could hear the vague thump of music seeping out. Through the glass double-door entrance, Aimee could see people crowded around inside, holding drinks and talking.

'What's with the all-white outfits?' she observed.

'I know! Like, they're a problem *every* summer. But I feel like this summer it's worse.'

'White pants?' Aimee squinted at the garments that, on her, would be a stain magnet. 'The sheer arrogance.'

Rob pulled open the handle on one of the glass doors, breaking the seal of the house and letting the music escape like a thousand dogs sprinting out to the street.

'I'm gonna go find our guy,' Rob called back as she slipped inside. Her boots clopped over the giant grey tiles and her long leopard print coat disappeared into the crowd.

Aimee hung back in the hallway. It definitely wasn't the kind of house that the people in her life hung out at but she was still paranoid about running into someone she knew. Like who? Town weirdos who gossiped. Narissa from the bank. She could tell the place was a rental. Modern furniture, generic artworks. No photographs or personal items. Kind of how her apartment would look when it was eventually listed on Airbnb. A toilet flushed and a timber sliding door rolled open behind her. Before she could move, the person had barged into her.

'Ugh!' Aimee shrieked as the guy placed a wet hand on her shoulder to walk past. She was on edge. It was like a haunted house – only, the ghosts and mauled bodies springing out of the dark corridors could be people she knew.

The guy laughed at Aimee's horror. 'It's not piss!' He held up his wet hand and yelled over the music. 'It's water! I just washed my hands!' He nodded to the basin in the bathroom.

She moved further down the hall to find some space away from the mayhem. Over the crowd, she could see a sprawling living room with soaring floor-to-ceiling glass doors and a fully-grown indoor palm tree that would had to have been craned in when the house was being built. Brooke would've been extremely jealous of the feat. Aimee squeezed and shuffled past people with breathy apologies until she reached the kitchen and took a seat on a tall timber stool at the marble-topped kitchen island. Her eyes had locked onto a giant canvas print of a highland cow – an accessory that everyone who wanted the Byron aesthetic seemed to have. Staring at the animal's trademark long tousled fringe, she realised it kinda looked like Bodhi the van guy.

'Aimee?'

She whipped around. Jules was standing on the opposite side of the bench. Her heart instantly started beating faster. With wide eyes, she worked hard to get her brain to catch up with what she was seeing. 'You!' she stated, hoping her horror would be misconstrued as surprise.

'Me,' he laughed. 'And . . . *You*.'

Aimee closed her eyes as she recited the excuse she'd formulated earlier while getting ready, should she accidentally run into someone she knew. 'One of the girls from the TV show was here and she texted and asked if I could pick her up.' Her voice sounded strained and anxious.

'Well, that's very thoughtful of you on New Year's Eve.'

'What are you doing here? This is . . . far away from your caravan.' She tried not to cringe at herself for sounding awkward.

Jules laughed and poured whisky into a short, heavy-looking crystal glass. 'Production party, remember?' He leant over the bench to give her a quick kiss before putting the lid back on the bottle.

'Oh, right.' She shook her head. 'Yeah . . . I just . . . thought it was on the Gold Coast.'

'Nah. Down here. Someone rented the house.' He smirked. 'I sent you a photo earlier.'

Aimee covered her face. 'You *did* send me a photo. I was driving when it came through . . . that's why I haven't responded yet.'

Things felt weird between them. Maybe it was just the circumstances of the night. Aimee felt like there were so many things she was trying to hide from so many people. Hide drugs from Jules, hide Jules from Rob. She'd rarely been out in public with Jules. Apart from the day they met in the bookstore and their blink-and-you'll-miss-it date at the annoying health cafe, they only ever really hung at his caravan. When they were together, it was always *just them*. In their own world.

Standing in the kitchen of a random million-dollar mansion, Aimee was aware the chemistry she usually felt with Jules had somehow evaporated – as if the walls of their private universe had fallen down and the winds of reality had blown out the spark. Now, all they had was random small talk. Aimee felt like she was forcing chit-chat with a colleague she had drunkenly slept with at the office Christmas party. She put the feeling down to the secret double life she was trying to keep under wraps that night.

Her phone buzzed and she glanced at the home screen. It was Rob, saying she was on her way back to the entrance. Aimee needed to get out quick. There was no way she was letting Rob near Jules after the almost-peen pic. And there was no way she was letting Jules near Rob for as long as there was a bumbag strapped to her waist filled with Ziplock bags of an illegal substance.

Aimee shook her head quickly and raced to talk, holding up her phone. 'That's my friend – the girl from the show, who I'm picking up. She's out the front, at the car. We gotta get her back to the New Year's party.'

She jumped off the stool and was about to run off when Jules grabbed her by the hand and spun her around with a laugh. 'Am I seein' you tomorrow?'

Aimee felt like there was an invisible clock ticking down and she only had seconds to escape. 'I'll message you later!' she called as she scurried back down the hallway and her body blended in with the crowd. Just as she was about to make her escape, the front door swung open.

'Freya's mum!'

Aimee almost shrieked at the sight. Luna was standing in the entrance with a cameraman. 'Hi?' was all she could manage as she tried to mentally consolidate all her worlds that were colliding.

'How did you get invited to this?!' Luna laughed. 'Sorry, I didn't mean it like that, babe.'

'Um, well . . .' Aimee shuffled back as the cameraman repositioned to get both girls in shot. 'Oh, no – I can't stay and film,' she hastily told the crew, feeling the clock count down faster. 'I was just dropping someone off.'

'Oh, who?'

'Ah.' Aimee squinted, but Luna didn't wait for a response.

'I don't know anyone here – just a guy I'm fucking,' she said nonchalantly.

'Oh, so you and Bodhi . . . not together anymore?' Aimee cursed herself for asking a question and delaying her exit more.

'No, we are.' Luna laughed. 'By the way, thanks again for saving me during my meltdown at Freya's party. It was just a phoenix moment. Go down in flames, then rise again.'

'Well, that's very Byron of you,' Aimee rushed, desperate to get away from the cameras and out of the house. Then a thought snuck into her mind. 'Wait, have you seen Freya tonight?' she asked, a little too directly. 'Because you came from Brooke's, right?'

Luna laughed, as if recalling an inside joke. 'Oh my god, when Nina and Brooke found out I was invited to a party where famous people would be, they basically kicked me out and told me to get here with a camera. Ever since most of the bars and restaurants banned the show from filming, Nina's desperate for parties to film that aren't just at Brooke's house.'

'But you saw Freya before you left?'

A voice called out from down the hall and Luna's head snapped to look. 'OK, babe, I gotta get in there!' She kissed Aimee on the cheek. 'You should come on the pod again!' The camera followed her into the crowd.

Aimee paused for a second before she remembered what she needed to do: get the hell out.

When she reached the bottom of the driveway and threw her body into the driver's seat of the Monaro, she felt like she hadn't taken a breath the entire time she'd been inside. The sound of Rob's boots clopping on the concrete echoed down through the dark.

'Sorry that took a while.' She flopped into the passenger seat and slammed the door. 'I got the feeling it was a famous person's house, so I had to take a photo of myself in their bed.' A white light lit up the dark as Rob swiped open her phone to reveal a photo of herself swathed in the owner's expensive-looking cream sheets. 'Just a second.' She clicked her seatbelt in and picked up the burner phone. 'I'll put the next address in Google Maps.'

Aimee held her hands up and closed her eyes. 'Look, we're not doing any more deliveries tonight. It's too risky. I just ran into someone I know.'

Rob's jaw dropped and she leant over to look up at the mansion through Aimee's window. 'Who do you know in houses like that?'

'Just . . . One of the girls from the show was there. With a cameraman. That was way too dangerous.'

Rob held up the burner phone. 'But all these people are expecting deliveries tonight.'

'It's cocaine, not milk. It won't expire.' Aimee started the engine and it let out a roar. 'I have an idea.'

Rob cackled at the unintentionally cool moment. 'Ooh ahh. You little villainess. C'mon. Do that again but this time while lighting a cigarette.'

Aimee swatted away the pack Rob was holding up.

'C'mon, smoke. All the cool villains do it.'

FORTY-ONE

'The Stevie?' a guy asked, a little hesitantly. He had one of those annoyingly neat haircuts that big city finance bros have. Probably went to a private school in Sydney when he was younger and now worked at one of the Big Four. The kind of guy who was always a dick to waiters.

Aimee and Rob sat before him in deck chairs behind a card table while the regular Sunday market nonsense carried on around them. They sipped on frozen cokes out of giant yellow cups that they'd purchased from the Night Owl down the street and smiled at the nervous finance bro, letting him dangle for a few moments and making him question if he was at the right place. A paper sign was sticky taped to the front of the table with the stall name scrawled on it: Cassette Collective Co-op. Laid out on top were the products. The afternoon sun brought out the scuffs and scratches on the well-worn plastic cases. You wanted eighties hits? You got 'em. Tom Jones. Diana Ross. Lots of those random compilation tapes with lame titles like, *Thru The Roof! Best of the Eighties!*

But customers only seemed to be making one request.

'Ah . . . someone told me to come here and ask for The Stevie?' the finance bro said again, scrunching his face a little.

Aimee reached under the table, pulled out a copy of Janet Jackson's *Rhythm Nation* and opened the case to make sure the right item was inside: a little zip-locked bag of white powder. 'It's a classic.' She held it out with a smirk.

'Eight dollars.' Rob held out her hand and the guy passed over a tidy wad of fifties. She flicked through the notes and counted three-hundred dollars, then shoved it in her bum bag. 'Enjoy the tunes.'

The guy tucked the tape into the side pocket of his chinos shorts and walked away while Rob giggled to herself.

'You're drunk with power.' Aimee sipped her frozen coke. 'And you're also way too proud of yourself for coming up with that code word.'

'The Stevie! It's perfect!' Rob laughed. 'Just like Luna is reclaiming the word "cunt", we're reclaiming The Stevie from Bree's annoying jewellery line. And *you* should be proud too. Coming up with this genius little idea.'

Aimee looked down and laughed nervously. She was still uncomfortable with the whole thing. But at least doing it this way was a little less sinister. Maybe it was the eighties hits. When she got home from the botched drop-off mission the night before, she had lain awake in bed and wondered to herself what Fleur would have done in this situation. Would this have even happened had she been alive? She shook her head and short-circuited the thought. 'Everyone been messaged?' she asked Rob.

Rob checked the Nokia. 'Affirmative. Only a few can't get here but most can. I've told them the code word. Said we'd be here until 3pm. It's just after one now. How many we got left?'

Aimee checked the milk crate of cassettes at her feet. The ones on top of the table were a decoy, should any weirdos actually *want* to buy a cassette. 'Hmmm. Still a few. We got Jimmy Barnes, *Freight Train Heart*. The B-52's, *Lucky Wild Planet* . . . The Kenny Rogers ultimate collection.'

'This has been fun.' Rob chewed her gum and smiled. 'Wanna hang tonight? I can come to yours and we can pack up your stuff into boxes. Or you can come to mine and we can pack up *my* stuff into boxes. Either way, we'll be packing crap into boxes.'

'I can't.' Aimee jabbed her thick pink straw into the icy cup. 'I've got a dinner – later. Something for the TV show at a restaurant. I've gotta go to it. And before that . . .' she paused, 'I gotta get some laundry done.' There was no laundry to do. There was a dinner for the show. But the open slot between dinner and selling coke-laced cassettes was carved out for Jules. She was desperate to see if the awkwardness from the previous night's run-in at the stranger's mansion was just a one-off. Afterwards, when trying to go to sleep, a thought had entered her mind that kept her up: was it awkward because they were out in public and Aimee was stressed with what she was there to do? Or was it awkward because she was now also sleeping with Heath? She told herself she wasn't *sleeping with him*. She'd *slept with Heath*. Once. But would it happen again?

'OK, I gotta run down to the salon and check in. You OK finishing up?' Rob unclipped the strap around her waist. 'I give you the magic bum bag.' She bent down and kissed Aimee on the cheek and ran off.

'Bye villainess,' Aimee called out.

'Hey.' A woman around Aimee's age approached the folding table. She was wearing black Bulgari sunglasses and a bold-print Camilla kaftan. 'I'm after . . . The Stevie?'

It didn't matter how many times Aimee did the transaction that day, it still felt weird every time. She reached down and pulled out The B-52's. 'Eight dollars,' she said, waiting for the payment before handing it over. The woman passed a bunch of fifties rolled up tight and Aimee did a quick count below the table. *One hundred, one-hundred-and-fifty . . .*

'Hey, you work at the bookstore, right?'

Aimee stopped counting and looked up.

'I was in there the other day with my kid.' The kaftan lady smiled. 'You've got great stuff.'

Aimee's heart sank. Now that a random customer had found her out, who else would?

'We didn't buy anything though. We found it cheaper online.' The woman winced and shook her head at herself. 'Shit, sorry. I didn't mean it like that. It's just, you know . . .'

Aimee finished counting the cash, handed over the tape and then tried to casually slide her sunnies down from on top of her head without looking like she was trying to disguise herself. 'Enjoy the tunes,' she said, a little flatly. She unzipped the bum bag and filed away the fifty-dollar notes with the others, attempting to be discreet. Just as she zipped it up, she jolted in her seat.

'Well, *this* is . . . *enterprising.*'

The passive aggressive tone could only be attributed to one person: Rozzie.

Aimee took a split-second to curse herself for not remembering Rozzie had a stall at the markets for the summer. 'Cassettes are the new vinyl,' she said, without looking up from the bum bag.

'I read that in the *New York Times*. They said it's part of a new trend to *switch off* and *disconnect*. Not sure it's going to fix *your* problems though.'

Her tone was dripping with the smugness Aimee knew too well.

'You come over here to gloat, Rozzie?'

Rozzie picked through the cassettes on the card table. 'Aimee, I came to *check* on you.'

'And what raised your concern?' Aimee faffed about with random objects.

'Well, I *heard* the latest *development* with you and Tim.'

'Well, you didn't *hear* it, Rozzie. You *instigated* it. You got what you wanted.' Aimee looked up sharply. 'Now, I really can't stand around chatting any longer.' She plucked a tape off the table and held it out sharply. 'Can I interest you in a little Tom Jones?'

Rozzie blinked slowly and smiled to herself. 'My offer still stands. A counselling session. You and Tim. Or just *you*. If you're still sceptical, take a listen to the latest episode of the Balls Deep podcast. Those girls are a riot. And Bree was an interesting case study. It was nice to talk to *one* person who appreciated my insight.'

———

Hey guys, welcome to another episode of the Balls Deep podcast where we get raw, uncut and brutally honest about all the things other people are too embarrassed to talk about. Today I'm joined by my Brats of Byron Bay *co-star Bree. She's currently dating a guy named Tim – who's the fiancé of Aimee, the mum of our other co-star, Freya. And we're also joined by Tim's mum Rozzie, who's a certified counsellor.*

Aimee had her headphones in and listened to the podcast while packing up at the markets. Of course she downloaded it the very second Rozzie left. She'd returned the card tables and was carrying the milk crate of leftover cassettes back to the Monaro. Her face cringed at what she was hearing.

It's definitely an unusual situation but, after Aimee came on and told us about the time-out she's on with Tim and what's involved, I had an insane amount of listener feedback with a lot of people saying they wish they could try it in their own relationship. And then I found out about Tim's mother being a counsellor who specialises in relationships . . . and thought it'd be fun to get her on with Bree – her sorta-daughter-in-law . . .

As Aimee reached the car, she saw Brooke across the road, standing with crossed arms, surrounded by the camera crew. Nearby, her G-Wagon was being towed off the median strip she had chosen to park on.

'Ai-mee!' Brooke sang out and twinkled the fingers of her right hand in the air. A Starbucks cup was held in the other.

Aimee could hear the faint sing-song cry over the podcast. She looked over at Brooke, refusing to acknowledge her, and propped the milk crate on one hip while unlocking the car boot.

'Ai-mee!' Brooke called again, clearly wanting some kind of assistance.

Aimee dumped the crate inside and slammed the boot. The sing-song voice continued to cry and passers-by – as well as the cameras – were now peering over. She rolled her eyes behind her sunglasses and paused the podcast as she walked over to the median strip.

'Well, Aimee. I am having a *day*.' Brooke laughed and tapped Aimee's wrist, apparently choosing to believe that the feud they were locked in didn't really exist.

The TV crew moved around to get Aimee in shot. An endless stream of cars rolled by and people gawked. The blinking yellow lights on the tow truck added to the circus.

'I'm running late and I need to get back to the farm. I've tried ordering an Uber and the next one's twenty minutes away. Do you have time for a lift?'

Aimee's face was blank. 'You bought my friend's business and home and kicked her out,' she said, flat and stern.

Brooke exhaled. 'Aimee, your friend slept with my husband.'

The cameras got in close.

'You know she didn't realise it was your husband – we hadn't even met you yet. And the only reason you went and blew it up into something bigger was so there'd be a stupid stunt to make this ridiculous show more interesting.'

Brooke pretended to be stunned. 'Aimee, are you not giving me a lift because you don't have time? Or simply out of spite?'

'*What*?!' Aimee squawked.

'Because, look, if this is some kind of petty payback . . .' She held her hands up in the air and shook her head. 'Need I remind you, you're a part of this show and, technically, it's part of your contract to appear when needed.'

Aimee felt the focus of the camera lenses zooming in. It didn't stop her. And when the tow truck engine turned on, she raised her voice over the grunts. 'But, Brooke, I *will* give you a lift home – because I am a decent person and I hope this simple act of kindness makes you feel even the smallest twinge of guilt when you're hanging out by yourself tonight and looking down on a half-built lake while your resentful husband gets stoned in a shed surrounded by DVD vending machines.' She jingled her keys and turned around to walk through a gap in the banked-up cars. 'I drive a coupe, so pick your favourite two crew members and tell 'em to hunch.'

By the time Aimee got back to the Monaro, Brooke was still teetering across the road in her stilettos. A cameraman and sound guy had beaten her and were already squeezing into the back seat. Brooke finally arrived and gracefully contorted her body into the passenger side where she insisted on sitting with perfect posture – like a ballerina riding a tractor.

Aimee turned the key and the motor revved. She wound down the window to let some air in but it was just as warm outside and the smell of fried chips wafted through. A couple of surfers in an old Subaru came to a halt and the guy behind the wheel nudged a finger up, signalling for Aimee to creep into the traffic ahead of them. The Monaro rolled forward, then came to a stand-still like the rest of the cars. Summer in paradise. Of course, the cameraman in the back seat ensured every second of the riveting piece of television was documented. Not a moment to be missed. Then, the new Bluetooth stereo that Freya had the mechanic install under the original tape deck connected automatically to Aimee's iPhone and the Balls Deep podcast continued playing over the speakers. Aimee's body seized up as Rozzie and Bree blared into the car. She felt Brooke glancing at her, but she refused to give a reaction and simply stared ahead.

'Now, Rozzie, I also thought it'd be good to have you on because this Tim-Aimee-Bree situation is super interesting to me and our listeners – and you're more qualified than anyone to talk about it. What are your thoughts?' Luna asked.

'Well, it's something *I've* been encouraging Tim and Aimee to do for *years*,' Rozzie bemoaned. 'The whole purpose of this experiment is to open their eyes to emotional and romantic – and *sexual* – things they may not have been able to experience as adults because they got together so young. Now, Bree – since you're a part of the experiment, I'd like you to tell me the most important thing: how often are you and Tim having sex?'

Aimee bristled. Her eyes flicked up at the rearview mirror and met those of the cameraman and sound guy in the back seat before she looked away again. She was acutely aware of Brooke to her left and refused to make eye contact or give her any satisfaction of an uncomfortable response. It was like they were engaged in a really twisted game of chicken – who could tolerate the discomfort the longest before one person gave in and switched off the dial? Of course Brooke wouldn't lose this game – Aimee was actually surprised she hadn't turned up the volume to make sure the cameras recorded the moment nice and clearly.

Bree was laughing awkwardly at the sex question.

'Darling, don't be *shy* – this is a *sex and relationship* podcast,' Rozzie chortled. 'I've listened to a few episodes before coming on, so I know what you girls talk about – no need to *tone things down*. This is what I *do*. I think it's admirable how you girls talk so openly – it's something a lot of people older than you aren't capable of, and it's to their *detriment*.'

Luna jumped in. 'Rozzie, girl – I hear you,' she laughed. 'And I can reliably inform you your son and Bree are having sex three times a day.'

Bree shrieked.

'Anywhere and everywhere!' Luna cheered.

Bree cut her off. 'Do not listen to her!' Bree laughed. 'We have sex . . . a healthy amount. It's summer sex. Everyone has more sex in summer.' She then gave in to stop the speculation. 'So, once a day. Maybe twice. *Maybe*. But that's also because it's a . . . *fling*, or whatever you want to call it.'

Rozzie was now flying high. 'Well, thank you for finally giving me an *answer*. That's not something my son is very forthcoming about.'

Aimee gripped the steering wheel tighter. The traffic hadn't moved the whole time.

'But, like I said,' Rozzie continued, 'I listened to some of the other episodes of this show – coincidentally, the one with Aimee, Tim's fiancée. And, if I recall, she admitted their sex life wasn't anywhere close to once a day. So, I mean, I think that's interesting right there. And so many problems can stem just from that one issue of not having regular intimacy. Have you met Aimee?'

'I have, she's lovely,' Bree said. 'I think it's very cool what she's doing with Tim.'

'You know, it's funny . . .' Rozzie said, as if a revelation had just come to her. 'You remind me a lot of Fleur. Aimee's sister. We sadly lost her but . . . you really have her spirit.'

Brooke lifted her hand up to the dial on the stereo and flicked it. The audio cut out. Staring ahead, with her giant bug-eyed Chanel sunglasses on, she snipped four words. 'Turn off the cameras.'

FORTY-TWO

'Fuck Rosie,' Jules said.

Aimee could feel the side of her face sticking to Jules's bare chest from a mix of tears and sweat, made worse by the humidity that had started to steam up in the caravan.

'Rozzie,' she corrected. 'But yes. Fuck her.'

She had been trying hard to withhold the details of her life from him – to preserve their fling in a perfect snow globe world where the white dust only fell when you chose and, when it did, it looked pretty. But the storms of real life had been rolling over relentlessly and started to leak through. Flicking away more tears, Aimee stared across the bed and out the open door of the van as layers of grey built up in the sky. Her face was still puffy from crying hot tears of rage on the side of the road after dropping Brooke and the TV crew back at the farm. The emotion had been building up with every passing white dash on the bitumen as everyone sat in silence for the half-hour journey after Rozzie's taunts had blasted over the car speakers. The cruel words played on a loop in Aimee's head. Even though Brooke had told the cameras not to film, Aimee didn't want to break down in front of her. Giving her that satisfaction wasn't an option. So she held it in.

After dropping off the unwanted passengers, she'd rolled down the dirt driveway, swung out onto the highway and accelerated – her body tightening as the hum of the engine threatened to break into a roar. That's when the tears started to flow. Then when they'd become too hard to see through, she'd hastily pulled over – a cloud of dust billowing around the car, making it impossible to see out of the windows. She'd gripped the steering wheel and let out a scream that stung the back of her throat. The clock on the dashboard showed it was almost a quarter past four – an hour later than she was supposed to meet Jules. She hadn't wanted him to see her like that. The sound of her phone buzzing vibrated on the plastic of the centre console. Jules:

You OK?

Hey, I'm really sorry. Got caught in traffic and some stuff came up. Just finishing now. Maybe we can do another day?

The three floating grey dots appeared under her reply.

I don't mind waiting :) Besides, I've got something I want to show you. Come over when you're done.

Aimee had looked up at herself in the rearview mirror and let out a frustrated sigh at the sight. Puffy eyes, red cheeks, hair a mess. She'd used her fingers to swipe and prod and tousle away the signs of her roadside breakdown so Jules wouldn't ask. It was all in vain. Still, her need to see him when everything felt wrong had become like her need to dive headfirst into the ocean. An escape. The outside noise drowning out. When she'd arrived at his van, he knew immediately she was upset. And her fury was so wild that it had all come spilling out.

Now, lying still on Jules' chest, the storm had passed and she was picking up the pieces.

'What did Tim say about it? Rozzie and the podcast?' he asked, his voice concerned as he traced a finger up and down Aimee's back.

'I don't know if he even knows about it yet,' she said, using a finger to nudge the gunk out of the corner of one of her eyes. 'He probably wouldn't care.'

Tim always batted down Aimee's claims that his mum didn't like her. And even with Rozzie's sideways insults now committed to tape, Aimee knew Tim would still find a way to ignore them.

'She sounds psychotic,' Jules said. 'It's not fair. How could someone let their mother talk about their partner like that?'

Aimee tried to remember why she'd been hiding so much from Jules. She'd been withholding stuff from so many people that the reasons for doing so had started to blur and muddle. She reminded herself: Jules was a fling and she'd wanted him to stay that way. Letting their feelings twist together and bond over the tiny, intimate details of each other's lives would instantly turn whatever they had into something it wasn't allowed to be. Though, that decision had been made when the end of her time-out with Tim was in sight – back when Aimee thought the time-out was simply a painful challenge they were putting themselves through before probably getting back together and continuing their lives the way they always had. Now, she wasn't so sure. What would her life look like without Tim and Rozzie and the problems that spread like gnarled tree roots through the life they'd built together? She felt Jules lean down and kiss the top of her head.

'Why would the TV show let this happen? Getting Tim's mum and the chick he's dating on a podcast that they knew you'd hear? Do you trust the producers?'

The question made Aimee zone out so much it must've looked like her soul had left her body.

Jules pulled back a little after feeling Aimee's body seize up. 'Am I OK to ask about that? The TV show?' he said. 'I know we agreed not to talk about the shows . . . it's just—'

'No, no,' Aimee rushed to say, placing a hand on his chest. 'It's fine . . . it's . . .' She trailed off.

Jules' questions had made her think of Heath. The drama of the afternoon's podcast was perfect TV drama – and while she had no doubt some of the other producers would've gleefully set it up, she couldn't help but feel defensive of him. His image barged into her mind in the same way he'd barged into her life at the beginning of summer and made himself at home. Like a stray dog smiling at the back door, wanting to be let inside, Aimee felt like her relationship with Heath had begun the same way. It started with shooing the scruffy fleabag off the back porch. Then persistence led to sympathy, with water bowls and the odd meal of leftovers shared. Eventually, that damn dog would charm its way inside the house. Heath wasn't at that final stage yet. Could he be? *Absolutely not*, Aimee thought to herself, almost offended at the thought. She didn't know how to explain what Heath was. All she knew was she hadn't hidden anything from him. He'd seen and experienced her worst. And still, he stayed. Snow globe towns might not withstand real storms, but Heath might.

Thup, thup, thup, thup, thup . . .

The sound of whooshing blades cut through the silence. Aimee cocked her head up.

'What's that?'

Jules groaned and covered his face with a hand. 'This is the worst timing.'

'Is this the thing you wanted to show me?'

The *thups* got closer and louder. A strong breeze started to blow through the open doorway of the caravan and some loose papers that lay scattered around the floor flipped up into the air. Then a helicopter touched down in the field.

Aimee clambered off the bed and pulled her denim shirt on over the white singlet she was wearing while walking towards the doorway.

Jules knelt up on the mattress and jokingly faceplanted forward. 'I should've cancelled it. It's just . . . when you got here, you were upset and . . . I forgot it was coming.'

Aimee let out a confused laugh. 'No, it's just . . . *why?*'

Jules looked up with a silly smile. 'Do helicopter rides need a reason?' He jumped off the bed, kissed her and started pulling on his black leather boots before grabbing her hand and leading the way out into the field.

Aimee's hair blew wildly and she laughed while trying to hold it in place. It made Jules laugh harder.

Something vibrated in Aimee's back pocket. She reached back and slid her phone out. On the screen was a calendar reminder.

Brats dinner – Mez Club @ 7PM

The notification made Aimee smack her forehead and cringe. She held up her phone. 'I forgot . . . I've got this thing tonight. I've gotta go to it.'

'C'mon.' Jules smiled and grabbed her hands. 'Wanna go for a ride?'

It was nearing 6pm. She knew she'd be late if she got in the helicopter. She breathed in the afternoon air and the sniffling sound from her nose reminded her of the tears she'd been crying just moments before. The question she'd been asking herself all afternoon still hovered: What could her life look like without Tim? She nodded and stepped up into the chopper.

'Let's go for a ride.'

———

Aimee's quest to escape one reality show had accidentally led her into another.

'This is like one of those dates on *The Bachelor*,' she yelled into her headset microphone while looking out the helicopter window as Byron Bay passed below.

'Ouch,' Jules laughed. 'I don't think that's a compliment coming from you.'

Aimee let out a big laugh. 'No! That's not how I meant it! But also . . . *kinda?*' She looked at him with a mock grimace.

'Point taken.' He pretended to sulk.

She continued to tease him. 'Look, as you can probably assume, I don't watch *The Bachelor* religiously. But my friend Rob has made me sit through enough to know that this is an Osher Günsberg-certified date from *The Bachelor.*'

In her mind, Aimee could also hear the passionate surge of orchestral music that producers usually soundtracked these dates to – forcing viewers into thinking the moment was more romantic than it actually was.

Jules continued to be mock-offended. 'Here I was thinking I'd present you with a lavish surprise to lift your spirits after a bad day—'

'You didn't know I was having a bad day when you organised this,' Aimee cut him off with a playful slap to the chest.

Even though the helicopter pilot was wearing sunglasses, Aimee could feel him bristle at the flirting.

'What is it exactly about my grand gesture that makes you cruelly compare it to a date on *The Bachelor?*' Jules committed to the faux argument.

'Well, from what I've seen, on *The Bachelor*, producers always somehow manage to choose the worst days to do a helicopter date – on an overcast weekday, when the weather's gross and everything's grey.' She peered out the windows at the never-ending greyness they were flying into. 'And it always feels like it's part of a sponsorship deal with RedBalloon or something.'

'And what happens on these dates?' Jules raised an eyebrow.

'From what I gather, they usually eat supermarket cheese and then make out on a deserted beach.'

'Is that so?' Jules leant in and kissed her.

He pulled back and they stared at each other for a moment.

'How do you feel seeing your town from above like this?' he asked.

The helicopter was gliding east, out of the mountains and towards the ocean. Aimee looked ahead and could see the city centre approaching. Everything looked expansive yet small, and whooshed by fast but also in slow motion – like one of those video games Tim would play on the big screen television he'd insisted on attaching to the wall of the living room.

'If you didn't know this was Byron Bay, would you recognise it from up here?' Jules' distorted voice scratched through the headset speakers.

Aimee sighed a half-laugh – not quite wistful, not quite weary – and stared down at the streets below. The streets she'd walked since before she could remember. If she tried, she could probably do it in pitch black darkness – like when you wake up in the middle of the night and need a glass of water but, instead of turning on the light, you let your memory guide you through the doorways and halls, relying on instincts built up over years to know how many steps to take and when to turn a corner. Then you stub your toe.

'If I didn't know this was Byron Bay, I wouldn't even recognise it on the ground,' she said softly.

'Do they get this cynical during dates on *The Bachelor*?' Jules teased.

She rolled her eyes and nudged her body into his. 'So. I have a question,' she said.

'I don't have any supermarket cheese.' He frowned.

Aimee ignored the joke. 'My question: why did you organise this?'

'Well . . .' He glanced up. 'I have a question for *you*.'

Aimee suddenly felt like she was in freefall.

'Filming wraps up in a few weeks and I was set to head back to the States. But I got offered another project filming here. It means I could stay another few months.' He reached for Aimee's hand, gripped his fingers between hers and looked into her eyes. 'Should I stay?'

Beams of sunlight started to shoot out of the long grey clouds stretching across the sky and an orange glow radiated in through the windows of the helicopter. Aimee squinted out at her hazy town and looked ahead as they soared out over the ocean. The water looked like miles of blue satin fabric, floating in the wind. A deep escape. In her core, Aimee felt the overwhelming urge to jump out of the helicopter and plunge into the blue unknown.

'Yeah.' She nodded, leaning in to kiss Jules. 'Yeah. You should take it.'

FORTY-THREE

Aimee rushed into the dining room at The Mez Club and looked around for the group of Brats surrounded by TV cameras. She was close to an hour late and her hair was still a bit wild after the helicopter ride but she'd ducked home to change into a new outfit. With nothing decent or clean in her own cupboard, she'd desperately flicked through Freya's wardrobe and chucked on a white linen jumpsuit. It was only on her way to the restaurant that she realised it was the one her niece was wearing on the night of her twenty-first. Maybe she hadn't recognised it immediately because she'd spent every minute since that night wishing it could simply be erased from history.

'Aimee!' someone called out across the room.

She immediately knew who it was from the gruff voice but she still couldn't see. It was one of those restaurants where the overhead lighting is dim and all the candles hurt your eyes. Then she saw Heath half-stand up and raise a hand. There he was. At a table . . . for two.

She cocked her head and laughed as she walked over, a little confused. 'I thought this was one of those big, disgusting group dinner parties where Luna makes people use vibrators and someone gets glassed.'

'Oh . . . um . . . no. I just thought . . .' He stood up properly and leaned in to kiss her but she turned her head slightly and his lips landed somewhere around her temple.

Aimee couldn't help but notice his outfit. Blue shirt, sleeves rolled up just a little. It looked ironed. But not ironed by a guy who was living out of a suitcase for a few weeks. It looked professionally ironed. Maybe even newly purchased. He seemed uncomfortable. In the shirt but also in the restaurant. It didn't seem like his kind of place. And it certainly wasn't Aimee's.

'So where is everyone?' she asked.

Heath shuffled the array of menus. 'Oh, this wasn't a group dinner – not for the show. I just suggested it because—'

'Oh! Sure.' Aimee shook her head and laughed. 'Sure. That's . . .' She reached over and placed her hand on his. 'That's nice. It's great.'

'I wanted to check—'

A waiter came up to take drink orders.

Heath looked at Aimee. 'Ah, white? Re—'

'Yes,' she blurted.

He laughed. 'Um. How about a bottle of champagne?' He ran his finger down the menu. 'Bollinger?'

Aimee shrugged in agreeance.

When the waiter left, Heath shook his head and tried to remember what he was going to say. 'Ah. Tim.' He cringed at himself. 'Sorry, I meant, I got told today that Tim's mum had gone on Luna's podcast with Bree. And . . .' He searched for the right words. 'She was *exactly* like you said she was.'

Aimee smirked. 'You saw the footage of what happened in the car,' she concluded.

He closed his eyes and smiled. 'No. Brooke called and flagged it with me so that I would be aware of it. If I didn't know about it, then it would be sent at the end of the day with all the other footage for Nina to sort through and she'd jump on it. Brooke said she didn't want it used. And I just . . . didn't want you to feel set up. I know this whole commitment with the show hasn't gone the way I told you it would. Because I'm the production manager I'm not always across the *antics* that happen.'

Aimee raised an eyebrow. '*Antics* is one way to describe what's gone on.'

Heath smiled and looked across at his dinner date. 'You look good. Did you get your hair done?'

Aimee shuffled in her seat and self-consciously touched the back of her head with a hand. 'Nope. Just . . . put some moisturiser in it.'

Heath nodded. 'It's nice.'

She looked back into his eyes for a moment before the waiter returned with the bottle of Bollinger and began pouring it into one of the flutes. The interruption gave Aimee a chance to look around at the influencers and the Bondi transplants who'd flocked to the restaurant. Aimee could never hide what she was really thinking – it always showed on her face.

Heath sat back and admired her – watching her watching everyone else. He followed her gaze around the room and assessed the scene as well. Then he held up a hand, just before the waiter could pour the second glass.

'Actually,' he said. 'Can we take the bottle to go?'

Like Aimee, the waiter was thrown by the question. 'Sorry, sir. All alcohol must be consumed on the premises.'

Heath pulled out his beat-up leather wallet and flipped it open. 'Don't tell anyone.' He winked and placed two crushed hundred dollar notes on the table. Then he grabbed the bottle, stood up and turned to Aimee with a grin. 'C'mon.'

———

'OK, this is so much better.' Aimee picked up another slice of pizza from the box that was laid out on the floor of the dark hallway.

'I think this is more our style.' Heath swigged from the bottle of champagne and passed it over. 'The *Brats of Byron Bay* HQ.' He stretched his arms out grandly. 'This is where the magic is made.' They were both sitting on the cheap office carpet and leaning against the wall. A few fluorescent lights flickered overhead. 'Admit it: You never imagined it'd be this glamorous.'

'And why exactly did you choose *this* place?' Aimee laughed. 'We could've eaten pizza in the park above the beach.'

'Well, the park doesn't contain the surprise that I wanna show you.'

Aimee gave him a curious look. 'It's not a helicopter, is it?' she said sarcastically.

'After pizza,' he said with a laugh while he chewed.

Aimee took a sip of champagne. 'You know, even though this building is in the middle of town, I have no recollection of ever seeing it.'

It was one of those five-level offices built in the early 2000s – all rendered brick and terracotta tiles. One of those buildings that would've been modern at the time but had aged quickly and now looked drab.

'I could see it wasn't your kinda place,' Heath said of the restaurant. 'I'm sorry I booked it, I shoulda known.'

'No, no,' Aimee rushed. 'It was beautiful. It was amazing. I'm sorry. I wish I enjoyed that kinda stuff more than I do. I'm not a very *fancy* person,' she laughed.

'It's what I like about you. And it wasn't my kinda place, either.'

Aimee dabbed some red pizza sauce off her mouth with a paper towel and smiled a little. 'Why'd you choose it?'

Heath shrugged. 'To impress you.'

Aimee smiled more. 'Well,' she looked around at the dingy office and the floor pizza, 'this impresses me more.'

'Now, now – don't make fun of HQ.' He laughed and looked down the hall into the shadowy work room. 'I wanna show you something.' He slowly got up with a grunt and jogged down to a computer. He jiggled the mouse to wake it up and the harsh white light of the screen cut through the dark.

The place smelt like Spray 'n' Wipe and instant coffee. Equipment, stationery and crappy office furniture was scattered everywhere but not put away or organised. The TV production was set to wrap up and leave town in a few weeks, so there was no point in keeping things tidy. Aimee could see a giant whiteboard with a grid drawn in felt pen. The days of the week were listed at the top by initial – M, T, W, T, F, S, S – and details of events and schedules had been scrawled underneath. Squinting to read it, she couldn't make out the words.

'Come,' Heath called out.

Aimee got to her feet, jumped over the pizza box and made her way down. As she got closer, she could see a browser window open on the computer screen with a bunch of file icons lined up in rows. 'What is it?' she whispered.

'Why are you whispering?' Heath whispered back, smiling to himself as he scrolled through the file names.

Aimee laughed and nudged her hip into his. 'It's dark. Everyone whispers in the dark.'

Heath traced the mouse around the screen and double-clicked on one of the files. A video player popped up and Freya's face appeared. He hit the space bar and the footage played.

Aimee's head flicked to look at Heath but he pointed back at the screen.

'Just watch,' he said.

I don't remember my mum – Aimee's probably the closest thing I had to one. Even when Dad got into relationships, the people he was with never filled that space. No one could. Except Aimee.

Freya was sitting on the beach talking to the camera, wearing one of those bucket hats that had become cool again. The wind picked up and whipped the ends of her wild hair. She tamed it with a hand.

But she did it in a way that wasn't forced. She didn't ever try to be my mum. And if she did, I don't think we'd have the relationship we have now. It's hard to describe. She was more than just an aunt. There was always excitement and fun around the idea of Aimee. When I was really little she was the special magical lady with all the books and toys. And then when I got older she was kind of a big sister who lived this cool life with cool people and she showed me movies and music and told me about my mum and nan and pop. It always felt like we had our own secret club. She's the most impressive person I know. Yeah . . . that's the word. I'm so impressed by her.

Then the video ended and a freeze-frame of Freya's face stayed on the screen. Aimee didn't cry. She just stared at her niece – sitting on the beach, with the Pepsi magazine ad looks that she'd inherited from her mum – and smiled.

'They recorded that when she first joined the show – just after I filmed your interview on the beach. But I only saw this footage of Freya recently.' Heath closed the video and the bright light from the blue computer background lit up his face. 'I just wanted you to see that.'

It wasn't a helicopter ride. It was better.

'Hey,' Aimee said.

Heath turned and looked at her – both their faces illuminated by the light of the computer screen.

She stared into his eyes. More than anyone else in her life, Heath had seen Aimee at her worst – outside, in the real world. No snow globe perfection. He knew her faults and shortcomings and endless list of problems. And he accepted it all.

'Thank you,' she said.

And then she kissed him.

FORTY-FOUR

Aimee woke to the sound of plastic vibrating on timber but that wasn't what made her open her eyes. It was the smell of hotel room mixed with Joop and cigarette smoke on the pillows. She inhaled deeply. It was the same smell Heath had left on her pillow the afternoon they first slept together at her place – the day he climbed over rocks and dived into the ocean to save Aimee's Def Leppard cassette. She'd let that pillow go unwashed for a few extra days. At night, going to sleep, when she'd roll over and smell it, she'd get *that feeling* – the one she hadn't felt for Tim in a long time. And it was better than that first hit of jasmine in spring. Heath had gotten in. Like smoke through the crack under the door. Aimee felt at ease. And then, for a second, she wondered if Jules would ever accept her the same way Heath had, if she ever let him into her real world. She stretched out and flopped an arm over to the other side of the bed, expecting to find him. Instead, it slapped down on the dense mattress – white sheets pulled down from when he'd gotten up. The phone vibrated on the bedside table again. Short, sharp rattles. A message alert. Aimee took a deep breath and rolled over to grab it. She squinted and held it up to her face. The auto-unlock facial recognition feature promptly rejected her but the message was still on the home screen.

Did I leave my laptop there? x

Aimee sat up and rubbed the corners of her eyes. She looked around the room at the matchy-matchy Scandinavian-style furniture. No laptop. She couldn't be bothered wrestling on the jumpsuit that was flung over a chair in the corner, so she grabbed Heath's blue shirt that was also in the tangled pile. Out in the living room, she squinted at the glare coming through the glass sliding doors. On her way to pull the curtains closed, she spotted the Mac on the coffee table. She was just about to snap shut the silver lid and text Heath that she'd found it but then she saw Tim's face on the screen. The image made her stand still for a moment and assess it. Her brow furrowed. It was a video clip that was paused, which must've been why the laptop hadn't auto-locked. She sat down on the couch and looked closer. From the frozen image of Tim, she could tell it was filmed on the roof of the surf shop. He was surrounded by construction mess and the big sign on top of The Dream Explosion poked up in the background from across the street. She hit the space bar and the clip began to play. From the very first few seconds, it was clear the footage was just a rough cut – like the clip of Freya that Heath had played her the night before in the office. It was a standard confessional interview – similar to the ones Aimee had done throughout filming with an off-camera producer asking questions. In the video of Tim, the producer's questions had been cut out, so it was just Tim's answers strung together in a chopped up monologue.

The time-out is to figure out a lot of stuff. I think . . . Our relationship is . . . complicated? We'd only been dating . . . maybe, six months, when her mum and dad and sister died. She was with me on a surfing comp – that's why she wasn't with them. And it hit her hard. Of course it did. She was only eighteen. I've spent most of my life since then feeling a bit guilty about it . . . Yeah, I was in comps – winning. I'd been training to do comps my whole life. It's what I thought my life would be. Surfing, having a family in Byron, start the surf shop after I retired from competitive surfing. Just . . . livin' the dream. Things didn't end up that way.

Then the footage suddenly cut to Rozzie. Aimee's body jerked at the harsh change. Rozzie was sitting in her living room with a painting of Buddha on the wall behind and a miniature Zen garden on the side table next to her. She was always talking about her miniature Zen garden. She loved it and claimed it soothed her. In the clip, she was dragging the mini gold rake through the sand, making a delicate pattern as she spoke.

As a counsellor, it's my observation that Aimee has a lot of undiag-nosed trauma from the death of her family. I think there's anger that hasn't been dealt with and depression that's just . . . continued to develop and progress. She refuses to ask for help and then refuses to help herself. Then things spiral even further out of control and I have had to sit on the sidelines and watch it sink further – all while biting my tongue. My son gave up his career for her. He wanted to be a champion surfer, he was good enough to be a champion surfer, everyone in the industry told him he could be a champion surfer. And he gave it all away, everything he worked hard for – just because she needed him to take care of her after the accident. She begged him not to leave and live his life. And then, after sticking around, she ums and ahs for years about whether she even wants to marry him – and then refuses to give him an answer about whether or not they'll ever have kids. It's terrible what happened to her family. She has dealt with a lot in her life and I truly feel sorry for her. But a tragedy is not a 'get out of jail free' card that allows you to traipse through life, doing as you please and dragging other people down with you. I've told him:

Aimee will not make you happy. Tim has told me several times over the years that he has wanted to end their relationship. And the only reason he doesn't? He says he's afraid of what Aimee's going to do to herself if he leaves.

The clip ended and froze on Rozzie glaring down the camera lens. Aimee was winded. Keys clinked and the door pushed open. 'Hey, I texted you befor—'

'Get away from me.' Aimee shot to her feet and clutched her stomach, as if she was about to be sick.

Heath held his hands up in shock and tried to walk over but she shoved past him into the bedroom where she ripped off his shirt and grabbed the linen jumpsuit off the chair.

'You know, she's not even a real counsellor,' she spat while shoving her legs into the outfit. 'She's done an online course and read some books about kinesiology. That's it! And she has not just *sat by* on the *sidelines* while *biting her tongue*. The woman has *never* bitten her tongue.' She tried poking her arms through the top but something was tangled and she kept having to yank her arms back out to realign it. 'And, my god, that all just fell out of her mouth so *effortlessly*. I have no doubt she's been rehearsing it every night in the shower for the past twenty-odd years. It was a *monologue*. I'm surprised she doesn't perform it at events for money.' The straps of the jumpsuit seemed to be getting more tangled the more she fiddled with it. 'Jesus!' She let go of the fabric and slapped her hands on her thighs.

'Here, let me.' Heath stepped forward.

'Don't,' Aimee snapped. 'Just . . . *don't*.' She held the top half of the outfit in place over her chest and slid her feet into her tan sandals while looking around for her bag.

'Aimee, the video, it's—' Heath tried to explain.

'I'm not a part of this show anymore.' She pointed a finger at him as she walked past. 'I will *not* be appearing in anything else and I don't care if there's a contract. I'll give you back the upfront fee and don't bother about paying the rest. You can sue me, I have nothing.'

She swung the door open and walked out into the hallway. 'And your documentaries weren't that good.'

FORTY-FIVE

'You haven't left me because you're worried about what I'll *do* to myself?' Aimee was standing in the tangled white jumpsuit at the top of the steps on Tim's shop roof. She'd stormed straight there from Heath's – right through town. She didn't care who saw. The morning humidity was hell but she'd been walking in such a rage she hadn't noticed. Standing still, underneath the sun on the rooftop, her body was glistening in sweat while a shirtless Tim got more golden by the second. She raised her voice over the clashy music that was blaring out of a Bluetooth speaker. 'What am I gonna *do* to myself, Tim?'

Tim threw the measuring tape he was holding onto a bundled-up canvas tarp and walked over to the speaker to switch it off. The music had just faded out and a lethargic-sounding radio announcer mumbled, *You're listening to Triple J,* before it all went silent. He sighed and closed his eyes, already exasperated. 'Aimee, what's goin' on?'

She crossed her arms and her bottom lip quivered. Where to start? There was so much going on. Aimee began with the most pressing issue.

'Why are you listening to *Triple J*?' she spat.

'I've always listened to Triple J.'

'Oh since when?' she rebuffed. 'Did you start listening to it around the same time you started wearing that ridiculous fedora?' She nodded to the moss green wide-brimmed felt hat that was perched on her fiancé's head. 'You look like you're in a really bad folk band for dads.'

Tim scoffed. 'So *I'm* not allowed to wear a fedora but *you're* allowed to wear an Akubra?'

'Yeah, I wear it to remember my dead sister. Not because I'm pretending to be twenty. Did she buy it for you?'

'Who?' he played dumb, choosing to make her say Bree's name.

'The Hot Ew Girl.'

Tim's eyes popped out of his head. 'Wow. Real nice, Aimee. Clearly I'm not the one pretending to be twenty. And remember – you're the one who signed up to a reality show. Did you just come to tell me I'm an asshole in a fedora – or is there a real issue?'

Aimee didn't even need prompting. She had no idea of the exact words she was about to say, but twenty years' worth of resentment came tumbling out. 'Your mum is awful. She has *never* been nice to me.' Her voice started to shake and she didn't fight it. 'And you just . . . *ignore* it and *make excuses* and talk to her *about* me. And say *horrible* things.' The tears started to fall. 'I've seen the videos of what you said about me on camera. On the show. What you both said. I didn't tell you to quit surfing. I didn't *make* you give things up for me.'

Tim exhaled and closed his eyes, losing his patience. 'You didn't really give me a choice.'

'I never asked you to do that!'

'You did, Aimee. In your *way*.'

'What's my . . . *way*?'

He ignored the question and zeroed in. 'Have you ever taken a moment to actually *think* about what I gave up for you? Even if you reckon you didn't ask me to. The fact is that I did. Have you ever even *noticed*?' He shook his head and chuckled a fed-up laugh. 'It's always about Aimee. Aimee, Aimee, Aimee. *Is Aimee happy today? Why is Aimee cranky? What tiny, innocuous thing is gonna set off Aimee?* These are all the questions I've gotta ask myself. Daily. *Everyone watch out for the eggshells that we've all gotta tiptoe on around Aimee!'*

'It is not *always about me!'* She raised her voice in frustration.

'Nichelle,' Tim blurted out.

'What?'

'Who we went to school with,' he spat.

Aimee scrunched her face and cocked her head. *'Narissa?'*

'That's not her fucking name! God, Aimee! Can you pay attention to anything outside of yourself?'

Aimee gasped and held her arms out. 'It's a weird name! I'm not an asshole just because I forgot some chick's name who we went to school with!'

'The problem isn't just Narissa.'

'I thought you said her name was *Nichelle,'* Aimee shot back.

'Fuck!' Tim kicked a pile of rubble. 'You just always wanna be right,' he dismissed.

'What do you mean *I* just wanna be right? *Everyone* just wants to be right. *You* just wanna be right. That's why you're so pissed off.'

He let out a laugh. 'I am *not* pissed off.' He tried to do that thing again where he'd act calm, to make her seem irrational.

'Then *get* pissed off! I *want* you to be pissed off! Tell me what you're actually thinking instead of just . . . bitching about me to your mum and to the Hot Ew Girl and some TV cameras. What other stuff did you tell them about me? And what have you told . . . *her?'*

'Christ, you've got issues, Aimee. Why can't you just be happy? Why is it so hard for *you* to be happy? Sometimes I think you're addicted to being unhappy. You just wouldn't know who you are if you weren't miserable.'

Aimee exhaled and walked over to the ledge of the rooftop, looking out over the street below. She wasn't sure if she was addicted to being unhappy. But she knew she was addicted to the loneliness.

It was the big gross stupid fight she'd secretly been wishing they'd have for years. Petty grievances hurled. Old resentments used as ammunition.

But it didn't end with them both bursting into laughter at how ridiculous they were being. Aimee wiped her nose and looked up. The giant faded red sign on top of The Dream Explosion awning rested in view. She could finally ask the question that'd been burning inside. 'Do you even *like* me anymore?'

Tim kept staring ahead. 'Do you even like *me* anymore?'

FORTY-SIX

Piles of cash were strapped in rubber bands and lined up on the faded Persian rug of Aimee's apartment while the Roomba hummed in the background, diligently zooming around the mess of scattered objects as it cleaned.

'We can watch a movie?' Rob kept counting the money as she glanced up at Aimee, who was sitting on the floor and leaning against the couch. 'Double feature. *Paul Blart: Mall Cop* – one *and* two.' She scribbled down on a notepad to keep tally of the dollars. 'Or if you like . . . I can put in a call, finally get Luna to shit in Tim's bed.' She looked up and raised an eyebrow. 'Is that a smile? Did I finally get one? I thought Paul Blart would do it but, of course, it was bed shitting.' She waited a beat. 'What about Rozzie's bed?'

'*No one's bed*,' Aimee mock scolded. 'But I'll take you up on your earlier offer to crimp Rozzie's fringe next time she comes into the salon.'

'What salon?' Rob commented dryly.

'Right,' Aimee remembered. There was no more salon.

'I can't believe what she said,' Rob switched the conversation back to Rozzie. 'The fact she even *thought* it is bad enough. And then to go on camera, *knowing* you'll eventually see the footage . . . it's psychotic. The woman is a psychopath. I mean, we always *suspected* it – but this is proof.

All of it – the podcast, the on-camera interview. And for Tim to have even had those conversations with her about you—'

'For *years*,' Aimee interrupted. 'To have those conversations with her for *years*. Acting like I *trapped* him. Like I'm a mental patient who needs a twenty-four-hour supervisor – and he was just *lumped* with the job. *Oh, how kind of you to sacrifice everything and save me from myself.* It's such an excuse. He was just too scared to end it. We were *both* too scared to end it. Things weren't great between us – but what if we split up and our lives just got worse? That was the real thing that stopped either of us from ending it. By staying together, we could just blame the other for why life sucked. But if we split up and life still sucked? Well . . . no one else to blame.'

Rob paused. 'Your life doesn't suck.'

'I know my life doesn't suck.'

'Tim's life will probably suck.'

Aimee fought a smile. 'OK.' She inhaled. 'No more Tim talk.' She was sick of talking about Tim and thinking about Tim. She needed to think of herself and what the hell she was going to do with her life. Looking down at the piles of cash on the floor, she wondered when she'd stopped feeling physically ill about the fact she'd done something illegal. The shock of everything – losing the store, the TV show dramas, Freya and now the break-up – had numbed her. Compared to all the other incidents that had happened over summer, her little illegal act didn't even seem like that big of a deal in the grand scheme of things. To Aimee, it felt like the only thing she'd actually had a choice in doing. Should she have felt more? Probably. But she'd started to treat all uncomfortable events in her life the same way she treated swimming in the ocean. Take it one stroke at a time, breathing in between. Eventually she'd be back at shore.

'Just one more question.' Rob bit her bottom lip and hesitated a moment. 'When's he picking up his stuff?'

Aimee took in a breath and looked around the apartment she'd shared with her fiancé for close to two decades. 'In a few days. It's not much.' She realised how small Tim's presence was in their home, even when he lived there. The weird antiques and collectables and cassettes piled high. All Aimee – just stuff he tolerated. 'He'll come by, put his remaining pairs of boardies and T-shirts in a reusable Coles bag and then leave,' she said. 'The rest of his stuff's already at Rozzie's.'

'And just one more question, but I swear it's not about him.'

Aimee looked up.

'Where are *we* gonna go?' Rob flicked her eyes around the half-packed boxes crowding the living room.

'Maybe we'll all have to crash on Charlie's drummer's couch.' It was a joke but also a likely reality.

The sound of the humming Roomba and Rob flicking through the fifty-dollar bills filled the silence.

'You know the guy I've been hooking up with? I think it might be . . . something,' Aimee said. Twenty-four hours before, this could've meant two people. Now, one. The beggy texts and phone calls from Heath had gone ignored. Aimee didn't want to hear what he had to say. She felt like a fool. Like the TV show, Heath had been a mistake. Realising that made her see Jules a lot more clearly. And by telling Rob about him, all the secret moments she'd enjoyed with him suddenly became something real and she finally let herself consider what their time together could be if she just let him in. The final alarm had sounded on the time-out, and whatever she had with Jules could be whatever she wanted it to be.

Rob dropped a wad of fifties in her lap. 'The guy who sent the almost-peen pic?'

Aimee gave her friend an unimpressed look.

'You were gonna let me sit through *Paul Blart: Mall Cop* one *and* two when we could've been talking about almost-peen pic guy?'

'*Jules.*' Aimee pushed a stack of cash to the side so she could stretch out her legs. 'It's . . . nice. Easy. All the good things that come with hanging out with someone who you haven't been with for decades.'

'Can you move in with *him*?' Rob raised an eyebrow.

'He lives in a caravan in a field.'

Rob sighed and closed her eyes. 'I feel like you're living in an Angus &
Julia Stone song. I'm repulsed but also jealous.'

'He's Irish. Only here for work over the summer. But he got offered
another job to stay in Byron for a few more months. And he asked me if he
should take it.'

'Well, *yes he should*. And now we just need to make sure *you* stay.'

The sound of a key clinked into the lock on the front door and Aimee
immediately whipped her head around, ready to rouse on Freya. She bit her
tongue just in time.

'Am I in trouble?' Charlie said slowly, standing in the doorway and
observing his housemate's stern face.

Aimee rolled her eyes. 'Sorry, I thought you were Freya, coming home
early.'

'Are you guys still not talking?' Rob asked.

'There's been *a lot* of floor stomping,' Charlie said, chucking his keys on
the sideboard and walking over to the kitchen with his shopping bags. He
tossed a pile of mail by Aimee's side on his way past.

'I've got her working at the bookstore when she's not doing the TV show.
Doing stocktake and packing things up into boxes before we close for good.
It's the only way for me to know where she is at all times.'

'So you've effectively grounded her,' Charlie laughed over his shoulder.

'How'd you ground a twenty-one-year-old?' Rob cackled.

'I told her I'd call her dad and tell him what's been going on up here,'
Aimee said, no-nonsense.

'And how are my little dealers doing?' Charlie teased.

'I reject that,' Aimee protested, tearing open one of the letters and
wincing as she checked to see if it was a bill. It was. She could tell by the
logo. Electricity. How much? Aimee was too scared to look properly. 'I'm
not a dealer. I'm . . . a super aunt.'

'Did you get the Aldi champagne?' Rob looked over to the kitchen.

Charlie used his foot to kick the fridge door closed and held up a
bottle. 'They're all bills, by the way.' He nodded to the stack of mail.

'We're moving out soon, maybe we can just not pay them and hope they never find us?'

Aimee sighed and shoved the pile of envelopes across the floor. 'I'm more than happy to try that.'

'Or . . .' Charlie opened a jar of peanut butter and dipped his finger in it, 'you could change your mind about giving back your TV show money?'

'Nope,' Aimee shot back decisively.

'Ooooh!' Rob interrupted. '*I* got offered TV show money yesterday.'

Aimee's brow furrowed and her tone became snappy. 'Did the producers seriously come and ask you to do a paid interview about me?'

'It's not all about *you*, Aimee,' Rob teased. 'A *different* TV show. *Buying Byron.*'

'Robertaaaaa,' Aimee groaned, anticipating what her friend had done.

'So, you know how my garage got sold for a ridiculous amount of money without even being on the market?'

'Yes, I remember the details of how our lives were unceremoniously upended,' Aimee deadpanned.

'Well, people at this new real estate reality series – *Buying Byron* – heard about it. A producer came to the salon and said they wanted to feature it as a storyline on the show – and then they offered me *a thousand dollars*, just to be involved!'

'You should totally do it!' Charlie cheered.

'No! You should totally *not* do it!' Aimee looked at her friends like they were crazy. 'Have you not been paying attention to what the *first* reality show did to our lives?'

'But it's free money,' Rob said, fanning out some of the cash on the floor in front of her.

'It's only a thousand dollars – that's not worth selling yourself to be a character on a stupid TV show.'

'*Only* a thousand dollars?' Charlie said. 'I'd *kill* for a thousand dollars.'

'Yeah, do *you* have a spare thousand lying around, moneybags?' Rob asked.

Aimee swatted her friend on the knee. 'You *know* I don't. But what I've learnt is . . . not all money is the same. Some money ruins everything.'

'Fine.' Rob sat up straight and smiled cheekily. 'I'll stop talking about the TV show if we can go back to what we were talking about before Charlie came home.'

Aimee shot her friend a look, anticipating where she was heading.

'Oh, were you talking about dick pic guy?' Charlie guessed.

Aimee's eyes sprang open. 'How did you—' She cut herself off mid-sentence and turned to Rob. 'You told him?'

'She texted me the moment she saw the photo on your phone!' Charlie laughed.

'I was excited for you!' Rob clapped her hands together.

'Can I see the dick pic?' Charlie jumped up and down.

'I wanna see it again, too! *And* a face!'

'No.' Aimee rejected their requests. 'As punishment you will not be seeing either.'

'Mean!' Charlie called.

'Yeah, big meanie!' Rob fake-huffed. 'Release the nudes!'

'Well if I can't see the dick pic then I'm just gonna have to move on to the next hot topic on the agenda,' Charlie sighed. 'For the love of God, Aimee: what the hell is going on with your hair?'

Aimee used her hands to defensively shield her slightly unkempt mane. 'I ran out of hair product!'

'A month ago,' Rob muttered.

'I've been using moisturiser temporarily to tame it!'

Charlie grabbed at the ends of his friend's hair and made a grossed-out face. '*What* moisturiser?'

'The one under the bathroom sink.'

Charlie thought for a second and then stared at her curiously. 'In the green bottle?'

'Yes,' Aimee said bluntly. '*That* moisturiser.'

'That's not moisturiser.'

'Ah, *yes it is*. The label says MoistSurge.'

'Aimee,' Charlie's voice turned serious. 'That's lube.'

Rob shrieked.

Aimee refused to believe it. 'It's not lube.' She doubled down. 'What kind of lube is white and pasty?'

'The kind you buy from one of the all-natural hippy stalls at the Byron markets,' Charlie said flatly as the colour drained from Aimee's face. 'I think it was from The Mermaid Collective.'

Aimee grabbed her frayed ends. 'I've been putting *hippy lube* in my hair?'

'Is there any left?' Rob said through howls. 'Because, if it's all-natural, maybe you'd also like to use it as a chip dip, Aimee?'

Aimee took a deep breath in – made a mental note to buy some Pantene – and ignored her friends' clear delight by attempting to move the conversation along. 'Has your drummer said you can definitely stay with him for a few weeks after we move out? And does he have room for us to crash? Just until we figure something out.'

'Well,' Charlie tiptoed around the give-or-take thirty thousand dollars that was stacked around the floor in separate piles. He flopped down next to Rob as they grinned at each other.

Aimee looked at him strangely. 'Well, *what?*'

'We might not have to do that . . .' Rob chimed in. 'I was waiting for Charlie to get here to discuss.'

'We have a plan,' Charlie finally spat out, like an excited toddler.

Aimee rolled her eyes and gave in. 'Lay it on me,' she sighed while slowly getting up off the floor to walk over to the kitchen and unpack one of the shopping bags on the bench. By the time she opened the fridge to start putting things away, Rob was already in the middle of her pitch.

'You're not gonna like it but all I ask is that you be quiet and just hear us out,' Rob said calmly. 'Because this could get us *a lot more* than just a thousand dollars.' She paused and took a breath. 'We do one more dial-a-dealer drop at Hot Canyon Nights.' She started racing to explain the rest in case Aimee cut in. 'Us three. Like what we did at the markets – but we'll do it inside the festival, from Charlie's taco truck. We'll send a text out to contacts and then they can spread it around. We'll all put in whatever spare cash we have saved and turn it into a windfall – like *this*,' she stretched her arms out over the piles of cash. 'I wanna make snow angels in this money so badly.'

Aimee had stopped unpacking the bags and was standing still, with her head inside the fridge. Charlie took the reins of what seemed like a rehearsed presentation.

'We secure the product, swaddle each baggie in wads of paper towels and then wrap it in tin foil – so it looks like a burrito.'

'We've still got that phone Freya gave us – and a lot of the clients on the contact list are in town for Hot Canyon Nights. We do a text out – like we did at the markets with the cassettes – telling them to come to the taco truck and use a code word. They buy a fake burrito and we take their money. Simple. And we'll be selling normal Mexican food anyway, so it won't be suspicious.'

'And at these events, we arrive early to set up and enter through the service gates, avoiding any checkpoints and flying under the radar of the cops,' Charlie added.

Aimee still hadn't reacted or said anything.

Charlie turned to Rob and tapped her arm. 'Now say your thing about Robin Hood.'

'Oh, yeah.' Rob cleared her throat and flicked her fringe out of her eyes. 'Like what Freya said about Byron in the summer – it's basically just rich people from the city coming here to party. They're gonna buy coke anyway. And they're ruining our town – so why not take their money? You'll be like Robin Hood – but with balayage and better shoes. And . . .' Rob leant over to rummage through a nearby box filled with Aimee's bulk purchase of wellness books, 'It's basically what all these self-help ladies are telling you to do. Shonda Rhymes says, "Say yes!" and all these other bitches are telling you, "Go for it, warrior woman!"'

'Also,' Charlie cut in, his tone taking a distinct turn from playful to serious. 'There's really no other option. None of us can afford to stay here.

We can't even afford to move towns. And trying to start new businesses? It's impossible. It worked out fine when you did it for Freya.'

Aimee had closed the fridge and was staring at the stainless steel door. Only one thing was on it: The slip of paper with the quote that Freya had stuck there after going to one of the fortune tellers when she first arrived in town.

If you want to win your life you have to go wild and jump into the fire.

Charlie was right. There were no other options.

She turned around and looked at her friends. 'OK,' she said, soft but sure.

It was met with stunned silence.

Rob squinted. 'Really? Cause . . . I gotta say, I'm a little disappointed you're agreeing so easily. I didn't even get to recite the poem I'd memorised from Matthew McConaughey's *Greenlights* memoir.'

Aimee shrugged, almost emotionless. 'Yes. Let's do it.'

FORTY-SEVEN

The Monaro sped west, down a road full of potholes, towards the hinterland. A sign – decorated with childlike paintings of flowers and trees and hearts – whooshed by.

WELCOME TO NIMBIN

'Now we both really *are* the Byron stereotype,' Aimee said as Rob furiously swiped and tapped at her phone screen.

Drugs to Nimbin were what croissants were to Paris or 'I heart NY' tees were to Manhattan. The easy access of substances meant Nimbin had long been a punchline for bad jokes. People would only have to scoff the word 'Nimbin' and everyone around them would laugh because of the connotations it held. Byron was also well on its way to being the one-word punchline to half-jokes. It was a caricature of itself. A geographical meme. In Nimbin, the town even had an annual MardiGrass festival, where hundreds of people would parade down the street in green wigs, dressed like marijuana leaves. The local newspaper always featured a big photograph of the event on its front page – usually involving the fifteen-metre long inflatable joint that took pride of place in the parade. Deep in the hills where hippy-dippy communes first popped up off the grid in the seventies, it was Australia's drug destination. No rules. At least it seemed that way. You could stand still on the main drag at any time of day and, in under a minuté, you'd be offered all different kinds of things. When Aimee told Charlie where they were heading that morning, he recalled the time he went to the Nimbin park and bought acid for ten dollars from a teenager in broad daylight while a new mum breastfed near the swings.

'We're not quite the stereotype. For us to be the stereotype, we'd need dreadlocks and tie-dyed outfits – like all these Nimbin locals.' Rob held up her phone and showed Aimee a dating app that displayed all the eligible men nearby.

Aimee glanced over from the steering wheel and squinted. 'I never understood the whole tie-dye thing.'

'I know.' Rob scrunched her face. 'Like, you can smoke a joint and still wear nice clothes.'

Aimee's Ace of Base ringtone started blaring and the phone's vibrations made it rattle against the plastic of the centre console where it was stowed. Rob looked down and read the name on the screen. 'It's Plain Jane Producer Girl again.'

'Reject it.' Aimee kept her eyes on the road. 'Jesus – between her and Nina, that's, what . . . four or five calls? And that's just since we left Byron. Brooke's even tried calling.'

'What do they want?' Rob made a face.

'I read one of the texts. They're trying to get me back to finish filming. *We just need to wrap up your storyline,*' she mimicked Nina's clipped British accent. 'As if it'd be that simple. After everything they've done, I can only imagine how they'd wanna *wrap up my storyline.*'

'I know, what else could they possibly wanna do to you? Set you on fire?'

'I *wish* that was the worst they'd done to me,' Aimee muttered. 'Hey, can you check Google Maps?' She switched off the stereo, cutting short Heart's

'These Dreams'. She'd been told by Rob to just follow the highway and the lack of specific directions was making her anxious.

'Aimee, the place we're going cannot be found on Google Maps.' Rob put on a placid one-with-the-earth voice.

'How *did* you find this place?'

Rob shrugged. 'Bada Bing.'

Aimee shook her head and sighed, clearly annoyed. It was only a matter of days before Rob's inquiry was used as a Guess Who, Don't Sue.

'Oh, it's completely fine.' Rob rested her elbow on the window ledge. 'All we gotta do is follow his vague directions to a remote commune and ask for The Artisan.'

'Well, that sounds reputable,' Aimee mumbled. 'Hey, I've been thinking . . . Do people even *do* cocaine at music festivals? I thought they did . . . MDNA.'

Rob snorted. 'MDNA is the name of the Madonna album.'

Aimee took a hand off the steering wheel to whack her. 'You know what I mean.'

'People do everything. A group of mates will buy a bag between each other. Pills, weed, ketamine. It's so crazy that ketamine's cool again. Anyway, we're being more *classy* with our product offering. Cocaine is more chic than falling into a K-hole.'

'How do you even know what people are doing at festivals?'

'There was a story on *Daily Mail* a few days ago about a Sydney festival – cops busted people with all kinds of stuff,' Rob said nonchalantly.

Aimee's eyes popped as she caught up with what her friend had just said. 'What if there's cops and sniffer dogs at Hot Canyon Nights? They'll *definitely* be there. Jesus!'

'Aimee! Seriously,' Rob talked over her friend. 'Cops at music festivals is not new information. We're not idiots – Charlie and I have already thought this through. We're going through the service entry early in the day to set up – we won't get checked. And when cops roam around the festivals, they're looking for punters behaving weirdly, exchanging shit in the shadows or hanging out around the bathrooms.'

'And what about sniffer dogs?'

Rob shrugged. 'If one comes close, we just throw a real burrito on the ground to distract it.'

Aimee glared at her friend. 'Very cute,' she deadpanned.

'I'm serious,' Rob laughed. 'I heard it on a true crime podcast. Cops went to do a bust and the dog missed the drugs because the guy "*dropped*" a ham and cheese toastie on the floor.'

Aimee let out a frustrated exhale.

'Byron Karen's a drug dealer,' Rob teased in a sing-song voice.

'Stop.'

'Oh, c'mon. It's funny. Let's not pretend like it's not what's happening.'

'I've been trying not to pay attention to what's happening.'

'I know. That's what you do.' Rob looked out the window and paused for a moment. 'When were you gonna tell me you hooked up with that TV hot shot?'

Aimee looked over quickly. 'How did you . . .'

Rob grinned. She didn't know. But now she did. 'I knew it was gonna happen from the start.'

'You did not.' Aimee rolled her eyes.

'You slimed his car and then he came back into your life as your boss. It's like the opening scene from a Sandra Bullock rom-com.'

'Then why doesn't my life feel like it's a Sandra Bullock rom-com?'

'I can *totally* imagine Sandra Bullock doing what you're doing.'

Aimee paused. 'That's the nicest thing you've ever said to me. You really think I look like Sandra Bullock?' She jokingly flicked her hair back.

'Well . . . that's not *exactly* what I said,' Rob laughed.

'I was at Heath's when I saw the footage of Tim and Rozzie,' Aimee shared. 'It was open on his laptop and I watched it. He wasn't there.'

'OK . . . *now* it's coming together,' Rob said slowly, filling in the blanks. 'So you *didn't* accidentally see it in the production tent while getting your make-up done.'

Aimee gave her friend a guilty look. 'I may have lied about that part.'

'And you think Heath set all that up? The videos of Tim and Rozzie saying those things?'

'Doesn't that seem accurate?'

Rob contorted her mouth, showing her scepticism.

'He produces a reality show!' Aimee said bluntly. 'Of course he concocted it. And I was a complete moron for trusting him in the first place. I'm just like all those other idiots who go on reality shows and then blame producers for screwing them over.'

'Well. You said he was different to everyone else on the show. And isn't his job to, like, handle the budgets?' Rob shrugged. 'Sounds like he had a crush on you from the start. Maybe it's not what you think. Did he try explaining the videos?'

Aimee sighed. 'After I saw the clips, he walked in and I stormed out. He's texted – said it was Nina who made the storyline producers pursue the angle about me and Tim and our history. Blah, blah, blah. I barely even read the messages before deleting them entirely.'

'Do you believe it?' Rob continued while tapping away on her phone screen. 'That Nina was behind it?'

Aimee inhaled. She wanted to believe it. And maybe she would have if there wasn't someone else on her mind.

'Well, you've still got your *other* guy – Jules,' Rob chattered away. 'And I hate you for not having any pictures of him.'

Aimee smirked. 'I did have a picture of him – but I deleted all evidence after you found the dick pic.'

'Ugh! Rude!' Rob slapped her thigh. 'Particularly because I'm sitting here showing you all these pictures of *my* boyfriends . . .' She held up the phone with all the hippy dating profiles. 'I was chatting to a guy on here last night and then he texted me a nudie pic of himself holding a broom.'

Aimee cocked her head and scrunched up her face. 'A *broom*?'

'Yeah.' Rob quickly tapped through her texts and showed Aimee the screen. She had not lied. On display was a naked guy taking a photo of himself in a mirror while holding a broom. 'Are broom nudes, like, a new trend or something?'

'How would *I* know if broom nudes are a trend?'

'Well, you're the one with two boyfriends. Have the kids on the show said anything about broom nudes? Maybe it's a new thing. Like . . . #BroomNudes.'

'Why a broom?' Aimee squinted at the photo again. 'Why not a mop? Or a rake?'

'It's like he's using it as a form of aspect ratio – holding up an object against his *other object* to show its size and scale.'

'Do guys really do that?' Aimee grimaced.

'They *love* to. I'm constantly being sent unsolicited photos by guys with their dicks next to things, just to show its proportions. A dick next to a Coke can. A dick next to a tube of Rexona. A dick next to the TV remote.'

'Ok, now I'm imagining all of them.' Aimee tried to shake the thought out of her head. 'Enough with the #BroomNudes.'

'Look, I may have to marry the #BroomNudes guy if I can't find a new place to live,' Rob joked. 'You can stay with us, if you like. Just don't use the broom.'

The sound of car wheels spinning over bitumen and tiny rocks spraying up at metal filled the silence for a moment.

'Last night I was sorting through stuff to throw out and pack in boxes when I started flicking through last year's day planner,' Rob said. 'Do you remember what we were doing in the first week of January a year ago?'

'Of course.' Aimee didn't miss a beat. 'We started that month-long meal plan to rebuild our gut microbiomes.' She paused and then turned to Rob with a blank expression. 'I didn't tell you this, but I only lasted a week.'

Rob stared ahead. 'I lied about even starting it.'

They both smiled. Rob glanced down at her phone to change the song and turned the volume on the stereo back up. A tinkly piano intro floated through the car.

Aimee laughed and shook her head. 'Toni Collette and the fucking Finish.'

'Just for you.'

———

Aimee already knew she was deep in a problem she couldn't escape, and that knowledge was validated when she saw three scruffy naked people scurrying into the forest that stretched along either side of the dirt road at the sight of her car. The Monaro had turned onto a private property and followed the track for about ten minutes. Dust clouded behind it. The canopy of leaves above was so thick it was hard to tell that it was the early afternoon. As the car rolled out of the darkness and into a clearing, white glare blasted down from the storm clouds that had started to gather. The brakes squeaked and the car slowed to a stop. Aimee and Rob looked out at the field. A weatherboard house was in the middle, bordered by rows of canvas huts. Scattered groups of people looked up from the gardening and washing they were doing. Kids with long hair and no shirts played in the dirt. The men and women had messy, mousy brown hair and wore basic, scrappy clothes in drab colours.

'Is that what cottagecore is?' Rob peered at them.

A man holding a shovel walked towards them. His head was cocked to the side and he stared at Aimee and Rob through the windscreen. When he got to the driver's side, he lifted the rusty scoop of the shovel and tapped it on Aimee's window three times.

She wound it down just enough to speak through. 'We're here to see The Artisan.'

The guy peered at them.

'#ShovelNudes,' Rob whispered.

The comment went ignored.

'I'm Aimee. What's your name?'

The guy didn't blink. 'I do not have a name. I am an entity.' He bent down to pick up a gumtree leaf off the ground. He held it up. 'This is my entity. This is who I am.' He opened his mouth, placed the leaf on his tongue, chewed and swallowed. 'Now I no longer exist.'

Aimee and Rob sat in silence. Fat droplets started to fall from the sky and splattered on the glass.

The guy still hadn't blinked. He nodded over to the house and started walking.

Aimee wound up the window and unclicked her seat belt.

'Spooky,' Rob whispered.

'Very.'

'Maybe we should move *here*.'

They could still feel all the eyes in the field on them as they got out and gently closed their doors. Aimee locked the car and they followed the guy with the shovel to the house. Its faded green paint was flaking and the corrugated iron roof was burnt orange from rust. The front door was open. The man who didn't exist led them inside. Aimee and Rob's shoes squeaked over the concrete floor and they squinted as their eyes adjusted to the dimly lit room filled with lamps and rugs on the walls. It sounded like a TV show was playing. Then Aimee recognised a voice. *Hilary Duff?*

A woman, maybe in her early fifties, was sitting at a grand turned-leg table in the middle of the room, writing on a notepad with a silver MacBook off to one side. She wasn't like the others outside in the field. Her skin looked like Cate Blanchett's in those SK-II ads and the kaftan she was wearing looked like it was from one of the boutiques in Byron where the cheapest things stocked are two-hundred dollar basic white tees. She flicked her smooth honey-coloured hair back, glanced up, put her pen down and assessed the two strangers. The guy who didn't exist left the room.

'Nice blow-out,' she said, her voice as smooth as her complexion.

Aimee's eyes flicked around as she tried to comprehend the comment. Hilary's voice kept chattering out of the laptop.

'Your hair. Did you get it done at that new blowdry bar in town? Blow Baes?'

'Um, she did it.' Aimee pointed at Rob.

'You got a salon?'

'I do. I *did*,' Rob corrected herself. 'It's closing down.'

'Shame.' The woman pushed her notepad to the side. 'You should apply to Blow Baes.' She hit the space bar on the Mac, pausing Hilary mid-sentence. 'I'm just getting into *Younger*. Charles is a cunt.'

'Hilary Duff really lights up the screen,' Aimee said, her voice shaking a little as she came to terms with the reality of the situation that was unfolding.

Rob shrugged. 'I just want the best for Hilary.'

The woman pressed a button on the side of the laptop and it spat out a round silver disc. Poking one of her long manicured fingers through the centre hole, she held it up in the air and used her other hand to flip open a DVD binder. Aimee and Rob stared as she flicked through the clear plastic sleeves with discs tucked neatly inside them.

'No internet here.' She continued to flip. 'So DVDs is all I've got.'

Just as the woman landed on a page with a spare slot and started to slide the disc in, Ace of Base began blaring from Aimee's back pocket and her body seized up like she'd just been shot. She rushed to pull out her phone to reject the call but, when she glanced at the screen, expecting to see Nina or Plain Jane Producer Girl's name, she paused. It was Freya. 'Hi,' she quickly answered before looking up at the woman behind the table, offering an apologetic wince and holding a finger in the air to show she'd just be a moment. 'Is everything OK?' She turned to walk over to a corner on the other side of the room.

'Yeah, just calling to say hi,' Freya said softly, a little shy.

'Well, *hi*,' Aimee replied, dragging the word out playfully. No foot stomping. No angry tone.

'Where are you?'

Aimee looked around the dark room of the remote shack with no known address. 'Just looking at new shop spaces.'

'All g.'

Aimee smiled to herself, remembering the first time Freya had replied to a text with 'all g' and how she had to google to see what it meant. 'Are you at the bookstore?'

'Yeah, stocktake's finished. I don't know if I did it right.'

'That's OK, I'm sure it's perfect.'

There was a pause. Then Freya let out a little laugh. 'Also . . . Meredith came in with a tape measure. She wants to move her crystal stall in here once you leave.'

Aimee snorted. 'Oh, of course she does. She'll probably *buy* the damn building.'

'Hey Aimee?'

'Yeah?'

'I'm sorry.'

Aimee's chest began to tighten. There was really only one thing to say. 'All g,' she replied.

They were both quiet for a moment.

'Meet you at the beach for a swim after I close the store?' Freya eventually said.

'You bet.'

Aimee hung up and looked at the photo on her phone's lock screen: Her and Freya sitting on the hood of the Monaro in the carpark above the beach. She tightened her grip around it and turned slowly to walk back to the woman at the desk.

'Sorry, that was my—'

'Niece,' the woman finished Aimee's sentence. 'Your friend told me. She's just turned twenty-one? Same age as my daughter.'

'Oh,' Aimee said, a little too stunned at the revelation.

'Didn't think someone like me would have kids?' The woman sat back confidently and smirked.

'No, no,' Aimee raced to say. 'That's not . . .' She trailed off. 'Does she live here?'

'God no. Both my kids did boarding school as teens. Now one's a lawyer and the other's studying engineering.'

'Do they know you do . . . *this*?'

The woman raised an eyebrow and stared into Aimee's eyes. 'Does your niece know you're *here*?'

Aimee looked down at her feet and thought about the lie she'd just told Freya.

'So,' the woman said, her tone swiftly switching to bright and upbeat. 'How can I help?'

FORTY-EIGHT

Aimee pulled the lever on the slushie machine inside Charlie's taco truck and filled a giant yellow cardboard cup with frozen tequila. Her hand shook. Partly from the whirling of the generator that powered the van and the vibrations of the music blaring from giant speakers across the field. But mostly from nerves. All three of them in the taco truck had lost count of how many slushies had been downed.

'It's always so weird when you remind yourself that a lot of the people who come to these festivals are accountants and teachers and physios.' Rob leant on the metal counter and looked out the serving window at the thousands of punters swarming around the paddock underneath flags and banners that read HOT CANYON NIGHTS.

Everyone looked like they'd coordinated their outfits with one of Brooke's Pinterest boards. The theme? Sexy space cowboy. Chunky military boots juxtaposed against floaty mesh sarong skirts embroidered with so many jewels and sequins they looked like galaxies. Earthy tones and pastel accents with pops of silver and gold swirled together in the crowd that sprawled between the multiple stages as a moody sunset glow settled overhead.

'Dammit.' Aimee jolted her body away from one of the cups and took her hand off the lever. 'My shawl dipped into the slushie-ness.'

Both Aimee and Rob were dressed as Stevie Nicks. Unable to agree on who would be Stevie, the trio came to a consensus that there was nothing wrong with having two Stevies on stage. Their outfits were same-same, but different – top hats, platform black boots and a flurry of excess fabric.

'You need to chill out,' Rob laughed.

'I can't. I'm . . . *freaking out.*' Aimee flicked the liquid off her sleeve and shook her head. 'I feel sick. You know what, I don't think I can do this.'

'You *can* do this.'

Charlie looked over his shoulder from the grill. 'You were *born* to do this.'

Aimee started doing a breathing exercise she'd vaguely learnt from one of the annoying motivational podcasts she'd downloaded in a particularly desperate moment. *Six seconds in. Nine seconds out.* Or was it nine seconds in, six seconds out?

'Jeez, if this is how you're reacting to the thought of just singing on stage, imagine what you would've been like if we went through with—'

'*Don't* finish that sentence,' Aimee interrupted, quickly turning to look at the service window to make sure no customers were listening.

Rob loved teasing Aimee when she was on edge. 'There's no issue if we're *not actually doing anything wrong.* But admit it: it would've been awesome to pull off another secret mission tonight. Code words, under-the-table dealings. Paying in cash. I forgot how fun *cash* can be. We need to start using *cash* again.'

'I love the *smell* of cash,' Charlie laughed.

Her friends' ridiculous tangent gave Aimee a moment to get her breathing steady again. 'Well, sorry to crush your dreams. I just *couldn't do it.* The first time was to get Freya out of her mess. A second time? Uh-uh. I don't even know how you convinced me to go to that house in the first place. I think I was just in shock – after everything that's happened, and then the breakup with Tim pushed me over the edge.' She took a beat and then fought a smile. '*Obviously* you both took advantage of my *fragile state* and that's the only reason I wound up there.'

'Liar!' Rob picked up Charlie's metal tongs and snapped them in the air at her friend.

'Get her!' Charlie started flicking a damp tea towel in the air.

Aimee swatted them away through a fit of laughter. 'My gosh! I am *shocked* at us. Going to *that house*. The fact we even *considered* following through with the plan here.' She held her hands out and waved them around the taco truck, laughing hysterically at the arrogance of the plan. 'And even doing what we did at the markets? It's the most idiotic thing I've ever done! That was *illegal. Illeeegal.*'

Rob looked at her friend like she'd just discovered what food and water were. 'Ah, *yeah.*'

Charlie laughed. 'I think she's got some kind of *delayed reaction* or something.'

Aimee caught her breath. 'I seriously think I've been in some kind of *clinical daze*. Like, I'm talking medically-certified craziness. But not anymore. Going to that house just *shocked* me out of it.'

The previous day, as The Artisan sat before them and offered to provide whatever they asked for, Aimee couldn't follow through with what they'd gone there to do. The only reason she went in the first place was because she thought her life was at rock bottom. Then came the phone call from Freya. As long as she had her, Aimee knew she wasn't at rock bottom.

'Rob, do your impression again!' Charlie giggled, turning back to the grill to shuffle meat around.

Aimee rolled her eyes. 'You've done it enough. It's really not that funny.'

Rob composed herself and stood with overly stiff posture. '*We're just browsing,*' she said in a funny voice.

Charlie screamed with laughter.

Rob fell to the floor. 'Who *browses* for drugs?' she wheezed.

Aimee pretended to kick her. 'Shoosh! And I *do not* sound like that!'

'*Browsing*! As if you were looking for laptops at JB Hi-Fi!'

Aimee leant on the counter to look out the service window and ignore her friends. 'You know my favourite thing about music festivals? Admiring the cultural appropriation,' she said flatly. 'Just when you think they've run out of cultures to steal from, they find something new.'

Native American feather headdresses were out. Maang Tikkas were in. Aimee looked over at the nearby Ferris wheel where a group of girls posing for a photo were all accessorised with the silver head chains.

'Ugh, I know.' Rob climbed off the floor. 'When I was lining up for the bathroom earlier, some drunk bitch whipped me in the eye with the beaded leather fringe on her jacket.'

'Are you *kidding* me?' Aimee spat, peering out through the crowd where a familiar sight caught her attention.

'I know,' Rob sighed. 'I think I'm gonna need prescription droplets. By the time my vision un-blurred, she'd skipped off into the Moët tent.'

'Not that,' Aimee huffed. Coming towards the van was a TV crew. 'Jesus Christ, I told them I'm not filming anything more for that stupid show.'

Rob leant on the bench next to her and peered out through the window. 'Ohhh,' she said, a little hesitantly. 'I forgot to tell you something.'

Charlie turned around from the grill. 'Rob now has her own TV show,' he tattled.

Rob picked up a tea towel and whipped him with it.

Aimee closed her eyes and slurped from her tequila slushie. 'That stupid *Bidding Byron* show?'

'*Buying Byron*,' Rob corrected. 'And, yes.'

Aimee slapped her cup down on the metal bench.

Rob raced to explain. 'Well, when we ditched our *old plan* to sell *other* products tonight, I realised I needed the extra cash. A thousand bucks! Easy! I can't say no to that.'

Aimee calmed herself. 'Just *please* be careful. I say that as someone who got screwed over by my own TV show.'

'And as someone who *also* got screwed over by your TV show, I believe you.' Rob raised an eyebrow and smirked.

'Ouch,' Aimee said. 'Look, I'm sorry—'

'No, don't be.' Rob kissed her friend on the forehead.

Aimee felt a buzz in the back pocket of her jeans and she reached around with a hand to slide out her phone. She froze for a moment when she glanced at the screen. Jules:

Come outside :P

'Look, I completely get your concern,' Rob kept talking. 'And I appreciate it. But this isn't like your show. It's not a dramatic one – it's just one about houses. Boring. I'm not gonna get screwed over. The EP said all they want is a Byron local who has been displaced by gentrification and had their livelihood stolen by rich out-of-towners.'

Aimee smirked. 'Translation: they want you to be Byron Karen.'

Rob clasped her face excitedly. 'I can only dream to be bestowed the honour.'

Aimee kissed her friend's forehead. 'I happily pass the torch.'

Rob looked out the window. 'Hey guys,' she greeted the crew before turning back to Aimee and lowering her voice. 'I will make sure to keep them far away from you.'

'Thank *god*,' Aimee laughed.

Rob turned to dash out of the van to meet the crew.

'I gotta duck outside, too.' Aimee followed. 'Have fun, TV star!' Slipping out the side door of the truck and clomping her boots down the metal stairs, Aimee squinted as she tried to spot Jules.

It took her a moment to realise the guy wearing the neon Lycra tights and the pink glasses with lenses in the shape of hearts was him. She burst out laughing.

'I thought I'd get in the spirit.' He held out his arms with a smile.

'And I thought I told you not to come.' Aimee slapped her hands on his buff bare chest.

'Well, I didn't wanna miss . . . *this*.' He grabbed her by the hand and spun her around, laughing as the reams of black fabric she was draped in picked up in the breeze.

'This is *exactly* why I didn't want you coming,' she laughed. 'I look like an idiot. And I'm gonna look even worse when I'm singing on stage.'

'And I'll make sure to film the trainwreck as it unfolds.' He held up his phone.

She leaned in close. 'Don't. You. Dare.'

He grinned and then surprised her with a kiss.

'Well, now that you're here, how about you come inside and meet my friends?' She twisted her fingers between his.

Jules squinted over her shoulder at the taco truck and nodded. 'What are they filming?'

Aimee glanced over and saw Rob holding court in front of the camera. 'Oh. Just a reality show – not the one I was on. A different one. With Rob.'

Jules grimaced and sucked in some air, like he'd just taken a shot of really cheap vodka. 'I kinda don't wanna be on camera. It's just *those shows*. I dunno. Do you mind if I meet your friends another time?'

Aimee stood up a little straighter. 'Oh, yeah.' She tried not to look taken aback. 'Sure. You can . . . meet them another time.' She forced a smile.

Jules took one more look at the cameras near the van then flicked his gaze back to Aimee and gave her a quick kiss. 'I better go push my way to the front of the crowd.' He smirked.

'No whooping!' Aimee warned as he walked away.

Just as she turned to walk back to the van, she heard the clang of the service window roller door smash down. Charlie burst out the side of the truck and tossed her a tambourine.

'It's time!' he boomed. 'We're on in ten.'

'Shit the bed.' Aimee cringed, wondering if it was too late to pull out. This happened every year. She knew they'd have to go on stage eventually, but that didn't stop her from praying an electrical blackout would surge and cancel their performance. 'Hey, are we sure this is the right song to do?' she asked Charlie, who was jumping on the spot and waving his hands in the air, trying to signal to Rob that it was time to wrap up her interview and leave.

'It's perfect,' he said. 'You always do this – you get nervous and then you end up having fun.'

'Oh shit,' Aimee blurted, staring at something in the distance.

'You're not pulling out,' Charlie automatically argued.

'No, it's—'

'Aimee! Hey girlfriend!' The annoying Plain Jane Producer Girl ran up and pulled Aimee into a hug as a cameraman and soundie clunked around with their equipment.

'Hi *girlfriend*,' Aimee replied sarcastically.

The Plain Jane Producer Girl didn't register the tone. 'Awesome night, right? Did you see Elsa Pataky and Luciana Barroso are here?'

Aimee's eyes flicked from side to side, waiting for an explanation. 'I don't know who they are.'

'Chris Hemsworth and Matt Damon's wives!'

'OK?'

'You've been hiding the past few days.' Plain Jane Producer Girl cocked her head and gave Aimee a fake sympathetic look.

'That's because I told you guys, *I'm not doing this anymore*.' Aimee tried to walk off but Plain Jane blocked her with the camera guy and the soundie.

'Well, we kinda need you, babe. It's just Bree and Luna and Addie here tonight. Freya's gone with Brooke up to the Gold Coast to audition five-year-old wannabe models at a shopping centre for that new Tutu Tribe campaign they're shooting.'

'Yes, *I know* that's where Freya is,' Aimee snapped, a little defensive. She had agreed to let her niece go on the trip and she had no issues with it. If Brooke's Oprah-style gift giveaway helped with Freya's future, then splash that cash. 'And don't talk to me in that fake-nice voice like we're best friends. I'm not an idiot – I know what you're doing. I told Heath and Nina *and you* that I wouldn't be on the show anymore.'

'Nina said you're contractually obligated. I know you don't wanna be filmed, but we're allowed to.' Plain Jane held her clipboard to her chest, like a doctor dealing with an unruly patient. The cameraman documented the standoff.

'Hey, can you guys move?' a producer from *Buying Byron* called out. 'We were filming here first and you're in our shot.'

'We have to go!' Charlie yelled and banged a tambourine, getting everyone's attention. 'Stevies! Both of you! Now!'

Plain Jane was still standing in a don't-mess-with-me stance.

Aimee turned to follow her friends. 'Do what you want,' she dismissed the crew. 'I don't care.' She tossed the end of one of her many shawls over a shoulder and disappeared into the swirl of sexy space cowboys.

———

The crowd waiting for The Girly Boys didn't necessarily match the ocean of people over at the main stage where Tones and I was performing in the exact same timeslot. Still, there were a couple of hundred punters who pressed their sweaty, glittery bodies against each other while a sugary-sweet deep fried carnival smell wafted around. A jangly guitar started strumming and then a waterfall of drum thumps followed. The lights shot up, illuminating Aimee, Rob and Charlie – all standing at three separate microphones in front of the rest of the band. The crowd instantly recognised the song and cheered. Charlie purred the opening lyrics to Fleetwood Mac's 'Go Your Own Way'.

Rob was banging her tambourine on her hip and waving a silk scarf. Aimee looked out at the crowd. Under the purple glow of the lights, she could see the reality show TV cameras in the pit below the stage. They were filming Luna and Addie and Bree, who were squeezed into the front row, against the metal barricades. They had appropriately beachy hair and wore outfits that made them look like extras from *Almost Famous*. There was no way in hell they'd have actually chosen to be in that mosh pit. Charlie's band was cool – but the attendance of Byron Bay Brats at a gig where Byron Karen was pretending to be Stevie Nicks on stage was clearly the work of Nina, who was probably hidden in one of her secret lairs while watching it all unfold.

That train of thought got run off the tracks when Aimee's eyes landed on Jules in the crowd. His sunnies and cap stood out – especially when he raised his arms and formed 'rock on' signs with his fingers as a joke. Aimee smirked and flicked her eyes away so she didn't laugh into the microphone. She was secretly glad he came – even if it meant looking like an idiot in front of him. A few years into this ridiculous tradition, Tim had stopped coming. 'You don't need me there,' he'd say. 'You guys just do it as a joke, anyway.' Standing on stage, her mind started to wander. *Maybe that's when I stopped going to the beach with him every Sunday. Some kind of unconscious payback.* That's when she saw it. A fedora. It bobbed up in the crowd and she recognised it immediately. Her eyes flicked just a little lower to the face it was perched on top of. Tim. He was standing behind Bree with his arms wrapped around her. Aimee's gaze locked with his. She could feel herself choking up. She jabbed a fingernail into the tip of her thumb. *Don't cry, don't cry. Not on stage. Not while you're dressed like Stevie Nicks.* There was a camera positioned firmly on Tim, and another pointing up at Aimee from the pit below. Their eyes were still locked. *Is he happy now?* she wondered. *And is he happier with her than he ever was with me?* She kept her eyes on her ex and felt the years of rage, upset and guilt start to swirl like sediment that had settled on the ocean floor only to be disturbed with a clumsy foot stomp – all the dirt and grime exploding up and clouding the water. Charlie was powering through the verse and racing towards the chorus, where Aimee and Rob were supposed to join in on the harmonies. The moment was somehow moving in slow-motion and fast-forward, all at once. She was going to have to sing. In five, four, three, two . . .

You can go your own—

Aimee ran off the stage.

FORTY-NINE

Aimee slumped onto the metal steps of the taco truck with her head in her hands. She heard her name, called from a distance. It was Rob's voice.

'I saw Tim,' Aimee said eventually, when her friend reached her.

Rob dropped to her knees and caught her breath. 'You saw Tim.' It wasn't a question. Just a statement, said with understanding and a little wheeziness from all the running.

The unmistakable sound of the truck's roller door being relentlessly rattled shattered the emotional moment. 'Hello?' It was a customer near the service window, which still had the BACK IN 20 sign taped to it.

'Just a minute!' Rob yelled impatiently before turning her attention back to Aimee. 'Why the hell did he even come? He knew we were here tonight. And . . . in that *stupid fucking fedora*.'

The customer started rattling the roller door again.

'Ugh. One second.' Rob jumped up the steps of the truck to deal with the interruption.

Aimee took a deep breath. She could hear the fuzzy music coming from performances happening on opposite sides of the field. Looking off into the distance at the stage she'd just run off, she replayed the scene in her head – but the memory wasn't from her point-of-view. It was like she was outside her body, looking at herself struggling to keep it together in front of Tim and the cameras before breaking down and running. A cover of Cyndi Lauper's 'Time After Time' began to drift over and Aimee recognised Charlie's vocals.

'Fuck . . .' Rob said, from inside the van. Her tone was different. Sharp. Serious. 'Aimee.'

Aimee got to her feet and turned around. Rob was holding her phone – staring at the screen with her mouth open, as if she was trying to find the right words but none were coming. 'One of the girls from the salon just texted me. A link. To the *Daily Mail*,' she eventually stuttered.

Aimee's heart sank as her pale-faced friend reluctantly handed over the phone. What had they photographed Freya doing now? Aimee squinted at the screen, her eyes adjusting to the bright light shining up at her. It took a moment for her to comprehend what she was looking at. Then she realised. She was looking at herself. On the *Daily Mail* homepage was a collage of photos of Jules and Aimee – naked, at the beach they went to on Boxing Day, after Brooke's disastrous Christmas party. The day Aimee didn't want to be around anyone. The day Jules took her to a secret place no one could find them – where he stripped off and then she followed. And where, after swimming naked together, they ran back up to their towels and lay in the shade while the sun set and Jules playfully pulled Aimee on top of him which led to a situation far more graphic than Freya's bikini-clad humping photos. The headline screamed:

WANG WATCH! *Oceans of Angels* heartthrob
JULES LAWSON busted in NAKED BEACH TRYST
with Byron Karen – as X-rated moment PROVES the
TV star's on-screen manhood is FAKE . . . See the photos!
WARNING: Graphic

Aimee couldn't take her eyes off the screen.

'Hey,' Rob whispered, trying to snap her out of her daze. 'Aimee,' she said a little louder. 'Look up.'

When she did, all colour had drained from her face. Jules was standing in front of her, hands by his sides, looking concerned.

'I saw you run off stage – are you OK?' He took off his hat and pink sunnies and walked closer to wrap his arms around her.

Aimee lunged back and held up the phone screen to his face. 'Who *are* you?' Her voice quivered.

Jules studied the screen. His mouth tried to move but no words came out.

'Who are you! And why am I *naked* on the internet?!' She started to break down.

'Hey, back off!' Rob yelled.

Aimee looked up to see her friend pushing one of the camera lenses away. She didn't know if it belonged to *The Brats of Byron Bay* or *Buying Byron* because, by then, both crews had arrived and were filming the scene like silent assassins. A flurry of action started to swirl around them.

'Oh my god! It's the guy with the massive dick from that TV show!' an onlooker screamed.

That's when the atmosphere switched from curious to pure pandemonium. More rings of people began to circle around and phones shot up into the air to capture the moment. Or more specifically, the person: Jules Lawson – apparently one of the hottest B-list actors in the world and the internet's thirsty new obsession. All Aimee could do was stare at the stranger she'd been sleeping with all summer.

Charlie pushed through the crowd and ran up behind the girls, grabbing Aimee to see if she was OK after her abrupt stage exit. Before he could look her in the face, he did a double-take of the man everyone was grabbing at.

'Holy shit.' He stared at Jules, recognising him instantly. 'That's—'

Rob handed him the phone. His eyes bulged.

'Aimee, can I just—' Jules began to say as he pushed past people but stopped when the rapid-fire stutters of a paparazzi camera started snapping away. 'We gotta get outta here.' Rob looked around at the growing crowd.

Charlie grabbed Aimee's hand and turned to run. 'Get in the truck.'

FIFTY

'Is it too soon to make a joke?' Rob looked up from her margarita.

'It will always be too soon.' Aimee's reply was muffled by the stack of damp Palace Hotel drink coasters she had smooshed her face into.

Thanks to the service entry at the festival grounds, the taco truck was able to make a quick escape while all the onlookers and TV crews were stranded. Still, as much as Charlie tried to rev his way through the gawkers, the cameramen jostled to get up close to the van, filming Aimee through the windows and banging on the glass as a way to startle her into looking at the lens. The trio couldn't go back to Aimee's apartment – it would be the first place the Plain Jane Producer Girl would direct her crew to go. *We just need to wrap up your storyline.* Aimee thought of what Nina had texted days earlier. There's no way the crew wouldn't pounce on this moment as a way to *wrap up her storyline.* For them, it was a gift from the reality TV gods. Aimee had to lay low. And she couldn't go to Rob's salon – that'd be the second place the crew would search. As the taco truck raced around town, Aimee remembered what Moe had told her at the mechanic about local businesses that were protesting against the reality shows. *If we don't grant permission, they've got nowhere to film.* The Palace Hotel was the safest place to be at that moment.

'Fine, I won't make a joke,' Rob said. 'But let me just show you one thing.'

Aimee looked up to find Rob holding her phone and using two fingers to zoom in on the pixelated crotch of Jules at the beach. 'I'll have *that*, with cheese.'

Aimee slumped back down and Charlie reached over to rub her head while getting a glimpse of the screen. 'Fuck. I'd have that with or *without* cheese,' he laughed.

'There are so many things I can't believe.' Rob tapped on her phone before raising the screen again to show the screenshot of Jules' racy full-frontal scene that went viral months before. 'How is *this* a prosthetic? HOW? It looks so real!'

Charlie let out a disappointed sigh. 'I feel like I just found out Santa isn't real.'

'I can't wait for the think pieces.' Rob shook her head. 'Also: I know you're sick of us asking this question, but I'm still not satisfied with your response. HOW DID YOU NOT KNOW YOU WERE DATING JULES LAWSON?'

'He said he was a stunt double!' Aimee defended herself.

'He *was* a stunt double.' Charlie had picked up his phone to do some googling and clicked on an *Entertainment Weekly* webpage, which he read aloud. 'And after years of working as a stunt performer, Lawson was finally cast in a lead role on *Oceans of Angels* – the Netflix soap about struggling actors in nineties Hollywood, whose cast is a sexy mix of *nobodies* who look like they could be *somebodies*.'

'Well that explains why the acting's so bad,' Rob mumbled. 'Anyway, Aimee, this is why I'm always telling you to read the news more. You have an iPhone. There's no excuse *not* to be informed.'

Aimee raised an eyebrow at her friend. 'You get your news exclusively from the *Daily Mail* and memes.'

'And *I* know who Jules Lawson is.' Rob smiled proudly.

'So he didn't *tell* you he was an actor?' Charlie was still trying to fill in the blanks.

'No!' Aimee furrowed her brow. 'He said he was a stunt double in town working on a really bad TV show on the Gold Coast.'

'And you didn't ask which show it was?'

Aimee exhaled. 'I didn't care what show it was. And we didn't talk about that stuff. He knew *I* was working on a stupid TV show. I knew *he* was working on a stupid TV show. We both made a pact to not talk about either of our stupid TV shows.'

'Then what *did* you guys talk about?' Rob asked.

'I don't think they did a lot of talking,' Charlie said out of the corner of his mouth.

'Pretty much,' Aimee responded to Charlie's crass aside. 'Jules didn't know the details about *The Brats of Byron Bay* or the time-out or the store or my money problems or Byron Karen or . . . Freya.' She ran her hands through her hair. 'I didn't have to talk about any of that. When I'd see him, I just got to be myself – away from my crappy old life. We just got to enjoy each other – without all the goddam noise.'

Rob squinted. 'So . . .' she paused before venturing forward. 'The photos on the *Daily Mail* are pixelated, but, how big is it in real life compared to the prosthetic?'

Aimee shot her a look.

'OK, not ready to talk about it.' Rob held her hands in the air. 'That's OK, it's been a big night.'

'You kids OK?' An older man walked over and collected the empty glasses. 'There's space upstairs if you wanna crash here tonight. I called the chemist under your apartment – they said there's a TV crew still waiting for you out the front.'

'Thanks Dusty.' Aimee exhaled. 'We might actually have to take you up on that.'

He placed a hand on her wrist as a sign of support and turned to walk away. Then, he hesitated. 'Hey,' he added, his voice strained, 'did you *really* not know who *Jules Lawson* was?'

Aimee screwed her face up at the seventy-year-old man she'd known since she was a kid.

Dusty winced, like he'd just touched a hot fry pan with his finger. 'I'm gonna start shifting people out and closing up – you kids stay as long as you need.' He ended the awkward moment and shuffled off.

Aimee pulled one of the margarita glasses closer and ran a finger around the salty rim, reflecting bitterly on the situation. 'I was sleeping with a guy for a month who lied to me about who he was. I'm such a goddam loser. It's like one of those stories you hear about on *A Current Affair* where a sad old woman falls in love with a fake hot guy on the internet and then gets scammed.'

Rob rested her palms on the table. 'As someone who has also been Dirty Johned, I sympathise. But this situation isn't quite like that. You're not sad or old and the hot guy isn't fake.'

'Even if he is someone *famous*.' Aimee cringed at that last word. 'That's just gross. Why wouldn't he tell me?'

Rob and Charlie looked at each other, silently deciding who would broach the subject first.

'Jeez, I dunno, Becker,' Charlie deadpanned.

'Yeah, gone on any rants about the Hemsworths lately?' Rob added.

'Oh please.' Aimee dismissed her friends.

Rob lightened her tone. 'Well, you do have a lot of opinions about that stuff. And . . . you're not afraid to voice them . . . *forcefully*.'

Aimee shot her a look.

'Passionately,' Charlie quickly corrected.

'*Passionately*,' Rob repeated. 'That's the word. You state your feelings very *passionately*. And that's why we love you! But it could also be why a guy like Jules might've felt like he had to withhold some stuff so you didn't judge him.'

'I wouldn't judge him!'

'Aimee.' Rob looked into her friend's eyes. 'We're the judgiest people in town. You would've judged him.'

Charlie nudged Aimee and smiled. 'He did it because he liiiiked you. It's sweet. I'd let him Dirty John me.'

Rob gasped. 'It's like a reverse *Maid In Manhattan*. But instead of pretending to be rich, he pretended to be normal. And I think he's the only person in the world who's sexier than JLo.'

Aimee inhaled and looked away. 'God, just . . . thinking about being in that caravan in the middle of nowhere with him.' She shuddered at the thought. 'Does he even really live there? Or was it all just part of the act to make it seem like he's a humble everyday guy, travelling the world and living off nothing? God, I feel *icky*.' She rubbed her arms, as if they were covered in grime. 'That I even let him *touch me* – and he was basically a complete stranger, the whole time.'

'I don't think he *was* lying.' Charlie flicked through his phone again. 'In that article about him, they describe him as very bohemian and Matthew McConaughey-ish.' He pointed at his screen excitedly. 'Here! It says back in LA he lives in Paradise Cove – a trailer park in Malibu.'

'A trailer park in *Malibu*?' Rob picked up her own phone to google it. 'Oooh . . . cool!' She held up her screen and showed photos of cute shacks and vans lined up in a field overlooking the Pacific Ocean, glazed with a golden Californian tint. 'It's a trailer park for famous people! It says Pamela Anderson and Minnie Driver have lived there. *And* Matthew McConaughey!'

'See!' Charlie sat up straight, satisfied with his argument. 'There you go – you bagged yourself a Matthew McConaughey.'

'Please don't either of you start quoting from *Greenlights*,' Aimee warned.

But Rob was still distracted with online articles about Paradise Cove. 'Hey, maybe we should start one of these here in Byron – a trailer park for famous people. Rich people are idiots – they'll buy anything.'

Charlie jumped in. 'Your phone has been buzzing ever since we left and I saw it's Jules' name on the screen – there's a *stream* of notifications from him. At least read the texts he's been sending you.'

Aimee paused. Just as she was about to give in, something across the room caught her eye. Heath was standing at the top of the steps – looking a little out of breath, as if he'd been searching for her all over town. His eyes widened a little when Aimee looked at him, and he walked over.

'Can I talk to you?' he asked before flicking a glance at Rob and Charlie, almost as if he was hoping they'd take it upon themselves to offer some privacy.

A waitress came over with a tray of waters and shuffled Heath out of the way to slide it on the table.

'No.' Aimee looked away from him and distracted herself by distributing the glasses.

Heath tucked his hands into the front pockets of his old jeans. 'It's important. I think it could help.'

Aimee let out a sarcastic laugh. 'Nothing you could do would be helpful to me.'

Heath closed his eyes. 'I know you don't like me.'

Aimee scoffed.

Heath paused briefly and then continued. 'I know you think I screwed you over. It's not the whole story. Just give me one minute. And, if you really want to, when I'm finished, you can throw one of those margaritas at me. That's something you didn't get to tick off your reality TV bingo card – throwing a drink in someone's face. Now's your chance. Just one minute.'

Aimee waited a beat. 'Those videos with Tim and Rozzie.' She shot him a withering stare. 'You set me up.'

'They're not what you think,' Heath raced to explain. 'Have you read my texts? Listened to my voicemails?'

'I don't wanna hear it.' Aimee waved him away.

'What I have can help you save your store,' Heath stated firmly. His wide eyes and heavy breathing were the signs of a man placing his final bet, hoping to win back everything he'd lost.

'Just give me *one minute*.'

Rob and Charlie gave each other a small look and silently agreed to move tables. They picked up their margaritas and shuffled across the room, leaving Aimee alone with Heath.

'I'm sorry for what's happened,' Heath began. 'With everything. And tonight, it's *horrible* . . . the photos.' He shook his head, clearly struggling to comprehend the gross situation. Then a little disappointment crept in. 'And, with *that guy*.' He exhaled. 'I didn't know you were seeing other people.'

'Oh, it was *one person*, Heath,' Aimee snapped. 'And you and I weren't *seeing each other*.'

The comment made Heath pull back a little, like a dog swatted on the snout by a cat. Aimee felt a pang of guilt in her gut. Had they been seeing each other? Every morning she woke up, she'd been wishing her sheets still smelt like cigarettes and Joop.

Heath relented and moved quickly to get his point back on track before Aimee walked away. 'I need you to know those videos of Tim and Rozzie weren't how they looked.' He pulled out his phone and started scrolling through emails. 'I didn't tell any of the producers to do that. One of the juniors told me Nina got her to pursue the storyline after she found out about the situation between you, Tim and Bree. It was just Nina being Nina. I was CC'd on the end-of-day email with the rough clips when it came through the night you stayed over.' He showed her the email chain on his phone. 'I saw it in the morning when I woke up and I went straight to the office to stop it. I'd left without taking the computer and that's when you found it. Those interviews, that storyline – it wasn't me. And it's not appearing on the show.'

Aimee zoned out. What Heath was saying was believable enough – she knew he might've even been telling the truth. But she wasn't letting herself go there again. She'd opened herself up for enough hurt and embarrassment that summer. She looked around the bar and tried to not engage with his attempts at begging for forgiveness. Then her eyes landed on something unexpected. *That fucking fedora*. It was like that stupid hat was haunting her. Dusty had shuffled out the stragglers for the night and Tim was one of the only other people left in the bar. Had he been there the whole time? He was by himself and Aimee could tell he was drunk. This had been their favourite bar – but the sight of him that night made her realise they probably hadn't been there together in close to a year.

'And,' Heath continued, reaching into his shirt pocket and pulling out a folded up slip of paper, 'I don't know if this helps. But . . .' He unfolded it and slid it across the table.

Aimee took her eyes off her ex-fiance and looked down to see a cheque, for $15,000. The amount was written in Heath's scrawl.

'No conditions, you don't have to appear on the show. And you don't have to take it but if it helps you find a new place or store it's there.'

Aimee was stunned. She looked up at Heath's eyes and recognised the softness she saw when he'd talk about Sadie – and how he'd do anything to get her presents to Sydney before she woke up on Christmas Day.

Before Aimee could respond, Tim started to stalk over, in his jeans and rubber thongs. *Slap, slap, slap.* 'Aimee . . .' He laughed to himself.

She glanced over, then looked back at Heath and shook her head quickly, trying to decide who to deal with first.

'How come *we* never fucked on the beach?' Tim slurred.

'Jesus.' She closed her eyes.

Heath stood up. 'Tim—'

'Aimee. I'm sorry. I just . . .' Tim stopped mid-sentence, clearly too drunk to remember what he was going to say.

'Why aren't you still at the festival with Bree?' Aimee shot back, already fed-up with the surprise appearance.

Heath held out an arm towards Tim. 'Mate—'

Tim raised his voice and stumbled backwards. 'I still wanna marry you!'

Aimee's jaw almost crashed onto the hardwood floors. Within an instant, Rob's boots were banging over as she ran to her friend's side with Charlie. Aimee stood in silence as she watched her ex-fiancé sniff and wipe his nose with the back of his finger, while still swaying a little on his feet.

Then he let out an almost menacing laugh. 'Hey!' He looked across the room. 'Aimee's average-dick boyfriend is here!'

Aimee whipped around and saw Jules standing at the top of the stairs. As he started to walk over, Tim scrunched up his face, like he was about to spit insults. Aimee could feel Heath move his body behind her, ready to step in if things got messy. Aimee wondered how, after trying so hard to keep all three men in her life hidden, they'd somehow started springing up uncontrollably, like Whack-A-Moles. Heath put a hand on her lower back but she pulled away from it and stood closer to her friends. Just as Jules got near enough to reach out and touch her, Tim stepped forward and hooked his right arm back to gather some momentum in a swing. But before he could follow through, the tension was broken by two men in jeans and business shirts who walked with purpose towards the group. Then those two men pulled out their badges.

'Aimee Maguire, Roberta Valentine, Charlie Tatler,' one of the men said, clear and swift. 'I'm Agent Harvey, that's Agent Jackson – we're with the Australian Federal Police. You're under arrest for conspiracy to supply prohibited drugs. You're not obliged to say anything unless you wish to do so – but whatever you say or do may later be used against you. Do you understand that?'

FIFTY-ONE

'Remember the last time I was in here?'

The question came from Rob. Out of the three friends, she was the only one who'd been held overnight at the local police station. No one remembered the exact details, but the incident involved tequila and Music Club.

Aimee wasn't in the mood for jovial memories. She kept thinking about the way Jules looked at her as the police arrested them.

'How did he even know where we were?' Aimee said aloud. 'Jules,' she added, shaking her head at the involuntary outburst.

'Well,' Charlie said, his face contorting into a pained expression. 'When Heath showed up and we moved tables to let you chat . . . I may have taken your phone and texted him where we were.' Just as Aimee shot him a look, he rushed to defend himself. 'I think you've got it wrong! Ever since you told me that night at Music Club that you'd been hooking up with someone, I'd noticed a change in you.'

Aimee fobbed off the observation as if it was crazy. 'There was no change.' She made a face like she'd just tasted expired yoghurt.

'Even with all the other stuff going wrong, there's a spark you've had back.'

'It's true.' Rob nodded. 'I think you gotta give him a chance.'

'Yes, he lied,' Charlie said. 'But it's not that bad. And you lied to him, too.'

The truth always hurt more coming from Charlie. Aimee thought of Jules' dark, sunken eyes – and cheeks pinched tight around his nose – as she was escorted out of the pub by the police. A look of clear disgust. Had she looked at him the same way earlier in the night when she found out who he really was? He might've lied about being famous, but she'd lied about something much worse. Little less glam, little more scam. Her body ached with the need to find Jules immediately so she could apologise and explain. The snow globe had smashed, and now maybe they could live in the real world.

But first, she needed to get out of the cell she was standing in. *How did the police know? And* what *did they know?* The two plainclothes cops didn't give much away at the pub but they were adamant that no one make a scene and draw attention. 'We have an unmarked car waiting in the back carpark. We will allow you to walk to the vehicle un-cuffed where you will be driven to the police station for further questioning.' Their voices were calm but assertive. No facial expressions. One thing was clear: *Do as you're told.*

'Why haven't they questioned us? It feels like it's been a few hours. They're gonna interrogate us at some point,' Charlie said before turning to the girls. 'Do we all have our story straight?'

'What do you mean, *do we have our story straight?*' Aimee tried to keep the volume low on her irritated whisper. '*What* story?'

'Do you think they found out about *Operation Burrito?*' Rob muttered.

'How?' Aimee replied. 'We didn't actually go through with it.'

'Did any of us tell other people about the plan?' Charlie suggested. 'People who might've told *other people.*'

Without missing a beat, Aimee turned to Rob. 'Bada Bing,' she stated firmly.

Rob dismissed her friend's claim. 'Bada Bing would never dob on us. He might like trolling people, but he'd never throw someone under the bus. He hates the cops.'

'Maybe it's the naked beach photos.' Charlie shrugged.

'What?' Aimee's voice went high-pitched.

'I dunno – is it illegal to be naked on a beach doing . . . *whatever it was* you two were doing?'

'I struggle to believe my naked body landed all of us in prison,' Aimee said with bite. 'Besides, they arrested us *on the suspicion of drugs*. That's what they said, didn't they? Suspicion? Or . . . conspiracy? Jesus, I can't remember. Just . . . Leave my naked body out of this.'

'I was just trying to think of reasons,' Charlie argued.

'*Suspicion*,' Rob said excitedly. '*Suspicion of drugs*. That's a good sign, isn't it? That it's *just a suspicion*?' Then her face dropped and she turned to Aimee. 'Wait, do you think it has something to do with the cassettes at the market?'

'What if it involves Freya?' Aimee panicked. Paranoia was starting to set in. 'Are we being recorded in here?' She looked up at the grey ceiling.

Charlie peered out of the holding cell and down the short hall, into the main office area. 'Hey, don't you know him?'

Aimee stopped inspecting the room for imaginary listening devices. 'Who?' She walked up behind Charlie and peered over his shoulder.

'The guy in the blue uniform.' He nodded.

Aimee squinted.

Rob joined the huddle and peeked out. 'Ohhh yeaaahhh . . . Norman Klump,' she said. 'That's right – you and Tim went to school with him.'

'No we didn't,' Aimee shot down the claim.

'Yes you did,' Rob insisted.

'How would *you* know who I went to school with? I think I'd remember if I went to school with someone called Norman *Klump*.'

'He's mates with Tim. I always see them talking at the pub,' Charlie said.

Rob widened her eyes and repeated herself slowly, as if her friends hadn't been listening. 'Yeah. *Because they went to school together*.' She tapped Aimee's arm. 'He's Nichelle's husband.'

Aimee only had time to let out a frustrated sigh before her alleged school-mate started walking down the hall towards them with the other cops.

'Shit the bed, they're coming,' Rob said. 'If they separate us for interrogation, our alibi is this: we were all at my garage watching *Paul Blart: Mall Cop*, one *and* two.'

The sound of thick rubber-soled boots clopped and squeaked down the painted cement floor and conversational murmurs bounced around the corridor. Norman walked behind the other two plainclothes officers, who, even out of uniform, seemed to carry themselves with more authority. One of them unlocked a square plastic casing on the wall and held a small round fob against an electronic pad. The door to the holding cell opened.

'You guys are almost free to go,' one of the arresting officers informed.

The trio looked at each other.

'Like, *go* go?' Rob squinted.

'Follow Senior Constable Klump and your lawyer will have more details.'

'Good to see you, Aimee,' Klump said over his shoulder, gesturing for the group to follow as he led the way back down the hall. 'Well. Not *good* to see you . . . *here*. You know what I mean.'

'Good to see you too *Norm*,' Aimee replied, distracted by the thought of what was going to happen once they reached the end of the hall.

'Nichelle said she saw you at the bank before Christmas.' His tone seemed overly chipper.

'Love Nichelle – great gal,' Rob piped up.

Aimee was just starting to comprehend the stuff the other cops had said when the cell door was unlocked. 'Wait. Did those guys say we already *have* a lawyer, or we need to *get* a lawyer?' she asked. 'Because we don't have lawyers. None of us even know any lawyers. Is there a special kind of lawyer we need to get? Like, one that deals with *the kind of stuff you guys think we did*? And who paid for the bail? *Was* there bail? Wait, are we *charged* with something?'

'I did . . .' Aimee heard Heath's voice as they reached the end of the hallway and rounded the corner into the office.

He stood up quickly from a swivel chair in the drab-looking room to greet her. The look on his face was all concern. 'I organised a lawyer,' he clarified.

'And there's no bail,' Klump said. 'You only need to pay bail if you're charged. Which you're not.' He sorted through a cabinet near the front desk before looking up. '*Yet.*'

'And I can sort out the bail if that's ever needed.' Heath nodded.

The disdain for him that had been raging through Aimee's veins for days started to drain a little. Maybe because she needed to reserve all her anger for Tim. There was too much going on for her to even think about his outburst at the pub. *I still wanna marry you.* Jesus. Did he mean it? Going by his absence at the station, the only thing she was certain of was that he'd blacked out on someone's couch for the night. There was a sharp pang in her gut as she realised the only person in her life able to help in that moment was standing in front of her: Heath. She wished it was Jules. Her thoughts were interrupted by the sound of another woman in the room – yammering into her iPhone and looking out the window. From behind, she was blonde with a short-ish skirt and matching blazer. She whipped around and pulled the phone away from her mouth for a second.

'Fuck me, it's bookstore Aimee!' her brash voice rasped.

It was the daughter of Lang – Aimee's dead landlord. She held an arm out and waved her fingers in the air before returning to the phone call.

'Her name's Bernadette – the lawyer,' Heath said, a little confused about Aimee's familiarity with her. 'I thought it'd be best to get one from the Gold Coast. She drove down right away.'

Aimee stared at him. 'Do you seriously not remember who that is?'

Heath turned to take another look at the woman. He cocked his head and thought.

Aimee ran out of patience. 'It's the woman whose Ferrari I slimed.'

'Huh.' Heath chuckled.

'I thought it was a Porsche,' Rob offered.

Aimee was exhausted. She had no energy to deal with the mess they were in. She wanted to escape. Find that secret place again where no one knew her.

Klump banged three zip-lock bags on the laminated desk, each jumbled full of Aimee, Rob and Charlie's possessions. 'Phones, wallets etcetera are all in there.'

Through the clear plastic, Aimee saw her iPhone screen light up as it got knocked around and her face sparked for a moment, hoping to see the series of texts and missed calls from Jules, desperately checking to see if she was OK. But the screen was empty. Impulsively, she grabbed the plastic pouch with her stuff inside and started fumbling with the zipper to open it while barging out the swinging glass door to the carpark.

'Aimee!' Heath called after her.

The bag and the rest of its contents dropped on the bitumen as she pulled out her phone and unlocked it with a trembling thumb. She frantically opened the message app and went to the text chain with Jules. The last messages were the ones that came through after she escaped the media storm at the festival – the ones she'd been too upset to read. There were so many and she was too overwhelmed to know where to start. Her eyes skimmed over a few as she quickly scrolled. Jules:

Aimee, please answer

Where are you? I just wanna talk

I only kept it a secret because of what you said when we met. That sounds stupid. Let me explain

Aimee, it's not as bad as it looks

Why hadn't he called or messaged since she'd been taken away at the pub? Why wouldn't he have come to the station? Was he disgusted with who he thought Aimee was? Her heart was beating fast and her thumb moved quickly across the screen – flicking closed the message app, swiping up her recent calls list and tapping Jules' name. She held the phone to her ear. Short, sharp sniffs from her nose filled the silence in the carpark as she waited for the dial tone. No ring came. Then the grating female voice of an automated message burst down the line.

The number you have dialled has been disconnected. Please check the number and try again. The number you have dialled has been disconnected. Please check the number and try again.

Aimee furrowed her brow and her eyes welled. She hung up and tapped his name again. No ring.

The number you have dialled has been disconnected. Please check the number and try again.

Her body dropped to the ground and she sat on the edge of the gutter, sobbing.

The heavy metal door of the station rattled open. Heath ran over, dropped next to Aimee and wrapped her in his arms.

FIFTY-TWO

'Hey, you aren't lookin' to sell, are you?' Bernadette glanced up from her phone and squinted at Aimee, who was seated next to Rob down one end of a laminated table under the fluorescent light of the police station's interrogation room. They were told they weren't charged but needed to be interviewed.

'*What?*' Aimee replied.

'Your house. Are you looking to sell your house?' Bernadette said. 'I figured, with your store gone, you might be looking to sell your house.'

Aimee didn't know if she was being trolled. 'I didn't own my store and I don't own my house. I don't actually even have a place to live anymore. My landlord's putting it on Airbnb.'

'Damn.' Bernadette made a face like she'd just missed out on an easy hole-in-one. 'I'm looking to buy a place around here so I can do the same thing.'

'Wait.' Aimee furrowed her brow. 'But . . . you're *selling* my store?'

Bernadette was half-distracted from the conversation and scrolling through the real estate app on her phone for recent residential listings. 'Yeah, commercial spaces are a headache. So much admin involved. In Byron, residential is where it's at. Buy a crappy house, plant a shitty pandanus tree in the driveway, whack it on Airbnb and it'll be booked most weeks of the year. I can't Airbnb an old bookstore. I need to fuck that building off, ASAP.' She glanced up at Aimee. 'No offence.'

'Are you gonna tell us any more details about why we're here?' Aimee firmly changed the subject.

'And why have they let Charlie go but not us?' Rob asked.

Bernadette paused the property search, leaned forward and crossed her arms on the table. 'Do you guys know anything about cocaine being sold in cassettes at a hippy market?'

Aimee and Rob shifted uncomfortably in their seats.

'Jesus,' Aimee eventually said, closing her eyes and exhaling. She had no energy left to pretend.

'They don't have proof it was you. But they *could* find proof,' Bernadette raised an eyebrow, '*if* you don't do what they ask.'

Aimee got a little frustrated that she had to ask the obvious question. 'What are they gonna ask?'

'It's best they explain it. It will sound shocking. But it's not as bad as it seems. I advise you to take them up on their offer. Because if you don't . . .' She shrugged and made a face, as if she'd just landed her point.

'If we don't, *what?*' Aimee threw back some attitude.

'Jail.' Bernadette gave Aimee a confused look. 'I thought that was obvious.' Aimee dropped her head onto the table.

Bernadette looked over at Rob. 'Hey, are *you* lookin' at sellin' *your* house?'

The door swung open and the two plainclothes agents entered, followed by Klump.

'We sent a patrol car to your apartment earlier and they've moved along the TV cameramen and photographers,' Klump said. 'Lotta interest – especially now with your new boyfriend.' He shrugged. 'Me and Nichelle watched an episode of *Oceans of Angels* a few weeks ago. It was very raunchy.'

'He's not my boyfriend,' Aimee said. 'We'll probably never see each other again.'

Rob reached over and grabbed her hand. 'You don't know that.'

'We'll send a car to drive by again before you head home to make sure it's clear,' Klump added.

Aimee sat up straight in her seat. 'So, we can go now?'

'Not quite,' Agent Harvey jumped in. 'You were arrested because we have reasonable suspicion to believe that you were in possession of and or selling illegal substances.'

'We're with the federal police.' Agent Jackson focused his attention on Aimee and Rob. 'A squad's in town for the music festival, doing drug searches. Our dogs made a series of busts. Several people in possession of illicit substances. Cocaine. And one of them pointed the finger at the . . .' he paused to get the wording right, '*hippy cassette mums from the market.*'

Aimee and Rob tried to sit still and not react in any way that could be perceived as guilty. Turns out, it doesn't matter what kind of facial expression you choose. If you're guilty, you feel like there's a big neon arrow above your head, pointing down.

'When pressed further, they said those two mums were also working in a taco truck at the festival.'

'Another person made a similar claim.' Agent Harvey crossed his arms and leant back in his chair.

Bernadette spoke up. 'It happens a lot,' she explained to Aimee and Rob. 'One idiot gets busted with a small amount, they panic and point the finger. It all snowballs from there.'

'And those people are arrested?' Aimee hesitantly asked, trying to hide the shakiness in her voice.

'They're usually carrying small amounts.' Agent Jackson shrugged. 'We're more interested in catching suppliers.'

Aimee's stomach sank. *What did they know?* All she wanted to do was find Freya and run far away.

'Now, we don't have proof of you selling at the markets – *right now*. But, if we dig, we could find it. CCTV cameras are everywhere. Transactions in public are very easy to spot and follow up on. Especially with amateurs.

They think they're slick, but they're making mistakes every which way. It's a very simple thing to piece together.'

Klump spoke up. 'These guys are the federal police, so a matter like this investigation is handled by them. But when I found out what was going on with you two tonight, I spoke with Agents Jackson and Harvey. Aimee, I've told them I've known you since we were kids. You're a good person. You've been going through a tough time. *If* you did happen to do something you shouldn't have, it would be extremely out of character. But, to be clear: I'm independent from this. I've said I know you – but I can't do anything to help you.'

'It's something we're seeing a lot of in areas like the Gold Coast, Brisbane and Sydney,' Agent Jackson said. 'People getting sucked into a world they know nothing about. Starts off innocent . . . Organise a bag for a friend and then your friend's friend. Then for people you've never even met before. You don't see yourself as a dealer, but you are. You don't see yourself as a criminal, but you are. A stranger who has stumbled into this new world and you have no idea how dark it really is.'

Aimee could feel her mouth filling up with saliva, as if she was about to vomit.

Agent Harvey pulled out some pages from a pale yellow manila folder he'd brought in with him. He slid the papers into the middle of the table. 'Wanna tell us why you were at this house in Nimbin?' Printed on the A4 pages were black and white photos of Aimee and Rob outside The Artisan's house – talking to the naked shovel guy, being led inside.

Aimee studied her face in the grainy pictures. She barely recognised herself.

'You're both small fish,' Agent Harvey said. 'Still, the way everything stands right now, you guys *could* go to jail. But that's no use to us. We've been doing surveillance on this property for a while. Know all about what goes on there.' He leant closer to the girls. '*They* are the big fish.'

'*Whales*,' Agent Jackson one-upped his colleague. 'Whales.'

'If you help us, we can help you,' Harvey added. 'And, if you agree, then we can write a letter of comfort that will be handed up to the magistrate if you're charged.'

'Are we talking full indemnity?' Bernadette asked.

'I don't have authority to grant indemnity. But your assistance to police will be able to assist you – and that'll be taken into account in any possible court matters.'

'Indemnity . . . Like Ashley Judd?' Rob squinted.

'That's double jeopardy,' Bernadette corrected.

Aimee took in a deep breath. She looked over at Bernadette, who gave her a wide-eyed nod of encouragement. 'And . . .' she cleared her throat. 'What exactly do we have to do?'

FIFTY-THREE

'I feel like that stupid fucking sign is just taunting us,' Aimee said as the familiar childlike paintings of flowers and trees and hearts whooshed by.

WELCOME TO NIMBIN

'I found another one!' Rob excitedly held up her phone screen.

'Stop it,' Aimee half-warned.

'C'mon! I'm not *trying* to find the bad ones – there's just so many! And, each time I think we've found the worst, three more pop up that are just as vicious.'

'I'm trying to be the bigger person.'

'It's got *one star* on Rotten Tomatoes! All up it has only a twelve per cent rating from critics! These are just facts!'

'I'm just not sure how I feel about hate-reading his negative reviews.'

Rob cleared her throat. '*Oceans of Angels* is about as sexy as running a pathology swab over a motel bedspread that hasn't been washed in fifteen years and sending it to the lab for testing.'

Aimee tried hard not to show her immense delight with the scathing takedown, but Rob's shrieking made her break into laughter.

'Cringe-worthy dialogue delivered by even cringier actors,' Rob read another. 'When it comes to Jules Lawson, his acting is so wooden it makes the comically-large rubber schlong he's forced to wield seem lifelike.'

'God, they really love ripping into the fake dick, don't they,' Aimee commented.

'I know, they're my favourite parts.' Rob put her feet on the dash. 'A relative newcomer in front of the camera, Jules Lawson is already at a low point: playing the sidekick to a scene-stealing prosthetic penis that has more charisma than the actor it's attached to.'

'Read my favourite one again.' Aimee looked ahead at the mountains in the distance.

Rob took a moment to scroll around and find it. '*Oceans of Angels* is like diving head-first into the shallow end of a pool that has no water in it.' She paused. 'I mean, it's brutal. Still, I don't know why that one's your favourite. It doesn't even make fun of the fake dick.'

Aimee ignored Rob's chattering for a moment and thought about those afternoons with Jules in his caravan – how they felt like diving into the *deepest* of swimming pools. Maybe she was wrong. She could've just had concussion.

That night at the pub was the last time she'd seen him. She hadn't tried calling, either. Not after the times in the police station carpark. It would've been too pathetic to hear the monotone voice of the automated message one more time: *The number you have dialled has been disconnected.* That lifeline was dead.

The Ace Of Bass ringtone began to blare from Aimee's phone. She looked down to where it was resting. On the screen was a name in white font: FLEUR. She swiped to answer and put it on loudspeaker.

'Hey guys,' she yelled over the sound of the wheels grinding across the gravelly road.

'Girls, we're travelling about ten kilometres behind you and the team's set up near the site,' Agent Harvey's fuzzy voice blasted through the speaker. 'And a reminder: It's important you don't have us saved in your phone by any names that could identify us as police, in case we need to call you while you're inside or you need to call us. Make sure you change us in your contacts to "Mum" or "Dad" or something. Have you done that?'

Aimee looked at the screen again. 'It's all taken care of.'

'Get your friend at the location talking as much as possible – but don't be unnatural about it. People in these situations swing one of two ways – they either babble too much about unrelated shit, or they try too hard and make it obvious that they're gathering evidence. You said you didn't buy anything last time you went to the property, so just tell the subject you chickened out but you're ready to go through with it now. Talk about the new order you want. Ask about what else they could supply you with and for how much. Anything. Get her to show you.'

'How do I ask all this?' Aimee shook her said. 'I don't know how to talk about this stuff.'

'Say you want coke and ask if it's good shit.'

Aimee cringed. 'I thought you said to talk naturally?'

'Just be aware . . . you wanna walk the line of getting as much information as possible but not making the situation more dangerous than it already is. Try to stay in open spaces. Don't get cornered.'

'What happens if we get cornered?'

'Try not to let them take you somewhere you really can't escape from.'

'Do we even have a choice if that happens?'

'We'll be hearing what's going on – just act normal. We'll get in there if we need to.'

Aimee and Rob gave each other a look. *How the hell did we wind up here?*

'You're both wearing wires – they transmit directly to us. We can hear everything that's going on inside.'

The matter-of-fact way it was all being talked about made Aimee grip the steering wheel tighter with her free hand and she rubbed her back against the seat, trying to scratch the itch she could suddenly feel where the thin microphone wire snaked out of the waistband of her jeans, up and around her torso to the centre of her bra. She felt like she'd gone from one reality show to another. Every moment being recorded.

'Remember, we're dealing with *gangsters*,' Agent Harvey warned.

Rob leaned over to talk into the phone. 'These guys aren't *gangsters* – they're just weird hippies with no shoes. And some rich lady who loves *Younger*.'

Harvey's voice came in firm. 'Where do you think they get their drugs from? Bikies. Peace and love only gets you so far.'

Aimee began to fret. 'So, what if they suspect us? I mean, you arrested us in public and took us to the station!'

'They don't know that,' Harvey said. 'That's why we kept things very low key – we found you at the pub after it had closed – no uniforms, no cop cars, no sirens. No cuffs – you just walked to an unmarked car. This hasn't been reported in the news – we've made sure a minimal amount of people know. Unless you've told people what's happened, there's no way anyone would know. Trust me.'

'You know how many people have told me to trust them this summer?' Aimee sighed.

'Good luck,' he signed off.

Fleur's name disappeared off the phone screen.

Aimee and Rob sat in silence and listened to the rumbles of the old car banging over the potholes.

'I can't wait to tell people we have indemnity.' Rob smirked, trying to lighten the mood. 'That's so punk rock. Ooh!' She pulled out her phone. 'New dating profile bio: INDEMNIFIED.'

'Are we even *allowed* to talk about it? Like, with *other* people?' Aimee squinted at the road ahead. They'd been told so much information over the past few days she could barely remember any of it. 'Or is it something we'll have to keep secret? Forever.'

'I was thinking last night about what our futures could've looked like. *Me* in jail? I couldn't go to jail. There's so much I still need to do in my life. Like, I swear, *this* is gonna be the year I finally subscribe to those online Masterclass courses. There's so many new skills I wanna pretend to learn.'

A sharp buzz came from Rob's phone. As she held it up to look at the screen, Aimee glanced over and saw a news notification banner with a headline.

JULES LAWSON JETS OUT OF BYRON AMID X-RATED BYRON KAREN BEACH TRYST

Just as Rob went to open her mouth, Aimee beat her to it.

'I'm fine,' she said. 'I'm . . . really fine.'

'Want me to read more bad reviews?' Rob smiled.

Aimee didn't reply. Rob put her hand on her friend's thigh and they sat in silence, staring ahead, for the rest of the drive.

After turning off onto the private property and following the dusty road through the bushes, into the middle of nowhere, they pulled into the clearing. The guy with the shovel who stared them down the first time they arrived looked out from one of the tents. Sunlight beamed down and dappled through the leaves. Aimee thought about how much she'd love to just be at the beach that afternoon. She unclicked her seatbelt and was the first to open her door.

'Hey,' Rob said.

Aimee looked over.

'You're my favourite person.'

They got out of the car, walked across the field and disappeared inside the house.

———

Aimee could feel the pumps of her heart beating down to the soles of her feet as she walked along the concrete floor. Then the sound of Kevin Spacey's voice drifted through the darkness.

When she rounded the corner with Rob by her side, her eyes adjusted to the orange glow of the lamps before her vision settled on The Artisan, who was perched at the table like last time, watching something on her MacBook.

'I've been waiting for you both,' The Artisan said slyly. She didn't even look up from her laptop screen.

Aimee's stomach sank as she wondered what The Artisan knew.

The Artisan raised an eyebrow and smirked. 'You scampered out of here so quickly last time without buying anything. Happens all the time. Usually takes people about a week to grow some balls and come back.'

Tap! Her elegantly long finger flicked at the space bar of the laptop keyboard, interrupting Kevin Spacey midsentence and silencing his voice.

'*House Of Cards.*' The Artisan glanced up. 'Just got the DVDs. Are we allowed to like Kevin Spacey again or no?'

Aimee still couldn't quite believe there was another human in the modern world who was almost as behind the times as she was.

'I think it's like Michael Jackson,' Rob said. 'We can all secretly listen to him privately but publicly we're supposed to pretend like we don't.'

The innocuous chit-chat somehow made Aimee feel sicker. Like she'd climbed the ladder of the world's tallest waterslide and was now just staring at the dips and curves of the long plastic tube, getting more anxious by the second. She'd hiked the steps for only one reason. Now, the only way was down. Eventually she'd have to jump. Delaying the inevitable only made it scarier. Still, she couldn't bring herself to leap.

'I went deep into an MJ rabbit hole recently,' Rob continued to ramble, doing exactly what the agents said not to do. 'Watched all the documentaries and concerts on YouTube. And old interviews – there's one with Oprah where Michael drives her around on a golf cart at Neverland. But my favourite video is from one of his concerts and, when the camera cuts to the front row, Macaulay Culkin, Elizabeth Taylor and Liza Minnelli are all sitting together.' She slapped her thighs and her voice went high-pitched. 'What the hell kind of conversation is going on between Liz Taylor, Liza Minnelli and Macaulay Culkin? It was like watching one of those viral video clips about unlikely animal friends – where a cat and a crocodile are just hanging out and shooting the breeze like it's no big deal.'

Aimee felt the urge to thump her friend to stop rambling but she resisted. Partly because she didn't want to seem suspicious. But mainly because, without the inane chatter, she wasn't quite sure what to say herself. She looked at her own unlikely animal friend sitting behind the table and reminded herself of what the cops had told them: Just get The Artisan talking.

'Before that, I went through an obsession with sharks,' Rob rattled on. 'Shark docos and Discovery Channel TV shows. All the shark movies – even that one where Blake Lively spends the whole ninety minutes sitting on a rock and befriending a seagull.'

'Sounds terrible,' The Artisan replied.

'My new obsession is drugs,' Aimee blurted.

Rob and The Artisan responded to the outburst with puzzled looks.

'You know.' Aimee closed her eyes and shrugged, trying to appear more relaxed than she was. '*Selling* drugs.'

The Artisan sat back and let out a small laugh. 'OK. Looking to *browse* again?'

'You were right,' Aimee said. 'About us needing a week to grow some balls. We got freaked out last time we came here.'

'It happens,' The Artisan said, flipping mindlessly through the clear plastic sleeves of her DVD folder. She had enough discs to fill one of the old vending machines in Brooke's barn. 'People get scared and run away. Then the idea creeps back in. They build up the courage again . . . find new reasons to justify their choices to make themselves believe they're not doing anything wrong.'

'Then?' Aimee asked.

The Artisan sighed. 'Then . . . you're back standing in my living room.'

Aimee resisted the urge to scratch and tug at the police wire under her shirt – the same way she had to ignore the tickle of the microphone cord while filming things for the TV show. She remembered how Plain Jane Producer Girl would scold her for mindlessly reaching to fiddle with it during piece-to-camera interviews. *Aimee, ignore the microphone cord. Also, remember: repeat the question in your answer. Explain it to me like I'm an idiot.*

Aimee felt a tingle through her entire body, like she'd just been pricked by some mystical electrical force that instantly gave her superpowers. *Explain it to me like I'm an idiot.* To get The Artisan to say what she needed, she would have to produce her into doing it.

'I guess . . . The reason we chickened out is we got so overwhelmed,' Aimee ventured, her voice taking on the same pretending-to-be-dumb tone the Plain Jane Producer Girl would adopt. 'We want to start up a premium dial-a-dealer network for high-profile clients holidaying in town. We found they don't usually feel comfortable with just getting their products from anyone, so we want to provide a selective offering and be an exclusive supplier who they can trust.'

Aimee didn't know where the words were coming from or how she even knew phrases like 'selective offering' and 'exclusive supplier'. She must've absorbed them while hanging around Brooke.

'We know there's demand and, for us, it's just about finding the right people to work with and source from. The way the town's going, we see business being steady throughout the year – and then skyrocketing during holiday periods, long weekends and festival season. Which means big business for us and, in turn, you.'

The Artisan sat back in her seat and smirked, staring up at the cracked paint on the ceiling while listening to Aimee's pitch.

Aimee looked over at Rob. 'Now, we have the business side sorted but where we need help is on the supply end. And, since we saw you last time, we've thought a lot more about our approach and have decided to do a full-service offering. We want to know every product you can get for us – how much, for what price, and how soon it can be in our hands.'

Then Aimee reached into her handbag, pulled out a giant wad of rubber-banded hundred-dollar notes and dropped it on the table. It landed with a satisfyingly solid thud.

'We'll take some product today. But I want you to walk us through everything you have – and explain to us all the details. I mean *nitty-gritty details* – explain it to me like I'm an *idiot*. We want to understand everything so we can optimise the customer experience for our clients.'

She could feel Rob beaming in amazement.

'Yeah,' Rob added, flicking her shaggy fringe out of her eyes.

The Artisan closed her DVD library binder, looked Aimee in the eye and gave a little nod – her old timber chair squeaking on the concrete floor as she pushed it back. She stood up.

'When I met you two, I thought you were morons. Just . . . two Byron Bay mums desperately trying to recreate whatever drama you've read in a Liane Moriarty novel in the hope of adding some interest to your boring lives. I still think that's partly true but, whatever. You want everything, we can supply everything.'

'Is it . . . *good shit*?' Aimee tried hard not to wince at herself for sounding like an idiot.

The Artisan smirked. 'Is *what* good shit?'

Aimee closed her eyes and shrugged. 'All of it. Is it . . . good shit?'

'Never had a complaint.'

'Well, we want it all,' Aimee said firmly.

The Artisan arched an eyebrow. 'OK,' she said with a half-smile. 'Follow me.'

Aimee shot Rob a split-second glance, looking for an excuse not to follow The Artisan to wherever they were about to be taken. No excuse came. There was no way to pull out now.

As Aimee took a step forward and her Converse squeaked on the concrete, the sound of doors crashing open thundered around the room and natural light from the outside world burst into the dank space. 'Police! Police! On the ground! On the ground!'

FIFTY-FOUR

One month later

Aimee heard the unmistakable sound of Rob's boots banging over the floorboards, towards their regular table at The Palace Hotel. Charlie's band had just soared into the chorus of The Go-Go's 'Our Lips Are Sealed' and the thumps on the floor almost threw off the beat of the drummer.

'Did you see the news?' Rob waved her phone in the air while simultaneously taking a sip from the margarita that was waiting for her.

Aimee shuddered. 'I have PTSD from you asking me if I've seen the news. Nothing good comes when you ask me that.'

Rob flopped onto the tall bar stool. 'Well you're right – it's not good news.' She flipped her phone screen around and summarised the headline. 'Olivia Newton-John's estate cuts last ties to Byron. She got rid of the house before she died and now the health retreat's sold for $30 million. You know – the one we always talked about going to but didn't because . . . well . . . it was stupidly expensive and we can just squeeze lemon into hot water at home for free?'

'Wow. End of an era.' Aimee craned her neck to look at the news article.

'And remember where her house was?' Rob raised an eyebrow. *'Ballina.'*

Aimee sighed. 'She truly was ahead of her time.'

'She was the OG Byron celebrity. Well. Her and Crocodile Dundee. Now, Shelley Craft carries the torch.'

A defeated exhale blew out of her mouth as she shook her head. 'That's it. She's gone. There's nothing left. Byron Bay is over. O-V-E-R. Over.'

Aimee knew where this was going. Rob loved nothing more than grabbing any opportunity to quote the Lexi Featherston monologue from the second-last episode of *Sex and the City* where the aging New York party girl laments the changing times before drunkenly falling out of a window.

'Nobody's fun anymore!' Rob yelled, committing to the impression. 'What ever happened to fun? God. I'm so bored I could die.'

Aimee laughed and shoulder danced as Charlie's band thrashed their way to the end of the song. 'Olivia Newton-John is officially gone. *It's a sign.*'

'I knew you'd say that.' Rob drained her glass. 'But you're right.' She raised her eyebrows. 'It's a *total* sign.'

The microphone screeched over the speakers and everyone shielded their ears with their hands. Aimee looked around at the core crowd of Music Club regulars. Summer was on its way out and the holidaymakers had gone back to their cities and office jobs, where they'd be forced to retire their all-linen outfits, lest they look like idiots in the real world. The change could be felt. The streets almost sighed with relief.

'Guess Who, Don't Sue . . .' came Bada Bing's rough voice. 'Which controversial Byron Bay reality star has avoided jail time after thwarting the dark underworld of which she almost succumbed to?'

The town Looney Tunes all turned to the back table. Aimee shrugged and sipped her margarita with a coy smirk.

Bada Bing was noticeably surprised at the lack of retaliation. 'Any thoughts or observations, Byron Karen?'

Aimee beamed, almost enjoying it.

Bada Bing exhaled. 'I liked you better when you were bitter.'

'Let's boo her anyway.' Meredith stood up.

The chorus of booing proceeded from the Power Players, seated down near the stage.

Rob used her palm to wipe a condensation puddle off the table as Aimee basked in the jeering. 'He's gotten so cocky since he went viral on TikTok. Have you seen his handle? @BadaBingOfficial.'

'I know. And did you see Netflix wants to give him a cameo on that new TV soap about Byron?' Aimee's voice turned smooth and slow as she recited the plot she'd read in the newspaper. 'A dramedy about five sexy singles who move to town for the summer and have to deal with all the cranky locals who hate them.'

Rob rolled her eyes. '*Boring*. No one wants a story about that.'

A mess of golden hair whirled over to the table and Freya wrapped Aimee up into a hug.

'You all packed?' Aimee laughed.

'If you mean, *have I shoved everything haphazardly into a bag at the last minute*, then, yes: I am all packed,' Freya replied.

'We taught you well!' Rob cheered.

'I really don't like the idea of you driving that gross old van back to Sydney by yourself,' Aimee said. 'Are you sure you can't just sell it to the @ThoseTwoVanGuys? I still don't understand what they do but I know it's *something* to do with vans.'

Freya went to roll her eyes and Aimee gave up.

'Fine.' Aimee held up her hands. 'Just text me every few hours so I know you haven't crashed into a highway rest stop. Are you gonna make it back in time for orientation day?'

'Nah, but I don't need to go. It's at the same uni I was at before.' Freya shrugged.

'I can't believe you're doing a master's degree,' Rob gushed. 'It sounds so fancy.' She slapped a palm on the counter. 'You just might be the smartest person I know.'

Aimee joined in the gush-fest. 'Is this one of those fancy degrees where you get to call yourself a doctor after you graduate – even though it has nothing to do with medicine?'

Freya nudged the margarita glasses away. 'I'm cutting you both off. And no. This is just a master's of photography.'

Aimee used her hands to tame the ends of her niece's hair. 'Well, it's still very impressive. How'd the rest of the campaign shoot go this arvo? Get it all finished?'

'Yeah, the little kids who were modelling the tutus were complete nightmares, but it got done. By the way, Brooke dropped me off here after we finished – she said she wanted to see you guys, she's just looking for a park.'

Rob let out a groan. 'Annnd I think that's my cue to go line up at the bar . . . at least until the crazy bitch with the lake leaves the premises.'

'No, no, no.' Freya grabbed Rob by the shoulders and playfully pushed her back down on her bar stool. 'I swear, you're gonna wanna be here. I promise.'

Rob put up a mock fight. 'Only if you show me photos of the weirdest-looking babies you found during your model search for the ad campaign.'

Aimee slapped her friend's hand.

'What? There are so many weird-looking babies these days and we're all just walking around, pretending like they're adorable.' Her eyes sparked. 'Ooh, you should see Nichelle's youngest kid.' She grabbed her phone and started tapping away. 'She keeps posting Instagram Stories about it—'

'*It?*' Aimee blurted.

'*The baby*. She keeps posting Instagram Stories about the baby and writing annoyingly cutesy captions in his voice, as if he were an adult.' She held the phone up to read one, in a British accent. 'Fanks cobber, next round on me.' The photo showed the baby suckling at Nichelle's boob. 'And what makes it worse is the baby looks like a seventy-year-old man.' She flipped the screen around.

Aimee and Freya gasped.

'Why are his eyebrows so bushy?' Freya covered her mouth in shock.

'His hairline already looks like it's receding.' Aimee squinted.

Rob nodded. 'Should I tell Nichelle that her baby looks like an elderly man? I should tell her.' She nodded. 'I'm gonna tell her.'

'You will *not* tell her.' Aimee issued the warning with wide-eyes. 'After her husband Klump helped us out of our . . . *incident* . . . I have nothing but kind things to say about Nichelle. See? I even learnt her name.'

'Finally,' Rob jabbed.

Freya looked down at the floor. 'Is now an appropriate time to issue my millionth apology?'

Aimee placed both hands on either side of her niece's face. 'You will be apologising to us every day for the rest of your life,' she joked.

Rob stared dreamily into the distance. '*The incident*. I love it. Ominous. Intriguing. It's how Liane Moriarty would refer to it in one of her books – and then I'd get impatient and just flip to the final pages to find out what *the incident* actually is.'

Freya clicked her fingers. 'I almost forgot . . .' She bent over to rummage through her stuffed duffel bag for a moment. When she stood back up, she was holding a gift – wrapped neatly in brown paper. 'For you.' She handed it to Aimee.

'Hmmm.' Aimee inspected the package with suspicion. Just from feeling it through the paper, she could tell it was a photo frame. 'This better not be a picture of me getting dressed up as Stevie Nicks. I saw you skulking around the apartment with your camera just before you left to drive up to the Gold Coast that day.'

'Just open it, Byron Karen.'

Aimee gently unwrapped it and flipped the frame around to see the photo inside. It was the front page of the *Byron Times*. The bold headline and kicker was emblazoned over it.

ULTIMATE HOLLYWOOD TWIST

In a scene that could've played out in a Hollywood blockbuster, two Byron Bay locals whose identities remain protected assisted police in a covert operation by going undercover to bring down a multi-million dollar drug supply chain.

'You're awful,' Aimee deadpanned to her niece.

Rob grabbed the frame. 'I still can't believe we have to remain anonymous and not get the fanfare we deserve. I've never felt more like Christine McVie.'

As Aimee studied the front page – now preserved forever behind glass – she started to smell something familiar. Floral and spice.

'There were no free car spaces so I just pulled up on a median strip,' Brooke huffed as she approached the table in her caped blazer, busily fishing a neat stack of papers out of her big buttery leather handbag. 'I can only be quick, sorry ladies . . . but all I need is a few quick signatures.' She plopped the files down in front of Rob and held out a pen.

Aimee and Rob looked at her, waiting for an explanation.

Brooke sighed. 'So, it turns out I need a bigger factory space for Tutu Tribe and can't use your garage. I thought you'd like to keep it for your salon. And home. The details of this contract are identical to your old one – rent will stay the same as what you were paying.'

Rob stared at her, mouth agape. Brooke looked uncomfortable and quickly moved on to other business. Whipping another stack of papers out of her bag, she gently tossed them over to Aimee's side of the table. They landed with a nice solid flop. 'I'll need your signature too.'

Aimee looked up in puzzlement.

'That's the contract for your new store. Now, I couldn't afford your old store because the potential for condo development skyrocketed the price. But there was this lovely little shop for sale just around the corner – on Jonson Street – and I snapped it up. It's perfect. Main street. Similar square-footage. I didn't know what you were paying for your old place but I've asked around some similar businesses in the area and I think the amount I've listed in the contract is fair.'

Aimee glanced down at the paperwork and saw the amount printed in bold. It was only a hundred dollars more than what she'd been paying for her old store. She closed her eyes and shook her head, stunned.

'I guess it's my way of saying thanks,' Brooke said.

'For what?' Aimee let out a small laugh.

'Fidgets.'

Aimee furrowed her brow.

'Ever since you told me about fidgets being the hot new toy, I started seeing them everywhere on Instagram. I did some research and the market's huge – kids are going nuts for them. I imported a stack of them, got the DVD vending machines refitted to accommodate the toys and then got them placed in Westfields and supermarkets up and down the east coast. They're a hit. I've even had to buy *more* vending machines.'

Rob let out a wry laugh and shook her head in admiration. 'The crazy bitch with the lake.'

'This is . . . wow,' Aimee said, flicking the pages of the contract.

Brooke shrugged and held out her fancy-looking pen for one of them to grab. Neither of them did.

'Really, it's *so nice*, Brooke. It's beautiful.' Aimee tried to think of how to word her response. 'But we don't actually *need* the stores anymore. Either of them.' She looked over at Rob and smiled.

Brooke squinted. 'You're getting married to each other?'

'Ahh . . . nope.' Aimee cocked her head, bemused. 'Both still single.'

Rob smiled. 'I guess you could say we've been inspired by Olivia Newton-John.'

FIFTY-FIVE

Aimee bounced out of the entrance of her apartment building and walked over to the Monaro that was parked on the street. She was carrying a big suitcase and, as she got closer to the car, her face started to scrunch as she saw how little room was left with all the other bags and possessions stuffed into the old coupe.

'We should've traded the Monaro for Freya's van,' Rob called out. She was sitting on the hood, organising a shopping bag full of different packets of lollies.

'It'll fit. You might just need to keep your bag of DVD boxsets on your lap.' Aimee dropped the suitcase on the road when she reached the boot. 'Or you could just get rid of them,' she muttered, knowing her friend would hear.

Rob jumped off the hood. 'I swear to god, those boxsets will be worth something very soon. First vinyl came back. Then cassettes. DVD boxsets are next. They're classic. A novelty! Mark my words: in a few years, kids will be going nuts over old DVD boxsets. The Artisan would kill for these DVDs!'

Aimee raised her eyebrows.

'The *Seinfeld* boxset is shaped like a fridge!' Rob's voice went high-pitched.

'It's true,' a guy's voice called out.

The girls looked over and saw Heath on the footpath. 'Don't throw out the *Seinfeld* boxset.'

Aimee walked over and hiked up the waistband of her jeans. 'Hi.' She nodded, standing close to him.

'Hi.' He nodded back with a smirk.

'Filming all wrapped up?'

'I can officially announce that season one of *The Brats of Byron Bay* is complete.' He held out his arms.

'Wow,' she laughed. 'Any word on a second season?'

Heath pursed his lips. 'Hmmm. Dunno.' He scratched the back of his head. 'Actually, I'm talking to the ABC about a producer gig they got goin'. Docos. So . . .'

'Nice.' Aimee enthusiastically whacked his chest with a palm.

'Eh. We'll see.' He got shy. 'Know where you're going yet?'

Aimee inhaled and looked up optimistically. 'Still figuring it out.'

'Well, call me if you get to Sydney. Or even if you don't. Lemme know how you're going.'

'I'll do that.' She gave him a lingering glance and turned to walk away. 'Hey, Heath?' She stopped. 'Thanks for helping me when you didn't have to.'

He smiled. 'I'd do it all again.' He looked down and kicked the toe of one of his ratty old sneakers on the footpath. Then he looked up and assessed her. 'Alright. Now, fuck off ya fuckin' hippy.'

Aimee rolled her eyes and turned around. 'Goodbye,' she laughed.

'We ready to roll?' Rob called out.

'Yep! I left something on the stairs,' Aimee yelled back as she jogged over to the building's door, painted yellow and blue and red to match the exterior of the discount chemist. When she emerged, she was using both arms to hold the carnival clown head. 'Just gotta make one stop.'

———

It smelt like it always did: old carpet and soggy wetsuits. The ding-dong alarm sounded when Aimee walked through the entrance and Tim stumbled through the back door of the shop, holding a new surfboard to hang on the wall rack.

His eyebrows raised and his mouth opened a little. Aimee's visit was clearly a pleasant surprise. But the clown head she was holding?

'That thing's haunting me,' Tim groaned.

'Parting gift.' Aimee bent at the knees and lowered it to the floor. 'Maybe it'll be less creepy if you give it a name.'

Tim thought for a moment. 'Rolfe.' He looked down at it. 'Nope. Even creepier.'

'Apartment's vacated,' Aimee said. 'All the antiques are sold and Rozzie's garage is finally empty. I'm sure she'll be thrilled,' she joked.

'I have no doubt,' he laughed. 'Charlie heading off with you guys?'

'Nah. He's lined up a small tour in the US with the band. One of their covers got picked up to be used in an episode of *Emily in Paris*.'

'Cool. Which cover?'

'Paris Hilton, "Nothing in This World".'

'Classic.'

Aimee noticed a long metal sign propped up against the wall. She cocked her head to read it.

'Ah, yeah . . .' Tim started to explain sheepishly. 'Changing the name of the store.'

Aimee read the sign aloud. 'Byron Boards & Bar.'

Tim smirked. 'Probably a better choice than Harley, Hawk & Co.'

Aimee shrugged. They stood in silence for a moment.

'I'm sorry. For the night at the pub. And . . . not being there for what happened after,' Tim said.

'It's OK. I sorted it myself.'

'Almost twenty years.'

'Almost twenty years.' She nodded.

He laughed. 'It's kinda insane.'

'It's *fucking* insane.'

'I think we did awesome.'

Aimee slid her hands into the front pockets of her jeans and smiled at the floor. 'I think we did, too.' The sound of the idling Monaro rattled into the shop. 'I've got the car running.' She pointed her thumb over her shoulder.

Tim nodded. Just as Aimee turned to leave, she noticed the fedora chucked to the side of the counter – on the floor with Tim's backpack.

She walked over, picked it up, then turned to face him. She looked at the lines around his eyes and across his forehead – etched into the tanned skin of the scruffily handsome face she'd gazed at for so long but hadn't noticed change. Popping up onto her tippy-toes, she reached over and plopped the hat on his head. She stepped back to take one final look at him. 'Better.' She smiled.

When she walked back out onto the footpath, she paused for a moment to feel the warm breeze on her face. She looked across the street at the empty windows of The Dream Explosion and the big SOLD sticker that had been slapped across the FOR SALE sign bolted to the awning. It was done. She jumped off the gutter, pulled open the car door and slid onto the vinyl seat.

'OK, what song do you wanna play?' Rob was shuffling through the music library on her iPhone.

'You can choose.' Aimee clicked in her seatbelt.

'Oh my goodness, I'm overwhelmed with choice. Neneh Cherry? No, Belinda Carlisle. Ooh, what if we do Madonna – but only her underrated deep cuts?'

'Nah.' Aimee smiled, dropping the gear stick into drive and pulling away from the kerb. 'How bout something we haven't heard before.'

ACKNOWLEDGEMENTS

Mum, Dad, Elizabeth, KJ and Julia.

Lisa Muxworthy, Oli Murray, Liz Burke, Kerry Warren, Stephanie Raethel, Kate de Brito. Publish the blacklisted columns upon my death.

Bluch and Caitlin. To the reams of prep. REAMS.

Beck. Because champagne is not just for special occasions.

Koubs. Guess who, don't sue …

LD. Coffee? JW.

Biggzy. Two lab chimps on the loose. #BroomNudes.

Gary. For not laughing at the dumb questions.

Jackie Henderson and Kyle Sandilands. For the stamp of approval.

Cassandra Di Bello, Michelle Swainson, Emma Nolan and Dan Ruffino. The manuscript will be with you within the hour … three months, tops.

ABOUT THE AUTHOR

James Weir is an award-winning journalist and the mastermind behind a popular reality TV column that has become a must-read. His recaps of *Married at First Sight* continue to crack record readership numbers and are appointment reading for fans of the show as well as those who never watch it.

Turning his sharp observation and irreverent humour to other areas, he has gone on the road to cover major events like the 2019 and 2022 federal election trails as well as Harry and Meghan's 2019 tour of South Africa – the couple's final trip before quitting the royal family. His satirical Sunday column is syndicated across Australia in the *Sunday Telegraph* and *Sunday Mail* newspapers and on the news.com.au and *New Zealand Herald* websites. Away from writing, he has been a regular contributor and fill-in host on KIIS 106.5's *The Kyle & Jackie O Show* for close to a decade. *The Hemsworth Effect* is his first novel.

To find out more visit www.hellojamesweir.com.